# HOW TO
# SAVE
## THE
# WORLD

**Tor books by Charles Sheffield**

*Cold as Ice*
*Georgia on My Mind and Other Places*
*Godspeed*
*How to Save the World* (editor)
*One Man's Universe*

# HOW TO
# SAVE
## THE
# WORLD

### EDITED BY CHARLES SHEFFIELD

**TOR**®

A TOM DOHERTY ASSOCIATES BOOK
NEW YORK

HOW TO SAVE THE WORLD

Copyright © 1995 by Kirkwood Research, Inc.

A Tor Book
Published by Tom Doherty Associates, Inc.
175 Fifth Avenue
New York, N.Y. 10010

Tor Books on the World-Wide Web:
http://www.tor.com

Tor® is a registered trademark of Tom Doherty Associates, Inc.

Library of Congress Cataloging-in-Publication Data

How to save the world / Charles Sheffield, editor.
     p.   cm.
   "A Tom Doherty Associates book."
   ISBN 0-312-85577-X
   1. Science fiction, American.   2. Science fiction, English.
 I. Sheffield, Charles.
 PS648.S3H69   1995                   95-20231
 813'.0876208—dc20                   CIP

First edition: September 1995

Printed in the United States of America

0 9 8 7 6 5 4 3 2 1

# TABLE OF CONTENTS

# HOW TO
# SAVE
## THE
# WORLD

# INTRODUCTION

When the friendly aliens finally arrive from the Lesser Magellanic Cloud, they will spend a couple of weeks examining the history, organisms, and customs of our planet. Then they will make a series of polite suggestions, along the lines of: If only you Earthlings will stop doing *this,* and begin to do *this,* everything here will be improved out of all recognition.

We, the people of Earth, will listen in dazed wonder and say, "Of course! Such insight, and such profound understanding! It's so obvious once you explain it like that. You are an Elder Race of super-geniuses, able to grasp in a few days what we have been unable to comprehend through the whole of our history."

And the aliens will look at us, slightly embarrassed, and reply, "Well, no, not actually. We have been civilized for rather longer than you, but we are not smarter. Actually, your basic intelligence may be a little higher than ours."

And when we get to know them better, we will learn that in truth they are no smarter than we are.

So how, then, are they able to solve our problems when we cannot? Simply because they are able to examine us from *outside*, without the emotional involvement that plagues us. How many times have you looked at what a friend is doing, and seen very easily and very quickly that it is self-destructive? He is embarking on a sexual affair that cannot possibly lead to anything but trouble and heartbreak; she is quitting a job for which she is well suited because of some minor irritation that if left to itself would have blown over in a few days; they are hell-bent on retiring to a place they don't know, leaving behind all the friends they have made over the past forty years.

And what am *I* doing that will later prove disastrous? I don't know. I need a sincere friend, emotionally sympathetic but not directly involved, to warn me and to guide me.

Unfortunately we, as a species, are on our own. We have no friendly advisor looking over our shoulder. We will have to make do with the next best thing: humans who are close *observers* of the actions of our species, but who are not directly involved in trying to run the affairs of humanity.

This, of course, is exactly what writers are and have been through recorded history. We can name well-known writers who held high public office: John Buchan Tweedsmuir was Governor General of Canada, and as John Buchan was also a best-selling writer. Benjamin Disraeli was a successful novelist and also Prime Minister of England. But such people are exceptions. Most writers fulfill the role of observer and analyst while remaining aloof from the messy business of running the show. This allows them to see, sooner and more clearly than the movers and shakers, what ails society and how it might be corrected. Unfortunately they are rarely able to persuade others to prompt action. In the words of Wilfred Owen, "All a poet can do is warn."

Even among writers, I argue that the writers of science fiction form a special sub-group. They tend to be interested in global problems, in the impact of science and technology, and in the long-term future of humanity. They are observers of events at the largest scale.

In addition it is a widely-held opinion (at least among science fiction writers, if not the rest of the world) that sf writers are smarter than all other people. Unfortunately, or some would say fortunately, science fiction writers are seldom given a chance to prove that fact.

This book is one of the rare exceptions. Its title, *How to Save the World,* is unduly modest. What our writers show in this volume is how to save a whole variety of worlds, all part of or derived from the world we live in today.

Is the big problem in our inner cities? Larry Niven points out how to solve that easily enough, in "The South Los Angeles Broadcasting System." Is our general nastiness to each other the main reason for misery? Then James Hogan has the perfect answer, in "Zap Thy Neighbor." Maybe we need rapid and reliable communications. That will come soon, as Doug Beason explains in "Defense Conversion."

Easy access to space will be provided—at a price—as in James Kirkwood's "The Invasion of Space." Are you worried about pollution? Consult Nick Pollotta, in "Raw Terra." Overpopulation? Try Arlan Andrews' "Souls on Ice." Racial intolerance? Brenda Clough, in "The Product of the Extremes," points out how things could be worse. Trouble with men? Well, there will always be trouble with men, but Mary Turzillo solves that problem in "The Guatemala Cure." How about problems with women? See "Choice," by Lawrence

Watt-Evans. Religion? Jerry Oltion, in "My Soul to Keep," provides this book with a good chance of being banned. Violent crime? "The Meetings of the Secret World Masters" offers Geoff Landis's eminently practical solution.

But maybe our troubles begin at an earlier age, when kids in school are supposed to be learning, and failing to do so. No worries. "Higher Education" provides the solution.

And if, of course, you happen to think that the whole place is going to hell, and fast, then you will find much to please and satisfy in "Buyer's Remorse."

Some of the stories in this book may offend. I certainly hope so. In fact, if every reader finds something disturbing in at least one tale, I will feel that I and the contributors to this volume have satisfied our objective.

Charles Sheffield
November, 1994

# ZAP THY NEIGHBOR

▼

## JAMES P. HOGAN

Mervyn Taub, editor-in-chief of the *San Francisco Daily Clamor,* turned his broad but gangling six-foot frame back from the window of his office overlooking the intersection of Geary and Market streets, and nodded a balding dome fringed by mutinous tufts of red hair above the ears.

*"Intolerance!"* he pronounced sonorously, making it sound like a revelation of the final secret that the universe had guarded obstinately to the end. "That's what's at the bottom of every problem left in the world. Nobody's hungry these days; everyone has somewhere to live; there's plenty of affordable everything. Science has solved all that it can solve. The problems left now are all social. And I just wanted you to know, Gary, that I'm proud to have somebody on the staff of this paper who not only has the guts to tell the biggest of them like it is, but names the names of the worst offenders too. This could do a lot for your promotion prospects."

Gary Summers was due to die sometime that day, and hence found it difficult to work up a lot of enthusiasm. Merv had a tendency to get carried away at times, and without meaning to seem insensitive could overlook things like that.

Taub raised a copy of the morning issue of the *Clamor*, folded back at an inside page to reveal an article with the head: A**HOLES I DON'T NEED IN MY LIFE: SOME PEOPLE THAT IT WOULD BE NICE TO START A DAY WITHOUT, over Gary Summers's byline.

"Intolerant people," he went on. "The ones who find it impossible to leave everyone else alone to just be what they want. They're the ones who are screwing everything up for the rest of us." Taub raised a finger for a moment, posing as if addressing a shareholders' meeting or a political campaign rally. "And I agree we've put up with them for long enough! It's time we made it plain that we're not going to let them get away with it any longer. This article of yours could be the beginning of a general tightening up of permissiveness to this kind of thing that's long overdue. I had a thought this morning that the *Clamor* could launch a public-awareness campaign based on the theme. What do you think, Gary? How about HELP STAMP OUT INTOLERANCE as a bumper sticker?"

For a moment Summers thought he could feel himself pitching forward out of the chair right then, but it was illusory, probably caused by autosuggestion. The official descriptions said that deactivation happened too instantaneously for any impression to register at all—and was perfectly painless. His still-dazed non sequitur of an answer was because he really had not been listening.

"It was never supposed to be serious. . . . Casey and I were out hitting the bars, and we had a couple too many. We only sent it in as a gag . . . but Casey appended the wrong destination code. It got slotted into 'Night Priority, Immediate,' instead of being held under 'File Editorial.' When I got here this morning it was already out. . . ."

The intercom on Taub's desk buzzed before Summers could ramble further. Taub moved from the window and flipped a switch. "Yes, what is it?"

The voice of Emily, his secretary, answered from the outer office. "Just a reminder that you've got lunch fixed with Morton Leland. Reception has just been through. He's here now and on his way up."

"Oh, right, I'd forgotten about that. Thanks, Emily. Gary and I are just about through." Taub looked across at Summers, showed his palms, and shrugged.

"I need to be getting along, anyway," Summers mumbled, straightening up in the chair and preparing to rise.

Morton Leland owned a left-liberal monthly magazine that held every evil to have been caused by capitalism, called for democracy within the ranks to choose military officers, and advocated world government as the solution to everything. The two men loathed one another's politics with a passion, invoked plagues and poxes upon the opposite house constantly—and had lunch together at least once a month.

Taub's face darkened as he flipped the intercom off. "The man's a public menace with that damn socialist rag of his," he muttered. "Give him his way, and half the country would be locked up in work camps for not agreeing with him. No concept of simply letting other people live how they want." He produced a pocket compad from his jacket and pointed at the red button set prominently in the lower right corner of the rectangular array below the miniature screen. "Do you know, Gary, there are days when some of the garbage that he publishes makes me so mad that for ten cents I could cheerfully punch his number in and—" He cut himself short, his face frozen in an awkward smile that was half grimace as he remembered that this was not the most tactful of subjects to be talking to Summers about today. An incoming call extricated him.

"Hello? Mervyn Taub here."

Summers began moving toward the door. "Well, I guess I'll be on my way, then."

"Owen! Say, what's up? Oh, excuse me just a second." Taub clapped a hand over the mouthpiece of the phone. "Hey, Gary, you didn't think I was just gonna let you walk off like that, did you? I mean, it's been a long time now." He shrugged apologetically. "I only wish there was something I could do, but you know how it is. . . . So, ah, well, all the best, eh?"

"Thanks." Summers opened the door to let himself out.

Taub returned his attention to the phone. "Hi, Owen. How are things? Got something for us? I was just thinking yesterday . . . wait just another sec. Oh, Gary." Summers paused and looked back. "I hope you didn't take me too seriously a minute ago—you know, about Mort. The guy can be a bit trying at times, but we wouldn't wanna do anything really bad to the old buzzard. It was just a joke, understand?"

"That's okay," Summers said.

"And if you could get any outstanding expenses in—you know, just to leave things clean and tidy before . . . well, I'd sure appreciate it."

"Yeah. Right."

"You still there, Owen? Okay, where were we? . . . "

Emily was gone from her desk when Summers emerged into the outer office, closing Taub's door behind him. He was halfway across the room when the scrawny, hook-nosed figure of Morton Leland appeared through the open doorway from the corridor. He had a bristly white beard that contrasted with florid, knobbly features, and was wearing a lightweight tan jacket with pink shirt and bootlace tie.

"Is Taub through there?" he asked Summers, indicating the closed door with a nod.

"Yes, but he's on a call right now."

"I was supposed to meet him for lunch."

"His secretary was here a moment ago. She can't have gone far. She'll be back shortly."

"Yes, I know Emily. . . . " Leland peered more closely. "I know you. You're Gary Summers, aren't you?"

"That's right."

"You wrote that piece this morning that said all the things we've been dying to read for years. Congratulations on your courage, my boy! Too bad you won't be around much longer to enjoy the praise that you've earned. But rest assured, there will be plenty of it—if that's any consolation." Leland moved a step closer. His voice fell and took on a harsher note. "The only one missing from it was that snake in there that you work for. Can't imagine how a person of your obvious intelligence ends up writing for a fascist propaganda swamp like this. Greed and corruption is all that the people who that man in there toadies to understand and worship. Give him his way, and half the country would be reduced to cheap labor for the industrial plantation." He pulled back a sleeve to uncover a communicator wristset. "Do you know, I must confess there have been days when for ten cents—"

The inner door opened, and Taub came out. His face creased like a rubber bendy doll's into a smiling picture of bonhomie and delight. Leland's mouth split into a wide, toothy grin.

"*Mort,* you old son of a gun! How've you been keeping?" They shook hands vigorously.

"Not bad, Merv, not bad. And you're not looking too bad yourself. . . . "

Summers hesitated, but neither took any notice of him. He

went out into the corridor and walked away toward the elevators.

The amazing thing was that it was almost lunchtime, and still, nothing had happened. Summers made a halfhearted attempt to finish a piece that he had been working on, but it was becoming increasingly difficult for him to concentrate, and he gave up. He retrieved his expense records with a view to clearing them as Taub had requested, but as he stared at the figures on the screen, a sudden upsurge of rebelliousness overcame him. "Screw 'em all," he muttered, and erased the whole file. He was still sitting and staring morosely at the wall of his work cubicle when a tone from the comterminal announced an incoming call.

The face that appeared on the screen was a man's, white-haired, heavy-jowled, and twisted with suppressed fury. The eyes blazed righteousness that could be felt radiating from the phosphor. Summers recognized him as the Texas TV evangelist Elias Broad, "Sword of the Lord," whom Summers's article had described (actually in one of Casey's contributions) as showing " . . . the compassion of a Rottweiler and about as much considered reason as a feeding frenzy of barracudas."

A hand in the foreground brandished a Bay Area communications directory open at one of the S pages. Summers was unable to make out the print, but a bright red ring had been scrawled around what was euphemistically termed the "Remote Deactivation Code" listed against one of the entries, alongside the regular calling numbers. A finger of Broad's other hand pointed to the circled item, while his voice trumpeted from beyond.

"Don't start having any ideas about getting away with this, boy, because you're not. We've got your number right here! *Nobody* takes the name of this defender of the Lord in vain. I just wanted to see you sweat a little before the divine retribution." The page was whisked aside and replaced by Elias Broad's glowering visage once again, framed behind a giant-size finger wagging accusingly.

"You're gonna burn in hell before today's out, know that? The Lord talked to me this morning, and he wants me to tell you what he said. Said them things you wrote were mean and full of spite, and that doesn't incline him to feel very kindly about you at all. See, he really wants us all to be charitable the way the Book says, but you think that means being nice to people who don't see things the right way. The unforgiving must be taught a lesson, and I am the instrument of his vengeance." The finger disappeared, and Broad's face enlarged as he leaned forward. "Did you ever stand close to an open furnace? Can you feel them flames lickin' around you already, eh? Gonna burn today, hee-hee!"

Summers licked his lips dryly. "All I really said was that it's a good thing that human fathers don't treat their children the way the all-wise, all-merciful One does his. And I didn't even say it. I got it from Mark Twain."

Broad studied him calculatingly for a second. "The Lord also asked me to tell you that in his infinite forgiveness, he might be willing to arrange a half-off remission. One small check wired through to the account of my humble church today is all it needs. Minimum's a thousand."

Summers tossed his hands up hopelessly. "Where am I supposed to get a thousand bucks from, just like that? It's a lot of money."

"For fifty percent off eternity? It works out to nothing at all," Broad retorted. "Anyhow, it won't be any use where you're going."

"But I don't have any. I got divorced six months ago. She cleaned me out."

"Don't you have a house? All you have to do is tap on the equity a little."

"It's an apartment, rented—along with the furniture."

"Got no car? There's gotta be something you can put up as collateral."

"The bank owns my shirt already."

"How about insurance policies, credit-card limits? The Catholics are pretty good with emergency loans if you can come up with a good line."

Summers blinked, wondering for a moment if he had missed something. "Well . . . if that's the case, how about your church? Couldn't we work out some kind of credit?"

Broad looked incredulous. "What do you think this is, a charity operation that I'm a-running? The Lord has entrusted me with his *business* here! And he's telling me right now that he'll give you until five o'clock to figure out something." The hand reappeared in the foreground, this time holding a portable communicator, with an index finger extended toward the red button. "Then it's curtains. Too bad you never learned goodwill and tolerance. We've got your number, boy. Have a nice day." The screen went blank.

Summers realized that he had broken out into a sweat. He brought up a hand and switched his own wristset to chronometer mode. The screen displayed 12:17. Even as he stared at them, the digits changed to 12:18. He had a feeling of time flying uncontrollably, like a smooth ice-slope rushing past beneath a falling mountaineer. Irresistibly, his eyes came to rest on the red button set prominently in the lower right corner of the rectangular array below the miniature screen and stared at it in fearful fascination. The answer was obvious. In all these years he had never considered such an option seriously, preferring—in what he now conceded readily to have been naive idealism—to believe that there had to be better ways of dealing with life's differences, which he would discover in the course of time with a little bit of work, and some patience and perseverance. But he hadn't made these insane rules of modern living. What choice was he left with?

He reached out and lifted the East Texas communications directory from one of the shelves beside the desk, opened it at the pages headed BR, and began running a finger down the columns. He found the name halfway down the third page: BROAD, REVEREND ELIAS J.; *Church of the Golden Fleece, Fort Worth*, followed by a regular calling number and fax number. And there right after it, staring him in the face, was Broad's Remote Deactivation Code: XXX-7951-26995-43WV-7KW. All that Summers had to do was enter the RDC into his wristset or any other personal communications device, press the red activation button, and follow with YYY when the screen requested confirmation. It really was as simple as that. And yet the enormity of even contemplating something so drastic overwhelmed him.

Well, actually, it wasn't quite as simple as that. As a safeguard against the whole thing getting out of hand, and to provide some curb over individual pettiness and impetuosity, the same RDC would need to be entered from at least five different personal-coded sources within a one-hour period to be effective. That meant that Summers would need to find allies, and that was generally no easy task. The ensuing tangles of suspicion and intrigue over who was secretly ganging up on whom tended to escalate into impossible complications, and the majority of people were—understandably—only too happy to stay clear of the whole business by attending to their own affairs and leaving others to theirs without censure or interference. It was different for somebody like Elias Broad, with a devoted band of followers marching in step for the cause. Summers had not missed the significance of his "*We've got your number . . .*"

He was still staring at the directory and wondering whether to try it, and if so, whom to start with, when Casey came into the cubicle through the gap in the partition. "Say, Gary, you're still here! That's great. I was getting worried. Look, about that twenty I lent you last night. Do you think we could kinda . . . well, you know, while you're still walking around. I mean, it's not as if it's gonna do you any good, having it in your pocket."

But Summers wasn't paying attention. Here, as if Providence were sending him a signal, was an obvious person to recruit if anyone was. He looked up at Casey with the intense, presageful expression of somebody about to bare his soul. Casey caught the vibe and frowned suspiciously.

"What?"

"I've never said this to anyone before, Casey. I've always been the kind of guy who tries to stay out of trouble—you know, mind my own business, let other people mind theirs, always look for friendly ways to sort out problems. But this thing this morning is something else. You can't just sit here and wait for it to happen. If they're not giving you any choice, then eventually you have to defend yourself. Know what I'm talking about?"

Casey looked at him uncertainly. "What do you mean?"

Summers gestured at the directory still lying open on his desk. "Elias Broad just called. He's mad as hell, got himself some co-sponsors, and they're going to key my number in at five o'clock. But that gives me an out, doesn't it, Casey? If I can get some seconders and go for him first. All we have to do is find three more—"

Casey stepped back and raised both hands in front of him

protectively. "Now *wa-it* a minute, Gary. What's this 'we' I'm hearing all of a sudden? Not me. This is *your* show, pardner. I'm sitting this one out."

"How can you say that, Casey? I seem to remember you as having a lot to do with it last night. In fact, the worst parts about Broad were your doing in the first place. And who was the genius who appended the wrong destination code?"

Casey looked pained. "Believe me I sympathize, Gary. But it wouldn't do you any good. We pissed *everybody* off, man, not just born-again Broad. Even if you do zap him, you'll never work the whole list before one of the others gets you. My life's complicated enough already. I don't need freaks looking my number up all the way from here to New Jersey."

Summers sat back heavily in his chair and slammed the directory shut. "Well, thanks for being a pal when I needed it. I really feel sorry that you've got complications. If that's how it is, why don't you just go and take care of them, huh?"

"That's what I figured. Only I've got this lunch date with that blonde in Classifieds, but I'm a bit short." Casey grinned sheepishly, at least having the decency to look moderately embarrassed. "Er, do you think I could have that twenty . . . please?"

Two o'clock came, and Summers was suffering from nothing worse than strained nerves. After a lot of thought, he had come to the conclusion that there had to be more to remote "deactivation" than the public at large were aware of—some inner angle that only a privileged few knew about. Surely, he reasoned, the people who controlled the system wouldn't leave themselves as vulnerable as everyone else. If anyone could tell him how the system really worked, it would be his ex-brother-in-law, Ted, who worked for the Effectuations section of the Justice Department, which administered the system. They had gotten along well together through the years of Summers's marriage, played golf, gone fishing, and fixed cars together, and Ted accepted the eventual split affably and nonjudgmentally as being none of his business.

Summers found him in the photo lab in the basement of the Federal Regional Building, located in the Financial District, and explained his problem. He concluded:

"I just find it impossible to believe that there isn't a way out of this, Ted. Nobody who thought up an idea like this would turn it loose without taking some kind of insurance. It'd be like firing off germ bombs without a vaccine for your own side. I just can't see anyone doing it the way we're all told. There has to be more to the story."

Ted showed a pair of empty palms while shaking his thinning, moonlike head. "Believe me, Gary, I'd help you if I could. But honestly, there's nothing I can do. There aren't any exceptions. The device self-assembles from nano-components that enter the brain via blood vessels from mandatory food additives. It's smart enough to find the right, key neural nexus to build itself around, which it disrupts on receipt of its unique transmitted code. That's really about all I can tell you. For the details you'd need to talk to one of the techs, or maybe read up on it . . ." Ted reflected on that for a second and added as an afterthought, rubbing his nose with a knuckle, "but then, I guess you don't have that much time left for reading, eh?"

Summers slumped back in the chair despairingly. "I just can't believe this is happening. I mean, am I really that bad? I've never hurt anyone. Yet everyone I talk to acts like it's nothing. You'd think they'd at least try to sound as if they cared. Were people always this way?"

Ted took a pipe from his shirt pocket and began filling it from a tin tobacco box that he took from his desk nearby. "Oh, don't take it to heart, Gary. It's just a front they put up because they can't change anything. Would it make you feel better to know what a nicer place the world is generally these days? 'Deactivation' sounds so impersonal. We prefer, 'Technologically Assisted Encouragement of Amiability and Courtesy.' Crazies were everywhere before RDCs were introduced: harassing people on the streets, closing down bookstores, dictating what movies you could watch, lobbying against everything, infesting City Hall, practically running the campuses. Now you don't hear from them so much—until somebody like you goes out asking for trouble." Ted struck a match, held it to the bowl of his pipe, and puffed several times. "I haven't seen the *Clamor* today. Out of curiosity, who else did you manage to upset apart from Elias Broad?"

Summers exhaled a weary sigh. "Oh . . . just about everyone there is: environmentalists, technarchs; anarchists, statists; lifers, choicers; militant gays, militant anti-gays . . . you name it." Ted groaned and shook his head. Summers tossed up his hands. "Casey and I did it as a catch-all. The ones who worry me the most are the psycho-feminists. I mean, to show that they're against racism and sexism they were telling women to punch in white male RDCs at random, even before we wrote this. It beats me why I'm still sitting here talking to you, on account of them alone."

"Who did you name, specifically?" Ted asked, looking across the room. "Melda Grushenstein?"

As the leader of a strident new activist movement across the Bay in Berkeley that had been getting a lot of coverage recently, she was the obvious first guess. The group wanted physics to be formulated differently because they held that terms like "force," "action," "thrust," and "power" carried masculine aggressiveness connotations. Besides calling for a random RDC blitz, they also demanded penile muzzling for single males over the age of eighteen.

Summers nodded heavily. "I think we said that she and her bunch need to worry about harassment from men about as much as Dracula needs protection at a convention of hemophiliacs."

"Well, I think I can set your mind at rest on that score, anyway," Ted said. "Melda's car went off the freeway and hit the base of an overpass early this morning. She won't be punching in your number or anyone else's."

Summers stared at him in astonishment. "You're kidding!"

Ted shook his head. "It was on the news. She had a couple of her diesel dykes with her. The police figure that whichever one was driving must have had a coronary or something." His eyes had a strange, half-amused twinkle. "Maybe it's your lucky day, eh?"

Summers shrugged in a resigned way that said in the long run it wouldn't make any difference. "But that's only one of them, Ted. Then there's that neo-Nazi nut down in L.A. who calls himself Siegfried—the one who has morons in jackboots marching up and down, and says concentration camps should replace welfare."

Ted waved a hand dismissively. "Oh, he's making too many enemies all over the place. He won't last long."

"But he's sure as hell likely to last longer than *me.*" Summers protested, jabbing a thumb at his own chest. "He's having another flag-waving rally this afternoon and says he's destined to follow in the steps of Hitler. We said we hope he does, and quick—all the way."

Ted sighed and puffed a cloud of smoke regretfully. "You're right. A guy like him isn't gonna just let something like that go by. They're all the same, these bigots: if you've seen one, you've seen 'em all. Gee, I only wish I could help ya." He pulled his pipe from his mouth and stared at it thoughtfully for a few seconds. Then he looked up. "I guess that means we won't be teeing off at eight on Saturday after all—and just when I was looking forward to trying out that new set of clubs, too. This has really messed up my weekend, Gary. I guess I'll just have to give Phil a call tonight and see how he's fixed."

Dr. Meckelberg was pale and thin-lipped with an angular face that accentuated the bone lines, hair stacked in stiff gray waves, and intense, colorless eyes peering through steel-rimmed glasses. He had just finished seeing patients when Summers arrived at the Embarcadero Hospital, and as good luck would have it, had a few spare minutes to talk without an appointment. There was probably no hope of even preparing for surgery at such short notice, but it was now three-thirty and Summers was past being rational. It turned out, however, that no solution was to be found in that direction, anyway.

"Ziss question I haff been asked before, unt it iss der insurmountable obstacle zat you face, I'm afraid, Mr. Summers," Meckelberg told him across the desk of his office in the Neurology Department. "Der nano-chip matrix forms itself inextricably into der interstices of der primary cerebral terminal ganglion. To take zem apart again, it vould be like separating ze vite parts out of der scrambled ekks unt leaving der yellow." He flashed a smile of silver-capped teeth, and the light glinted off his lenses. "Unt if ve try to remove all, you end up just ze same, anyvays."

Summers swallowed. "So, that's it? There's nothing you can do?"

"*Nein.* Not possible, vat you ask. For you, all iss kaput."

"Oh." Summers stared numbly at the pen turning idly between the talon-like fingers above the desk.

Meckelberg tilted his head, pursed his lips for a moment,

and shrugged. "Or maybe der luck today, you are haffing. Since ziss morning der Nazi in L.A. you are vorrying about, but him it iss who goes kaput."

Summers looked up with a start. "What do you mean, him? I don't understand."

Meckelberg looked surprised. "Ach so, you don't hear about it, *nein*?"

"Hear what? I don't know what you're talking about."

"Today, der marching rally mit der flags unt der *sieg heils* he was supposed to be haffing, *ja*? I make der time between surgeries to vatch on der television, but all ve get is der ball-game from Chicago instead. Zen ve find Siegfried haff der stroke late ziss morning, unt iss rushed to der hospital. Vat happens to him afterward, I don't know."

Summers was shaking his head disbelievingly. "Two in the same day? My luck doesn't work like that. This isn't real."

Meckelberg raised his voice to call through the open office door to the nurse outside. "Joyce, iss it true vat I say about der Nazi? Vat happens to him after zey take him avay? Do you hear any more vile I am operatink?"

Joyce appeared on the far side of the doorway. "Storm trooper Siegfried? He's out of it: DOA. I guess he made Valhalla."

Meckelberg spread his hands. "Him, it seems you do not need to vorry yourself over. Unt to show zat my sympathies are viss you, Mr. Summers, if you don't make it past tonight, zen I von't bill you for der consultation. Vat you zink? Iss a gutt deal zat I make for you, *ja*?"

Summers walked the streets back toward the offices of the *Daily Clamor* in a daze. First Grushenstein, then Siegfried. Coincidences like that didn't happen. Yet the clock outside the Bank of America HQ building read 4:07, and still nothing had happened to Summers.

Surely not.

Was it possible that it had really worked this way around all along? His mind boggled at the implications. . . . Or was he inventing the explanation in his mind through some instinctive defense mechanism, creating an illusion of hope where there was no hope? He didn't feel that he was any longer capable of judging. There was only one way to test it out. His pace quickened as he came onto Market Street and turned west.

He sat in his cubicle back on the third floor of the *Clamor* building, rubbing his moist palms on his thighs and vainly trying to coax some moisture into his mouth. The lines of text showing on the screen were just to make it look as if he were doing something—he hadn't even registered which file he had loaded. His eyes were fixed on the numbers showing in the time-of-day box at the end of the header line, in the top right-hand corner of the display.

4:56

He had never understood relativity—nor really thought about trying to, for physics was not his subject—but he knew it had something to do with time running at different speeds. How could anyone ever have believed that time always ran at the same speed? He remembered that when he was a boy, a whole morning seemed to last forever and what happened after lunch was another world away. As people got older, time ran faster until there was never enough of it to get anything finished anymore. Then, at times like this, it could stand still.

4:57

He was feeling nauseous. The phone rang. He lifted the receiver momentarily, then put it down again to cut the call. An old saying came to mind about watched pots never boiling. Seemingly, watched digits never changed, either.

Maybe it just took some people—depending on their circumstances, or just plain whether they thought about it enough—longer than others to figure the deactivation business out. Very likely, some people never did. So had Merv known all along? And Leland? Maybe, maybe not. There really wasn't any way to tell. Summers tried to ask himself how he would react—if it turned out he was right. Very probably, he'd just smile, make bad jokes, and keep it to himself too.

Then he realized with a start that despite the moment his mind had wandered, and the display was showing 4:59. His hands tightened on the armrests of his chair. The tensing of his jaw made his teeth ache.

4:59 . . . 5:00 . . .

His shirt was soaking, his breath coming in short gasps. Knots were tying themselves in his stomach. A miniature preview of eternity. Then:

5:01

He had resolved to allow five full minutes past the hour, but he could wait no longer. He picked up the phone and called the number in Fort Worth that he had already looked up.

A woman's voice answered, "Police Department."

"Emergency dispatcher, please."

With barely a delay, a man answered. "This is Emergency."

"Hello, look, I hope this isn't an awkward time to be calling, but I have a question that's urgent. My name is Gary Summers. I'm with the *San Francisco Daily Clamor*. We have reason to believe that there may have been a recent incident involving the Reverend Elias Broad, who's well known in

your city. Could you confirm if you've had any report, please?"

There was a short pause. Then the voice spoke again, sounding incredulous. "I don't believe this! Are they giving you guys crystal balls or something, out in California? We only got it ourselves less than a minute ago."

"Then you can confirm it's true? What are the details?"

"We don't know yet. Heart attack, something like that. The ambulance has only just left. It's on its way there now."

Summers almost dropped the phone in his excitement. "Let me try just one more hunch," he said. "By any chance, did you get any other calls at about the same time . . . several, maybe?"

"No, I can't say that we . . . wait a second. What's going on over there? Well, I'll be darned! You're right—there's one coming in right now, from the other side of the city. . . . Now, would *you* mind telling *me* just what's going on around here?"

Summers was unable to stifle a guffaw of relief. "It doesn't matter. Just an item that I wanted to verify. I'm tying up an emergency line. You have a good evening, officer."

He hung up and looked around him, feeling the last shreds of tension falling away like dead leaves, and a swelling, intoxicating sense of well-being surging up inside to take its place. He sat back, thumped the rests of his chair repeatedly with both hands, leaned his head back, and sent a delirious *"Yeeaaahhh!"* up to the ceiling. Then he sat forward to the phone once more, checked his personal directory, and called Ted's number.

"Photo Lab. Ted speaking."

"Hi, Ted. This is Gary."

"I was just leaving. What's up?"

"You were holding out on me. I think I've figured this thing out."

"You have, huh?" Ted didn't sound overly surprised. His voice fell to a confidential murmur. "Well, for Christ's sake don't go spreading it around. It works better than God ever did. The world's a much better place than it used to be."

"There's one thing I don't understand, though. It's the people who try to zap you who zap themselves. But how does the system know who they are? Their numbers aren't entered."

"It doesn't matter," Ted replied. "The numbers don't mean anything. If somebody presses a button for real, it simply fires any deactivator that's within a two-foot radius."

Summers frowned. "That could be a bit dangerous, though, Ted. I mean, what if somebody's just having a bad day? I almost tried going for Elias Broad myself earlier today—I might have done it, too, if I'd gotten some seconders."

"Did you try finding any?"

"Just one."

"Any luck?"

"Not really."

"See, people who don't want to do that to anybody stay around. That's why it's set up that way. But you'd still have been okay, even if you had found another four. The computer gives you three chances. Try it more times than that, and it decides you're a bad guy."

"Well, I just wanted to tell you not to bother calling Phil. I'll be there at eight sharp on Saturday. You'd better be in good form, Ted, because I'm feeling just great."

"Who are you trying to kid? I could lick you with a shovel."

"We'll see. Want to make it twenty?"

"Twenty. You're on."

"See you Saturday, Ted."

"Take care. And don't go upsetting any more people, okay?"

Summers was humming to himself as he walked along the sidewalk away from the office, when Casey caught up with him, ashen-faced and breathless, and grabbed him by the sleeve. "Gary, you've got to help me. I'm in trouble."

"Why, what's up?"

"That eco-freak woman who we said has got more boobs than IQ points—I just got a call from one of the believers. They've found out that I was the cowriter on it, and they're gonna do my number."

Summers fought hard to look concerned. "Gee, that's too bad. I wish there was something I could do."

"You said it earlier today," Casey gibbered. "All we have to do is find three more people who—"

"Hey, now, *wa-it* a minute, Casey. How did you suddenly figure me into this? I'm doing okay as things are. Why rock the boat?"

"You don't seem to understand. This time tomorrow I might not be here."

"That's true." Summers looked contemplatively into the distance for a few seconds, as if weighing his options. "I guess you won't be dating the blonde in Classifieds, then. Want me to take care of it for you?"

Casey shook his head wildly. "Hey, I'm not hearing this. How long have we been buddies, Gary? And this is what I get? If things were the other way around, do you think . . . " His voice trailed away lamely.

"Yeah?" Summers challenged.

"Well, that was different. You're on borrowed time anyway."

Summers shook his head. "Sorry, no dice. I'm going for a beer. I'd ask you along, but if you're gonna just keep on about your problems all night, it'll spoil the evening. If I don't see you around, well . . . something else would have happened eventually, anyway."

"You can't do this, Gary. Okay, maybe I was a bit hasty this afternoon. But if it was the other way around, I'd give a guy a break. Do you think I'd . . . " Casey's voice faded in the crowded sidewalk behind as Summers strolled on his way, whistling silently to himself, enjoying the city and watching the evening diners, shoppers, and people just out on the town.

"Excuse me, *sir*!" the man coming out of a doorway exclaimed, smiling apologetically as he bumped an Oriental walking on the sidewalk.

"Thank you, ma'am," the black going into a restaurant acknowledged as the woman ahead of him waited, holding the door.

"You're welcome."

Farther along the street, two men arrived simultaneously at a waiting cab.

"Go ahead, please," one invited.

"I'm not in a hurry. You take it," the other insisted.

"Why don't we share?"

Ted was right. The world was a nicer place these days. Summers had never really noticed it before. And people seemed to enjoy it.

There were still those who would mess things up if given the chance, of course. But for some strange reason they were a lot fewer than they used to be, and they tended not to be around for very long.

It was a fine evening, with the air balmy and the sky clear. A good evening for a steak and a bottle of burgundy to wash it down, Summers thought. If he'd thought a bit quicker, he could probably have talked Casey into giving him the twenty back.

# CHOICE

▼

## LAWRENCE WATT-EVANS

The drive from the airport had her pretty worked up. I wasn't surprised. She probably hadn't liked the guards' manners, either—or the fact that she received an escort in the first place.

One guard in particular was eyeing her with unhealthy interest—or at least, a more intense interest than she or I was happy with.

"Ms. Pellegrini," I said, opening the door wider with a bit of an Old World bow—it's a habit, and I should know better with American feminists, but I forget. "I'm Mohammed Raheem; welcome to our city."

The guards stepped back a bit. Three of them kept a wary eye down the hallway, just in case; that other was still watching his charge.

"Mr. Raheem," she said, staring at me, clearly trying to decide whether to blame me for her treatment, and for what she had seen, and not seen—with her particular interests she would undoubtedly have noticed what she did not see—on her ride.

"Won't you have a seat?" I asked.

"You're . . . it says on the door you represent the World Health Organization."

"That's right," I said. "Please sit down."

She made no move toward the chair I indicated; she didn't even let go her hold on the open door.

"I don't know why they sent me *here,*" she said. "I expected to speak to the Minister of Education, or to a human rights commissioner of some sort, or perhaps some propaganda agency."

"Well, if you'll come in and sit down, perhaps we can straighten that out." I gestured at the chair again.

She gave it another second or two of serious thought, then gave in. The door closed when she released it, leaving the guards outside. "I'd always heard that Third World people had their own ways . . . " she began, as she settled onto the chair. I took my own seat, then interrupted her.

"Culturally pure," I said, "not 'Third World.' The current jargon is 'culturally pure peoples of the world.' " Before she could reply, I added, "I know it's foolish—there's nothing any purer about a country's culture just because the economy hasn't kept up, and you'll find the locals who can afford it wearing Levi's, drinking Heineken, driving Toyotas, and listening to the New Commissars, same as anywhere else—but 'culturally pure' is still the polite term at present." I shrugged. "It'll change again next year, in all probability."

"Culturally pure, then," she said. "I'd heard that culturally pure nations had their own customs, and that everything would be easier if I went along with what was expected of me, as far as possible. They expected me to come here, almost *ordered* me to come here, so here I am—but I still think it's a mistake."

"You aren't concerned with the health of the people here?" I asked.

I knew she wasn't. Nobody ever comes to see if we're giving the kids their shots. They don't care about that.

And they don't seem to know what else WHO has done, here and elsewhere.

"Not directly, no," she said. "Mr. Raheem, I represent the Gender Issues Group, an international organization dedicated to ensuring the fair treatment of women in all nations, regardless of cultural heritage. I'm concerned with basic human rights, not just health."

"Isn't health care a basic human right?" I asked mildly.

"It's just one," she said.

"Well, in any case, you're here," I said. "Why don't you start with me? What is it you're here to do? What is GIG's agenda?"

"I'm here," she said, "to see just what the human rights situation is here, to report back to GIG, and to make recommendations as to what action, if any, we should take. We maintain an active mailing list of over eleven million names, Mr. Raheem; if we call for a letter-writing campaign or a boycott, sooner or later the governments of the wealthier nations will listen. And when they do, the government here, with that President-for-Life whose face is all over the billboards, will have to listen, as well."

I nodded politely.

She stared at me. "Do you even understand what I'm talking about?" she demanded irritably.

I smiled. "Don't let the traditional robes fool you, Ms. Pellegrini," I said. "I was born and raised in Maryland. Princeton class of 'sixteen, Harvard Med 'twenty-one. I know *exactly* what you're talking about."

"You don't seem very concerned—but then, why should you be? You're a U.N. doctor, in charge of vaccinating kids against AIDS and measles, and trying to keep the local strain of syphilis from spreading, right?" That old image again. "Why am I *talking* to you?"

She started to rise, but I held up a hand. "Please, Ms. Pellegrini," I said, "sit down. Bringing you here was not a mistake. It was quite deliberate. You aren't the first women's rights advocate to come here, and I'm sure you won't be the last."

She sat again, and waited. I launched into my usual speech.

"You came here to observe women's circumstances here," I said, "and just in the brief time you've been here, despite the inconvenience of being under armed guard, I'm sure you've seen enough to enrage you. Let me mention a few things."

I ticked them off on my fingers.

"You saw no women in any positions of importance—no women holding any jobs whatsoever, in fact. No female clerks at the airport; no women working as baggage handlers, concessionaires, cab drivers, or even sweepers.

"You saw men lounging around the streets, but no women—not on the sidewalks, not in the markets if you came that way, not anywhere in the city. The men stared at you in a way you probably found insulting and frightening; chances are a few exposed themselves to you, or made lewd gestures. No one bothered you, since your guards had their guns ready, but just the looks must have been unpleasant—and your own guards were looking at you the same way, I saw that in the hall just now.

"Everywhere you looked, you saw billboards, placards, newspapers, and graffiti trumpeting the President's propaganda—and it's all offensively sexist. References to our nation's sons, our young men, our warriors, our fathers—never daughters, women, mothers.

"If you *did* see any women, they were heavily veiled, walking with eyes downcast, always escorted by at least one armed male, in fact always with male hands on them, guiding and guarding them; some may have been leashed or even chained to their husbands or fathers.

"And if you saw any children at play, you saw only boys.

"And this doesn't even mention whatever implications you may have seen in the fact that here in this room is the first time since your plane landed that you've been out of sight of those four soldiers in the corridor.

"Am I right?"

"You *know* you are!" she burst out. "I am absolutely *horrified*—I'd heard that conditions here were a bit backward, but I had no idea . . ."

I held up a restraining hand.

"Ms. Pellegrini," I said, "do you know what you *didn't* see?"

"I didn't see women taking their rightful place!"

"Besides that."

She looked at me in blank anger, and I finally answered my own question.

"You didn't see starvation. You didn't see fly-blown bodies in the streets, children bloated with kwashiorkor following your car begging for pennies, men with guns guarding food you wouldn't offer your dog and having to *use* those guns."

"No, the men were guarding *me.* If you're going to lecture me about priorities, or boast about how your organization has been too busy . . ."

"Not exactly." I sighed. "You didn't see any real hunger at all, though, did you?"

"No," she admitted. "So with *that* solved, Mr. Raheem,

it's hardly time to rest on your laurels, is it?"

"Ms. Pellegrini, do you know any of the local history?"

"I don't *need . . .* " She caught herself. "I know some of it," she said. "I know about the old empires, and the spread of Islam, and the colonial period, and independence after the Second World War. But that was a long time ago—people don't have to be trapped by history, they can outgrow it!"

"If they don't die first," I agreed.

"What's your point, Mr. Raheem?"

"My point," I said, "is that back in the nineteen nineties, there *were* children dying in the streets here. If you look at the wall behind me, those three marks are bulletholes from the 'ninety-five Insurrection—I've preserved them as a reminder. And do you know why there *aren't* children starving, now?"

"I presume that the crops have improved. Mr. Raheem, what does this have to do with women's rights?"

"Crops haven't improved significantly," I told her. "Besides, if there was one thing that the last quarter of the twentieth century demonstrated in this part of the world, it was the ability of human beings to outbreed *any* food supply—or to mismanage it so that people starved amid plenty."

She had realized, finally, that I was going to explain in my own way; she just waited for me to continue.

I could see from her face that she was determined to hear me out so that she could say she had given me a fair chance, but that she had no intention of being convinced of anything.

"There have been changes here, all right," I said. "Major changes. But they've had nothing to do with food crops; they're WHO's doing. We've presented the people here with choices, and they've chosen." I stood up. "I'd like to show you something, Ms. Pellegrini."

She came along, with a barely-tolerant expression plain on her face as I led her out of my office.

In the corridor I waved off the four guards—they didn't like it, but they stayed clear. One in particular, the man who had stared so insolently, seemed annoyed, and I saw him fingering his weapon, but he backed off.

Of course, they followed us, about fifty feet back, as I led the way downstairs. They stopped, though, at the entrance to the connecting passage to the New Order Hospital—as it was now called; it was the Hope Clinic when I first arrived, and St. Mary's before that.

These four weren't allowed in the hospital; that was secure turf, outside their jurisdiction. They waited at the checkpoint.

I could feel the one man staring after us.

By using the tunnel, as we call it, we avoided the regular security check; the guards at the tunnel checkpoint all knew me, and saw that I was with a woman, and let us pass.

Along the way I chatted a little.

"If you're trained in gender issues," I said, "I'm sure you remember those studies from the nineteen eighties and nineties about sex bias in classrooms—that if women contributed more than fifteen percent of the responses in a classroom situation, they were seen as dominating the conversation."

"I remember," she said bitterly.

"That was the first real documentation we had of something that's obvious when you think about it." I held the door for her; she glared at me, and I said, "You can get the next one, if you like; I'm not being sexist, merely playing the host."

She wasn't much mollified.

"As I was saying," I continued as the door swung shut behind us, "those studies showed that what people see isn't inequity, it's deviation from what they've experienced in the past. People who have always lived in a particular situation see it as normal, if they perceive it at all. One can't judge one's own culture until one has seen something else—if then. Do fish see the water they swim in?"

She ignored the question, just as she was ignoring the intense stares of the white-jacketed men down the corridor.

"You'll want to remember that when you hear my complete explanation," I told her. "Here, we need to take the elevator—and you'll notice that the elevators all work, that there's reliable electricity, none of which was true twenty or thirty years ago."

"I should hope things have improved in the past thirty years!" she burst out.

"Oh, but you know, they *didn't* improve, for quite some time," I pointed out. "Between the nineteen sixties and the turn of the century conditions deteriorated badly in much of the culturally-pure world, and for twenty years thereafter improvement was spotty, at best. Up, please."

She pushed the call button, and the door opened immediately. We stepped in, and I pushed 7.

"Fine," she said. "So poverty's been alleviated, the infrastructure is sound, the country's relatively peaceful—but there are men with guns everywhere, and the women are all kept out of sight. Isn't it about time to pay some attention to human decency?"

"We do," I said. "Believe me, we do everything we can for the women here. The men with guns are an essential part of that."

She made it plain, wordlessly, that she didn't believe it for a second.

We stepped out on the seventh floor, and I led the way to the maternity ward. The guards at the entrance raised their guns, then recognized me and waved us through. I think one even saluted.

The nurse on duty glanced up at us, then stared. I waved to him and walked on past, leading the way to the nursery window.

"It's not very clean," my guest remarked. I shrugged.

"It's still the Third World," I said, "whatever they're calling it this week. And you should have seen it when I first got here."

Then we looked through the glass at the babies. No one can resist that.

"A lot of empty places," she remarked. I nodded. There were half a dozen babies, but a score of unused bassinets.

The attending nurse looked up at us through the glass, and I waved to him. He'd known me for years, and he'd seen me bring western women here before.

He waved back.

"You can't tell by looking," I said, "but those babies are all boys."

She glanced at me, then back at the newborns, at their tiny brown fists and squashed-looking faces, and their white blankets and diapers. "They even separate the babies?" she asked. "Where are the girls?"

"They don't separate the girls," I told her, slightly annoyed that she hadn't yet figured it out. "There *aren't* any girls. If there were any, they'd be in there, too—with red blankets."

"Red?" She stared at the white-wrapped infants, then turned to me. Her angry certainty was finally shaken; she looked at me with open puzzlement for the first time.

I nodded. "The color of blood," I explained.

"And you knew there wouldn't be any? I assume there's a point, it's not just coincidence."

"It's not coincidence. It's what I do. What WHO does."

For a moment she stared blankly, then I saw the inevitable suspicion form.

"No," I said, "We don't murder the girl babies." I sighed. "We don't have to. We just give the mothers a choice. That's all we've done since the nineteen nineties—give the mothers a choice."

She looked at the babies, sudden comprehension dawning. "Sons," she said. "They all want sons."

I nodded. "They're culturally pure—and it's a culture that measures a mother's worth in sons, not daughters." I waved an arm. "Every drugstore in this city sells sex-selective spermicides, half a dozen brands, all U.N.-subsidized—and all of them designed to only kill X sperm, none to kill Y. They've got trade names like 'Only Boys' and 'Sons for Certain.' And we provide free prenatal care to anyone who asks, so long as they permit us to do a genetic analysis of the fetus, and the very first thing we tell them is always the baby's sex—even before we mention defects, or verify paternity. And yes, we do point out hereditary defects, and yes, we report on paternity—there's an advertising campaign, telling men to be sure they aren't supporting another man's get. About half of all the pregnancies we see wind up in abortion—and we do that for free, too."

"You're trying to keep the population down. That's what you were talking about, with the starving children."

I nodded.

"And it's working, right? No one's starving. So why do you keep it up? And why do you let the women be mistreated?"

I sighed. "No, you still don't understand. We started this program back in the nineteen nineties, with methods far more primitive than what we have now, and yes, it succeeded—long ago."

"So you kept people from having too many children—so why . . . " she began.

I interrupted. "No, no. That's where the pioneers in population control went wrong. We let people have all the children they want. Sociologists knew back in the nineteen eighties that the best way to convince people not to have too many kids is to make everyone affluent—the poor will always have kids, because they have nothing to lose and much to gain, and besides, most of them will probably die anyway, while the wealthy are generally content with one or two—if they bother to have any at all. In a modern society, kids cost time and money; in a tribal society, sons *are* wealth. The best way to stop overpopulation is to make everyone well enough off, and modern enough, that kids become an expense rather than an asset. But the poorer countries had too many people, and were increasing the number too fast; there was no way to make them affluent faster than they were breeding themselves back into poverty. Population control had to come first, but there was no practical way to convince the poor not to have children short of shooting them—and nobody was willing to go quite that far."

"But then . . . " She stopped, puzzled.

"We told them to have all the children they wanted, Ms. Pellegrini. We even helped them to be sure that they'd have the children they wanted—strong, healthy sons.

"And only sons. We couldn't stop them from bearing children, but it was *easy* to convince them to stop bearing daughters."

She looked at the six babies, in their white blankets.

"We don't *force* them," I said. "We just give them the choice. And sometimes an added incentive—a token payment of a hundred dollars for every son, for example, but never anything for a daughter. And we reinforced the cultural pressures that were already present."

"But I don't understand," she said. "How does that help? You'll have almost as many babies, won't you?"

I nodded. "Of course. They did. Thirteen live births per hundred population they had here, in 2000. And eleven of those thirteen were male. And that was thirty years ago. The women who had those babies are out of their childbearing years, and their sons are grown men—and they had no daughters. Or few, anyway." I gestured at the glass. *"That's* why there are no women working at the airport or in the market, no women on the streets, Ms. Pellegrini—there *are no women.* The population of this country is roughly 85 percent male, 15 percent female, and many of those 15 percent are old, grandmothers and great-grandmothers."

"But . . . " She looked at the babies, then at me. "Don't they realize what they're doing? They're *still* only having sons?"

I nodded. "The population is now dropping steadily—and per capita income is rising steadily. We estimate that if current trends continue we'll be seeing an actual population crash in another twenty years."

"But don't they *see*? If everything's improving, don't they *know*? You've educated them, haven't you?"

"Oh, yes. They know. They're becoming steadily more educated, more affluent—and the average number of live births per mother has dropped from 4.8 to 2.1 since the turn of the century. Two sons, 0.1 daughters."

"But . . . it's *genocide*!"

I shook my head. "It's free choice. To be honest, I think we're near bottom now; I expect the trends to shift. The economics are there. Dowries are long gone, of course. A typical bride-price has now reached the low seven figures in American money, and even an ugly prostitute—yes, there are still prostitutes, of both sexes, but the females are all high-priced courtesans, not streetwalkers any more. At any rate, the going price for a roll in the hay with a real woman, as opposed to a transvestite, is around fourteen hundred dollars. I expect parents to begin realizing this—they'll have a son to carry on the family, and then daughters to sell. So far, though, they haven't trusted the market to last."

*"Sell?"*

I nodded. "Supply and demand. Women are scarce, and that makes them valuable. A girl of six is now considered marriageable. Only a millionaire could afford the traditional polygamy, and the last one to try it was lynched. And of course, that's one reason that we aren't seeing daughters—the men who can afford wives don't *need* to sell their daughters."

"Mr. Raheem, this is all appalling!"

"I won't argue with that," I said. "But children starving in the street were pretty appalling, too. This was a slow, long-term solution, and it had some drawbacks—but it worked, here and in half a hundred other countries. And the people directly affected don't seem terribly upset."

"I can't believe that," she said.

I shrugged. "They've lived with it all their lives," I said. "The men here grew up without any sisters or other girls around; they've never known anything else. Remember I mentioned those studies about women in the classroom? To the people here, 15 percent seems the normal percentage of women; most of them can't imagine a fifty-fifty society. If you transported them to New York, they'd . . . well, we don't have to guess; haven't you heard foreigners talking about how it seems as if there's no one in America but women, how our whole civilization is effeminate? Isn't that one reason that organizations like GIG form in the first place, because it's so obvious that the rest of the world is so backward about gender issues?"

We'd seen what I wanted to see in the nursery. I turned away from the window. "Come on," I said. "There's something else I want to show you."

She was struggling to absorb it all as we found our way through the corridors, past the guards, to the prenatal care and screening unit.

No patients were in at the moment; the room was empty and dark. I turned on the light and pointed at the big poster.

"I can't read it," she said.

I'd forgotten—she was an American. Probably only spoke English.

"It says, 'Give your daughters a chance to live,' " I explained. "We've stopped our original campaign; now we're trying to swing the balance back toward normal. But it'll take years—and one reason is that no sane mother would want her daughter to grow up here."

"But if they *all* had daughters . . . "

"But they won't. No one wants to be first. It'll happen, though. Once there are a few girls, there'll be more, and more, and eventually we should get back to normal. Or even swing slightly over toward excess females—and that'll be fine, because they can be exported to other countries that aren't as far along. We did our best to encourage isolation here, with propaganda about cultural purity and foreigners carrying diseases, but it's time to let up on that, too."

"But if they have daughters, won't that start the whole thing over again?"

I shook my head as I fished behind the counter for what I wanted. "By then, this country will be advanced and wealthy enough that the birth rate will be harmlessly low." I found the folder and handed it to her. "You might want to read these," I said. "It's transcripts of the interviews with pregnant women—in English, we keep several translations. You can see for yourself the reasons they give for aborting daughters."

She didn't really read them, just flipped through enough to convince her that I was telling the truth.

"All right," she said, "I believe you. The women aren't being hidden away. But why aren't *any* of them working?"

I stared at her in surprise. "Why *should* they?" I said.

"For personal fulfillment, of course!" she snapped. "Obviously, any woman can land a husband capable of supporting her in comfort, but don't any of them *want* to work?"

"Ms. Pellegrini," I said, "I don't think you understand." I gestured at the guards at the door. "What do you think they're there for? Why do you think you had four armed guards escort you from the airport to my office?"

"I assumed there's some sort of danger from . . . from outlaws of some sort," she said.

I shook my head. "No, just from men," I said. "Any woman seen in public unguarded is assumed to be asking to be raped—usually gang-raped. Gangs will sometimes carry off any woman they can find. It's become part of the culture here—these men still have the normal interests, but without the normal outlets. Like sailors, before ships were integrated—when they get a chance at a woman, they take it. As for this place, by its very nature, everyone knows this hospital has women in it. No woman could possibly work at an ordinary job without armed guards around her the entire time," I sighed. "And an unmarried American woman—there are a million men in this city who would love a chance to seduce you into marriage, and the customary local method of seduction is indistinguishable from rape. The theory is that if one's sexual prowess is sufficiently impressive, that rape will turn to love. And marrying an American is the next thing to paradise—not only will you gain admission to the third-wealthiest country on Earth, where you'll have a computer on your wrist and a dozen robots to wait on you, but it's a country run by women, where you'll see beautiful women everywhere you turn."

"That's utterly appalling," she said.

I shrugged. "I know."

"This whole thing is a disgrace, a perversion—it's *sick.*"

"Oh, I know. We've distorted and destroyed whole cultures here. We've created an abomination—and I haven't even mentioned the inter-tribal raids, the catamites, the desperate attempts at emigration. We were afraid for a time that with all that testosterone we'd be responsible for a major war, but that, at least, never happened—apparently women aren't a moderating influence at all. If anything, they give men more to fight for. It's still ghastly—but, Ms. Pellegrini, we averted perpetual famine and got the population under control, which allowed the creation of a stable economy and the preservation of the local environment. And it's temporary."

She held up the folder.

"Is it?" she asked.

I didn't have an answer to that beyond, "We hope so."

That ended the tour; we rejoined her escort, and I saw her safely to her hotel.

When the hotel staff had learned that an American woman was coming they had, of course, given her the Presidential Suite, and I could just imagine the infighting over who would be providing whatever services she might need.

She saw the faces on the street on the way there. She saw the men at the hotel watching her. She was overweight, like most Americans, and not particularly young or attractive, so far as I could see, but that didn't matter here.

She saw the faces, and now she knew it wasn't hatred—it was lust.

An entire country of sailors just in from the sea.

We got her to her room without incident; her luggage had arrived separately, and the guards helped her unpack.

That same one I'd noticed before seemed particularly eager to help, and that worried me, but there wasn't much I could do about it. Guards are usually chosen very carefully; if possible, the army chooses gay men, who wouldn't be interested in their charges, just as WHO and the other international organizations do their best to use gay personnel here. If they can't get gays, they look for eunuchs, or just men who aren't interested, but sometimes someone has the necessary political connections to land a guard job without any such qualifications.

But he was just one out of four, and what could I do?

As I prepared to leave, she stopped me.

"Will I be safe?" she whispered.

I gestured at the guards.

"That's the fox guarding the henhouse," she said, with a quick glance at the suspicious one—clearly, she'd noticed his interest, just as I had. "How do I know I can trust them?"

"That's why there are four," I said. "It's likely at least one will stay loyal, and keep the others in line. And if not—well, they won't want to hurt you."

I walked out and closed the door before she could get over her shock sufficiently to react to that last remark.

She probably thought I was just being cruel, that I was angry with her, returning her hostility.

I wish she'd believed me. And I wish I'd been able to do something.

We still don't know how he managed to kill the other three single-handed; maybe he had help from the hotel staff. A busboy turned up dead as well, so that was probably it. The guard was shot trying to escape, so we couldn't ask.

She wasn't hurt, beyond a few bruises and the emotional damage. And she wasn't interested in talking about it; she took the next plane back to Europe, and I assume she went home to the States from there.

I hope she talks about it there.

I thought she had enough to absorb that first day, so I hadn't mentioned the problem I wanted her help on. If she'd stayed the three days she had originally planned, I'd have shown her the records of what happened to the last planeload of western women who thought it would be fun to visit a country where there are six men for every female.

Why they expected those men to understand the traditional mating dances of our species, to respect their rights and customs, to tolerate any sort of sexual teasing, I don't know. It's hardly a traditional society here.

But at least it's still a society, not a death camp. I keep telling myself that. And it'll readjust someday. We haven't destroyed it forever.

All we did was offer them a choice.

That *was* all we did, wasn't it?

# THE MEETINGS OF THE SECRET WORLD MASTERS

▼

## GEOFFREY A. LANDIS

*Experimental Set-up*

Frank Gordon loved his big Harley. He liked them quiet, and his was the quietest bike he'd ever heard. It had a special custom muffler he'd gotten from a specialty shop in California; it was so quiet it was frightening. Gordo liked the way it would come up on you without warning, like a shape coming out of a nightmare. He gunned it, coming around the ramp onto 82 at almost eighty, heading for Brigadoon's.

Brig's was the biker bar. There were already half a dozen choppers parked outside. Gordo put his next to them and walked into the dimly lit interior. A couple of the guys greeted him. He picked a stool at the bar next to Big Al and ordered a beer. Gordo and Al were almost opposites; Al big and sloppy, Gordo slender and neat. Al was built like a football player gone to seed, but uglier and meaner. In contrast to Gordo's meticulously brushed suede, Al habitually wore a black leather jacket with ripped sleeves festooned with chrome studs. He was a nasty son of a bitch. They got along perfectly.

He looked Gordo up and down. "You're smiling. Bet you had some fun today."

"Damn straight."

"Ha. Way you use 'em up, pretty soon there ain't gonna be any left. What'cha lookin at next?"

"I ain't worried. There's a chicken I got my eyes on, real fine piece. Little momma type. She gonna squirm real good when I stick it in. Real good." He nudged Al in the ribs and pointed to the TV. "Hey, listen to that. They talking 'bout me."

" . . . And it looks as if the Providence serial rapist has claimed yet another victim, this one in Central Falls. Details at ten."

As the commercial came on, Al and Gordo chuckled, as if at a private joke.

## Laboratory Protocols

Katherine Tabor sat back in her chair, sipped her coffee, and watched David Kantrowitz tinker with the microscope. If there was a Nobel prize for tinkering, she thought, he'd certainly be a contender. The X-ray microscope had been designed for metallurgy. He'd modified the sample chamber to accept hydrated samples—wet goo, like the nuclei of living cells—so it could do biological crystallography. With some help from the computer postdoc that he'd persuaded Irwald to hire, he'd hooked the microscope interface to a PC networked into the Cray. The Cray crunched the datastream, extracted the DNA sequences from the mess of data, and then followed the DNA forward into the coded proteins.

Kate didn't know much about X-ray microscopes—computers either, for that matter—but she knew DNA backward, forward, and sideways. What they'd put together was easily the world's fastest DNA sequencer.

She thought about inviting him over to her apartment and seeing what he could do with her broken toaster, but she wasn't sure if she was ready to deal with whatever it would be that he would make out of it. Or if she was ready to deal with *him,* not that he wasn't kind of cute in an awkward, but tall and dark-haired way. Not awkward when working with equipment, though, not at all.

An automated DNA sequencer. Now *that* was really something.

She shook her head. She'd set aside today to get the introduction done on her dissertation, and drinking coffee and mooning over the lab staff wasn't going to get her anywhere. She turned to her computer. Time to get to work.

"The sad fact of the world," Kate wrote, "is that it is far easier to break something than to fix it. It is much easier for a virus to cause a disease than it is for us to cure one. To cause a disease requires one to attack only one vulnerable point; to prevent one we have to defend them all. So if we only know, say, one percent of all there is to know about human biochemistry, we don't know nearly enough to cure diseases; but we know plenty enough to cause them."

She stopped and looked at what she'd written. That wasn't what she wanted to say. She deleted the paragraph and started again.

"Contrary to popular opinion, viruses are the most highly evolved, and the most highly efficient, living organisms on the planet." She looked at it. Better. "They are built to reproduce, and, given the right conditions, are nearly perfect at doing so. Causing disease is at most a side effect: in terms of evolutionary success, a virus doesn't want to harm its host." She thought about that one for a moment. A virus doesn't *want* anything, strictly speaking. But let it stand. Her thesis committee would know what she meant. "Now consider taking a virus and making genetic modifications. Our modifications can't help the viruses at replication; Mother Nature has already worked a billion years to make them very efficient at that. The modifications must be harmful to the virus. The point, however, is that in general modifications will also be harmful to the host. At best we only modify exactly *how* they make people sick." She looked at it again. Still not quite what she wanted to say, but what the heck. If she kept deleting every paragraph after she wrote it, she'd *never* get the thesis written.

Time to get to the lab and check her cultures anyway. She saved the file and headed for the door.

### Experimental Set-up (continued)

Nancy wasn't too surprised when Mrs. Gundich didn't meet her at the door. Normally if Mrs. Gundich had to leave early, she'd give a call to the bank to let her know, but occasionally things came up without warning. Chrissy was old enough to take care of herself for an hour. She fished out her key and let herself in. "Christine? I'm home. Hello? Chrissy?" No answer. She walked into the kitchen.

She saw the knife first, then the man behind it. The stranger held it at Christine's throat. The child was wide-eyed with terror, struggling to say something, but the adhesive tape over her mouth didn't let her. The man had a mask on, so she couldn't see his face. Then she saw Mrs. Gundich, gagged and blindfolded, bound tightly to a kitchen chair with strapping tape.

"Hey there, pretty momma," the man said, in a surprisingly soft tone. "If you're real good and behave yourself just right, maybe I'll leave your little girl alone. I think we could both have a little fun, don't you? Now, why don't you just start out by taking off your clothes? *Now.*"

Mr. Gundich was beginning to get annoyed. It was fine with him if Hilda earned a little extra pocket money baby sitting, but they had tickets to the opera, and she still hadn't come home. He tried the number once more. Still busy. What in the *world* could they be doing over there?

If he waited any longer they'd be late for sure. He was getting really angry now. He decided to get in the car and go over himself.

She hadn't been any trouble. Gordo had her blindfolded and strapped down to the kitchen table real good. He removed her bra and pink nylon panties with his knife, caressing her softly with the edge, not quite hard enough to draw blood. He took off his mask and was about to unzip his pants when he noticed that she had somehow managed to work the blindfold off. He reached over and picked up the knife.

"Now, that wasn't a very smart idea, little momma, was it?" he said softly. He put the blade up to the side of his face and rubbed it slowly against his cheek. "I wouldn't want you to be able to identify me, now would I? Just what do you think I should do now?" Her eyes rolled up in terror. He grinned. "I'm sure I'll think of something. But first . . . " He put the knife down again and started to unbuckle his belt.

Outside, a car started to honk. First a couple of short honks, then one continuous blast. It went on and on. A dog started barking.

"Shit." Gordo walked over to the window, crouched down where he couldn't be seen, and pulled aside a corner of the drapes. An old guy in a blue monster caddy (the kind he hated) was looking over at the house and leaning on the horn. To either side, neighbors were opening their windows and shouting. The old guy shouted back, but kept right on leaning on the horn. Two guys from across the street walked out to get on his case. Good for them, hope they pound his ass. The old guy let off the horn to argue, gesturing toward the house. After a moment all three of them started walking up to the front of the house.

Damn. Did she lock the front door behind her when she came in? He couldn't remember. He crept quietly down the cellar stairs and out the back door the way he'd gotten in. The Harley was still there in the alley, hidden behind the Dumpsters. He kicked it to life and made his escape as the men tried the front door.

The police didn't catch up with him until Monday morning, when she picked his photo out from the file.

### The First Meeting

Sitting around the lab Tuesday morning, drinking coffee, everybody was talking about the news.

"Castrate the worm, that's what they should do," said Kate. "With a chainsaw. Give the slimy little nematode a batch of his own medicine."

"And then dip him in boiling asphalt," said Jacob Rankin. Jake Rankin was a research professor in Irwald's lab and, technically, Kate's boss. His position wasn't tenure-track, but he still outranked everyone else in the lab—except, of course, for Professor Irwald himself. Irwald, however, had a marked tendency to spend his time in Washington, or off somewhere giving lectures, or almost anywhere, it seemed, other than in his own laboratory. Jake had an annoying tendency to pontificate, Kate thought, but otherwise seemed to be a decent enough boss.

"Hey, guys, come off it," David said. "The man's sick. He can't help it. They should lock him up, sure, but let's don't get too sicko ourselves, okay?"

"Well, what do you think they should do, huh? Put him in jail and have him eligible for parole in a year or two? You think that's punishment?"

"No. You want to know what I think they should do to the guy?" He paused a moment and looked around.

"Actually, I don't give a damn," said Jake, "but I suppose you're going to tell us all anyway."

"Well, for one time in your life, Jake, my buddy, you're right. Now, I think they should take the guy and give him an injection. A special injection. Everytime the guy gets a hard-on, wham. He gets real weak. Can't stand up. *Now* let's see him go around raping people."

Kate looked up. "Say, you may have something there. You could do even better than that. Tie it in to the adrenaline level. Only happens when he's excited. Double whammo."

"You guys," said Jake, shaking his head. "Great drug you got there. Funny, guess I missed seeing it in the PDR last time I looked."

"Not a drug, a disease," said Kate. "Say, a genetically tailored virus, special made for the purpose. Responds to the gene pattern. Be a little tricky to make it, but it could be done."

"Say, I like that," said David. "Designer diseases."

"Think so? How you gonna get something like that past the NIH watchdog committee? They scream bloody murder when we even ask for permission to do a little gene doctoring to *cure* people. You think they'll let somebody have permission to release a *disease*? No way, Jose."

"Well, they ought to. Save the public a lot of money; they wouldn't have to keep the guy in prison. Make the bug trigger only on a single gene pattern. To anybody else, it would be harmless."

"Yeah, and try to convince the NIH of that. Besides, who could tailor a virus that precisely?"

Kate looked at him. "*We* could."

Jake looked thoughtful. "You know, if we all pooled our talents together, I think maybe we could at that. David on the mike; your skill at splicing . . . maybe we could. But, I'll tell you—nobody else. None of the other labs have all the right kinds of people in the same place."

"Wouldn't even be dangerous," said David. "We've got the sequencer; we could key it so tightly to this one guy's genotype, even if it got loose it would never infect somebody else in a million years—"

The doorknob turned, and the group scrambled to pretend to look busy. Doctor Irwald walked in. "Talking about the rapist, eh." He laughed. Maybe he'd heard some of the conversation. He tossed a newspaper down on the lab bench and left again. "Take a look at that."

David walked over and looked at the headline:

VICTIM DROPS CHARGES AGAINST ALLEGED SERIAL RAPIST.

There was a sudden silence when he showed up at Brig's. The mirror behind the bar reflected him darkly, and in it Gordo could see a dozen eyes watch him walk up to the bar. He walked confidently. He figured that in a pinch he and Big Al could take down any six of the weekend outlaws. The bartender he wasn't so sure about, but hell, this was his place, and damned if he'd be driven out without making trouble.

The bartender picked up a whiskey bottle and started polishing it with his rag. "Heard 'bout you on the TV. Having some trouble with your old lady?"

He shrugged with elaborate casualness. "Some. Not any more."

"She over eighteen?"

He gave the bartender a sharp look. "Damn straight. I like 'em young, sure, but not *that* young."

"Well, all right then." The bartender put the bottle back behind the bar and drew him a beer. "No babyfuckers drinking at this bar."

He could feel the tension drain away. A couple of the regulars bought him beers. He looked around at the crowd and found Big Al at a table in the back. He walked up to him and punched him in the arm. "You?"

Big Al leaned back in his chair, way back until the chair almost tipped over, and showed his yellow teeth. "Yep."

"Thanks, big guy."

"No problem, amigo." Big Al smiled. "Anything for a friend."

"So, tell."

"You shoulda seen it, man. You just shoulda been there when she saw that puppy. The pigs put her in this motel room, you see, said it would keep her safe until she testified, you know it?" Big Al had visited the hotel room and left her a present, a basset hound pup that he'd bought from a couple of kids selling puppies in one of the rich suburbs. He described the look the little momma's face had when she found it in the motel room. He'd left it dissected across the motel's double bed. The puppy had still been whimpering and trying to lap his hand when he left it. "Now, *that* changed her mind about talking, real quick," he said, and laughed. "You gonna go back to it, or hang low for a while?"

"Hang low, I think. Maybe cruise around a bit out of town, if you know what I mean?" Big Al laughed.

Yeah, hang low. On the other hand, there was this chicken he'd had his eye on lately, some sort of researcher worked at the university hospital. Hell, he'd seen her walk back toward the student section of town a lot of nights after midnight. It would be so easy. Wouldn't hardly be rape, even. On the streets after midnight, it was just like she'd asked for it, how he figured it. Not hardly even sport at all. He smiled. Yeah.

### The First Experiment

It hadn't even been very hard, although the lab work took two solid days of straight sleepless effort, sandwiched into bits and pieces of time between "real" work.

The police laboratory had a blood sample from the alleged rapist, and had sent it over to the university hospital for analysis. Kate simply walked in dressed as a lab tech and logged it out. David's machine sequenced it, and Kate programmed the attack DNA sequence with a big dollop of help from their computer assistant, Herbert, doing the simulations. That done, she spliced RNA together to the specs the simulations had indicated would work.

The plan they'd finally come up with involved lactic-acid poisoning in the muscles to produce the weakness whenever the trigger stimulus was present, along with production of a detumescence hormone and a few enzymes that deadened sexual desire. They'd managed to tie it to female pheremone as a trigger, as well as the usual biochemical tags of sexual arousal, "just in case he decides to try the other side of the street," said

David. "No way this sicko is going to go rape *any*body after we've gotten at him. Are you ready with the host virus?"

"Got the undergrad assistant mass-producing it in the cell-culture."

"Good enough. What are you using? Influenza?"

Kate shook her head. "Epstein-Barr virus."

"EB? Why that?"

"Well, first, because it cultivates well in human tissue and is mostly harmless. But, mainly, because we have a good sample available that's already well characterized."

"Mostly harmless?" said David. "What's the mostly part?"

"Hell, if he doesn't like it, let him sue me."

When Kate had the handmade RNA ready, she gave it to Jake, who used a dash of reverse transcriptase according to the method he'd worked out and spliced it into the ready virons. He and the assistant then mass-produced the altered virus in the tissue culture.

When enough had been made, they spun down a pure sample and gave it to David to sequence. Kate and Jake waited anxiously as Dave whistled tunelessly over the X-ray microscope. Finally he leaned back from his console, smiled, and gave them a thumbs-up. "Per-*fect*-o. Not a codon out of place."

"We're in business," said Kate. "Let's boogie."

He'd followed his chicken coming home late. She was begging for it, all right. It was after two, and the street was deserted. Gordo cruised around ahead of her, and as she passed the alley he made his move.

Or tried to. His legs collapsed right under him and he hit the asphalt with a grunt. It was as if all his muscles had turned to wet newspaper, like he had just tried to run a marathon carrying his Harley on his back. He was on his face in the alley before he'd even known he was hit.

She'd walked right on past; hadn't even glanced at him. He crawled back to his hog and threw up.

What the hell? He couldn't figure it, not then, not later in the week.

Hang low was right. Way low. He could joke and pretend everything was the same, but, tell the truth, looked like cruise around a bit was about *all* he was likely to do. Christ, if he even *thought* about doing it to a chick, he got the wobbles and had to sit down. Couldn't get a hard-on even with a pro, and for *damn* sure that means you got trouble. He'd even descended to the level of having to use his own hand for relief, and he hadn't been forced to that extreme since he'd gotten his first switchblade at seventeen.

Maybe the damn cops had put some kind of drug into his food? Would the cops do something like that? Rough you up a bit if no reporters were watching and they thought they could get away with it, sure, that was just part of the good times. But he'd never even *heard* of anything like this.

Hell, he must just be getting old. Could he have shot his wad so often he'd used it all up? Everybody knew geezers lost it long before they started taking Geritol and listening to ooze music.

Maybe he ought to just sell the hog and move down to Florida. Get a job, maybe do car repair or something. No way he could keep pretending hanging with the rowdies much longer—pretty soon one of them would bring in a loose momma, and then he'd be shown up pretty, for sure, for sure.

The only thought he had was to go on a drunk. A long, ugly, three-day falling-down stupid drunk. For sure.

## The Second Meeting

It couldn't possibly have worked, Kate insisted. They'd been too carried away by the excitement of the illicit experiment to realize that. It was common knowledge that a rapist isn't really interested in sex, but in domination and humiliation of a helpless victim.

But after two weeks of carefully watching the news and scanning the headlines for signs of the serial rapist, she had to admit it apparently *had* worked. One day when Dr. Irwald was gone to Washington looking for funding, Jake brought balloons and a beerball to the lab for an impromptu party to celebrate. The three of them agreed that Irwald should be kept strictly in the dark, but they filled Herbert and the undergraduate assistant Beth in on the conspiracy after both of them swore secrecy.

One thing led to another, and somehow the party didn't break up until about two. Jake fell asleep on the couch in the corner and couldn't be woken up. Beth and Herbert had both left a bit earlier, and David staggered back to his apartment trying to whistle around a bad case of hiccups. Kate was left to carry the debris from the party out to the garbage. She dumped it on the pile of week-old newspapers when a name in a discarded paper caught her eye. She pulled it out of the bin and took it back to the lab.

The news wasn't on the front page, and it didn't mention rape at all. Just that the motorcycle had been doing well over a hundred when it hit the bridge embankment.

So it had turned out to be a death sentence, after all.

At last Kate turned off the lights in the lab and stood alone, looking into the darkness at the glow of power supply lights and indicators.

"But it doesn't stop here," she whispered. "That was only the beginning. We can do anything to anyone, anywhere, any time. We can assassinate presidents, decimate armies, dictate rules to popes. We're, we're masters of the world. The secret masters of the world." She was silent for a while. "But where does it all end? Where in hell does it all end?"

The lab answered with the quiet whirr of vacuum pumps and the dim glow of lights. After a moment she closed the door and went home.

## The Third Meeting

It was a week later, and Katherine Tabor was—as usual—working late when Jacob walked into the lab. She had been slowly reading her way through a stack of photocopied papers on synthesized DNA sequences. It was boring but important work if she wanted to keep up in the field. At the electronics bench across the lab, David was messing around trying to fix a circuit board. They both looked up as Jake came through the door.

"The First World War was a war of chemists," he said. Just like him to not bother to say hello, Kate thought. He leaned against one of the sample refrigerators and looked at them with a tiny smile on his face.

"The Second was won by the physicists," Jake continued. "The next, I predict, will bring the triumph of the biologists. Namely, us."

"Crap," said David. David Kantrowitz was an engineer, not a biologist, but they all knew that it was his tinkering with the lab equipment which made Irwald's lab capable of an astonishing range of biological syntheses; well beyond what should be expected from a second-rank biology department, given the university's chronic funding shortages. "A war of chemists? Don't you think trenches and guns have something to do with it?"

"Poison gas," said Jake. "Synthetic rubber. Chemical explosives. Chemistry was how the real war was fought. The rest was just—dying."

"Zeppelins," Kate said. "Biplanes. The Red Baron."

"Tanks," David added.

"Nope," Jake said. "None of those made the slightest difference to the war. That one was a war of chemists. World War II was won by physicists—radar, the bomb. This next one—"

"Yeah?" said David. "Are you making some kind of a point, here? So what?"

"So what?" Jake leaned against one of the stainless-steel twelve-tube centrifuges and stared back at David as if with astonishment. "So what! So, we're the masters of the world, don't you know it? Carpe diem, you guys! We've got the power! Let's use it!"

Well, I'll be, Kate thought. He realizes it too.

"We, meaning we biologists?" David asked, stressing the second "we" ever so slightly.

"Or meaning we, this particular lab?" Kate said.

"Both! This lab—yeah, this lab! We could do it, you know! We could rule the world!"

"Oh, really," David said. He folded his arms. "You guys can tailor viruses, sure. I've seen that. You want we should put an announcement on the tube, tell people that if they don't do what we say, we release a plague and kill everybody?"

"It's a thought," Jake said. "But we don't have to kill *everybody*. We're way past that now! We can tailor viruses specifically. Attack whatever group we want to target. Specific people. We can target anybody at all, if we can just get a specific enough genetic handle on them."

"Yeah? So we just kill—"

"—incapacitate. Could be non-lethal." Jake nodded at Kate. "We've shown that."

"—incapacitate anybody who opposes us?"

"Why not?" asked Jake.

"Well, Irwald probably would tell us to get back to work," Kate said. "It *is* his laboratory, you know."

Jake smiled. "So who was planning to tell him?"

### The Fourth Meeting

When Kate got to the lab, a few minutes late, the rest of the lab was already waiting. Jiao Jiang, wearing a frayed Bruins sweatshirt, was slumped back in the easy chair reading a comic book, while David Kantrowitz was at the bench behind her, busy taking apart an auxiliary power supply for the X-ray microscope. Kate looked at the serious expression on Jake's face and suppressed a giggle, and he gave her a stern look. Herbert, the computer jockey, looked befuddled; but then, he always looked befuddled. Only Beth, the undergraduate assistant, looked attentive.

"Now that we are all here," Jake said, looking directly at her, "the policy meeting will now come to order."

They were all seated in the outer room of the lab, where they could relax in their street clothes without worrying about biological contamination. The outer room contained a hodgepodge of chairs and equipment that didn't require full biological isolation: microscopes, centrifuges, freezers full of biological probes and Eppendorf tubes of cell cultures, antique gel electrophoresis units for DNA sequencing, a lead-lined safe for the radioactively-tagged bio-probes, with the combination written on a yellowed piece of masking tape stuck to the door, and hundreds of laboratory notebooks in various stages of completeness. Inside, in the clean labs, the recombinant work was done, but the clean labs were no place for relaxed discussions.

"Before we start, is everyone clear that nothing said here leaves the room?" Jake looked around. "Anybody have problems with that?" No one raised an objection. "Then we're open for anything. Any suggestions?"

"Maybe we ought to talk about whether trying to change the world is right," Kate said. "I mean—"

"Kate, babe, don't be naive," Jake interrupted. "Everybody wants to change the world. You can be honest and admit it, or you can lie, but why the hell are you here, if you don't want to make the world a better place? Did you watch the news yesterday? You think that this world couldn't use some changing?"

What had been on the news last night had been, as usual, violence. The feature story had been a poorly-focussed, but clear enough, home-video clip of a white man whose car had broken down in the wrong portion of Cincinnati. The clip showed him being dragged out of his car by five black youths and being clubbed nearly to death, apparently in retaliation for earlier violence against blacks elsewhere in the city. Kate started to reply that she wasn't sure how Jake thought they would stop events like this. A single rapist was one thing. But before she could frame her thoughts, he said, "Now, let's quit the bullshit and get to work. Any suggestions—real suggestions?"

To Kate's surprise, the computer jock Herbert was the first to speak. Grinning wickedly, he said, "Sure, I know how we can make the world a better place. How about we start by wasting that jerk in Iraq?"

And then everyone seemed to be speaking at once, too fast to make out who said what:

"Seconded."

"What jerk in Iraq?"

"Hell, every Arab in the whole damn country's a jerk."

"Hey, now, just wait a minute," David said. "There are probably a lot of people in Iraq who don't have anything to do with Hussein. Most of them probably hate their government just as much as we do. Don't go stereotyping Arabs just because Saddam's a warmonger, okay?"

"Jeez, Kantrowitz, don't they pull your Jew license if they hear you talking like that?" Jake said. "What is this, be kind to towelheads week or something?"

"Saddam," said Herbert, "*that's* the jerk I want to waste."

"Amen! Let's do it! And the jerk in Iran, too—the Ayatollah. What's his name, Khomeini."

"Hey, just because I'm a Jew doesn't mean I'm a knee-jerk chowderhead. Unlike some people I could name. Present company excluded, ha ha."

"Khomeini? He's been dead for years."

"But not this other ayatollah, what's his name, I forget?"

"Yeah, right. Him, too."

"Hell, and how about the jerk in Liberia?"

"Liberia? You mean Libya? Khadaffi?"

"Yeah, that's the guy."

"Wouldn't hurt to get the one in Liberia—he's a real jerk too, far as I can tell."

"Fine by me."

"Then what about South Africa?"

"What I hear, the guy in South Africa's okay, trying to change things."

"Not trying too damn hard."

"And what about Israel? Get rid of the hard-liners, bring in some guys who are willing to compromise, might solve a hell of a lot of the world's problems. Oops, sorry, Kantrowitz—you were in that one, weren't you?"

"Just because I was there doesn't mean that I agree with all of the government's policies toward Palestinians," David said. "They're getting better, but the hard-liners are still going to have to make some more compromises. But—if you haven't been there, you really don't have much of a notion of what's going on. The news here is garbage, it doesn't even pretend to tell you the real stories."

"Right!" said Jake. "Let's delete a few of these biased reporters—"

"They've got a lot of hard problems over there," David continued, ignoring Jake's interruption. "They have to act tough; if they appear too willing to compromise, boom, the Arabs take it as weakness and boom, next thing you know a million people are dying. There are no easy solutions. Don't pretend you understand the situation. You don't know even the least little bit of it."

Jake raised his hands. "Okay, Kantrowitz, okay! You don't need to lecture!"

"And what about the PLO? You want to solve the Middle East problems, why don't you kill off the PLO?"

"Don't know how we could do that," Jake said. "I mean, PLO isn't a specific genetic trait. Maybe we could get that guy Arafat with a tailored one-shot, though."

"Hey, Arafat's mellowing out," Herbert said. "He signed that peace treaty, didn't he?"

"Yeah, right—how many people did he kill? Mellowing

out, what does that mean? He only kills people on alternate Thursdays now? Waste him and do the world a favor."

"And what about back here?" Herbert said. "How about doing something about Senator Jerrison?"

"Huh? He's a jerk, sure, but why waste him?"

"Why waste him? You crazy? He just cut the funding for the new space shuttle. If it wasn't for his anti-science attitude in general, that alone would be enough to justify a little therapeutic homicide. Yeah, and while we're at it, maybe that Senator Studerville as well. The guy who just about killed nuclear power in the U.S."

"And the television evangelists. Get them all, the whole rotten bunch."

"Ku Klux Klan!"

"Right to Lifers."

"The NRA."

"The automobile company executives!"

"Mr. Potatohead!"

"Who?"

"You know, the president!"

"Oh."

"Jeez," said Jake in disgust. "Get real, you guys. This is serious business, get that through your heads. We gotta get some order here."

In the silence, David said, "I'd like to hear what Jiao Jiang has to say. Everybody else has been talking two miles a minute, but Jiao hasn't said a word."

Everybody turned their eyes to Jiao Jiang, who had been sitting quietly at the back. She nodded slightly toward David and waited for the silence to gather for a moment before speaking. "Thank you. I am of two minds on this matter. I have been watching your working very carefully, and I have seen that you have come up with some very impressive techniques for tailoring viruses—yes, I've seen what you have done. You are very clever in disguising the real purpose of what you were working on, but you have not been that clever. And I, too, watch the news."

Jiao Jiang was an unknown factor in the lab, a postdoc virologist from Cornell who had been working with them for only six months. Jake had argued that they shouldn't let her into their conspiracy, but Kate and David had convinced him that there was no way that they could hide what they would be doing well enough that she wouldn't suspect. Besides, Kate had watched her in the lab, and she knew that they could use her expertise.

"I have visited many laboratories. Many are more capable in specific fields, but I have seen no other laboratory that has designed viruses the way you do. But I am still wondering how you intend to use this power. I understand that all power, if it exists, will ultimately be used. Perhaps it is better by us than by others."

"Right!" said Jake.

"I have been thinking about my own country. There are certainly many people in my country, politicians and generals, that it would be better for the world if they quietly died. I know that you have learned to make a virus so specific that it would only attack one single person. Is this what you intend? To find the evil people in the world and make them sick and die?"

"Well, I wouldn't put it quite exactly that way," Jake said.

"Then just how would you put it?" asked David. "It's what you're talking about, isn't it?"

"But, I think you Americans do not understand my country very well," Jiao continued. "What do you know? Maybe you have heard of Chiang Kai-Shek; maybe you understand communists and capitalists. I do not think you could understand which people are doing evil, and which are doing the best they can in a very difficult situation, with too many problems and too few tools to solve them. I do not even know if I would trust myself to make such decisions, and there are very many countries in the world."

"Well, sure, we gotta do some research," said Jake.

"Yes," said Jiao Jiang earnestly. "Very much research."

"Okay—Beth. You will come up with a list of major world problems. By next meeting. Okay? Everybody—" Jake raised his voice. "Dismissed!"

"And, Jake," Kate said, just before he left. "Remember, we don't *have* to solve problems by killing people. There are other ways."

"Namely?"

"We could be clever."

### The Fifth Meeting

Kate yawned and stretched her legs out on the couch. Jake sat up straight on a lab stool, the only one of the men wearing a tie, looking earnest. Jiao Jiang, wearing a denim vest over a Rolling Stones tee shirt, sat next to the electron microscope, while Herbert the computer jock sat at his terminal, as always, tapping his feet while listening to the conversation flying around him and occasionally making a barbed suggestion. Beth sat behind him, clutching a neatly ordered folder of notes in her arms. David sprawled out on the floor.

"The policy meeting of the secret world dictatorship will now come to order," Jake said. "First item of business: a report from the committee on immediate world problems." He looked at Beth and nodded. She stood up.

"There are many pressing problems of concern to all of us," she said. She was wearing a pink cotton sweater and reading from an index card. "The ones which I think are most important are, in order:

"One, the threat of nuclear war. It's lessened now that the cold war is over, but it's still a problem that hasn't gone away.

"Two, overpopulation.

"Three, various minor wars and probable wars, including in the Middle East, Central America, Southeast Asia, et cetera.

"Four, world hunger, especially famine in Africa and Asia.

"Fifth, the depletion of natural resources, especially fossil fuels, and the greenhouse effect.

"Sixth, racial prejudice, in the United States and elsewhere."

That would be something to stop, Kate thought. The news that night had shown a video clip over and over featuring a blindfolded black man being hanged by his feet from a tree and then beaten to death by men in white sheets. She was still shuddering. The videotape had been quite graphic. It had been mailed anonymously to the three major news networks, accompanied by a note saying it was "justice" for last week's attack on a white motorist. The entire world has gone nuts, she thought. That people would not only attack an innocent person, but deliberately videotape it . . .

"And finally," Beth was saying, "human rights in repressive regimes, in the Third World, states of the former Yugoslavia, etc." She put one hand to the thin silver chain that suspended a tiny crucifix from her neck and rubbed it with a thumb. "There's more, but I think those are the most urgent."

"Well," said Jake indulgently. "You certainly aren't afraid to think big. Comments, anyone?"

"Yeah," said David. "I agree that all this is well and good, but there are a whole bunch of problems on that list that we really can't do a damn thing about. The greenhouse effect, for example. Sure, it's important, but what do you think you're going to do? Invent some widget to make a car run on water? You guys are a bunch of biologists, for Chrissake, not engineers."

"The point is, Kantrowitz, that all of these problems are amenable to political power," Jake said. "We don't necessarily have to solve them ourselves. We just have to get the right people moving in the right directions. And furthermore, I think that as biologists, we have a unique perspective on problems of natural resources. After all, we *know* what things like the burning of coal do to the Earth's environment."

"I agree with Dave," said Kate. "We can't talk about problems independently of what we're capable of doing about them."

At that moment, Professor Irwald walked in the door. He rarely ever went into the lab except when he called a meeting of his graduate students, much less at nine in the morning, but this morning they were apparently unusually lucky. He blinked owlishly, and said, "Problems? Are we having problems? Perhaps you had better tell me about them."

"Nothing, Dr. Irwald," Jake said hastily. "We were just talking hypotheticals here."

"Right," Kate jumped in. "Problem solving. I mean, figuring out a plan of action, what we *would* do if we *did* have a problem."

"Oh," said the Professor. He blinked again, and then said, "That's negative thinking, students. Negative thinking has no place if you want to get results. Positive! Think positive! Plan for things to go right, not things going wrong."

"Right," said Jake. "Results! Don't worry, Dr. Irwald. We're going to get you some results. We're going to get some results like you wouldn't *believe*."

## *The Sixth Meeting*

"The meeting of the secret masters of the world is now called to order," Jake announced. They were meeting in the back room of Penguin's Cafe this time, figuring it was unlikely that Irwald would unexpectedly walk in. They usually met there to discuss labwork over lunch anyway, and, although it was a bit earlier than their usual time, the proprietor knew enough to lead them to the back and leave them in peace.

"Not more of this parliamentary procedure crap," said David. "Who needs it?"

"Our first order of business is—"

"Move we skip reading of the minutes of the last meeting," David said. "Move we suspend parliamentary procedure and just get it over with."

"Move we skip the meeting and proceed immediately to the refreshments," suggested Kate.

"Move we skip the refreshments and send for pizza and beer," Jiao Jiang added, grinning widely.

"At nine in the morning?" said Beth. "Yech."

Jake sighed and drummed his fingers impatiently. "Can we quit the joking and proceed in an orderly fashion?"

Kate sat up and looked at him. "Oh, cut the Roberts Rules of Order crap. Which world problem are we going to solve this week?"

Jake looked at his notes. "Uh, on the agenda for this week is, racism."

"Racism? I thought that war and the environment were higher up on the list."

"Jeez, Kantrowitz, haven't you been watching the news? Besides, I thought we'd start with something simple first, then work up to the big ones."

"Prejudice? That's what you call simple? What do you consider hard?"

"What I want to know is," Kate said, "do we really think we can make a significant dent in world problems? I mean, really. In our spare time?"

Jake shrugged. "Look, we've got to learn to think big. If we decide to make a difference, we *can* make a difference. Lots of people talk about solving the world's problems. Let's *do* something."

"Yeah? So how do we eliminate racism?" David said. "Brainwash people?"

"No problem, Kantrowitz. Eliminate the color, eliminate the color prejudice."

"You gonna make all the races of the world alike?"

"Nah—anyway, not to start with. We'll just start with black and white."

## The Second Experiment

Kate still hadn't decided if she wanted to go along with Jake's plans, but this one she agreed with wholeheartedly. In the last week there had been race riots in half a dozen cities, and sickening video footage across all the major networks. If she could do something to stop it, how could she justify standing idle? She devoted all her spare time, and much of the time she should have spent on other projects, to the work.

It was simple in principle, but took long and painstaking effort. Two weeks of all-night sessions by Herbert had gotten them unrestricted access to the Hugo data banks, the central research repository of the Human Genome Organization. Using the Hugo data as a map, she localized forty-three segments on twenty chromosomes that controlled the majority of racial somatype expression—the major visible characteristics of race. Many of them were simple on-off switches that regulated flow of the chemical agents that produced melanin, or other chemicals that controlled appearance. Then it was a straightforward task to devise ribozymes that would find and deactivate one sequence, while splicing in the other. She picked a T2 bacteriophage as her workhorse, a simple virus that didn't normally attack human cells, but would flourish and multiply among the *e. coli* of the intestinal track. Her modification added a tiny snippet of DNA, an instruction tape that made it seek out epidermal cells and inject tiny snippets of DNA to be incorporated into the nucleus and co-opt the cell's programming.

"This one is really sweet," said Jake, when they had it all finished. "No symptoms at all. Not even a runny nose. You go to bed white as Nixon, and wake up black like the Queen of Sheba. Zap!"

"It does a bit more than that," Kate said. She had made three variant strains of the virus, with different amounts of change, to cover genetic variation and natural immunity in the population. Herbert had calculated that about fifty percent of the Caucasian population should be infected by at least one strain. "Over the period of about a month or so, as cells produce a modified RNA message, the soft tissues are modified as well. The facial characteristics will actually be reshaped."

"Even better," said Jake.

"You do realize," Jiao Jiang said, "that we are breaking every biological containment regulation there is if we let this loose."

Jake shrugged. "So?"

"I've heard a hundred people say that they don't care what color a person's skin is," Herbert said, "but just watch 'em. It's the very first thing they notice. You can tell."

"No more L.A. riots," David said. "I'm sure people will still beat each other up, but not because they don't like the color of somebody's skin."

They released the test run at a KKK rally in Cincinnati. Then, for good luck, they sent Herbert to Kennedy Airport to stand in the departure lounge, sneezing on the passengers of a flight to Capetown. It took two months to act, but when it did, was all they'd hoped for, and more.

## The Seventh Meeting

"Seriously, now, everybody?"

"Okay, okay. Hey everybody—SHUT UP!"

"Okay, okay, Jake, you don't have to shout," David said.

"Okay, then," Jake said, when everybody had finally settled down. "The environmental committee—what is the worst problem on the list? The greenhouse effect?"

Beth stood up, holding her notes in one hand and unconsciously fingering her silver chain with the other. "Number one," she said, "is Third World deforestation."

"Okay. You mean cutting down the Amazon rainforest?"

Beth nodded. "Brazil, sub-Saharan Africa, Indonesia."

"Get real," David said. "How are we going to do anything about that? What's next on the environment list?"

Beth looked at her notes again. "Environmental effects of burning coal."

"Coal? How about fossil fuels in general?"

"Coal is the worst," Jake said. "It's a dirty, polluting, killing substance. It kills miners, kills people who breathe the pollution, kills whole forests and ecosystems from acid rain. Not to mention the ecological devastation of strip-mining."

"Hey, sounds like you got a bug up your backside, ol' buddy," David said.

"I grew up in coal mining country," Jake said curtly. "You want to hear how coal makes America great and mine workers are the greatest Americans in the world, talk to my unemployed cousins; don't talk to me."

"I still think we should be thinking about targeting a few world leaders," Herbert said.

"We agreed on no killing," Jiao Jiang said. "If we are going to change that ground rule, I will withdraw my participation."

"Wait one minute here! You can't do that!" Jake said. "We agreed that everything we did here was a secret!"

"Then no killing," she said.

"Well, it's still better than nuclear power," Beth said suddenly.

Jake turned on her. "Better? In exactly what way?"

"Well," Beth said, "I mean, radioactivity. Nuclear waste—"

"That only shows that you're an idiot," Jake said. "Coal emits a thousand times worse poisons, and spews them right into the atmosphere."

"Although Jake is rather obnoxious about it," said David, "he may have a point there. Coal does contain minute amounts of thorium, which enter the biosphere from the combustion products and the slag. Cumulatively, it's probably put more radioactivity into the biosphere than nuclear plants have."

"But what about if there's an accident?" Beth said.

"Honey," said Jake, "there are coal accidents just about every week. Thousands of people get killed."

"Thousands?" said David dryly.

"Well, hundreds, anyway. If a nuclear plant emits one microcurie of radioactivity, it's news. If a coal mine explodes, it doesn't even make the front page.

"Let's quit jawing about the problem, and do something."

"About coal-burning?" said Kate. The research she'd done to come up with the black-white virus had left her with dozens of ideas for new ways to use viruses as a tool. She leaned back in her chair, her eyes half-shut. "If we wanted to, we could do something about that pretty easily."

"How?"

She opened her eyes and looked at them with a slight smile. "I've got plenty of ideas."

### The Third Experiment

It was amazing, really, how easy it was to synthesize a virus to make people allergic to coal. This one was even easier than the black-to-white virus, and they made it completely unselective. The beauty of it was that they didn't even have to stealth it past the immune system—the virus was designed to sensitize the immune system, and the immune system itself did the work. Long after the virus was vanquished from the bloodstream, the allergy remained, like an immunity, forever.

"You are absolutely brilliant, Kate," said Jake.

"Jiao Jiang did much of the work," said Kate. Jiao looked up as Kate said her name, but stayed silent.

"I mean it! The both of you! This is Nobel-quality work!"

"If we were ever able to tell anybody about it, that is," David said.

It still surprised Kate every time she looked at Dave and saw a black man. He had argued that it would be suspicious if none of the group had been affected by the race-blending virus, and allowed himself to be infected. The campus had a lot of black faces recently.

"Are we sure this is a good idea?" said Kate. Her head was buzzing from Jake's praise, but she wasn't sure that she'd been wise to let her enthusiasm for the work get the best of her. She wondered if it wouldn't be wiser to just drop the samples of the new virus into the autoclave and set it for maximum. "Don't we all depend on coal? Nobody will be able to mine it any more. Nobody will be able to shovel it, or *anything*."

"Kate, the fact is that there have been alternative sources of energy available for *decades*," Jake said emphatically. "The problem has been that coal is so cheap, they've never gotten a foot in the market. Coal is *cheap*! It's just a rock that you pick up out of the ground! Did you know that there's nothing you can buy that's cheaper in bulk quantities than coal? Not even sand!"

"Have you seen the effect of acid rain?" Beth said. She seemed to have switched sides completely in the month it had taken Kate to work out the virus, perhaps due to her developing what seemed to be a serious crush on Jake. "Whole ecosystems have been wiped out in Eastern Europe. Even if clean-burning coal plants are beginning to come into use, it's too little, too late."

"Hey, climb back into the twentieth century," said David. "There are lots of new coal-fueled generating technologies that are ultra-low emission. Coal gasification, fluidized bed combustion—"

"*You* climb into the twentieth century," Beth said. "You think that America is the whole world? Open your eyes."

"The Third World isn't going to buy all that crap," Jake said. "They don't have any money. They want to industrialize, and they're doing it now. Look at China. They've got lots of soft, brown coal, stuff it would be *illegal* to burn over here, that's almost like burning dirt. Jiao, you tell 'em."

Jiao Jiang nodded. "There is much coal burned on the mainland. It is very ecologically unsound. It is used for heating and cooking."

"And they're building power plants as fast as they can,"

Beth said. "India, too. They don't give a rat's fart about what comes out of the stacks."

"Do you know how many people are killed by coal every year?" Jake asked. "Thousands! Maybe even millions, with emphysema or whatever aggravated by pollution. I'm talking about mining disasters, about black lung disease, the whole works."

Kate turned to David.

He smiled. "Well, since Beth brought the subject up at the meeting last month, I've been doing a bit of homework. I think Jake's exaggerating a little."

"The heck I am. Anyway, not all that much."

"It's not as quite bad as all that. There are a lot of ways to avoid pollution problems—heck, you been to Pittsburgh recently? It's clean and serene. Sooner or later, the technology will even filter down to the Third World."

Kate nodded. "So we—"

"But," he said, raising a hand, "you still get carbon dioxide. However clean you can burn it, it can't help putting out that CO two. Just how severe the greenhouse effect is is a matter of controversy, but no matter how you slice it, if we keep on increasing the rate we burn coal, we're gonna pay some hefty consequences.

"So," he said, "bottom line, I say—let's do it!"

"Well, I still don't know . . . " Kate said. She felt a little betrayed—she'd thought that Dave and Beth were the two reasonable people on the team, the ones most likely to listen to the idea that maybe they should think a bit more about the implications of what they were doing. She was pretty sure that people would get hurt if they released the virus, and wanted to be absolutely sure that the results would be worth it, that was all. But it seemed that they were all eco-fascists now.

"We're talking saving lives here," Jake said. "Saving hundreds of thousands of lives. We're going to be heroes."

And put half of Appalachia out of work, Kate thought, the half that isn't *already* out of work. But maybe it was worth it. She kept her doubts to herself, and let them release the virus that she and Jiao Jiang had made.

### The Eighth Meeting

Kate decided she liked Dave's new dark-skinned appearance. His facial features were still Caucasian, but she knew that if he stayed black for another few months they, too, would begin to shift. Maybe she should think about the change herself. Would Dave notice her more as a black woman? He certainly didn't seem to now. Maybe when summer rolled around. Better than getting a tan. She would cut her hair real short as soon as she got infected, she decided, let the new hair grow in curly.

Jake—who was still white—passed around the secret scrapbook. It was mostly filled with newspaper clippings about the spread of the mysterious "contagious melaninitis"—white people turning black—throughout the Midwest and the South, but the last few pages were devoted to news clippings about the outbreak of a new disease, already being called coal-miner's syndrome. There had been a few deaths, Kate was surprised to note, coal miners who had continued working until their bodies went into complete histamine shock.

"Hey, if they were stupid enough to keep on working in the mine even after it was *obvious* it was killing them, they deserved to die," Jake said. "Cheer up. Evolution in action."

So much for your talk about saving lives, Kate thought. But, "It's about time to release the melanin-suppressing virus," was all she said. "The one that turns black people white."

"That'll confuse people," said David. "Which is good. People need to be confused sometimes. Too much regularity in life."

"But so far we've been attacking symptoms," Beth said. In the course of six months, their undergraduate assistant had been studying world problems almost continuously, even— to Kate's annoyance—neglecting her work in the lab. She was becoming the most serious conspirator of them all. Kate wondered what was driving her. She didn't think Beth had any social life outside the lab at all. But then, between their real work and their secret project, none of them did. "The real problem is overpopulation," Beth continued. "The world population is doubling in less than thirty years. If we don't reduce the size of the population in thirty years, when the population hits ten billion we're going to face a massive die-off, like the dinosaurs."

"And what we do is?" Herbert asked. "Involuntary sterilization?"

"Make the population smaller," said David. "Obvious."

"Obvious."

"I mean the physical size," David said, grinning. "Let's redesign people to grow to only four feet high, maybe four six max. Smaller people use less food, require less oxygen, less energy, can use smaller cars. Our society tends to be prejudiced against short people, but there's no logical reason for it, since small people use fewer resources than big ones. Let shorties be the entire population. Humans used to be smaller a few hundred years ago anyway."

"But it won't solve the problem," Beth said.

"Sure will help the space program," Herbert said. "But why stop? What if people were six inches high?"

"Well, there's got to be a limit somewhere," David said, "if you want to keep brain function."

"Not if you had nanotechnology—"

"Nanotechnology doesn't exist," Jake cut in sharply. "Hello, everybody? Could we get real here? Maybe, talk about a solution that's actually *possible,* instead of re-engineering people from scratch?"

"Well," said David. "It'll be possible *someday.* Maybe ten years, twenty."

"And maybe a hundred. But not yet."

"We need to limit the population now," Beth said. "It's the most important thing we can do."

"Wait a second," Kate said. She was looking at the tiny silver cross Beth wore on a chain around her neck. "It sure sounds like you're talking about birth control."

"So what if I am?" Beth suddenly saw what Kate was looking at. Her left hand stole up to her throat and clasped the cross protectively. "My mother gave it to me," she said defensively. "I don't believe that stuff. Really. I don't even go to mass any more, except when I go home. Besides, it's only a sin if people do it for themselves. If we did it for them, then it's like an act of nature or something."

"Herbert is right," Jake said, breaking in. "We need a virus to cause sterility."

"Yeah, right," said David. "You figure the Earth is better without humans at all? But you know there will always be a few natural immunes. Unless you're going to count on natural immunes to continue the race?"

"It's an idea. No, what I'm figuring is something more subtle. We want a virus that sterilizes after the second kid."

"Now, that's tough—how are you going to teach a virus to count?"

"Not a problem. What we do is, we make a virus sterilizes women, but only after pregnancy, and only if it's a *female* child. That way, on the average, every woman only has two children. Zero population growth, guaranteed."

"Hmmm. Actually slightly negative," David said. "Some women don't have children, some children die, et cetera."

"Slightly negative is good."

"Wait one second, buster!" Beth said. "Why only women? Why not one that sterilizes men?"

"Jeez, Beth, just think about it for a second, will you?" Jake said, exasperated. "It can't work for males—how smart do you think a virus is? There's no way a virus is gonna know whether a guy's knocking up a woman or just beating off. How could you get it to count how many kids a guy has?"

"Wait," Herbert said. "You said the virus sterilizes after the first female child? Won't it skew the sex ratio?"

"No. Work it out."

"But . . . if women are sterilized after the first girl child . . . a woman could still have a whole string of boys . . . there'll be more boys than girls born, right?"

"Why does it have to be girls?" Beth asked. "Why not boys?"

"Wrong, wrong, wrong!" Jake said. "Work it out. Those long strings of sons are precisely balanced by the fifty percent that have a daughter and no sons at all."

"Give me a minute." Herbert tapped on his calculator. After a while he said "It doesn't seem right, but I just simulated a sample population of a million, and it sure looks like you're correct."

"Of course I'm right." Jake turned to Beth. "It would work the same whether you pick boys or girls. I just picked one."

"No," said Jiao Jiang. "It should sterilize after boys, not girls."

"It doesn't make any difference."

"But it does. You see, in many cultures, it is very important that a family have a boy child. If you sterilize after a boy child, then regardless of how many girls the family has, they will be at least a little happy. But if you sterilize after a girl child, half the families will be disappointed."

"So?" said Jake. "That's their problem."

"That's sexist thinking anyway," Beth said. "They should learn to be just as happy with girls."

Jiao Jiang shook her head. "If you are trying to solve the population problem, I agree this is a serious problem. If you are trying to change every culture in the world to make it more like America, I think you are very foolish. You do not know how much disruption you will cause."

"So, okay, already," said Jake. "It works either way. Boys it is."

### The Fourth Experiment

It took them six months before Kate admitted to herself that they'd picked a problem that they couldn't solve, and another two months for even Jake to give up.

It had seemed so simple compared to other problems that they had solved, but eventually she just ran out of approaches. She'd tried a dozen likely lines of solution, and one by one each one had proved too tough to handle. The problem was hard in too many different ways. It proved to be impossible for them to make a virus that sterilized reliably, one that wasn't too easily destroyed by the immune system, one that didn't have other, fatal, side-effects, one that triggered only on a pregnancy—much less one that was specific for sex of the fetus.

"We just don't have good enough tools," Kate concluded. "We've got our repertoire of virus tricks, maybe half a dozen clever things we've worked out, and this time it just happened that none of our methods does the job. We need some new tricks. It's the secrecy that's killing us. We can't just give a progress talk at Cold Spring Harbor and see if anybody has any ideas. If we had a hundred people working on the problem, tried a hundred approaches—"

"Absolutely not," said Jake.

The lab funding was in jeopardy. All federally funded laboratories were in trouble because of the budget cuts. The fact that Professor Irwald—nominally the director of the laboratory—had been ill for most of last term hadn't helped. This year's budgets were even worse than usual because of the depression. The steel industry had virtually shut down due to the skyrocketing cost of coal, and the resulting price hikes had hit the automobile and building industries especially hard. The unexpected bankruptcy of several of the largest electric utilities had also sent shocks through Wall Street, sending utility stocks—usually considered the bluest of blue chips—plummeting. The results, augmented by the sudden hit on insurance and workman's compensation for diseases nobody had anticipated, had cascaded through the economy.

"It'll get better soon," Jake assured everybody. While Professor Irwald had been sick quite a bit recently, he had gotten well enough to take a trip to Washington to argue for their budget. "This is a transient. Environmentally friendly energy sources will take over from coal generation, and fortunes are going to be made. The economy will take a turn for a better, and federal research funding will be back on track."

Beth still carefully made clippings for the scrapbook, but they were not as cheerful as they had been. The civil war in South Africa was threatening to spread across the rest of Africa. Another dozen people had died of coal miner's syndrome, and this time not coal miners, but ordinary people who just happened to be unusually sensitive.

"We're saving the world," Kate said. She wondered if it was true.

"Right!" said Jake. "That's the attitude, kid. That's it exactly."

### The Ninth Meeting

"I don't know," Beth said. "I mean, I thought I wanted to go into biology because I could help people, you know? But we're making new viruses. Are we really helping people?" Beth's eyes were shadowed, but then, in the candlelight it was hard to read anybody's expression. Tuesdays and Thursdays were their days to get electricity, and so they were holding their conspiracy meeting on a Wednesday. Jake had asked Irwald to get their lab onto the list of emergency facilities exempt from power rationing, but so far without success.

"Tell you the truth, I'm not so sure myself," David said.

"You just have to take the long view," said Jake.

"But if we just devoted our resources to finding cures for diseases—"

"There are a hundred labs doing that, with thousands of times our resources. We're a drop in the bucket."

"I don't know," Beth said. "To tell the truth, I've been thinking about going somewhere else for graduate school. Stanford, maybe."

Jake froze. Kate had never seen him at a loss for words before. Then he said, "Doll, I think—"

She turned on him. "Don't call me doll! And don't tell me what you think! It's my life, and I'll do what I think is best!"

"All I mean is—"

"I don't care what you mean! Leave me alone!"

After a long moment, in a voice that was smaller than Kate

had ever heard him speak in, Jake said, "I thought we were a team. In this together."

"Well, maybe we ought to think again." After a long pause, Beth added, "Besides, I don't even know if I could get admitted here. My grades haven't been so good, you know. I've been spending too much time in your stupid lab."

Jake went over and put his arm around her. "I think we can work something out."

### The Fifth Experiment

"Chimpanzees," Kate said, "are humanity's closest relatives, differing from us in less than one percent of our genetic heritage. Genetically, humans diverged from chimps only five million years ago: barely an instant, evolutionarily speaking."

"Speak for yourself," Jake said. "Are you going somewhere with this, or just talking?"

"An important way in which humans differ from chimpanzees is on chromosome 17," Kate said, ignoring the interruption, "in a section that codes for the protein HGH, human growth hormone. In fact, genetically, it can be argued that human beings are a species of gigantic, hairless chimpanzees. The giganticism is due to the effect of the HGH enzyme."

"Really," David said, interested. "Are you saying—"

"HGH is a protein which is 191 amino-acids long, and its production and effects are now very well understood," continued Kate. "We know its co-enzymes; and last year its complete structure and binding sites were published."

"Which means?" asked David.

"Which means we can synthesize a blocking factor," she

said. She held up a test tube. "Twenty-two amino acids, and we can make it with a simple plasmid. You want smaller humans? I've got them right here."

"Holy shit," said David.

### The Tenth Meeting

"I just think we should talk this one out a little first," Jake said, leaning back in his chair. "I mean, talking about breeding shorties is one thing when Kantrowitz is joking around, but you're *serious.* I mean, don't any of you want to have children someday? Do you really want them to be *dwarfs*?"

"Why not?" David said.

"Don't you care?" Beth said. Her face was white. "It's real people you're talking about here. You want to make children grow up into freaks. Don't you even care?"

David shrugged. "If all the other children are the same, I don't see how you can call them freaks."

"It makes a difference," said Beth, each word enunciated separately, "when it's about children of your own."

"Yeah?" said David. "So, how would you know? You don't have children."

Beth looked away.

Jake's chair came down with a thump. "Shit," he said. "Tell me you're joking."

Without looking at him, Beth shook her head.

"I think Beth and I had better go outside and have a talk," Jake said. "A long talk."

David turned on him. "You meathead, she's an undergraduate! Jacob, just what the hell were you thinking about?"

"I figured she was . . . taking precautions."

David thumped back into his chair, his fists unconsciously

clenched. "You moron. You idiot. You complete, idiotic . . . moron."

In the silence after Jake let the door swing shut, Jiao Jiang said, "Perhaps, with Dr. Jake gone, this is a good time to let you know that I will be leaving the laboratory in a month."

"What?"

"My postdoc. It was not a permanent appointment, you know."

"But—"

"You *are* aware that my research grant is to do gene sequences on lambda-phage DNA to determine the spontaneous mutation rate, not to design new viruses?"

"Of course—"

"I've been falling behind, and I've decided that a change of environment will do me some good."

"I'm sorry," Kate said. "We've been—"

"No," said Jiao Jiang, "It is not just the time spent doing your—our—virus synthesis. Dr. Irwald has been sick, and that too has slowed down my project. I would appreciate it, by the way, if you would not mention to Doctor Jake that I will be leaving. I do not think he will be happy."

"How can you not tell Jake?" Kate asked. "He'll need to know—"

"Jake Rankin is not the head of this laboratory," Jiao Jiang interrupted her, "although I can see how you might have forgotten that point. The lab belongs to Dr. Irwald."

"Of course it does. But—"

"I work for Dr. Irwald. It is his job to inform Jake that I will be leaving, if and when he decides to do so, and I'd appreciate it if you would leave this to him."

Kate nodded slowly. "If you'd prefer, sure. But I still don't see why it's important to you."

"Because you are so naive. Do you really think that you and I are the only ones in this laboratory synthesizing viruses?"

"Well—yes."

"It hasn't bothered you that Professor Irwald has been sick almost all semester?"

"That's ridiculous."

"And the lab is being run by an ambitious research professor who would do just about anything to get a tenure track position?"

"Just what the heck are you saying? Besides—"

"Have you noticed, by the way, that a lot of world leaders have taken quiet leaves of absence due to health problems? Libya, Iran, Serbia . . . I could name quite a few."

"Jake doesn't have the background to synthesize a virus. Besides, seriously, I rather doubt he's smart enough."

"If you say so."

"I don't believe it."

Jiao Jiang shrugged. "Just as long as you don't tell Dr. Jake that I am leaving, you may believe what you prefer."

"You wouldn't—you don't intend to tell people what we've been doing, do you?"

"She's not stupid, Kate," David said, breaking in. "Even I've heard about NIH regulations for recombinant DNA experiments. She doesn't dare tell anybody."

Jiao Jiang nodded. "I am no longer so sure that what we have been doing has been wise, but I would not be so rash as to discuss it with outsiders. If it comes out just how loose we have been with the NIH containment protocols, I do not think that any of us could get a job, not even as bottle-washers, in any laboratory in America. And I think I would prefer to stay out of prison, as well."

"They wouldn't send us to prison for violating NIH regulations?"

"No?" Jiao Jiang asked. She shook her head. "Not for the regulations, maybe. But it hasn't occurred to you that people have died?"

In the silence that followed, Kate thought through the implications of what Jiao had said.

Then Herbert—who had been listening quietly through the whole thing—said, "I guess I ought to tell you my news, then, too. I won't be doing your computer work in a month, either."

"What?"

"What, are you surprised? You know that I finished my master's six months ago. I mean, these bio-molecular simulations you've been having me program have been real interesting, and I've learned a lot, but it's not exactly a thing I can put on a resume. I've been sending job letters out for months. We don't have any funding for next year. I'm surprised you're not sending out resumes yourself."

"And you want us to avoid telling it to Jake as well?"

"I just got the job offer yesterday." Herbert shrugged. "I was planning to let everybody know at the meeting today. Tell you the truth, I think Jiao's a little paranoid. Go ahead and tell Jake; let everybody know. They'll have to know soon enough anyway."

### The Sixth Experiment

"I just don't believe it. He was so young."

Jake shrugged. "A heart attack can hit anybody. It's more common in older people, but sometimes even children get them. Especially if they're genetically susceptible, or . . . "

"Or what?"

"Well . . . you know, there are certain, predisposing factors for myocardial infarction, such as chemical stimulants, you know? Just maybe—now, I'm not saying—"

"Herbert?" Beth said. "Herbert, use drugs? That's crazy. Only stimulant he needed is—was—a computer screen."

Jake shrugged again. "I guess you never really know for sure." He looked around. "I'm really surprised that Jiao hasn't come to the funeral. I wonder what's keeping her?"

Probably the fact that she's on an airplane over the middle of the Pacific, Kate thought; on her way to Hong Kong as fast as she could go. Jiao Jiang had not even bothered to pack her belongings; just grabbed the most important of her lab notebooks and left the moment she had heard of Herbert's death. She'd called from the airport and asked Kate to pack up some of her things. Kate thought she was overreacting.

Viruses didn't cause heart attacks, Kate thought. A virus that kills its host quickly would be an evolutionary dead-end. But an engineered virus, one designed for only one host? There were a thousand ways a heart could be made to fail.

"Surely she's smart enough to realize that we all have to stick together," Jake said. "Especially now. We've got our secrets to protect."

Kate felt a chill sweep through her. "What do you mean by that?"

"We can't break up the group. I would think that would be obvious to you." Jake was looking at her steadily, so intently that she had to lower her eyes. "We've gone a little far to have people jump ship now, you know. Herbert should have known that."

"You're implying just what, exactly?"

Jake kept on looking at her. "Nothing," he said. "I'm not implying anything at all."

\* \* \*

On David's television, news commentators were discussing the civil war in Iraq. The one with the toupee was suggesting that it was likely to go nuclear soon. Kate wondered if it had really been Jake who had triggered the inexplicable, sudden illness that had toppled the government and led to the chaos, and, if he had, what he thought about it now.

"I have to talk," Kate said, "and you're the only person I trust."

"So talk," said David. He had been watching the television with only half his attention anyway. He turned it off and looked at her.

"Jiao Jiang thinks that Jake killed Herbert."

"What do you think?"

"I just don't know. It would have to be a virus . . . maybe the coal allergy virus, modified. I can't believe it, but . . . I talked to Jake at the funeral, and it almost sounded like he was trying to hint . . . I don't know."

"What would you do if he did?"

"I don't know."

"Would you kill him?"

"No! Of course not! I'd—I don't know. I just don't know."

"Jiao Jiang is a pretty smart lady," David said, "and the secrets we know could blow Jake right out of the water. I don't think that he's the kind of guy who would let somebody have power over him, unless he had some sort of hold on them."

"So what are you going to do?"

"I've started writing down everything I know," David said, "and giving it to somebody I trust. I suggest perhaps you might do the same."

## *The Eleventh Meeting*

It had never been her style to leave important questions unanswered. She found Jake in his office. "I've written down everything we've done, right from the beginning" Kate said. She put her palms on Jake's desk and leaned forward. "Every virus we've made, and how we released them. I've made several copies. I've left these with a few people I know."

"What?" said Jake. "Just what the hell are you trying to do? Do you want to destroy everything? You want to spend the rest of your life in jail?"

"These are people I can trust," Kate said. "They won't read it unless I tell them they can. Not as long as I'm alive."

"You're crazy." Jake shoved his chair back and stood up. "You go and get them back, immediately." When Kate didn't move, he said, "Do it! That's an order."

"And who appointed you to give orders?" Kate asked. "Jiao Jiang didn't think you can be trusted. Maybe she was wrong. Prove it to me."

"That lying Chink bitch! Where is she?"

"Far away."

"She's a lying, worthless, cheating slant-eyed whore. I never should have trusted her." Jake kicked his chair backwards, made a fist and moved up close. "Now, where is she?"

Kate altered her stance slightly, bending her knees and centering her weight over the balls of her feet. She made sure her arms were free, and forced her breath to become even and regular. "If you think you're going to hit me," she said, trying to project calm strength, "I believe I will break your arm."

Jake shuffled his feet microscopically, looked at his hand as if he'd just noticed he was holding it up, and then brought it up to his neck to scratch a suddenly-appearing itch.

Kate let the tension in her shoulders relax slightly, but didn't let it show. She couldn't have taken him, but there was no way he could have known that. As it happened, she had gotten a postcard from Jiao that morning, but she wasn't about to tell Jake. "I don't intend," Kate said, "to tell you anything about where Jiao went."

"You bitch." Jake took half a step backwards. "You're nothing but an ugly, stupid cow. If it weren't for me, you'd be nowhere, and you know it. This is my lab, and I say who comes and goes. If you don't cooperate with me, you can be damn sure you're going to get what's coming to you. Now, one more time: just where did she go?"

"I don't believe I want to continue this conversation any further, Doctor Rankin. I suggest that you count me out of your future plans."

"Damn right I'm counting you out, you stupid cow. I should have known you couldn't be trusted. You're out, do you understand?"

"Fine."

"Fine? I'll show you fine. I mean out of the lab, out of a job, out on the streets. I've got connections, and I can make sure you'll never be trusted in a bio lab again. You can just try to make a living selling your precious ass on street corners, you stinking slut. I knew you couldn't be trusted. And don't make a lot of long-range plans. You're gonna get what's coming to you, and I promise that you're not going to like it, either. Have you ever heard of a cofactor virus? Do you think that the Chink bitch got away? Think again, you ugly cow. You're not half as smart as you think you are. I don't have to know where she is to get her, and I don't have to know where you are, either. I promise you that you're going to come begging back to me. Crawling, do you hear me? Crawling!"

\*    \*    \*

Jake's words had rattled her more than she'd realized. If she'd been thinking straight she would have gone straight to the lab, to make sure her lab notebooks were safe. Instead she had gone home, to spend an hour pacing up and down her apartment, staring at the walls and replaying the conversation in her head.

She'd thought she knew him. This was a side she'd never seen, although, in hindsight, she should have realized how carefully controlled Jake had been, wondered what he was hiding.

Cofactor virus.

They'd talked about it enough; a virus that would wait dormant in the body, inhibited as long as the victim's environment contained some keying chemical. If he'd given them such a virus, and spiked the laboratory with a minuscule amount of the suppressor chemical, it was the perfect tool to keep her trapped here, at least until she analyzed what the cofactor was. It would kill her if she left.

Jiao hadn't even had a warning.

Could she sample her blood? Could she find and recognize one virus among the hundreds of usually harmless viruses typically resident in human tissues? That was a task for teams of virologists, taking years to identify a single virus.

It might be easier to find the cofactor. It would have to be a small molecule, high vapor pressure, something not found in most environments, easily taken up in the blood serum. She could think of a dozen candidates off hand.

In any case, she had to get to the lab.

The door was locked. It was an electronic combination lock, a precaution required by the biological containment protocols to keep unqualified personnel such as janitors and curious students from unintentional exposure to potentially hazardous materials. She'd known in principle that the combination could be changed, but it had been the same for all the time she'd been there. She punched her code in again, hoping she'd just mis-keyed it the first time, and then a third time.

At last she realized it wouldn't do her any good.

Her lab notebooks were in there. All the equipment, all the supplies, Herbert's computer terminal, their bio-design simulation. She had allowed all her tools to be taken away without even a protest.

She couldn't get hold of David. Jake picked up his phone, but only laughed when she told him she needed to get into the lab.

She had nowhere else to go, so she went home.

She wasn't totally locked away from her work, she realized. Her home computer could dial in to the university computer, and access the bio-simulation that she and Herbert had made.

If Jake was designing viruses, he must be using this program. It was their secret weapon; it was the best in the world. Jake had watched them do it enough times, he might have learned to run it himself. But he would have stored his results on his own machine, not left them on the mainframe. No way she could figure out what he had been doing.

Tape backups? Unlikely: the default output mode went directly to the terminal.

She stared at the program for a long time. There was always the question of ethics, but they had answered that question long ago, the first time they had let a virus loose. They had replaced the question of ethics with one of power: not, *should* we, but *can* we?

There was one thing she could do. The magnetic tape with their DNA sequences was still loaded in the machine. She copied the files she wanted, logged off, and then went to sleep.

### The Seventh Experiment

"He was bluffing about the cofactor virus," she told David, "the same way I had been bluffing about writing down what we had been doing."

"But how could you know for sure?"

"Well, I don't think he was smart enough. I could see Jake maybe grabbing one of the viruses we'd worked on already; possibly picking up on a design we'd abandoned because the simulations showed fatal side effects. But not designing a virus from scratch."

Dave shook his head. "That was taking a big risk."

"Not really. I'd gotten a postcard from Jiao. If he'd actually done it, Jiao would, at the very least, have been sick. She'd been gone for days. No, the cofactor business was something he made up on the spot to scare me, try to intimidate me into backing down."

"He might have come up with it later," David said, "after Jiao left. To keep anybody else from leaving."

Kate shook her head. "Didn't have time."

"It could have gotten ugly," David said. "We were lucky your friend Jake wasn't as careful in the lab as you and Jiao. Makes me shudder—one slip, and that could have been any of us."

"We weren't working on lethal viruses."

"Still, mistakes can happen. Beth was pretty shook up about what happened to him."

"She's resilient. She'll get over it."

"You're sure that the one that killed Jake isn't loose? I keep thinking we should have raised an alarm."

"The cremation will be enough. And it isn't contagious—it was a one-host virus, with no natural vector."

David shook his head again. "At least he died quickly. It's just hard to believe Jake would make such an incredible blunder, and accidentally select a section of his own genetic code as a triggering cofactor."

"It was a simple computer error. The system had DNA files on all of us. I expect that he just copied the wrong file."

David whistled. "Then we really are lucky."

"Lucky." Kate turned away so David wouldn't read the conflicting emotions on her face, or the fact that she was trembling slightly. She felt at the same time relieved and sick, guilty and afraid. He had been after them. She had copied Jake's DNA code into all of the computer files that used to hold their DNA. It hadn't mattered who he had been trying to hit; the virus he had targeted for her had struck him down himself. Suicide, she told herself. Call it suicide. He had been killed by the virus he had been trying to aim at them.

"Lucky?" she said, slowly. "Lucky? I guess we were."

### The Last Experiment

At the university, life went on. In only a few weeks graduation day had arrived. Kate sat in the back row, on a folding chair set on a lawn packed with parents, siblings, and well-wishers, and wondered if any of their well-intentioned changes had done any real good. Perhaps it was too early to tell. Fighting still raged across South Africa, and Iran and Pakistan had entered on opposite sides of the Iraqi civil war. In America, several important black—formerly black—journalists had propounded a theory that the melaninitis virus had been deliberately designed by the CIA to destroy black culture and destroy affirmative action, without solving any of the urgent problems of poverty and repression. The coal depression was entering its second year. Someday, perhaps, the promised new energy sources would arrive and solve all their problems. Nobody could say when.

She looked at the perfume sprayer in her hand.

She'd asked Beth, right before Beth had left for her seat up front, why she had joined with them in the conspiracy. Didn't she worry about playing God?

Beth had only shaken her head. The nuns at Immaculate Heart, she had said, instilled in each of their charges a strict sense of duty. Everyone can change the world, they'd told her. It is important for each of us to improve the world, in little ways or great ways, and the sin of omission, not to try to make things better with whatever means you were given, was far less forgivable than to try, and fail.

The valedictorian, when she could hear his words, seemed to be saying the same thing.

Kate looked at the perfume sprayer again, and then out at the seated rows of people, the graduating class, young and earnest and eager to change the world. There was a slight breeze at her back, blowing into the crowd.

Smaller people. It would give the world a pause, one more generation before humanity suffocated in their own wastes, perhaps time enough to learn to solve our problems. Time, at least, for this generation to have its chance to change the world.

Had they learned anything at all? She smiled wryly. None of those were the real reasons. They had changed the world, she thought, for one reason: because they could.

Shaking her head, still smiling, she started to spray.

# THE INVASION OF SPACE

▼

## JAMES KIRKWOOD

There's a starting point for everything. Every great development has a "Big Bang," a moment when it all begins. But we may not agree on the pivotal event.

For one of us—I *am* one of us, although for reasons that will be apparent later I will not say which one—it was January 28, 1986, with the loss of the *Challenger*. The technical failure of the shuttle's solid rocket boosters was a symptom but it was not a cause. The cause was management failure, bureaucrats placing politics ahead of engineering.

For another it came four years later, when the Hubble Space Telescope, which he had hyped hard in his writings and awaited for years, was finally launched—and was found within a couple of months to be badly flawed. The primary mirror had been ground, with infinite care, into the wrong shape. Again, it was a management failure. Sanity checks on mirror shape had been neglected because of schedule and budget pressures.

Two other members of our core group were not much worried about the shuttle or the space telescope. They were planetary science nuts. They lost it when the Galileo main antenna refused to deploy after launch, and then a few months later the Mars Observer disappeared. Bang went a couple of billion dollars; vanishing with the money went the best opportunity to study Jupiter and Mars during the twentieth century.

These facts and feelings did not emerge systematically. They came to light when the group who would later call themselves the Gang of Seven held a long, random meeting over Labor Day weekend. And by another quirk, the catalyst for everything that followed was not a member of the group at all. He was an outsider (and not me; I will give away that much). Sid Rawlings had his own union card, but his Ph.D. was in English literature, with a dissertation on the works of J.G. Ballard. The other six of us were authentic techies, practicing scientists and scientist/writers. But Sid was a science groupie who liked to hang around the rest of us, so he was tolerated.

Tolerated because he was pretty quiet, at least around scientists. The other six were more than ready to talk about anything, and a listening member was rather welcomed. And tolerated also because, although none of us would ever admit it, Sid was a better *writer*. We could all do the far-out visionary stuff and the grand climaxes, what Sir Walter Scott referred to as "the big bow-wow;" but Sid was lyrical, compact, passionate, and poetic, all at the same time, in a way that was beyond us.

The day of our meeting had been a bad one for Sid. None of us knew it at the time, but his live-in girl friend of two years had dumped him that morning for a chain-smoking attorney "more my own age." Sid was a physical fitness fanatic. He worked out every day and climbed mountains whenever he had a chance. He was in terrific shape. He would probably outlive his nicotine-addicted rival by decades. But he was eleven years older than Carol; a point not disputable.

So although Sid was not a drinking man, on that evening he drank. Drank in Jason Perrine's suite, while we watched the videotape that Allen Anderson had brought with him of the latest Delta Clipper single-stage-to-orbit tests. Drank while we all "oohed" and "aahed" and gloated over their success. Drank while Dick Banning, who had done a two-year stint at the White House and kept up his connections there, gave us the bad news: we were watching the last tests, because the funding had dried up. If the program were to go on it would have to be turned over to NASA.

"Which means it's buggered." Chris Scarborough had been sitting with his right hand pressed to his forehead. He had arrived late the previous night from Washington, and was suffering from lack of sleep and a sinus headache. "Turn it over to NASA, you might as well flush the money down the toilet."

"You still knocking NASA?" Bill Findlay was sometimes referred to by the others as a NASA shill. On the other hand, anyone who bought a house on the extreme northeast coast of Scotland, as Bill Findlay had done, in order to spend the *winters* there, had to be a little strange.

"You talk about NASA's failures," Bill went on. "Well, I can cite dozens of *successes.* Apollo, Pioneer, Landsat, Skylab, Viking, IUE, Voyager, Magellan—how many do you want? Compare that with the record of Housing and Urban Development, or Health and Human Services, or Drug Enforcement, or Education. Or what about the Department of Energy, supposed to clean up the nuclear sites in the next decade—"

"My favorite is still EPA," Geoff Binton said. We had known each other for a long time, and interruptions were taken for granted. "EPA spent billions, and they haven't cleaned up a single major toxic waste site. They ought to be called the Environmental *Pollution* Agency."

"Don't change the subject." Bill Findlay turned again to Chris Scarborough. "Come on, Chris. You know the Washington scene better than anyone. Admit it, the trouble isn't NASA, it's Congress. They won't fund anything in a systematic way. The House and Senate are equally bad, all pork-barreling and corruption."

"Hey, don't blame *me* for Congress." Chris stuck a cortisone spray up his nose and sniffed hard. "I just live there. You won't find me defending them. They only care about two things: re-election, and lining their own pockets. But I agree with you and Dick, the other agencies are as bad. I sometimes think the signs they have around Washington offices, 'This is a drug-free work zone,' have it backwards. They should say, 'This is a work-free drug zone.'"

"So Chris agrees with me—for once." Findlay addressed himself to Jason Perrine, usually NASA's harshest critic. "It's not NASA."

"I never said that!" Chris Scarborough had not been drinking at a rate to match Sid Rawlings, but he was not entirely sober. That combined with his headache to take away a little of his usual smoothness. "You gave a list of NASA successes, Apollo and Voyager and the rest. But you didn't mention that everything on your list was done decades ago. Voyager didn't reach Neptune until 1989, but it was launched in 1977. IUE is still functioning and returning data, but it was launched in seventy-eight. You tell me something that NASA has done *recently* that's good. Don't say the Hubble fix-up—

correcting your own mistakes doesn't count. Not communications, either. That's all commercial. You want to try and persuade us on Space Station? Where they've already spent the original eight billion dollar estimate, and still don't have a *design?* Where are the NASA success stories since 1980?"

That's when everyone started to talk at once. All the personal frustrations and disappointments and obsessions came to light, until finally, in the middle of the hubbub, Sid Rawlings spoke. He wasn't loud, but his voice was so intense that everyone else stopped talking at once.

"It is NASA. But it's not *only* NASA. Want to know what's wrong with NASA and with the whole space program? I'll tell you. It's the same thing that's wrong with all of you." He turned on Jason Perrine. "You've got your books and your lecturing and your computer columns. How much money did you make last year?"

Jason recoiled, as though Sid had reached out and hit him. "What the hell has that to do with anything?"

"A lot. Never mind an exact number. Say it's three hundred thousand dollars, say it's a million. Do you work any harder now than when you made thirty thousand a year?"

Jason turned red. "I work damned hard. I always have."

"I believe you. But you didn't answer my question. I'll answer it for you—for all of us, including me." Sid glared around the group. "We all work hard. But not quite as hard as we did twenty-five years ago, because we're all lucky. We made it. Even the poorest of us has his house paid off and a comfortable pile of money. How long since one of you watched every mail delivery, waiting for a check so you could pay the rent or buy groceries?"

"Hey, I'm not a best-seller," Allen Anderson protested. "I don't make a fortune."

"No, but you're comfortable. And you're part of the *problem.* You work for the enemy, and that's worse than being a fat, pompous, pontificating writer."

Jason bristled, but Allen Anderson was in before him. "Damn you, Sid, I work for a private company, not the government or Congress."

"Yeah. As part of a federal facility support contract." Sid turned on Allen, more savage than ever. "Your paycheck comes from a company, sure, but everything you do and have—paper, computers, phone bills, travel—comes straight out of taxpayers' pockets. The private companies are worse than the feds. You listen to their commercials, you'd think they care about the space station or SSTO or EOS. But when you look closely, all they want is to suck on the government tit. They're no more interested in Mars than in missiles. And if they don't smell a contract, they're gone before you can blink."

"You're talking big companies." Chris Scarborough spoke up. "I work for a little one. We don't have anyone looking out for us, the way the government looks after Lockheed or Martin. We have to make it on our own."

He should have kept quiet. Sid Rawlings swiveled in his seat to face him, almost falling over as he did so.

"On your own? Don't give me that. You're worse than anyone. Do you think the rest of us are idiots? We know you're part of the tightest old-boy network of all. You do top secret classified work, where everything is clearances and sole source contracts. *And* you slap a high security label on a project if it's a major screw-up. Chris, if *anyone* feeds off the system and has their own built-in safety net, it's you. And Dick and Allen and Bill are just as bad."

The lack of logic in the final sentence didn't prevent Chris

Scarborough from turning as white as Jason Perrine was red. "You're pissed, Sid. You should learn to keep your mouth shut when you've been drinking. Maybe then *you'd* be trusted with something important. Maybe—"

But Rawlings was not listening. He had continued to turn, expanding his attack to everyone in the room.

"You lot. You think you're the elite, scientists and writers both. You know the terrible thing? You *are* the goddamned elite. Kids want to meet you, they listen to you, they hang onto your every word. They know you're rich, but they don't realize you're complacent. You and NASA, there's no real difference. Their top layer is full of over-the-hill bureaucrats, avoiding risk, slowing things down, marking time until retirement. You're no better. You all talk well enough, but tell me a cause you'd give everything you've got for—your money and time and energy, even your family. Tell me a cause you'd *die* for. I've got one—but have you? The hell with all of you. I'm getting out of here."

It was a long, drunken, impassioned speech, and its appearance from Sid's mouth seemed to startle him. He stumbled to the door, went out, and slammed it behind him. The rest of us stared after him in silence, until Jason said, "He'll find it a tight exit if he tries to leave through there. That's the bathroom."

"Is he all right?" Geoff Binton stood up. "Maybe I'd better see—"

He paused. Dreadful vomiting sounds were coming from beyond the door.

"On second thoughts, maybe I'll wait until he's finished. Though I do feel a lot of sympathy for Sid." Geoff preened himself, staring at his reflection in a mirror over the suite's bar. "Did you notice, he didn't say anything bad about me?"

"That's because he didn't need to." Jason, deprived of Sid, switched targets. "You've got tenure. That's the ultimate sinecure. You'll never work again."

"Don't I? Well, fuck you, too."

But the spirit seemed to have gone from the group. After a few minutes of desultory argument, all of us except Jason hurried away one by one.

He would have left, too, but he couldn't. It was his suite. Whatever Sid was doing in the bathroom might be his fault, but clearing it up was going to be Jason's responsibility.

That might have been the end of it, except that Jason Perrine, Chris Scarborough, and Allen Anderson happened to eat breakfast at the same time the next morning, and naturally sat together.

Chris looked warily at Jason. "How's Sid?"

"He's in wonderful shape." Jason poured coffee and looked around for the cream. "He must be. Anyone who can vomit that long and hard and not die of heart failure has to have a great cardiovascular system."

"What time did he leave?"

"He didn't." They paused as their food arrived, and Jason continued, "He's in the other bed in my suite, still snoring. He's all right."

"Good." Allen reached for the salt. "Not like Sid, was it. Something must have been eating at him."

"Something was. Carol. She broke it off."

"Sounds painful. Who's Carol?" Chris didn't keep up well with the California scene.

"Woman. Longtime relationship." Jason sniffed. "I never thought much of her."

"You mean she never thought much of you." But Chris's tone was mild, and the three ate in silence for a couple of minutes until he went on, "I've been thinking a lot about what Sid said."

"Me too."

"And me." Jason paused, laden fork in hand. "You know something? When I got over being mad, I decided that he was right."

"Yeah. Not only that, he rubbed our noses in it."

There was another substantial silence, until Chris said softly, "Well, gentlemen. What now? Nothing? Business as usual?"

They looked at each other. At last Allen shook his head. "Sid was on the mark, at least for me. I won't accept nothing. Not if it can be something."

"Do you know where the others are staying?" Jason frowned at Allen.

"Dick Banning and Bill Findlay are at the same hotel as me and Chris. I don't know about Geoff Binton. Or Sid either, if you think he should be included."

"Definitely." Jason dropped dollars on the table and stood up. "He started it, he stays with it. He says he has something he'd die for, let's find out what it is. I don't think you need to worry about locating his hotel. I'd be amazed if he moved since I left him. I'll find Geoff. Call me as soon as you talk to the others."

Sid Rawlings did not look like the man who had climbed the Matterhorn and made it to twenty-three thousand feet on Everest. He looked like a man who had spent the night embracing a toilet bowl.

He had sympathy but no relief. The others had been there often enough themselves, in the days when hard drinking was pleasure and future pain did not count.

"All right." The spokesman, not for the first time, was

Chris Scarborough. "Sid, you told us what you thought of us yesterday. We're rich, we're lazy, we're full of waffle. We sit and we pontificate, but we don't do anything. So what should we be doing?"

"I didn't say you pontificate."

"You sure as hell did." Jason Perrine had a voice to carry over the general outcry. "Fat, pompous, pontificating, you called us."

"I was shit-faced drunk."

"Which is no excuse. This isn't Japan. Chris is right. Put up or shut up."

"All right." Sid stared around him. "Coffee?"

"Six flavors, right there. From Len. I talked to him. He'd like to be in on this."

"So why isn't he? He has more money than any of us."

"He's on a panel. And he values his personal time."

"So do we all." That was Chris again, who wasted more time tilting at windmills than anyone in known space. "Hit it, Sid. Jason will snare Len when we need him."

"All right." Sid took a long, steadying breath and stared around him. "Let's start with the basics. What's the most important thing the space program needs?"

It was a rhetorical question. We had agreed on that long ago. It wasn't the space station, or a solar power satellite, or a better science program.

"It needs a single-stage-to-orbit, reusable, low-cost spacecraft with rapid ground turnaround." Jason spoke, but he spoke for the whole group. His comment met nothing but vigorous nods of agreement. "Once we have that, everything else follows. SPS, the Moon, Mars, the whole solar system; you name it."

"And without it, we have nothing." Sid nodded. "All

right. I agree. Now I'm going to tell you a story. About NASA."

"Another one?!" "Screw NASA." "Ah, a *horror* story!" *"NASA delenda est."* (That last from Chris, who before coming to the U.S. had suffered a classical education.)

But Sid went on, ignoring the storm of comments. "It isn't a true story, but I have no trouble believing it.

"NASA developed a new rocket too dangerous to fly under U.S. regulations."

("Yeah, and it took 'em fifty years to do it." "Oh shit, OSHA." "Let the man *talk*, for God's sake.")

"So a NASA representative was sent abroad to find an astronaut candidate. First he went to Germany. He asked the German candidate, 'How much do you want to fly this very dangerous rocket to the Moon?' "

"And the Kraut—"

("Racist, racist." "Nah, politically incorrect!")

"And the Kraut says, 'Three million dollars.' So the NASA rep says, 'Why three million?'

"The German says, 'It is a fair price. One million for me, one million for my wife and family, and one million for *the Fatherland.*'

" 'Right,' says the NASA guy. And he flies on to France. He says to the French candidate, 'How much do you want to fly this dangerous rocket to the Moon?'

" 'I want six million dollars.'

" 'All right.' The NASA rep makes a note. 'And why six million dollars?'

" 'Two million for me, *n'est-ce pas?* And two million for my wife and family. And two million for my mistress.'

" 'Fair enough,' says the NASA negotiator, and he flies on to Iran.

"He meets with someone at Mehrabad airport, an oily type he wouldn't normally go near. 'How much,' he says, 'to fly this dangerous rocket to the moon?'

" 'For you, my friend, an exceptionally good deal. Only nine million dollars.'

" 'Nine million?' The NASA guy looks at his notes. 'Isn't that a little high?'

" 'Not at all.' The Iranian leaned close. 'First, my friend, there is three million dollars for *you*. And then there will be three million for me.'

" 'But you said *nine*. What about the other three?' "

"The Iranian shrugged. 'Well, we still have to pay that crazy German to fly your rocket to the Moon.' "

Sid stopped. The others waited, until it became clear that he was done.

"Well?" Allen Anderson said. "Or do I mean, what?"

"I'll tell you what." Sid Rawlings glared around, no less fiery sober than when he was drunk. "You don't need to do the world tour. I'm the crazy German who's willing to fly the rocket. Get the money, and I'll sit on top of my own funeral pyre if it goes into orbit. Hell, I *want* to do it. But don't you see what's missing?"

There was a long, blank silence, until Sid sighed and said, "What's missing is the three million dollars for *you*—I mean for the American people. We never told them where *their* three million dollars is, and how they'll get it. What's in it for *them?* Until we spell that out—and *you* have to do it, not me, 'cause God knows you famous chain-talking experts have a thousand times my technical credibility—but until we do it we have no driving force. We'll sit on our rear ends until Doomsday, right here on Earth. You sell books easily enough, all of you. Can you sell people?"

"I do nothing *but* sell people." Chris spoke first, although

Allen, Dick, Bill, and Jason chimed in at almost the same time. "Selling people is my specialty. How can I do more?"

"By putting more on the line." Sid looked at the rest of us, one by one. "Maybe you already think you give up something. But you give up fat. I'm talking bone and sinew. I'm not talking two inches off your waist. I'm talking two inches off your dick."

"Pu-pu-pu*leeze.*" Dick Banning went into Roger Rabbit mode. "Two inches. Half of all I have."

"Right." Sid didn't take it as a joke at all. "One half will be enough. Half your time, half your money, half of everything. I'm willing to put in a hundred percent. I'm willing to *die.* Find a way to build that sucker, I'll sit on top and ride it wherever it goes. But I can't tell you how it gets built, 'cause I don't know. That's up to you lot."

There was a long silence; not of impotence, but of thought.

"Fifty-one senators," Allen Anderson said thoughtfully. "And two hundred and eighteen representatives. That's for starters."

"With a core group of pushers. Say, four House, four Senate." Jason Perrine's tone was gentle, almost philosophical. The tenor of the meeting had changed. Thought and planning had replaced emotion. "I can get a couple, maybe three on the House side. Chris? A couple more?"

"Jesus Christ." Scarborough looked stricken. "Do you realize how long I've worked to build up favors in Washington?"

"Great. What do you propose to do? Die with them uncalled, or wait till your buddies are shunted out of office?"

"I get the message. All right. I'll find a couple on Appropriations. Better than that—I'll deliver staffers. They're the ones who really tilt Congressional thinking. But they can't do a thing unless the people back home send the right signals and messages. I said it yesterday: Re-election is the name of the game."

"We'll get to that." Sid, mysteriously, had become the leader of the group. Given the strong egos involved, that in itself was a miracle. "Public opinion, grassroots support, and a defined strategy and schedule. All vital.

"But first we have to deal with something unpleasant. You all pride yourselves on being broad-gauge, multi-faceted people. Don't bother to argue, I've heard every one of you say you are. But if you're serious about this, we have to become what we all despise: one-noters. Until we succeed we have to be single-issue advocates, plugging the same thing over and over."

"But anyone like that loses—"

"I know. You have to do it so cleverly that no one knows it. We can't afford to be like the one-note fanatics at the airports or out on street corners. Our message has to be ninety percent subliminal."

"The planetary program." Geoff Binton spoke in a whisper, almost drowned out by Bill Findlay's groan of "Advanced propulsion methods!"

"No." Sid did not raise his voice, but there was finality in it. "You are either in this, or out of it. No partial entries. We'll be planning an invasion, and war has no time for spectators. But if we win—when we win—you'll get everything else on your wish list as a by-product. Planetary exploration *and* advanced propulsion."

Silence. At last—

"I'm in." That was Jason. The rest of us slowly nodded, one by one, all except Chris, who said, "I'm probably in, too. I'll even be a one-noter, though I hate the idea. But I have to know the rest of it. What does 'in' imply?"

Sid nodded. His hangover must have been fading. "Fair

question. 'In' means a commitment. At least twenty-four hours a week from everyone." He smiled grimly. "That's twenty-four *real* hours. Grinding, concentrated, maximum-effort work. Not the sort of half-assed effort that three man-days buys on a government contract."

That's the point where I, personally, almost backed out. I knew from experience that most people didn't do twenty-four hours of real work in a whole month. Useful time was diluted by coffee breaks, social conversation, review meetings, brief-ings, phone calls, vacations, and the thousand-and-one dis-tractions that seem to come with professional success.

But then Sid added, "I'm willing to promise more than that. I'll guarantee every hour and every minute of my time. One day we're going to die, all of us. And when we lie on our deathbeds we may be thinking to ourselves, in my life I did many things but no one will remember any of them in ten years or a hundred. Or we may be thinking, I was part of the most important event of this century and the next."

Sid wouldn't get his wish, but not for any reason we could have predicted. We went on to make plans, without any sort of formal vote or agreement. It was time to define the hard work and divvy up the chores.

A real and scrupulous historian, devoting as much effort to describing the next four years as I have done in talking of the first twenty-four hours, would produce a monumental text of ten thousand pages.

Fortunately I am not an historian. I am allowed to—obliged to—summarize.

Thus: first came two months of confusion in which each of us saw our own roles more clearly. I suspect that in the same period each of us also had the urge to back out. I know I did. And if I stayed in, it was only because in some strange sense my honor was at stake in the eyes of people I felt to be my peers—the only group, really, who mattered.

We all stayed in, and we started to work harder than any of us had worked for fifteen years. I gave up many of the "essential" things that used to fill my days and weeks. For years I had stored within my computer a list of statements that appeared when it was first turned on. One of them was, "I could achieve great things if I did not fill my days with small things." At last I realized what that statement meant. And I erased from my computer list another old maxim: "Time is money."

Time isn't money. Time is more important than money could ever be.

We also learned, by hard experience, to submit our actions for group review. We could not afford false statements or, worse, reveal too much of our agenda. That was the toughest lesson of all. Every one of us was used to thinking he knew best. But we didn't; and we learned.

Our reward? A full year of huge frustration. Not one of us seemed to be making progress. Worse than that, Sid had a positive genius for pointing out other areas that needed work. We were, he said, all white males over forty. How could we win the hearts and minds of the American people if we excluded more than three-quarters of them? *First, there's three million dollars for you.* We had to reach out.

He was right. Our cozy clique was not enough. The Gang of Seven by careful expansion became a gang of twenty, forty, sixty, a hundred, mixed in gender, race, and background. I no longer recognized all the members on sight, or knew quite what they were doing for The Program. That's another reason I am obliged to summarize.

We never did give The Program any other name. If we were to succeed, it would finally include everything that any of us could think of, and more. Why limit it, by a restriction to one vehicle, or to work within a one or two-year time frame?

Perhaps that was just as well. Because the dam never did break. There was not a moment during four full years where the original Gang of Seven could call each other and say, "Success! We made it."

Yet we did—at last, slowly and painfully, never the way we wanted it. The House and Senate found a hundred and fifty million of funding, somehow, for one more year of single-stage-to-orbit development. When that was done we found ourselves in the same position all over again, facing a next-year cut-off, always on the edge of the steep slope to cancellation. We worked on that, and at the same time on public opinion. I remember attending the first convention at which every science panel, by some strange confluence of viewpoint, *assumed* that an SSTO vehicle was the natural next step in space. I remember the first time I read such a statement in a newspaper editorial. I do not recall the first time it was taken as a given during a congressional hearing, but it certainly happened.

After the first year we were all too busy to follow what everyone else was doing in any detail. I know that Jason Perrine, with the help of Len Norris, managed with one hand to deliver the entire science fiction fan community, Trekkers and gamers and all, while with the other hand he and Chris worked Washington. The National Space Society, American Astronautical Society, and Young Astronaut Council fell into line early, thanks to a little internal lobbying—I hate to say "manipulation"—of their boards of directors. The Planetary Society was a tougher nut to crack, but by the end of the first year the case we had put together was overwhelmingly convincing to the three people who mattered.

One nice thing about scientists and engineers, they are highly susceptible to logic. Geoff Binton, Bill Findlay, and

Allen Anderson by a coordinated effort delivered, in succession, the American Physical Society, the American Association for the Advancement of Science, the American Institute of Aeronautics and Astronautics, the National Academy of Engineering, and the National Academy of Sciences.

Generals and admirals are less impressed by logic than by territorial claims and the need to command the high ground. I have no idea what Dick Banning *did*, but I still regard his delivery of unqualified Defense Department support for the SSTO as "vital to military operations" as the *tour de force* that put all our other achievements into the shade. It took him two and a half years; but as Dick said, "What's time to a pig?"

The person left out of all this is Sid Rawlings. He didn't have the cards to play that the rest of us had, the accumulated equity that we were busy cashing in. What he did was very different, and we didn't find out about some of it until later.

We all knew that he had been steadily upgrading his flying qualifications. Before we began he held a commercial pilot's license. He added to that by going through rigorous astronaut training. Dick arranged it, but it was Sid who was pricked, probed, spun, and centrifuged. Finally, as the manned launch test came closer to reality we realized that he had been totally serious in our first meeting. He expected us to pull the strings so that he was on the first mission to carry a crew; and since the prototype was built for a single person, he intended to *be* that crew.

I suppose we could have argued with him. We didn't. We worked the problem. It was almost a point of honor. The deal had been struck in our very first meeting. We would all live up to our piece of it. So Sid had to be the "crazy German" who rode his funeral pyre (though we hoped it wouldn't prove to be that) into orbit.

"Orbit" is an overstatement for the first planned ascent. The pilot would rise fifty miles to the edge of space, perform a few simple maneuvers, and return to the launch pad. Rapid turnaround was part of the agenda. The *Ben Franklin* would be readied to fly again within forty-eight hours. Orbit would be attained on the second flight. Sid was to pilot both the first test and first orbital flight. Then he would be happy to bow out—having proved, as he put it, "that anyone can fly the *Franklin*."

Even though this is a summary, a word has to be said about the name. *Ben Franklin* was a great choice, but it was also a compromise. Of all the tricky pieces of The Program, the naming of the ship in many ways called for the most finesse. I suppose it's a mark of the progress we had achieved that *everyone* was claiming the SSTO as theirs, and thus the right to name it.

Here is a partial list, which I include only to show the diversity of our support: *Goddard, Edison, John F. Kennedy, Einstein, Mahatma Gandhi, Oral Roberts, Martin Luther King, Mickey Mouse* (from guess who), *Jefferson, Elvis, Walt Whitman, Madame Blavatsky, Eisenhower, Robert Heinlein, Aaron Copland, Washington.* These were probably all serious suggestions. Some others, like *Monty Python* and *William Proxmire* and *Jack D. Ripper,* were clearly intended as jokes. *Adolf Hitler* I'm not so sure about. That one came from Iowa accompanied by a long handwritten letter explaining that the era of "space-rockets," as the writer described them, began at Peenemunde, in Germany, during "the reign of Adolph Hitler."

This is just from the list of people names. I'll skip the suggested institutions and objects and commercial products, except for the *Titanic,* which in retrospect foreshadowed events.

\* \* \*

Time marched on. The launch date grew nearer. I won't say nothing went wrong. It is more accurate to say that a thousand things went wrong, but nothing stopped The Program's progress.

As things moved forward Sid also had to admit that he was wrong. The contractors who were building the ship *did* care. We could feel it when we went to the plant. It was like a fever, something had hold of them, something that maybe they had not felt for many years. They were like an old warhorse, pricking up its ears as the trumpet signals the charge. The contractor engineers didn't want cost over-runs, because then they might have to stop work. *Ergo,* no cost over-runs. I don't even want to know how much time and money was stolen from other contracts and given as a secret freebie to the construction and testing of the *Franklin.* I do know that, problems both technical and managerial notwithstanding, the team hit each milestone on or ahead of schedule.

Every member of the Gang of Seven missed either the first roll-out or one or more of the unmanned tests. We were all at Kingman Island, though, when it was Sid's turn.

We were not allowed closer than a mile. From that distance the *Franklin* was a little curved bullet of matte silver, standing on its flat end. To our right were the Press and the banks of cameras, crowding against the barrier as though a single foot nearer made a difference. On our left was the VIP section. The six of us, from pride and an inverted snobbery, avoided that. We sat together. During the last few minutes we did not speak. I am not sure we breathed.

At last we saw the blur of heat at the base of the *Franklin.* Then the white jets of flame. And then there was no point in speaking. The thunder of engines made communication impossible.

Heads tilted back as the ship rose, sedately at first but soon faster and faster. The *Franklin*'s ascent was vertical rather than tilting its path to the east like a launch to orbit. We followed it until the plume became a speck of light, merging at last into the bright sky background.

Sid was on his way. Fifty miles up, fifty miles back. The whole flight would be less than thirty minutes.

How long did it seem?

I doubt that any one of us could answer that question in a meaningful way. From one point of view it was an eternity, longer than any day. It was also no time at all. It formed a hiatus in our lives. Discussing the event later not one of us could recall either hearing or saying a word, until there was a kind of communal breathless sigh when the *Franklin* appeared again, steadily descending on its long stalk of flame.

It landed; exactly on schedule, precisely where it had taken off. The waiting fire trucks to our left set off with the other cars toward the ship, but that was no more than a routine precaution. Before ten minutes had passed Sid was heading towards us sitting in the back of an open jeep. He had already removed his helmet.

A wave to the VIPs, then straight to the press. We had talked this over a thousand times and we knew the priorities. First: the public had to get *its* three million dollars worth. So publicity was number one, then medical with its inevitable tests. Our own turn with Sid would come later and out of sight. The rest of us in the Gang of Seven took a huge and perverse pleasure in our anonymity and secret importance.

Sid had paused in front of the banks of cameras and was wiping his face with a green cloth.

"You're sweating!" called a woman reporter near the front, before Sid had time to open his mouth.

He raised an eyebrow at her. "It's over a hundred degrees out here."

"You mean you weren't frightened while you were on the way down?"

Sid grinned. "Did I say that?"

And suddenly everything seemed relaxed and casual. A ride in the *Franklin,* judging from Sid's attitude, was no more dangerous or nerve-racking than taking an elevator.

He didn't fool *us* for one moment, but then he didn't need to. He chatted—that's the right word for it, even though his comments had been carefully scripted—with the press for five more minutes, then jerked his head to the medical units waiting off to their left.

"Sorry. I'm obviously fine, but the doctors want to get at me." A general mutter of disappointment. "I'll be going up again in two days. Tell you what. It should be quiet in orbit. Arrange for continuous radio and TV hook-up, and I promise you as much time as you like."

That invitation to continuous access sounded like an ad lib. It had not been in the script that we had all reviewed. But if Sid didn't mind giving the media night and day access to him in orbit, we were not going to argue. *Publicity is number one.* First, there's three million dollars for *you.* The public comes first.

"You really think you'll be ready in two days?" That was a parting question as Sid moved away.

"Hope so," he said over his shoulder. "But even if *I'm* not ready, the *Franklin* will be. Refuel the ship now, it could fly again within the hour—and take you with me into orbit."

The media people probably thought he was kidding. They had become used to shuttle launches, with endless interrupted countdowns, delays for weather, super-qualified astronauts, and twenty or thirty thousand dollars for every pound of payload to orbit.

We knew Sid wasn't kidding. He wasn't even exaggerating. Thirty years had made enormous differences in materials, engine design, and computer control. The *Franklin* would take payload to orbit for a hundred dollars a pound. It had been designed for twenty-four hour ground turnaround, and at a pinch it could land, refuel, and fly again at once. We had done just that in the unmanned tests. The only reason for two full days this time was that the ship was still officially in prototype evaluation.

We chafed at the delay.

The second manned launch was more ambitious. It was heading all the way to orbit, and the speeds and stresses on the ship would be much higher. But the media coverage at Kingman was less.

Had we failed? Was public interest already diminishing, or was it only the media's *perception* of the public?

We sat at the launch site in breathless pre-dawn stillness, gritting our collective teeth as the *Franklin* at last lifted, tilted toward the east, and vanished into the sunrise on its extended plume of fire. We hovered in suspended animation until the telemetry reported that the ship had exceeded necessary orbital velocity. Ten more minutes, one small maneuver, and an in-space burn; then Sid was in a stable, four hundred kilometer circular orbit.

He could stay there, if he chose, as little as one revolution or as long as a week. He might even find it boring. Apart from in-space tests of equipment he had no real duties.

The radio and TV linkage began on the second orbit. We watched and listened. Of course *we* listened. But we questioned how many other people were doing the same. The big networks apparently shared our worries. Their first broadcasts were nothing more than short sound bites from Sid, interrupted and talked around by the regular television hosts and newscasters. CNN was the only one to offer long, uninterrupted stretches of coverage.

I wonder how long it took for the radio and TV station managers to catch on. Was it when they found their own program monitors watching CNN? Was it when egotistical talk show hosts who insisted on intruding their usual babble got real-time feedback of a diminishing audience? The smart ones sensed the truth very early. They kept quiet and let Sid talk with minimal interruptions. They knew a good thing when they heard it.

We knew more than that. We were all experienced writers and speakers. We listened to Sid's quiet comments about Earth, stars, space, and humanity as the *Franklin* circled the planet. And we knew, even if the audience did not, that no one spoke like that *ad lib*, off-the-cuff, without preparation. No human could do it; not Cicero, or Demosthenes, or Shakespeare, or Abe Lincoln.

Sid had been preparing for four years, reviewing images of Earth and space, selecting the words to go with them, writing and endlessly rewriting. His broadcasts from orbit, designed to sound impromptu and even casual, were an inspired combination of real-time stimulus building on intense prior thought.

We realized what was happening after the first couple of hours. Since the first human went into orbit the nations of Earth had placed in space people of many different skills; pilots, engineers, physicists, doctors, chemists, biologists. They were all brave, talented, and articulate. But they were no more than that. We thought we had sent to space an amateur astronaut. What we had actually sent, for the first time in human history, was a great poet.

I will not offer a sampling of Sid's words. For one thing, they are readily available, anywhere in the world and in any language. For another, they would remain his words. Neither I, nor any other of the Gang of Seven, could speak or write like that. We admitted the truth to each other, rejoicing at the same time as we wanted to cry. The public was finally getting its three million dollars, and a million times three million.

Sid broadcast, with little pause for rest, for thirty-four hours. He talked of the scenes passing below him, of individual countries, of seas and mountains and lakes and cities and forests. He talked of space, of its endless resources and huge potential value to human life. He talked of life and death, and of the dreams that transcend both. His words were heard live, recorded, and rebroadcast to a waking world as sunrise moved around the globe. By that time all networks in all countries were offering near-continuous coverage.

Finally Sid signed off. He would rest for a little while, he said, and then the *Franklin* would return to Earth. The ship was scheduled for a 7:00 P.M. touchdown, descending in twilight as it had risen at dawn, one day and an era ago.

And finally we could rest, too. Or try to. Rare levels of adrenaline flowed in all our veins. I don't know about the others but I could not sleep. I tossed and turned for a few hours on a narrow bunk at the Kingman Island dormitory, until at six o'clock I gave up the effort. I had a drink of water and went outside. I found the rest of the Gang already in place, sitting and staring up at the sky.

It was perfect weather for the return, clear and still. Light bands of cloud, far off to the west, striped the sky with pink and grey. We knew just where to look for the *Franklin*'s first appearance. It was impossible not to stare in that direction, although the radio reports told us that Sid and the ship were far beyond the horizon and still a few minutes short of re-entry.

The dangerous part came next. This was the *Franklin*'s first return from orbit, facing temperatures and stresses beyond anything that the ship had been exposed to before.

Ionization around the hull cut off telemetry at the crucial time. The only reassurance came from ground-based radar, telling us from its range and range-rate data that the *Franklin* was exactly where it ought to be, moving at just the right speed.

We waited through long minutes of radio silence, until at last the shipboard telemetry cut in again. Then we all looked at each other and couldn't stop smiling. Jason reached out to grip Chris's hand, who in turn took Geoff's. After a few seconds all our hands were linked. Even if for some reason the engines of the *Franklin* were to fail now, abort system chutes would operate. Sid Rawlings, *our* Sid, first poet of space, was almost home.

The sky overhead was a clear, dark purple, still a little too light for the first stars, when we had visual contact. A tiny white fleck appeared, growing as we watched, changing into a stubby bright spear of light. The *Franklin* was descending, its rocket jets foreshortened because it was heading almost directly toward us.

I glanced toward the pad where the ship would land, and found that I could not see it. My eyes were so filled with the bright afterimage of that flaring jet, anything else was invisible.

Or almost anything. As I stared back up to the steadily descending *Franklin*, from the tail of my eye I caught a thin bright streak of orange off to the south. It moved across the sky with incredible speed. Almost before I realized what it might be and where it was heading, it had reached its destination.

Orange flame met white flame. A great fireball swallowed both of them. The sky filled with light.

Within a fraction of a second I knew many things without understanding them. A surface-to-air missile. Launched from maybe twenty miles to the south. The abort system was designed to handle ship malfunction, not deliberate attack. I knew that Sid was dead, even as I realized that we were all still holding hands.

There was no longer a Gang of Seven. The dream was over.

Others can write what they choose. I will not give the mindless, moronic terrorists who killed Sid Rawlings, or their incomprehensible cause, the publicity that they so craved. I will not identify them.

In any case, they totally misjudged the public response. They had been too busy with their destructive plans to watch Sid's broadcast from space, or to realize what it was accomplishing back on Earth. They had sought international recognition. Instead they achieved worldwide condemnation and anger and a complete cutoff in their sources of funding.

But we too, we who thought we were so smart, had also misjudged the public. The dream was not over.

We realized that when the pressure started—pressure not for the production of a single replacement ship, which was actually almost finished, but for a whole fleet like the *Franklin*. Pressure for long-term programs and commitment. The call came at many levels, in many countries. No leader who wished to remain a leader dare ignore that call. Sid's words had reached out and grabbed people at the deep level where the most important decisions are made. You do not marry, or have children, because cost-benefit analysis recommends it.

You do it because you want to do it, because it is part of being human to do it. Expanding beyond Earth is part of being human.

I said it was Sid's words that did all this. But perhaps it was the fact and manner of his death. It does not matter. What matters is that *something* did it.

Or rather, *someone* did it. When I began this summary, I said that I would not identify myself. My reasons were good, and they seemed sufficient. I did not matter. It was Sid who mattered. He was the key element. He was the force for persuasion.

As for me, I had been lucky. I was in the right place at the right time. If it had not been me, it would have been someone else.

But now I wonder. After the Gang of Seven's formation, four years ago, I did things that only I could do. I used my ideas, exploited personal contacts, shamelessly pulled every string I could reach. There was nothing unique in that. Everyone in the Gang of Seven, and the extended gang of hundreds and thousands who were later drawn into the effort, had done the same.

And maybe we *all* mattered. Maybe we were all crucial. Maybe, without every one of us, the effort would have faltered and failed.

I don't know. And that doesn't matter, either. It's enough that I did it. We did it. The way to space is open.

The surviving six members of the Gang of Seven meet regularly. How could we not, when we are bound to each other by ties as strong as family? And I notice an odd thing. We don't drink any more. Instead of meeting in hotel bars we are as likely to meet in hotel gyms, on treadmills and exercise bicycles.

We tell each other that it's our duty, we have to remain in

fighting trim. The battle is not over. The first wave in the invasion of space is breaking, but there may not be another one if we don't keep pushing.

That's what we tell each other. I suspect there's another reason behind our new focus on health and fitness. We want to *go,* every one of us. We can afford it. As soon as the fleet is big enough we'll be able to do it.

Risky?

Maybe. There's risk in everything. Access to space is easier, but it is not yet routine. There will be casualties. People will be killed.

Perhaps my life will end as Sid's ended, in a flash of incandescence too brief and violent to know what is happening. Or perhaps I'll live to be an old man, and die quietly in bed. I'll die either way. As Sid assured us, long ago, one day we're going to die. All of us.

If I go the second way, slow and peaceful, at the very end I hope I'll get to think Sid's thought for him, the one he was never able to use for himself: *In my life I did many things that no one will remember in ten years or a hundred. But I was part of the most important event of this century. And the next.*

Not many things matter. But that, you see, that *does* matter.

# THE SOUTH LOS ANGELES BROADCASTING SYSTEM

## LARRY NIVEN

There had been a bench here. It was a bus stop, labeled as one anyway; Monney remembered the bench, but it was gone. Maybe some rioters had picked it up and run it across the street to the Vietnamese grocery and thrown it in to burn.

So they sat on the curb, and Monney sat with them because he was tired. It wasn't that Charles and Harold and Nolan had anything to say. They were only repeating old words.

"Who's gonna pay for it all?"

"We are. It's our homes."

"Well, Harold, you were the one who threw—"

"I didn't burn down a thousand buildings and carry off a, what, a million—"

"Carried off what you could."

Four of the buildings were black rubble. Across the street men in suits moved purposefully around a great black rectangle; they measured, they talked, they made faces of disgust at each other. One stepped carefully through what had been a double door into what had been a market. His footsteps crunched. The others were calling him back. Dangerous.

You could see the same on other blocks. Insurance men and owners and city officials in little clusters, pretending to be thinking about rebuilding.

"Who's gonna pay for it all?" Nolan asked again.

"*This* time," Monney added. Monney was the oldest of them. He remembered Watts burning twenty-seven years ago. Money had flowed into Watts to rebuild, to turn a slum into a civilization, to see to it that this never happened again, *that* time.

Harold burst out, "How could they do that? How could they say those cops weren't guilty?"

"It was taped. It was taped."

"That jury saw the same thing we saw, didn't they?"

Long pause. "No."

"Charles?"

Charles was slow to answer. "Well, think about it. They saw the whole tape. You know anyone who saw the whole tape? On the TV they only showed that one little part."

"Beating him and beating him—"

"Wait up, Harold. Charles, you don't really *know* anything."

"You think they showed the whole tape?"

"What if that's all the tape there was? Eighteen seconds. It isn't as if the guy took that had time to set up the camera first."

They others nodded thoughtfully.

Monney hadn't been planning to speak, but that did it. He said, "I saw it. One of the networks showed the whole thing."

"What? I never saw that!"

"After the riot started. Don't know what *you* were doing,

Harold. *I* went home and locked my door. One of the . . . it was CNN. They showed the whole thing."

Charles was vindicated. "Yeah! How could they let all of them cops go like that if they only knew what we know?"

"That's what's burning my ass—"

"Hold up, Harold. Monney, *what*?"

"Well, some of it wasn't like the part all the TV news was showing. King, he *runs* at the cops. They beat him down and he's up again, like nobody can stop him. Not like that poor bastard truck driver. You seen Rodney King? He's big."

"So they say they thought he was on drugs," Charles said. "Well, maybe not. But somehow they made the jury think the cops were afraid of Rodney King, right? And it was all on tape, so . . . see? Either the tape backs them up or it doesn't."

Monney said, "Sergeant, we have captured Conan the Cimmerian. You will see to his questioning under torture." They looked at him dubiously. "Like, you know you're really in trouble when. He kept getting up and coming at 'em. And then of course he didn't, but they kept beating him. But the TV never showed why."

They mulled it. Nolan said, "You're saying Channel Four caused the goddamn riot?"

"Well, I didn't . . . um."

Harold loved it. "Well, that what you're *sayin'*, isn't it? They showed some of the tape and they didn't show some of the tape, and now there's—there's fifty dead and two thousand injured and a billion dollars in damage. If it's like you said, then that's—"

"Yeah."

"So find a lawyer and sue!"

Charles shrugged angrily. Monney said, "Class action?"

"You couldn't find no lawyer to take that," Harold said. Which made Monney laugh. Charles nodded glumly.

"No no no," Monney said. "You stand at any crosswalk in any city and throw a brick, you hit six lawyers before you ever break a window. Look, all the law offices here are burned down, what are the lawyers gonna do? Damn right you can find a lawyer. Class action, yeah. You was asking, who's gonna pay to rebuild?"

Nolan said, "Channel Nine sent someone down here, he asked, why aren't you rioting? And they did. With a helicopter right over them to take the pictures."

"Could have been famous, Harold," Monney said.

Charles was looking doubtful. Starting to take this seriously. "It's . . . no, look. A billion dollars in damage, right? This isn't one of those things where you never worked in your life but you want six million dollars 'cause you fucked up your knee slipping on somebody's lawn—"

"But you settle for six hundred—"

"—There really *was* a billion dollars burned out here. You can see it just walking around, *smell* it, and it's more if you count up hospital bills too, funeral expenses. You couldn't ask for less, man, they guilty or they ain't. A billion dollars."

Monney was chuckling quietly. He said, "The networks don't have that."

"Yeah, yeah, that's what I mean. You couldn't wind up rebuilding shit!" Charles, shouting, stood and waved with both arms at the rubble around him. Within the great black rectangle, the owner and insurer and city official stopped crunching around, looked at him, then looked away. "Wouldn't build anything. You wouldn't get money. You'd wind up owning one of the networks."

Monney stared. "The ghetto owning the news?"

Harold said, "Ghetto. I been in other cities. I seen—well, maybe it's a ghetto now."

You couldn't *breathe* without knowing where you were.

Charred wet furniture stuffing and wood and glue and plastic. A war zone smelled like this.

"Could turn interesting, couldn't it?" Charles stood up. "A law office is what we want."

Nolan's wide white grin. "A building still standing is what we want."

"No," said Monney. They had him now, they'd sucked him in. He stood, looked around him. "Look for a new car and a suit. That won't be a pimp, not here, not yet. If it isn't a big group like *them*, it'll be a lawyer."

"And he'll look at us coming at him—"

That made a picture, all right. Still. "We can try. Charles, what is it you think you'll lose? There's nothing left."

Charles nodded; Harold shoved his hands hard into his jacket pockets like he was trying to crush rats; Nolan started walking. There weren't any new cars in sight. They would have to look elsewhere.

Monney said, "Fuck, can't you just see it? Live from beautiful downtown Watts, it's The Tonight Show!" And among the blackened shells, under the sooty sky, he tried to make himself see it.

# BUYER'S REMORSE

## KATHE KOJA
## & BARRY N. MALZBERG

*God is already perfect. Me? I try to improve.*
—Mischa Elman

Dear Courtesy & Advisement Person:

Let me begin at the beginning: my friends have eventuated both this communication and its bare, vulnerable necessity; I myself remain patently unconvinced of that necessity for reasons which will become apparent, nonetheless I defer to my friends as do we all in this perilous and increasingly polarized and nasty time. My query, at any rate and such as it is, is this: after a period of deep, not to say unhappy self-communion and a degree of introspection quite unusual for me (I am a holographer, an externalizer, a statutory creator of desires through the shaping and layering of images elegant and without the stain of individuality) I have emerged into an overwhelming new appreciation for and enjoyment of the pleasures available through virtuality. Ah, virtuality! It was as though a sweet gooless placenta of desire or birth had poured from me behind the neonate of insight: a new world, a world of immersion in not only leisure activities (and oh there are so *many,* from core-diving to synchronized cycling to cruelty-free vivisection; even I who consider myself a fairly well-informed if not jaded consumer had never even suspected such a menu; it just goes to show what can be found when one, as they say, *lets it all go*) but those that reach beyond the merely recreational, that encompass the whole of life in all its functions and versatility; in fact and in short I now eat my meals in virtuality, I experience virtual sleep, I even copulate virtually (and superbly, if I may say so, and say further that the experience has in its unexpected slicks and textures provided for me a whole new definition of the verb conjugation *to emit*) and I am very happy about all of this, in fact I do not care if I die wearing these slim well-fitting instruments, in fact I think I would *enjoy* the possibility of experiencing virtual death if that were in fact possible (and I assume in some quarters it must be, if one has the wherewithal).

So, you must be asking yourself, what then the problem?

In a word, *two* words: my friends. My warm, loving, forward-thinking, well-meaning friends, who refuse to cease in their maddening attempts to drag me back into the world *materiel,* who with their sensible fingers keep trying to rip the virtual caul from my eyes, who with their bullying and endless messages overrode the peace and security of this tensionless womb I have created (and at such cost of concentration!). They harangue, they insist that I must not let myself become a fully virtual person, a VP, an object unrelated to the physical, that I must in their words "be for real." Be for *real*? And what is that, and why should I? It was my last attempt to (re)create peace (and through peace the solitude that I not only crave but now demand) that led to this communique but as far as I am concerned I have the answer already.

Virtually Perfect

Dear Virtually Perfect:

Acts and nominations, shadow and act, the cross-transference of time and the uncertainty, one might say, the lack of *viability* of the real: this is the holographer's tomb, the airless dungeon which awaits they who too long work with representations and refractory media and are at the end unable to distinguish between the modular and the slender, necessitous forms which they would imitate: they can no longer tell a peep from a groan and it is this which has occurred, you have (as so many holographers in mid-career, truly it is a syndrome the existence of which Courtesy & Advisement Person can verify as well as deplore) not so much abandoned as been *evicted* from reality, and the delights of virtuality, so thrilling for the constitutionally craven and worthy for the judicious, have overwhelmed you. Your friends are correct, they have neither misled nor misjudged the situation; you are enacting a perilous course between the fragile hold upon what remains of your life and that swamp, that Charon's stew of motive and loss, lust and untrammeled terror which may at any time burn out the remains of the brain pan and leave you, vivisected and ever so much more alone than you might think, to the thunderous, odorous passage of temporal sensation as it obliterates what is left of your personality. Oh, the situation—omitting the question of virtual copulation which is, whether you accept it or not, the *least* dangerous of the virtualities since it presents at least the illusion of choice, a counterweight to entrapment—the situation is perilous, you have not been to the well of Courtesy & Advisement too soon, in fact it may already be too late; temporality is after all a function of perception and brutal chronology and chronology has been squashed and flattened within those slick tunnels to which you casually refer.

But how to—what could be the expression wanted?— how to handle the *je ne sais quoi*, the sheer *insouciance* of the situation: your reflexes, you may note, are already dominated by escape, you have already fled the century as well as the holographer's bogus justification for a reality of which in this Greenhouse Time you already know to be noxious . . . the clever beasts and Comforters of virtuality will be whispering in your shell-pink ear this moment, even at the condition of query; *your communication to Courtesy & Advisement Person is itself a form of virtuality:* locked in cube and receptors you are in virtual communication with virtual Courtesy & Advisement Person and this too is part of the inverted bowl of experience. How to convince and by convincing lead you out the other end, to make of this *je ne sais quoi* a certain *chose* of the effable and the purchased? Courtesy & Advisement Person, overwhelmed by the paradoxical and hermetic nature of the trap, feels no less overwhelmed than you: virtuality is its own reward and often enough its own cancellation because *eviction* can itself be a form of virtuality; does the ouroboros turn for you, too?

But one must deal with the situation as best as one can.

*Stop.* Stop machine immersion. It is one of the cunning traps of our difficult time, that which will lead the citizenry not away but toward the tyranny which they think the wires and hoods, the shapes and peeping cries of the imposed experience will overcome. It is now possible to fool all of the people all of the time because it involves both collaboration and consent, both of which you must cease immediately. Make holographs. Return to holography, make shadows on the walls of the eternal caves, seek signs and talismans, cast them against the light and use that light to move with purpose toward the exits. *Egress* with all dignity. It is not in the end virtuality which will evict you so much as the spurred congealments of self, and in the dawn—bright if not rosy, fresh if not original—which will come from the forsaking of such slick and soulless comforts you will undergo (restored and humbled by the dangerous nature of your experience) the *real* thrill of living within the twenty-third century rather than in some exculpatory and mean little tunnel of false darkness or foolish light. The century awaits! and while not perfect it is real, and earnest, and the values of causality as opposed to dreams are not to be minimized. Or overvalued. Or to be mediated, friends or not, in any way. This advice is *not* that of virtuality which (were such the case) would be to "burrow deeper." Our ancestors tried that and look what it got them.

Dear Courtesy & Advisement Person:

If, as we are often told, health and moral sanity are available to all, if what was once considered to be rankest and most evil perversion is now merely a marketing niche without stain or strain, percussion or repercussion, if all is not only fair in love and war but in bed and under it (not to mention beside or above), why does my third wife (the alliance itself begun as a result of some very sophisticated circumstances which cannot be here explicated due to prevailing privacy laws) insist that certain sexual practices are not only distasteful to her but actively, if not legally, "perverted"? "I don't do that," she says; nor does she; but how can this be? If this is truly the most meaningful of all worlds, if every taboo and spiritual shortcoming have in fact been both overcome and neutralized by the judicious and loving application of gene therapy and medication, if it is true that there are no longer any bad people, only incautious attempts at pleasure, then I suppose what I am seeking is a workable, defensible definition of perversion, if such is not too much to expect or if the question does not in fact negate itself with its own kind of hopeless, if helplessly innocent display of naivete and old-fashioned, not to say unappetizing, kink.

Happy to be Alive

Dear Happy:

A long time ago some wit defined the moral as "that which feels good"; the corollary, one might infer, being that if it feels bad *that* is immoral not to say perverse and that aphorism had its attendants for some time although we must remember that the wit at issue blew out his brains with big rifle in big kitchen in Big Ketchum a long, long time ago and sees neither fish nor dreams nor Pretty Big Trouble in that sacristy which presumably he now occupies, that clean well-lighted place of bulls and *cojones* and the places where all the soldiers at the end of their time must go. We must forage, then, beyond this simplistic principle for a definition of perversity: come to the surface of the planet, don the proper protective gear and take a look at the suckholes, the sinkholes, the thick transformative ooze, the hulk of expired animals more grotesque than can ever be dreamed hurtling through the stinking, sad design of what the previous century did to the shell of our humble and divine place of residence. Consider this as one definition of perversion; for another consider the plight of a holographer turned virtually perfect who in the chancy tunnels of imagined possibility turns in (and in, and in: the crippled whorl of the shell, the broken and eternal wheel) upon that which should long ago have been properly extracted. Consider, in fact, Courtesy & Advisement Person, still seeking in these tumultuous, unspeakable times to proffer considerations of linearity, motive, explication, causes and effects in a modest and unassuming, logical and extrapolative rhetoric which will bring to command all of the sense and reason which Courtesy & Advisement Person *has* to know passed from the earth, the great wounded globe itself so long ago. *These* are concepts of the perverse, certainly not the innocent placement, extraction and surge which constitute what your (regrettably naive) third wife finds so reactively unpleasant.

Perversion is what has been done or what *cannot happen;* all the rest of it, spread before us as pale and innocent as the snows of Kilimanjaro consists of those layers of possibility and dream in which, even in this time of entrapment and burrowing, we can still take ourselves to gambol and gambol, driven and sustained by the thin and tremulous heart of all design.

Dear Courtesy & Advisement Person:

Being as I am a decent, humble, unassuming sort, I am the last person in what I laughingly call "this world" or any other to wish to cause or prolong dissension but a situation has developed in my biosphere which I can seemingly neither solve nor ignore, rectify nor endure, and frankly it is ruining my life. The particulars are simple, so simple that I suppose it might be comic to the casual observer, but it is not comic to me. I shall try to explain without passion or disgust, though I have had occasion, much occasion, to feel if not display plenty of both.

In this biosphere in which I live and have lived without incident for nearly four years, the atmospheric situation has remained stable and relatively serene; we have had an imbalance here, a rule bent ever so gently there. We are not, we Consulting Residents, here to punish or restrain, to order or deny, we are here, we exist merely to keep the ecological scales in true, as it were, to keep the trinity of oxygen, nitrogen, and loving kindness (or at least civility which is never too much to ask, especially not in such a close, not to say cramped, arrangement as our little biosphere out on the edge of the deeps, surrounded by cracks and caverns, in the silence and blue dread of our known enclosure—an enclosure from which no one, *no one* wants to depart: how could we? what else is there?) in triangular felicity: to mediate: to ameliorate: to solve and to serve. Being a consulting resident is not, let me assure you, a task to which much thought is given by others or gratitude either, but I (as well as, I am sure, the other consulting residents) am not in this for the gratitude; we exist solely to serve in our appointed capacity, to keep the biosphere stable, to keep ourselves and our other (small *r*) residents safe.

Imagine our chagrin then at discovering within our midst, our mulchy, warm, yeast-bearing, and comfortable midst a potentially *toxic* situation! One of our residents has been, without sanction, without approval, without even the knowledge of the Consulting Resident Board, conducting experiments of the most dangerous and dangerously volatile sort. One day it is the cultivation (not to mention wanton application) of "artificial" contraceptives, the next it is a new kind of renewable fuel (as if one were necessary, here in this almost painfully balanced biosphere in which we Consulting Residents so heroically seek to maintain both peace and breathable air in equal proportions), the next day something else equally combustible and arcane, not to say dangerous, not to say absolutely mad. The only reason we are here, the only reason any of us are *alive* is because our principles, our biospheric laws are rigorously safeguarded and maintained: and now here comes this irresponsible, ungrateful, leering, sneering ne'er-do-well—whose admittance, I would like to state right now and explicitly, was achieved by the casting of one consulting resident's swing vote, said voter having since seen the considerable error of her ways; too late, too late, but if repentance cannot redress the wrongs its original wrong has caused at least it can provide some interesting modes of attempted reparation... do I digress? I am agitated. So here is Toxicity, come among us like a bloodborne irritant to infect our healthy and serene circulation, that is what I think: consequently *molto agitato.* This may not seem to be a Courtesy & Advisement problem but upon your deeper inspection (and I trust you will grant it) you will see that the very principles of courtesy are being violated here in our once-happy biosphere; it is the good of the many being sacrificed on the altar of the toxic-bearer by whom these principles and mores are daily, if not hourly, violated: and it is in the spirit of last-chance, last-ditch, last-gasp hospitality to this resident who has so brutally abused *our* courtesy that I present my query here: how do we cleanse our biosphere of this human irritant without violating both the sacred code of the hutch as well as international, not to say regional, law?

Consulting Resident

Dear Consulting Resident and Bearer of Toxicity:

Because that is the situation, of course, the little bleached cells of Courtesy & Advisement Person, chronically underrated for their inferential ability and their necessitous grasp of proper clues have long since led to that deduction: it is *you* who are the bearer of the (undefined: and how interesting that that should be so!) toxicity who, leading a double life, perhaps even a single life innocent of your own duplicity and multiple motives, have introduced into the biosphere the stinking and shrieking Egg Infestation which as all of us in these external corridors know to have already laid the biosphere low, to have dragged the unhappy project to the precipice of an unfortunate end.

The egg infestation! But how could you have done otherwise, Consulting Resident? something mad and purposeful within you—all of this has been discussed in creed at the levels of consultation to which Courtesy & Advisement Person, last and least but still present, is privy—something immersed in terror and revulsion at the wreckage which had been made of the closed crevices of this our time and to which the biosphere had represented a sane alternative . . . something within you said, "What right do *we* have to flee the general distemper, when we no less than any of the others have been driven to these hidden cities within the moaning and dying planet?" Such questions—and they are *good* ones, Consulting Resident, nothing frivolous here and Courtesy & Advisement Person should (and does, oh, does indeed) know—wracked you in the fresh and scented biosphere nights, appealed to you without possibility of answer in the sterile biosphere days and crept (crypt?) within you on little dead feet until you could no longer avoid the temptation irresistible and with smuggled eggs, elemental chemistry and the power of juxtaposition produced the living, burning cells of ova toxicity which have turned the biosphere into a reeking, bubbling, abominable, untenable sinkhole and have left the authorities with no recourse save to go in and clean out the project, to save however harshly (oh, ever so harshly) what must be saved.

In the midst of this, your frail and presumptive shriek of culpability disguised as an anonymous complaint against an unnamed infiltrator speaks of the degree of dysfunction not to say profound pain which must have been yours: a pain which came from your own apprehension in the first whickers and peeps, stench and homicide of the Egg Infestation that you had gone too far and destroyed not only the biosphere but your own belief in any possible future outside these domes in which we must chase our own chronology and eventually confront it only to die. How you must have felt in the wretchedness and yet compensatory splendors of your self-revulsion as eggs and stink crawled in and out of the tube of memory and loss, consideration and repose and left you at last stunned and in no position to do other than appeal to Courtesy & Advisement Person seeking not only concealment and an alibi but—understandably, understandably: it is here where the tenderness and the horror lie like doomed lovers or hens and eggs entwined—some way out, some true way out of your predicament which you had come—it is all clear to Courtesy & Advisement Person now and soon to you as well—to identify with the human predicament itself: grandiose, if psychotic, to contemplate such while entwined like those lovers, those screeching hens in the vines and the possibilities, the aborted languishing air of the biosphere itself . . . oh, it is almost too much even for Courtesy & Advisement Person to consider and we must spare ourselves, in the interests of professional detachment, further meditation upon this scene.

Cleanse the biosphere? Remove the human irritant? It was said that there are no second acts in human lives—perhaps Courtesy & Advisement Person misquotes but in your shoes, Consulting Resident and Biospheric Assassin, you more than likely do not care—and one might add no firsts either in this century which has been so sadly concocted, so brutally served. You must suspire, you must live, you must smell eggs, you must be overcome by the fumes of sulphur and desire, you must sink and dive amidst all of the consequences of your own folly and in the dismantling of the corpse of the biosphere you must, grandiose or not, reenact our own loss of the century, the starkness of our certainty, the swaddling illimitable nature of our eggless and plangent doom.

One can, however, and even as one is dragged off in shackles toward the Extermination Hutch confront the situation with courage if not hope. Courtesy & Advisement Person is enclosing herewith the special pamphlet on courage and calls your attention to the 833rd entry, that dealing with the constancy and fumigation of eggs.

Dear Courtesy & Advisement Person:

My mate to whom I usually defer in all ways has taken to ingesting huge quantities of aphrodisiacs and questing the tubes at all hours, looking for, as she puts it, "fun." Whether or not she is successful in finding satisfaction is not my concern; what *does* concern me is not the phobic specter of possible disorder or disease, but the hideous cost of these ridiculous drugs which she sullenly maintains she must use even in our home and in my presence because she needs them to "feel" something. I cannot even frame a query, my confusion and dismay are so great: I leave it to Courtesy & Advisement Person to sort and cogitate, to disassemble and refigure my true question and its answer.

Disappointed in Love

Dear Disappointed:

The issue of induced "feeling" is complex and interesting; it falls outside the purview of Courtesy & Advisement Person—who is able to maintain this position only through the rigorous, not to say obsessive use of powerful emotional blocks; try *this* one cycle without such suppressants and see what happens—but it is an era not so much of feeling as of *activity*. Fortunately and in that regard it would seem that you have less of a problem than you think. In her search to "feel" your mate seeks not the passivity of, say, virtuality nor the shock of personal "intimacy" but instead is, as you say, questing the tubes and using drugs; this indicates an active if querulous state, much more promising than the emotional numbing, the wreckage and catatonic revulsion with which so many if not most of your contemporaries have sought to deal with what they perceive as life. Searching for feeling is perhaps itself a value (although not for Courtesy & Advisement Person who, as above explained, would be unable to practice even on an occasional basis without the blocks and suppressants) and the use of drugs has been not only socially approved but *analogous* to feeling for a long, long time, predating even the retreat from the surfaces of the distant past and appears to have been part of the Apocalyptic Culture which drove us here. It is our suggestion—we will not be pornographic here although Courtesy & Advisement Person feels twinges leading in that direction, maddening little pulses and explosions of feeling responding to the question which strongly hint some suppressants might be overdue—that you do *this* with your partner and perhaps *that*, talking hallucinatorily all the time and perhaps even with a little (cautious) virtuality to spend your way toward some kind of climax; in the sheer this-and-thatness of your mission you might find that very expenditure of "feeling" so sought by your troubled mate. That of course could lead to a perilous emotional state of another sort but to deal with this would be to deal in a projective, and therefore inconstant, circumstance and Courtesy & Advisement Person can advise you only to await the moment and seek further counsel if then necessary. In the fullness of our being, in the purchase of all these little anodynes, awaits the death which awaits us, the *lux* and the drift of the surfaces and the stars. Or something like that. Ah, the candle burned at both ends which will not last the night! In our beginning, in our *thisness* is our end; our *that* as Kant might have said on the wheel, culturally speaking, and one does not need an aphrodisiac to assume more than the position after all.

Dear Courtesy & Advisement Person:

Whether it is advice or merely mercy I seek I cannot be wholly sure, but, awed by and familiar with the rigors both endured and dispensed by the Courtesy & Advisement Person (who is known to be very stern, not to say merciless, on occasion) I will attempt to make my query interesting if not brief, digestible if not nourishing, stoic if not brave: and my query is this: When the iron vicissitudes of modern (if not postmodern) life become insupportable, when the prospect if not the fact immediate of chaos absolute becomes in some hideous way *more* desirable than less, when the long pale arm of terrible need reaches out to enfold, encircle, and haul the helpless but unresisting (oh, note that they do not resist, that for them who are us the word *no* or even its possibilities do not exist within the perimeters of this most impossible of circumstances, this world so dressed by specters, so hung about with the mosses and red ropes of our desires), haul and drag those racked and desperate into its unquenchable embrace, why then, *then* tell me if, in this zone where reason and the heart collide, in this enclosure, this abattoir of light and pain, whether that monstrosity of pain dressed in the concealing rags of life and circumstance is constructed, is *intended* purely to be the vehicle to further knowledge of self: intended to ultimately create as well as utterly destroy: and if all this is so then how does one go about paying the fare? One pays and pays it is suspected but in this realm, what is the proper coin?

In Waiting

Dear In:

The coin is the self, the payment is extracted piece by piece and through all the pockets and crevices of implication, and as was said by Epictetus, Erasmus, Harry the Flat (or perhaps they spoke in tandem, Courtesy & Advisement Person is no scholar of *historie concrete*): "Pain, drop by drop falls on us like rain and from that pain comes the beginning of knowledge, the apprehension of the true role of the favorite, knowledge of the underlay and the overlay, the great and terrible machinery of the tote which blinking and winking in the vital and suspended, the electrical and inconstant darkness floods us at last—losers and winners, graceless and graced, broken and spent all together now—with the light that shines from behind the millennium, the light that fell in the beginning and will fall forever, the light of our hearts on fire, burning and burning, unconsummated and unconsumed" to which Courtesy & Advisement Person can only add that the recognition of pain, unlike the recognition of disease, leads not to treatment and possible cure, but is—as it must be—its own treatment and reward: for no cure is possible, nor would it be applicable if it were.

Dear Courtesy & Advisement Person:

Here I sit, muddled by the ravages of chronology, entropy, madness, dusk, dessert, and wine, the mixed and mingled detritus of a long day's journey or perhaps I mean night, surrounded by remorse, regret, and the distant shrieks and giggles of the third millennium, the anteroom of the apocalypse finding neither comfort nor the ghost of resolution in the air. One might call me a paradigm of these difficult times except that I am not self-aggrandizing, simple person, singular, *Wayt Humble* as is my *nom de guerre* here in the Seniority Hutch: *Wayt Humble* for the darkening which signals the dawn even as those emblems of our time—shriek and giggle, tremble and retch—rattle like bone chip castanets in the background.

I plead to a certain amount of reactive depression, a regressive diagnosis but one in key with the times. *Quelle dommage.* What do I do? What is the name of the game? Where doth the pleasure emit? And various other questions from the humble Wayt Humble as in the coils and snares of his (medically undiagnosed) reactive depression he crouches in the Seniority Hutch, feeling the glazed tumble of his days slowly extract from him those inner fires and thunders, those retchings and gigglings now so shockingly refracted to the outside.

Perhaps I expostulate. It is a familial disease; my father ran off to the equator with something not of his species. I try to reassume control, put the question coldly: the millennia soar, the centuries parse on their way and in the bleakness and salvage of the valley of the shadow of the Hutch I ask: *what do I do? what do I do?*

Wayt Humble

Dear Wayt:

Reactive depression is, or could be understood to be, Courtesy & Advisement Person's *nom de guerre* if such things were capable of being adequately understood at all. Which, circumstances agree, they are not: Courtesy & Advisement Person, as free of bitterness as of cant, as past self-pity as self-help understands this as well as all the many other intangibles, reactive and dysfunctional, undifferentiated and vast with which the concept (if not the lowly, the stricken, the heart-broken and tenacious embodiment) of Courtesy & Advisement is bombarded every day, every gray new hour, every vicious and sterile dawn. One might even argue that if depression were not the result as well as the cause of one's miseries one might be in such a way as to be past all help, hope, succor medical, pharmaceutical, devotional, or beyond: what is not truly apprehended here is what must be: to wit: it is *supposed* to bewilder, it is *supposed* to depress, it is *supposed* to *hurt,* Wayt Humble or Wayt Forever, as witness testimony both to and from that earlier correspondent who is also in waiting, who is also bewildered by pain but whose query is both more and less applicable to the real question of our and all times: and so what you *do* is only what must be done: empty the dumpster of the heart and the bowels, the mind and the shrinking soul to fill it all anew each bright and stinking morning: recycle, reboot, retouch, retrace: react if you must, retrench if you can, relinquish if possible but more possibly not; and remember: *remember:* the shudder of impact which maketh the soul, the collision of flesh on flesh which engenders anew like each false dawn the body and the blood. Ripeness is all and all is almost certainly lost; only memory (and its sweet crippled offspring, desire) is sacrosanct and works, like the tender and innocent organs of reproduction and elimination, both ways. *Both* ways: forward and backward: in and out: hopeless and helpless and in both depths and dawning one discovers—refracted, reflected—the light of the fire which cleanses as it consumes and in that fire and that light we see the huge pageant of our folly and our loss narrowed at last to a locus, a focus, an aperture of remembrance as tiny and

precarious as our own existence and it is in and by the bene-
diction of that memory—if ever redemption can be possible,
if ever reclamation can exist—in this world, this time, this
hour or any other, in transcendence and humble agony, finally
and exquisitely we are healed.

Remember the green. Remember the green and vast, the
rolling expanse of the earth of our desire, unreeled beneath us
in lost and lost and lost time as a dream.

# SOULS ON ICE

▼

## ARLAN ANDREWS

The revivification chamber was cool and dark and damp, *A lot like an ancient tomb,* Dr. Vivian Crook thought, shivering at the similarity. Soft amber lighting only added to the unpleasantness. Per the oft-repeated instructions from the loudspeakers, she didn't touch anything—not the slablike operating table that hovered above the floor at waist height, not any of the jungle vine–like apparatus dangling haphazardly from the low ceiling, certainly not the shiny octopoid robots that dwelt silently, ominously, in each corner, with only the throbbing reddish glow of their optic sensors distinguishing them from any of the inanimate instruments embedded in the walls. She was thankful not to be alone in here, grateful for the company of the other White House observer, even if he was only a lawyer. She would be extremely happy to leave the cramped and creepy laboratory as soon as possible. *I'm glad I'll be outside, looking in. I don't like this at all.* She shook her head, vainly trying to dispel her uneasiness, lest the politico with her pick up on her irrational mood.

*There has to be a first time for everything,* she thought, *but the idea of bringing back someone from the dead stirs primal fears, even in my enlightened twenty-first century!*

"Please leave the chamber," came a syrupy synthesized voice on the loudspeaker. "You must all be seated in the observation room before we can seal and sterilize the ReViv area." Gratefully, Crook shuffled out of the chamber with her compatriot and took her seat on the other side of a one-way mirror.

The man to her right, Beele Dougson, a political appointee in the Technology Office, leaned over and whispered, "Viv, what do you think so far? This guy Roderick on the horizontal? I mean, calling us out here, saying it's a dire emergency, getting the President all stirred up like she was?" Stiffening, Crook nodded, not welcoming the insistent intrusion on her troubled thoughts. Dougson didn't take the hint, and inclined his head toward the mirror as a gray mist swirled in, filling the chamber on the other side. "I don't see any Deity-damned 'emergency,' do you? I think I'm going to recommend to the budget staff that we zero out this one's research appropriations, just for wasting our time in this mortuary. All the corpse-sicles are already frozen for good, you know, and they're not coming out. Why spend more money for research? The public doesn't *want* ReViv to work. What in the hell would we do with a coupla billion more people?"

Turning to her companion, Crook smiled and said sweetly, "You mean, Beele, that *elected officials* all over the world don't want them ReVived, not with those billions of votes already locked in forever by Cryo-Proxy." Dougson frowned and turned away, his verbal prey having successfully resisted him again. *Hell, unfreezing the cryomated millions in*

*this country alone would undermine the uninterrupted power
our party has enjoyed for thirty years,* Crook mused. *I mean,
what if they were to change their minds when they wake up?
You'd have to have political campaigns and all that stuff
again! Not to mention how we'd ever pay them those trillions
of dollars in Social Security annuities they were all promised.
Besides that, eventually some of the ReVived cryos would die,
and where would all those locked-in votes be?* The heretical
possibilities in such treasonous suppositions almost stimulated her back to her normal, cheerful disposition. But then,
rising amber lights in the observation window returned the revivification chamber to a simulated circle of Hell. From the
left, swathed in green, a demon entered.

*No, a Damon,* she corrected herself. "Dr. Damon Roderick, general manager of this ICE facility," the synthesized an-
nouncer intoned. *ICE—International Cryomation Enter-
prises, the world's leading—and only—cryomation service,*
Crook thought. *Solve all your problems by putting them on
ICE....*

"I welcome our White House guests for this important
demonstration," the short, bearded Roderick said, bowing toward his unseen audience. He introduced two other attendants, big burly green-gowned males, as they wheeled in a two-
meter tall, vertical cylindrical tube, its glistening metallic
surface covered in a thin layer of dissipating vapor. "Distin-
guished visitors," Roderick began, "this is the standard cryotube in which are stored, at today's count, four point six eight
three billion of our fellow human beings—"

*Grandpa a little senile?* Crook added mentally. *Put him in
storage and you'll all meet in the "Great ICE-and-bye."
Meantime, ICE'll guarantee you a percentage of his Social Security to alleviate the pain. Don't worry, he'll have billions
when he's healed and thawed!*

"—two-plus billion fetuses of various stages of development—"

*Abortion a problem? Freeze the little sucker-to-be till a more convenient time.*

"—and several hundred millions of animals of every species—"

*Pet getting old and sick? Put her little paws on ICE until the nano-vets figure a way to make her young and well. Even the poor old Greenies had supported this one, once upon a time—"Save the whales," they'd said. Too bad that by now all the whales are just fertilized eggs, ICEd somewhere. Along with all the lions and tigers and bears. Oh my!*

Roderick said something to the attendants and the men started operating hand control panels. The cryotube cylinder was hoisted over the hovering operating table and gently lowered until it was just above the sheeted surface. Meanwhile Roderick had donned sterile gloves and facemask, like an old M.D. from the last century about to "operate" on a patient. Disgusted with the visual parallel and with the euphemism, Crook was once again thankful that her birth century provided microscopic robots and fiber optic lasers that corrected most human abnormalities in place, with a minimum of unintended effects. *Surgery,* the barbaric practice of cutting through perfectly healthy tissue to effect gross changes on internal organs, belonged to the last millennium. It was almost extinct as a medical practice, along with leeches, drug therapy, psychology, and other discredited quackery.

While the cryogenically-frozen person was being unwrapped by Roderick's helpmeets, the scientist gave a short discourse on how he had applied molecule-sized robots safely to freeze and then to thaw human bodies. Dougson interrupted him. "Dr. Roderick, how can you be sure this cryomate will survive? And even if he does, can you heal what killed him?" With a self-satisfied smile, the politico looked at Crook for approval. The glance she gave back was colder than the patient on the table. Dougson shrugged.

"Protection features are integral to all nano-robots," the cryoscientist replied from his chamber, "and the nanoes are monitored continuously in each and every cryotube on Earth. With the advanced simulations available by computer, I am assured the ReViv process is perfectly safe. This procedure has been done only once before, on one other human. No, the *procedure* is safe enough, and the *body* is healed. There are other circumstances, however . . . " His voice trailed off, ominously. "That's why I asked the President to send observers for the second ReViv."

"You did this already, on a *person*?" the lawyer said, shocked.

"We weren't allowed to use test animals, you know." *Did they ever use animals for testing?* Crook thought. *How perfectly repulsive! What a horrible century!*

Dougson retorted sarcastically, "But the cryo you've got here, according to the display data, was frozen thirty years ago, one of the first. Your little nanoes have got to be three decades out of date. Won't they be so primitive as to be useless?" The man felt he was moving in for a kill.

Roderick replied quite curtly, Crook concluding that he was pressing his point to ensure that the non-scientist—Dougson—understood. "We knew, when we began cryomation thirty years ago, that the first ICEing procedures would be primitive compared to later technologies, so we built in a method to ensure that we could take advantage of the continuous progress of technology. The cryotubes have microscopic hollow fibers that access the frozen bodies, and through which we can insert—and remove, if need be—the ice-bug nanoes that service our cryomates. In this way, our bugs receive continuous updates on new advances in medtech, in ReViv tech, in ICE-maintenance procedures. In short, each ice-bug is essentially reconfigured every hour or so, reflecting the latest improvements in cellular repair and so forth."

Dougson cringed; Crook bet that Roderick could see that body language even through the one-way glass. "Everywhere on Earth, Dr. Roderick?" he barely whispered. "*All* of them?"

Crook expected the cryoscientist to trill with triumph, but he kept that emotion out of his voice. Something was bothering him, Crook felt. "All of them, Mr. Dougson, every one of them. Every ice-bug nano is exactly like all its sisters around the world, each and every incorporating the latest technologies." Uncertainty was not one of Roderick's weaknesses, Crook noted.

And there was the problem. For whatever the "emergency" he had brought them out for, this Roderick was nevertheless a true believer. Didn't he understand that nobody really cared if the cryomated ever came back? That the ever-more-powerful "Living First" Party had clamped down on the first ReViv attempts immediately after the first round of cryomations? First, they'd used the argument that nano-tech wasn't good enough to bring every cryomate back out, much less heal what had killed them. Nowadays, however, they argued that the ICEd should stay in frozen limbo until "the Earth is clean and beautiful and the stars are in our grasp." It sounded good, but every cryomate going under meant more proxy resources and property in the hands of the L. F. Party leaders, not to mention the "frozen Proxy" votes that automatically tallied for the L. F. at every election.

Polls showed that by next year's elections, the L. F. would gain control of the presidency and both houses of Congress. It had happened in other countries already. She wanted to tell

Roderick flat out that there would never be a mass movement for ReViv. Cryotubes were cheap, politicians were satisfied, and though the public at large still gave lip service to the vision of cryomated immortality, she felt that few really believed in it.

Rather like a comforting, though nebulous, religious dogma, it felt good as long as one didn't investigate the claims too closely. With cryomation, Crook had long ago decided that her generation was the first with the perfect solution to the impossible and embarrassing situations of death, senility, unwanted children. Put them on ICE and forget them; just deep-freeze your responsibilities and cryomate your conscience!

Maybe Dougson's murmurings of R&D funds cut off was the "emergency" for which Roderick had called them out here to the heat-stifled wilds of upper Minnesota on the spur of the moment. Dougson was right about one thing: Madame President didn't rile easily, but when she did, the staff jumped, never asking why.

"—rotting in the grave, without hope. At least in our material world, leaving religious beliefs out of it." Roderick was continuing his monologue as the attendants went about their mysterious duties. "This cryomate died of cancer and was frozen immediately, a rather backward method by today's standards. It ruptures many cells. Some of the nanoes are operating right now, going in to determine which molecule on each side of every crack should mate with which other." The one-way mirror became a displate, where an animated body pulsed with a soft glow. Trillions of nanoes were doing a nearly infinite amount of repair work in just a few seconds.

"Being virus-sized, they bore right through cell tissue without causing much damage. They repair their boring holes behind them, and once they're finished, they inert themselves to become food for the wakening cell in which they have re-mained." The cartoon-body was glowing, golden, in less than a minute.

"The cell damage caused by freezing rupturing has been repaired," Roderick announced. "So right now, I am bringing the subject up to just above liquid water temperature, so the cancer-fighting devices can traverse his blood stream and lymphatic systems." Real-time video superimposed over the scene of the chamber, showing swarms of tiny robots attacking cancer cells and rebuilding damaged ones in their place. "With today's technologies, the cancer cure is easily done, and I'm even taking care of the baldness and obesity." Onscreen, hair follicles sprouted and tree-sized hairs sprang to life, a forest of red shafts, bamboolike.

"After waiting a few minutes for these nanoes to effect final repair, we start the subject's heart, and warm his brain." In animation, hundreds of physiological parameters pulsated: the man was coming back to life. Crook gulped; somehow the animated version gave more reality to the situation than did the now-breathing body she could see directly through the glass.

"All is going well, so far," Roderick said, suddenly waving the attendants out of the chamber. "For the rest, I am afraid I must leave the chamber and let our friend arrive at consciousness alone." He turned to face the mirror. "I will let you see for yourself, to experience for yourself, the reanimation, the ReViv.

"Then we will discuss my 'emergency,' Mr. Dougson." He turned on one heel and left, the chamber door sealing behind him. Crook wondered at the rapid change in Roderick's demeanor. Something was about to happen, and suddenly she was afraid. Did Dougson feel it, too? She was about to ask him when the lawyer started mumbling about being treated like a child. "Damn science types," was all she could make out. She shut her eyes, shook her head and turned to watch what was unfolding under the amber lights of Hades.

The ReViver's breathing increased, the chest expanding rapidly. Limbs twitched, moved; it looked as though someone were waking from a light sleep. Because his face was turned away, Crook couldn't see the man's appearance, though a montage of viewing angles on the displate showed every angle. She stared right through them, wanting to concentrate, real-eyes, on this person brought back from the dead.

The ReVived turned his face slowly toward the one-way mirror, either to see himself, or, Crook feared, to look directly at her. In that instant, she knew that the image burning into her brain would never leave her memory: though originally handsome and still bearing the strong, dignified features of the politician the man had once been, the face was a horror from the depths of the subconscious. Eyes were rolled back and bulging, only the whites visible, like boiled eggs protruding from their sockets. The tongue was an obscene organ thicker and longer than she would have thought possible, like some unnatural reptilian life-form, coiling and twitching insanely. But then came the worst.

He screamed.

The sound that came through the speakers was Chaos set loose, the symphonies of hell made audible. As part of her mind struggled to retain sanity, Crook desperately sought to find something with which to compare the inhuman roars from the cryomate's distended throat. In defensive panic, her memory dredged up an analogy. "An absorption spectro-graph of the sun," an old physics professor was saying on the *verch* learning channel. "How do you identify individual ele-ments burning on the surface of the sun when there's all that overwhelming radiance pouring forth into your instruments?

The secret is, some of that full-spectrum background is attenuated by the element you want to identify." Desperately, Crook's mind ticked off the milliseconds until salvation came. The roar chilled her body and her mind, and she feared for her unbelieved-in soul. "The signal is found only by the absence of the background. What's *not* there is what you're looking for."

In this case, Crook's fearful mind told itself, the analogy worked, was very apt. The man's humanity, his actual screams, were evident only where they absorbed the full-spectrum shrieks of Hell that poured forth in an unholy roar. *Black noise, she told herself, the marching song of the legions of hell!*

Abruptly, the sound ceased, but Crook, shaking and ill, jerked quickly to her feet, barely able to stand. Intermittent sobs, punctuated with vomiting and a hideous odor, told her that Dougson was face forward on the floor, a victim of the unbelievable scene still taking place on the other side of the mirror. "Roderick has shut off the sound," she whispered in surprise. *Thank you, Dr. Damon.*

But the horror wasn't over. At a sudden thudding noise, she turned toward the mirror and screamed. With incredible quickness, the patient was pounding on the mirror, and cracks were appearing. He was after her personally, this shrieking banshee from Hell! "Oh God! Stop him! Roderick, stop him!"

Instantly the octopoid robots seized the thrashing patient, coiling him in a rat's nest of tentacles. A grimacing Roderick appeared in the room, grabbing one of the dangling cables from the ceiling and pressing it against the insane man's arm. The ReVived jerked from the contact, his head swinging wildly back and forth, bloody froth gushing from around his swollen tongue. His muscles relaxed and in seconds he was quiet. Crook, still shaking and fighting back sobs, fell back into her chair. At her feet, amidst his own effluents, Dougson mewed for his female parent.

"Roderick, you knew this was going to happen, and didn't warn us, you—you—*Deity-damned non-PC!*" Vivian Crook cursed aloud, calling up the only epithets she could recall. As the octopoids placed the quiescent madman back into his cryotube, her anger built on outrage, replacing the trauma of unspeakable fear. Crook waited for the cryoscientist to dare to show his face.

"The attendants are taking care of your Mr. Dougson, Dr. Crook," Damon Roderick was saying as he stood in front of her observation seat. He handed her a cup and saucer; the smell told her it was InstaCalm. "You just have some tea, calm down, and I'll explain."

Crook nodded without answering. He'd better have a good story; otherwise, a complete holo-video of the incident would be on Madame President's desk in a matter of minutes. She sipped the welcome warmth and immediately felt the nanidote's familiar soothing.

"The same thing happened to the first patient who revived, that was last week." Crook didn't blink. *So?*

"But last week, the ReViv was spontaneous." Crook blinked.

"*Spontaneous?*" she gasped.

"My *emergency*," Roderick said with a frown. "The instrumentation said the ReViv was already underway, so we had to bring the person, a woman, into the revivification chamber immediately, so as to be sure the proper ReViv procedures were followed. If she had totally revived inside the cryotube, she'd not be healed. And the safety features of the tubes—which cannot be overridden—would have let her out, to roam the facility at will." He shrugged. "And the doors to this ICE house—like all of the others—would have let her out onto the street, screeching insanity and all."

"God almighty," Crook spat out, unaware that she herself even knew any religious oaths. "What a horrible way to wake up. And to die!" The thought struck her. "But, spontaneous, you say? How in the world—"

"I've spent the last week trying to find out. That's why I called Chels yesterday, to get you out here to see for yourselves."

*He calls the President by her pet name! A real First Friend! He does have clout.* Crook would remember these perks of power, once this episode was over. And she wouldn't be so quick to try to intimidate this little man with her position, either.

"What is the answer?"

"Two parts, Dr. Crook. Part One, what causes the ReViv? And Two, the real problem—why are they so hellishly insane?" Crook nodded again. *Of course, if they don't ReViv, we don't have to worry about Two, do we?* Roderick was reading her mind as though he were telepathic. Smiling sadly, he turned to look through the mirror. The upright cryotube was back in operation, already covered in frost, with a fog of white mist beginning to pour down the sides. The octopoids slowly wheeled the apparatus out the far door.

"But both things *are* happening, and we have to have help—extensive government help—or those billions of cryos will inundate our underpopulated world uncontrollably, spreading their insanity."

"Spreading, what do you mean?" Crook asked, fearful of the answer.

"You felt your own reaction, Dr. Crook, and you're an educated, experienced woman." He jerked a thumb toward the open door where Dougson had just been evacuated. "Your

friend, there, Mr. Lawyer, how do you think he'd react to a
hundred patients running around him? A thousand? A million?"

"But if we can keep them away from us, so we don't see
them . . . " It was more of a prayer than even a hope.

"The insanity *radiates* from them, Dr. Crook. Even if you
hadn't seen our thawed friend in there, hadn't heard him, the
waves of revulsion and fear would have hit you anyhow." The
White House representative had never heard anything so hideous. Even the experience of a few minutes ago paled beside
the implications of the scientist's other statement.

"That's why the attendants and I left, Dr. Crook, to get
outside the facility, as far away as possible." He looked into
her eyes with pity and with pain. "You see, last week, we experienced the full force of the first ReViv close at hand, and we
nearly went mad ourselves."

"Dougson's at the ICE hospital in Minneapolis, and they
think he'll recover nicely," Roderick said, stretching his arms
and yawning. They were sitting in his plush office. "Hope his
mind heals, as well." Behind him, a full-wall holo showed the
Minnesota ICE house, a giant golf ball surrounded by the
transitional trees of the newly-forming rainforest. Hadn't it
once been cool up in this part of the country? Crook wondered.

She said, "I'm recording this, Dr. Roderick. Please, quick
and to the point. Parts One and Two, if you would."

"Part Two, first: Why are they insane? I don't know. But I
can suppose that consciousness is somehow tied into factors
and phenomena external to the body."

"Wait a minute, a *soul*? I don't believe that for a moment."

"I didn't say that, and I don't care what you believe. You
asked my opinion. I think that cryonically freezing a person's

nervous system somehow affects these external factors, like causing total and complete sensory deprivation." Roderick pursed his lips. "Until last century, humans had never been taken down to cryogenic temperatures, so there's no experience with the effects. Hell, maybe it *is* freezing the soul."

Roderick stroked a control panel on his left forearm and the wall behind him became a displate. The holo volume was filled with thin, nearly invisible white threads, all more or less parallel. Crook could see that they were all vibrating very slowly, very much like a stop-motion video of violin strings. The cryoscientist narrated. "Cosmic strings, ultrathreads, constitute the universe. They penetrate and probably compose our personal consciousness just as they penetrate and comprise all other matter and energy. And they vibrate." Another control stroke and one of the threads turned a bright red. A pair of fingers held it at the middle, and its vibration rate increased.

Crook recognized the similarity to a stringed instrument—you changed the frequency by fingering it, or by touching it with a bow. Simple enough. Roderick continued. "By ICEing people, I think we have frozen one node of the vibrating ultrathreads and have distorted the intended modes of oscillation. What we're hearing from the poor ReViveds is what their minds are experiencing as a result." Crook shuddered; InstaCalm couldn't handle every contingency.

"What makes the madness *radiate,* to use your word?" Onscreen came the answer: as the red thread continued its new, rather chaotic vibrations, the adjacent lines appeared to resonate in kind. *Again, like an instrument,* Crook thought. *One badly out of tune.* She didn't like what was forming in her mind. Not at all.

"What's on the displate: resonance." Roderick answered,

chewing a thumbnail nervously. "It's just a guess, but something is damned sure happening. And we need research to find out."

*Maybe you do, at that, Roderick. We sure as hell can't have all these billions of screamers set loose on the world, emanating insanity to us all.* "So we fund your research, Dr. Roderick? Do you also give us the answers to Part One—why are they Reviving spontaneously?"

"That one, I know the answer to. It's just the solution you're not going to like."

"Try."

"The nanoes are subjected to hourly upgrading, new reconfiguration, to provide the most progressive sensing and analysis technologies approved of by the leading researchers."

"You told us that. So?"

"So, Dr. Crook, somehow some of the ice-bugs were able to determine the damage being done to the cryomates by the freezing process." Crook's puzzled glance stimulated another effort by Roderick. "The longer they're in cryomation, the worse the damage to the 'soul' or whatever it is."

"So what we saw today was after thirty years?" Crook didn't like the direction Roderick was leading.

"That's right. Every one of us in cryomation will be like that in thirty years. It might get even worse, you stay in longer."

Crook shuddered. Worse than what she'd seen? How could it be? "How long before a minimum amount of damage, then? Do you know?"

"Can't say. I would guess a few months, maybe a few years, before the 'frozen node' gets so far out of synch with the vibrations of the ultrathreads so as to cause such madness." He shrugged his shoulders. Crook could tell the scientist was bearing a heavy load. *Saving lives, losing souls?*

"Back to the ice-bugs. What about the fetuses, the animals?"

"Monitors show the fetuses developing into babies. The robots in each facility are moving them into larger cryotubes as they grow. The animals? I can't tell. Something is being done to their brains. Maybe they're being made intelligent, like humans. Again, I need research help. We just don't know now."

"And how did it all happen? Spreading from one cryotube to another, all over the world? Is it like a virus?"

"No, as soon as one set of bugs determined the mental injuries—or spiritual, if you will—being done to the cryomates, the information went to the medical section of the worldweb, was analyzed and then transmitted to every cryofacility and hence to every cryomate on the planet. Don't ask me how they did it, that's our one hopeful research direction."

"When will they all start—ReViving?"

"One, last week. This one, today. The old ones first, the newer ones later, I would suppose. Today Minnesota, in a few weeks, the world."

*A few weeks.* Crook exhaled. Chels would have to know, immediately.

"And that's my story, Madame President." Receiving a taped acknowledgement from the holo-screen, Dr. Vivian Crook waited as the President's holo–message recorder broke the connection. "You think she will believe it, Damon?"

"It doesn't matter, does it, Vivian? In a few weeks the world will go insane, incredibly insane, won't it?"

"But what if they decide to bomb the cryofacilities?"

"Viv, someone's going to let them melt old Grandpap on the merest suspicion he's coming back as some kind of monster? Don't be silly. Besides, who knows what might happen if a cryo died? Might break a few ultrathreads, drive more people nuts. We can't take that chance.

"Not to mention killing all those babies and those newly-intelligent animals," Crook added softly. "No, I think the governments of the world can't let out the knowledge of what's about to happen. Interesting times ahead, Dr. Roderick?"

*Do the effects reach off-planet?* she wondered. *If the budget holds, they're taking a dozen or so new settlers up to Gore City, Luna Sector, next week. Would one more attractive woman be acceptable?* She'd have to make discreet inquiries. . . .

Roderick waved a hand toward the exit. "*Very* interesting, Dr. Crook. And now, if you'll excuse me. While you're back in New Columbia rounding up emergency funding for my latest ICE research, I need to get back to my charges." He smiled. "To make sure the natives don't get restless."

Crook didn't smile.

The President did smile, onscreen. "Thank you, Damon, that was a perfecto performance, it even scared me, all over again. But you've got my most agnostic, cynical staffer convinced, and you'll have to do the same for a couple of Congress-critters in a day or so. Then we'll be in business, I believe. But Damon, do you honestly think the situation will go so far, get that bad?"

Dr. Damon Roderick put down his Scotch and water, blowing a kiss toward the holo-screen. "Chels, from what you tell me, world society is deteriorating rapidly from the depopulation made possible by ICE houses. All the talented and intelligent people are going on ICE to take their chances later, and soon there won't be enough educated and trained ones to run the infrastructure.

"Just take electric power, for instance. The solar power satellites are derated by half; the nuclear electric sites are all going the way of surgery, and what power is left is intermittent. If the ICE power supplies become any more irregular than they are now, I predict we could have irrecoverable temperature excursions in two years or less, with horrible results.

"And if we have to keep on building more and more ICE facilities, even the reliability of nanotechnology won't be adequate to ensure quality control. There are bound to be failures, millions or billions of deaths in the tubes.

"On the political side, the radical NewGreens are already calling for the shutdown of all ICE houses, since 'the cryos are dead already.' All of these scenarios result in disaster. We can't have that, now, can we? Deaths by the billions?"

The President wiped back tears that matched Roderick's own. "No, we can't, Damon. You're a perfect example of why. There's too much humanity at stake, both for those ICEd and those fully alive." She sighed. "We'll hold up this end. Just make sure, my old friend, that your mass-production ReViv technology is ready. I'll get the legislation handled through some other friends here—you know which ones, those with ICEd loved ones whom they still love.

"We'll call the cryomations a health hazard or something, leak just a little bit of your horror story, get the system slowed down and stopped. On the positive side, you'll have to bring out a few beloved celebrities—*after* you announce a breakthrough or two.

"Six weeks okay, Damon? Or do you need longer?"

Roderick smiled. "Two months, Chels. Then we start bringing out the old ones, our friends and compatriots, the famous and the talented first. We can have them all ReVived and out in two years or less. But how is the world going to handle it all? I really haven't been out very much in the last couple of years."

"I know that, love. But you will be, soon, I guarantee it. The deICEed, the ReVives, they'll still have friends and relatives, many of them. We'll ease in the Social Security windfalls and tax them to death with one excuse or another, so the economy can absorb it. Population-wise, we need them all. The country's going to hell, we've been losing too many brains too fast. We've got abandoned towns and farms, and consumer markets are drying up because there are not enough people to buy new products. Or invent them."

Roderick said, "So the solution is a new wave of immigration—from the past. Proven, experienced people, healthy and educated and ready for a new life here in the future. A net plus, don't you think?"

The President smiled broadly. "You should know, my fine frozen lover. Goodbye."

Damon Roderick waited for his old friend to break the connection, then sipped his drink, savoring the flavors of both the Scotch and of the just-ended conversation. Indeed, the performance in the ReViv chamber had been quite good; low-frequency vibrations to induce nausea, psychological and pharmacological influences to stimulate fear. The charade nearly duplicated the same fears he'd felt two years ago, when he had been the first person ReVived.

Two years ago, on the President's discreet orders, he'd been brought out of twenty years of cryomation, healed of his Alzheimer's and rejuvenated until his body was as it had been at age thirty, back when he had been married to the woman who was now President. A political genius, she had seen the enormity of the effects of continued, near-universal cryomation, and had seized upon her dead husband's scientific expertise to try to stem the accelerating degradation of humanity.

Even for a Nobel Laureate polymath, it had taken two years of intense, *verch*-fed learning to catch up to the state of the art, to formulate a solution to the problems the President proposed. He'd finally done his part, the technological side, the easier of the tasks. And now the hard part, the politics, had to kick in and complete the equation. She'd be able to handle it from here on; Chels had always been extremely savvy.

Just before breaking off the President had said, "I know the insane patient act with the tongue and eyeballs was all special effects, but that hideous scream, it really did sound like something from hell. Are there really any side effects of ICEing, Damon?"

"The primary side effect is that I'm thirty years old again, Madame President, dearest, and with the advances in nanotech I've been able to accomplish since you ReVived me, you will soon be, too.

"As for the sound effects, I used the computer and played with sound mixing a little, *subtracting* my own fine singing voice from the roaring chaos. For the background noise? I just took the latest *verch*-net rock song and played it backwards!"

# RAW TERRA

▼

## NICK POLLOTTA

"Ladies and gentlemen, we're almost there!" cried Erik Kaye into his hand-held mike, while hanging out the open window of the antique style train engine.

The cool Titan wind whipped his curly gray hair into a wild frenzy, totally unlike the usual neat perfection his billions of TriD viewers were familiar with, and for the first time in his life Kaye didn't give a good goddamn. They were going to make it! The story of the year! Hell, the decade!

If only he knew what *it* was!

Alongside him in the cabin was Dr. Alice Bentley, a pretty brunette in a lab jumpsuit typing madly on her wrist secretary with one hand, a computer stylus clamped tight between clenched teeth. Behind the scientist was Sergeant Valkilmar Zane, a stout United Planets' police officer nervously fondling his service laser, rigidly formal in his stark white uniform, the red and blue emblem of this independent colony emblazoned on a shoulder. Filling the fore of the open cabin was a rocky gray bipedal mountain, whose nimble alien hands were frantically working the controls of the rumbling steam engine. Birth name: (assorted grunts, snorts and a rude flatulent noise); social name: Rocky. Which was the equivalent of calling an Irishman 'Red' or an African pygmy 'Shorty'. Not quite exactly an insult, but hardly original thinking for the alien Choron.

Adjusting the gain on his transceiver, Erik sighed internally. These four were the only ones to brave this final leg of their perilous historic journey. A mere four out of the trillions filling the Sol system. That didn't say much for the courage and dedication of the average UP citizen. Then again, it was sweeps week on the TriD. And, sadly, saving the worlds was hardly a match for Nude Celebrity Mud Wrestling. Art will always triumph. *Rat-a-clack, rat-a-clack.* The iron wheels of the environmentally correct locomotive clattered over every rail joint of the Earth-sized moon of Saturn as the convoy steadily built speed, bio-degradable black smoke pouring from the tall fluted chimney. Filling the horizon overhead was the ringed glory of the gasgiant mother world. On either side of the rattling train were the ragged cliffs of a low ravine—an arroyo actually, thought Kaye, although few folk knew the word these days. But then, the shame of modern education was next week's story, not today's. The terraforming of Titan had started a hundred years ago, and today was its ultimate culmination. If only they could crash this train into a toxin-polluted lake before they were all killed by accidents or terrorists.

Titan, your vacation wonderland. Whee.

"Dr. Bentley, how's it going?" asked Kaye, holding a hand before the floating HoverCam before him to signal a break in the story flow.

Her long hair an auburn Medusa's nest, Alice glanced up from her wrist work. "Statistically, the events plaguing us have almost exceeded any possibility of random causation and risen to the mathematical point of certainty," she shouted.

In the far distance, something exploded in the gray sky with violent results above the mountainous Titan garbage dump.

"Yeah, well statistics will only help you so much against anti-personnel Gotcha! missiles," remarked Sergeant Zane, flicking his gun safety off/on/off.

A rocky smile from the inhuman pilot. "At least the protective umbrella from the Titan Defense Corp is still in operation. We're not dead yet, officer!"

" 'Yet' being the operative word, citizen."

At their feet, the train engineer and chief technician of the scientific project snored peacefully on top of each other. Both of their PocketDocs had mysteriously given them a massive overdose of "Don't Worry, Be Sleepy!" tranquilizers just as the train was going around Deadman's Curve. They should have crashed. Just another amazing coincidence in an endless stream of them. And they would have, too, if not for the timely intervention of the Rocky, a tourist who had inadvertently gotten on the wrong train at the right time.

Plus the assistant train engineer had never showed up. All of the doors, windows, and garbage chute of his home had became bizarrely jammed this morning and after he managed to wiggle out the doggie door, his car wouldn't start from the relatively simple but unsolvable problem that its entire engine had been removed by thieves during the night.

Curls to the wind, Erik snorted. Thieves, his butt! The reporter had no damn idea who their unseen enemy was, but they really gave a new definition to the word persistent. And added a few lines to the description of ruthless. Webster and

184 ▼ NICK POLLOTTA

Roget would have been proud of them. Just before they shot the bastards.

Whoever the nameless enemy was.

At the broomhandle throttle, cramped in the small human size control booth was their two meters of scaled alien muscle, whose living granite fingers were nimbly operating the iron control rods and wheels with a surgeon's delicacy. Or more precise, the knowledgeable touch of a being who loved machines.

Dressed only in a bulging tool belt and pre-space aviator scarf, the Choron tourist had been pressed into service as the impromptu chauffeur of the hundred-ton train by Bentley and Zane when the railroad engineers had resigned from the job by hitting the floor and snoring in stereo. Although not specifically interested in this human endeavor, saving a world was a noble deed! Besides, (assorted snorts, grunts and a rude flatulent noise) was getting paid by the hour for the task.

Jammed into the back of the cabin so it would have enough room for a good picture was a flying ceramic egg; aerials, antennas, and an array of telephoto lenses covered the exposed surface. A Geraldo-class HoverCam floated effortlessly above Erik's shoulder like the hologram parrot of a cyborg pirate. The effect was augmented by the fact that one of the three lenses of the Toshiba camcorder had been broken recently by shrapnel from an inexplicably exploding film vending machine and the TBBC news reporter had temporarily covered the cracked glass with a tiny eyepatch.

Why would anybody want to stop a reclamation project?

"Gods above and below!" cursed Rocky, thumping on unbreakable gauges and thus proving that the manufacturer's claim was correct. Inexorably the train began to slow.

"Oh, what now?" demanded Dr. Bentley, dropping her stylus.

The Choron turned to face the tiny human without bothering to move his shoulders. "The main drive rod appears to have disconnected itself. We've losing all motivational power!"

"How about using Scientology, or EST?" joked the Titan officer dryly.

"Ha. I laugh. You're fired," snapped Alice.

Wisely, Erik covered the built-in microphone on his camcorder as he spat twelve of the fourteen dirty words you still couldn't say on television. Even in the twenty-fourth century. Funny cops. Just what they needed.

Craning her neck out the window, Bentley could just see a dark flat mass ahead of them, as her nose hairs started to curl and burn. Lake Underdunk, without a doubt. So close and yet so far.

"Ideas!" the scientist barked loudly, trying desperately not to breathe. Phew, what a stink!

While the officer and the reporter scrunched their faces in thought, and then gagged as the smell of the lake hit them like a nasal injection of sewage, the alien brandished a wrench.

"I'll free the rear carriages," he said and charged off into the empty passenger compartment. "Momentum equals mass over gravity plus velocity."

True enough, at least for media work. "But who's going to drive this thing?" demanded Erik gasping for air or any reasonable facsimile.

"It's a train on tracks," wheezed Sergeant Zane, arching an eyebrow. "Where's it going to go? Off for a pizza?"

*Rat-a-clack, rat-a-clack.* And then from the rear of the train there came a metallic noise, half crunch, half snap and all loud. Instantly, the last two of the passenger compartments started to drag behind and the train drastically increased speed. The noise was repeated twice more and in short order there was nothing remaining of the once mighty convoy but the environmentally safe, wood burning, steam locomotive and the stainless steel tanker car holding the fifty-five thousand gallons of the mutant brew, Y.U.M. 123.

Again, Dr. Bentley fumed over why anybody would want to destroy such a benign project.

Soon Rocky returned. The alien had encountered no problems disconnecting the rear carriages, as all of them were empty. The plush seats, massive buffet, and robotic bar remained cold and untouched. Although he bitterly hated cowards, Kaye really couldn't blame the local politicians and bigwigs from passing on this trip. Amalgamated Water had been a horror from the word launch. Crashed computers, lost mail, burst water pipes in the middle of conferences, power outages, miswired diagnostic machinery, improperly labeled chemicals, vicious pencil sharpeners which worked too damn well, and sub-zero bathrooms. Nothing violent, nothing direct. No single act that would plainly state outside interference—that was why Zane was the only cop they had as protection—only endless little problems which bled the hope and drive from the people involved as efficiently as . . . ah, disconnecting the drive rods of a steam locomotive.

Holding onto a stanchion, Erik stuck an Irish Coffee flavorstick into his mouth and sucked a dozen millimeters of color from the confection, as the HoverCam automatically fed a prerecorded commercial into the AV loop. Faintly he could hear himself saying, "If it fits in the palm of your hand, is made of plastic, costs under ten dollars, and breaks in a week, it's another fine product from . . . the Gunderson Corporation! Makers of Murphy's Law Soap . . . whatever can be cleaned, will be cleaned!"

Truth in advertising. What a concept.

Scanning the sky and the ravine around them, Zane loosened a collar button. "What's the status?" he barked in a military manner.

"We'll make it," said the returning alien, throwing his wrench aside tiredly. "Although stopping may be an interesting procedure."

"Interesting, how?" asked the officer.

With a grating noise, an eyeridge was raised. "Don't crashes always make good TriD viewing?"

Oh swell. Continuing to build speed, the train crested the arroyo and started hurtling down the tracks towards the horrible quagmire of Lake Underdunk. It was, officially, the most polluted body of water in the fourteen worlds of the Human Solar System according to the Ecological Survey of 2207. And considering Boston Harbor, White Sands nuclear test site in New Mexico, lower south Marsportville near the sulphur plant, along with most of the take-out restaurants in Bombay, India, that was really saying something.

With one silicate hand on the throttle, Rocky kicked open the firedoor and reached across the cabin to grab ahold of a log in the aft tinder box. But as the tree trunk passed in front of Sergeant Zane, the man went stiff.

"Hold it!" shouted Zane, his 1mm. Bedlow laser pistol out of its shoulder holster and leveled at the lumbering leviathan.

Just to be polite, everybody else also froze motionless.

"I'm a cyborg," the officer enunciated slowly, his blue eyes narrowed to dark slits. "And this log throws a radar shadow."

"Impossible," snorted Bentley, crossing her arms. "Wood couldn't do that unless," her voice started to fail, ". . . there's something metallic inside."

Gingerly, the alien placed the innocent-appearing log on the floor and Zane went to work with a Venus Army Knife. With a click the rough wood broke in half, the two pieces separating with a hydraulic sigh. Lying on the floor was a nasty looking assortment of steel tubes, fiber optic cables, digital timer, and four large blocks of a grayish clay compound. Nobody had any doubt as to what the infernal device was. It was classic. Prototypical of its kind.

"That's a bomb, isn't it?" asked Rocky, nudging the explosive with a toe.

Flavorstick dropping from his mouth, Kaye pushed the alien back. "And it's live!" he shouted in rising fear, as the internal indicators started winking and blinking wildly. Holy prack!

"Not anymore," said Zane calmly, ripping a red wire free from the technological spaghetti. In a sad ratcheting sound, the indicators turned off and the internal electrostatic supports of the device went limp.

While the rest sighed in relief, Rocky quickly picked the fifty-kilo charge up in a hand and heaved it over the side of the train doing his very best impersonation of Knute Rockne as the Statue of Liberty.

Arching into the distance, the log/bomb hit the middle of Lake Underdunk with more of a sploot than a splash and disappeared instantly into the watery morass.

"Better," smiled the alien.

Alice cocked an eyebrow at the Goliath technician. "Do you really think that was necessary?"

That was what she intended to ask, but before the words could leave her mouth the whole lake seemed to heave upwards, the putrid waters parting in a strident roar of hot gases and dead fish shotgunning into the air as if the world itself was vomiting. Smelled like it too. Whew!

Peeking out from behind the Geraldo, the scientist apologized for doubting the technician.

"Agreed," said Zane, his eyes glowing a faint blue as he

stared real hard at everything. "Now we're safe."

"For the moment," noted Kaye, scanning the horizon with a pair of trinoculars. Ever since he had been on this damn story, somebody, or bodies, had been systematically trying to stop it. And now their efforts had escalated from slashing the tires on ground cars and stealing clothes to outright murder.

"Although we didn't include guardian in our original contract," said the alien, facing the tiny scientist. "And I do think we should renegotiate for that."

"My station will kick in an extra thousand for the exclusive rights to the bomb story," snapped Kaye impatiently.

A stalactite grin. "Done."

Geez! Reluctantly the reporter was starting to get the feeling that somebody, somewhere, was probably paying the Choron to use gravity. He didn't do anything for free!

With a grateful nod to Erik, Alice glanced backwards at the massive refrigerated tanker trailing behind them just to make sure it was still there, safe and secure. That precious tank. It was the total capital worth of her company, EnviroInc.

For inside that container was a new form of artificial life, and one even more useful than the previously created Bacteria 1040, which specialized in eating income tax forms.

Environment Incorporated had long been bothered by the fact that when Humanity went into space, they left all of their garbage on Earth. And as each colony matured, so did their pollution level. So EnviroInc had created a sub-company, Amalgamated Water, whose brilliant staff spent the next two decades in a sanitized space lab high above Jupiter inventing Y.U.M. 123.

Y.U.M. was a genetically unstable organism with a total life span of six hours, and it ravenously ate anything suspended in water that wasn't alive. How the technicians got the stuff to make the distinction between a sluggish fish and an oil slick was beyond even their normally lugubrious ability to explain. But she had seen the test, and the stuff worked. About all it didn't consume was concrete and steel, and thus, was no danger to bridges, tunnels, or floating boats. Although a scuba driver caught unawares might find himself suddenly stark naked, wearing only his air tank and a waterproof watch.

The end result was if Y.U.M. was introduced into a water system, like a polluted river, the water would be rendered clean, absolutely chemically clean, drinkable, without any damage to the fish or plants—should any still be living in target cesspool. The scientists at AmWa had started experimenting upon Kool-Aid, then beef stew, working their way up to raw bathroom sewage, and finally to industrial sludge. But the fluid contents of Underdunk was a sublime combination of all these with the muck of a swamp, the waste of a toxic chemical dump site, and the dissolved inventory of a garbage heap! Even the field testing in New Jersey hadn't prepared them for this.

"Plane," said Sergeant Zane, pointing towards the horizon.

Kaye pivoted and his HoverCam focused on the approaching speck. He had just found the correct focus when a dozen other specks rose from the ground and the aerial dot blossomed into a quite spectacular fireball.

"Whew. Nice missile work," commented the alien.

"The gang at Titan Defense are masters of destruction," boasted Zane proudly.

Erik grumped, "Your tax dollars at work. And maybe now the cops will believe us."

"I sure do," commented the officer.

"Why?" demanded Dr. Bentley petulantly. "Why would anybody not want a lake cleaned?"

Only the *rat-a-clack* of the train and the sounds of the syrupy water lapping sluggishly against the mottled beach answered her question.

"It'll make the property values go up," suggested the alien, shoving logs into the furnace, but only after Sergeant Zane had given him a nod for each one. "Perhaps the source of the attacks wanted them to go down so he could purchase the land cheaply."

"The government owns the property," answered the Titan officer. "It's going to become a park. If this works."

"Yes, if!"

Rounding a bend in the tracks, the mixed crew could now plainly see their final destination. The infamous Lake Underdunk. There were no flies in the swampy air above the murky waterway because nobody made gas masks quite that tiny.

"So what's the plan?" asked Kaye, hoping the fumes wouldn't dissolve his camera.

Rigidly at attention, Sergeant Zane turned around from saluting a passing Titan flag. They were now officially on government property. "As we pass by the lake, we open a series of nozzles and spray the entire eastern bank of the sludge pile."

"So stopping is not necessary?" asked Rocky curiously.

"Not until we want to get off."

Surreptitiously, the granite giant hid the broken brake wheel behind his back. "Sounds good!" As long as they didn't charge him for breakage. Even a locomotive probably came under the universal axiom, "Nice to look at, nice to hold . . ." etc., etc.

"The Y.U.M. is at operational temperature!" called Alice, minutely adjusting gauges on the tanker by tapping commands onto her wrist secretary. "In range in thirty-five seconds . . . twenty . . . ten . . . no!"

"What?" snapped Kaye, extending his mike.

Frantic tapping. "The release control is stuck!"

"Allow me," rumbled Rocky. Reaching for the emergency manual release handle set among the engine controls, the alien used fingertip pressure to shove the bar forward one single notch. The rod broke off completely, falling to the floor and shattering like glass. Which it was.

"Ghtqz! This is a real fifteen-cent operation!" cursed the huge alien rudely. Or was the human phrase nickel and dime? Well, whatever, it was definitely time for some change!

"Son of a bitch!" corrected the furious Titan agent, drawing his Bedlow laser and pointing the weapon at the tanker.

"No!" cried Bentley stepping between him and the tanker. "At this range the Y.U.M. fumes would kill us before they disperse! Even with the wind factor!"

At those words, Kaye slumped. So their unknown foe had succeeded. Amalgamated Water had spent every cent, pulled every string to get this one test into operation. Its failure meant an end to the whole operation. There was nothing more to be done. What a terrible end for the story.

"Do you mind?" asked Rocky plucking the laser from the officer's hand. As the startled humans watched, the alien bent ridiculously far out of the cabin and fired one long burst from the energy pistol at something far ahead of them.

"Thanks," the stone said, tossing the weapon back.

"Hey, the power pack is empty!" gasped Zane in surprise.

"What did you do?" gasped Kaye, scanning with his trinoculars.

"I destroyed the Underdunk inlet bridge," came the calm reply.

"What?" chorused the carbon-based life-forms.

Below them the steaming mire of the horribly polluted basin flashed by like a vista from hell.

An avalanche of a shrug. "If we can't reach the lake properly, then we shall crash into it."

"We'll all die!"

"Nonsense." He snorted. "We will only be going fifty, sixty kilometers per hour." A short pause. "You humans can take a crash at that speed onto concrete without damage, can't you?"

Their expressions told him different.

Oops.

"How soon till the bridge?" demanded Kaye, making a fast duplicate of his video disks and tossing them overboard for safe keeping. The rainbow flats scattered to the wind, a few landing in the lake and dissolving.

"Oh, right about now," said Sergeant Zane in a falsely calm poker voice.

"Jump!" cried Dr. Bentley, and she did.

It was death one way or the other, so having little choice in the matter Kaye and the rest joined her. Hugging his Geraldo for protection Erik followed suit, hoping and praying that his insurance premiums were paid in full. This was definitely going to hurt.

The fall was short, and ended in a hard squish as the ex-passengers landed squarely in a large drainage ditch full of what drainage ditches were usually full of.

"Shit!" sputtered the spattered Zane, waist deep in stinking brown goo. Everybody agreed. Yep, that's what it was, all right. Good ol' non-toxic crap from Oberon City. What a relief!

Rocky pulled himself free from the pit his landing had rudely formed in the concrete embankment and walked over to the edge to give a hand to the quagmired humans. Soon standing on the cracked but solid lee, their three Gunderson

Corporation PocketDocs extended mechanical spider legs and produced belt pouches to begin assorted repairs and start the cleaning process. Gagging and retching, the battered humans watched as the thundering train roared past them on the track atop the steel girder trestle.

Barreling by at ever-increasing speed, the steam engine tilted over dangerously as it took a gentle curve in the track and then leveled out just in time to soar straight off the still glowing end of the ruined bridge.

For almost a full second the chugging train was suspended in the air, then it began to arc downward, rapidly descend and then plummet like a lead safe full of dead bricks.

Engine broke apart from the wood bin, which came free from the tanker, and the three hit in a triad of meteoric impacts. A triangular geyser formed which made the precious bomb blast resemble a fishy fart. Sewage and biological toxins soared skyward forming for a brief moment a muddy mushroom cloud, the sight sending chills down everybody's spine.

In ragged stages, the aquatic undulations ceased, the aerial sludge rained back down into its steaming home and visibility returned. There, roughly in the middle of the lake was the refrigerated tanker bobbing like a steel hotdog. Under the trinoculars, there appeared to be not even the smallest crack in its adamantine hull.

"The damn thing is still intact!" roared Kaye furiously.

"Yeah? Well, not anymore," said Zane, and the Bedlow was in his hand. The first shot merely cleansed the firing lenses in a harmless pyrotechnic display of lights. But the next emitted a shimmering beam of rainbow colors which stabbed out from the maw of the dire weapon and a neat line of puckered holes appeared in the resilient metal container, as if it was being attacked by a giant, invisible sewing machine. Steam wisped into view from the punctures and then a slick purplish fluid streamed out into the brownish-gray sludge of the lake.

Trying not to breathe too deeply as the air made their lungs burn, the battered group waddled hopefully to the sticky beach for a better look. A minute passed. Another. Another.

Nothing was happening.

"Prack!" cried Dr. Bentley, and she pulled a tiny vial of oily fluid from a pocket. "The activator!"

Recording everything, Eric lowered his mike and looked at the twenty meters of pungent chemical sewage that separated them from the sinking locomotive and surrendered. Whoever their unknown foe was had finally won. There was no way anybody could cross the morass of bio-toxins and survive. Not without spacesuits, which were hours away.

Both hands holding the vial to her heart, Dr. Bentley kicked one leg forward and lunged into a crouch, her right arm doing a hard fast whip forward.

The vial cannonballed towards the bubbling mess, and only a foot in front the vial dipped a bit and to the left, then crashed loudly on the metal hull. Like a glass comet, the tiny vial shattered into a million glistening pieces. Instantly, the purple goo underneath changed from white to brown, then green. Glorious green!

And then everything sank from sight.

Standing on the beach, the group stared at the woman.

"A curve ball. Sorry. Old habit," said Alice sheepishly. "I was the relief pitcher for the Luna Miners during my college days for three years running."

Straightening his filthy clothes, Erik took a stance before the lake as the HoverCam reached out a mechanical arm and combed his hair into place. It then powdered his nose, adjusted focus and flashed the on-air signal.

"So, ladies and gentlemen, this is it. We have finally

reached Lake Underdunk in spite of colossal odds. For any new viewers who may have just tuned in, this is Erik Kaye for TBBC, reporting live from the independent moon Titan. Long a haven for chemical research, industrial dumping, and nuclear storage, the people of Titan, like those on Earth, have only recently started the odious job of cleaning up their incredibly polluted environment."

A half-turn to the stage left to show his good side and display a section of the bubbling cesspool. "And the scientists of Amalgamated Water have been plagued by mysterious problems from the very beginning. Missed shipments, mismarked containers. Computer virus, scrambled phone lines. Nothing violent, or overt. But a steady destruction of this totally innocuous project. Coincidence? No."

The anchor glanced over his shoulder at the smooth expanse of the dead lake.

"Due to their ever-growing population, Titan Central has domed over this site and is attempting to reclaim this lost bit of biology. A noble task. Exemplary! Only," his voice lowered dramatically, "can it be done?"

Tense moments passed, as Dr. Bentley wiped her face clean with a pocket handkerchief. And prayed. After ten years of hard work, the incredible project was starting. Alice glanced at her watch. Correction. Had started two minutes ago.

Standing on an old abandoned aircar engine, Zane pointed, "Look!"

"Wait a minute, I seem to see something happening. . . ." said Kaye for his blind or inattentive viewers.

Something was swirling below the slimy surface. A bubble rose to the syrupy surface of the lake, then a second, a third, fourth. Then a series of bubbles, then the center began to boil furiously. As fast as it started the process stopped, and a great calm engulfed the hundred domed hectares of deep space refuse park.

Had the Y.U.M. worked? Was that it? A measly bubbling. A can of fizzy soda pop could have done better!

"Hey, I see something," said Rocky, his crystalline eyes extending on louvered stalks from inside his head. "The center of the lake . . . yes, it is . . . it's changing color."

"It's doing what?" demanded Dr. Bentley, pulling out a set of pocket trinoculars and dialing for computer enhancement.

Under the magnification, the blackish fluid had now formed a green area in the general vicinity of the crashed train. Was it an oil leak from the hydraulic system? Had the bar ruptured? Or . . .

But as she watched, the green section turned aquamarine, dark blue, light blue, and then clear.

Perfectly clean water!

Dumbfounded by the extreme change, her wrist secretary ran a diagnostic on itself and sent an angry letter to the manufacturer for such obviously shoddy workmanship on its sensors.

Inch by inch, the circle expanded into the stygian, nigh impregnable Underdunk, centuries of industrial pollution rendering it little more than a pool of mud.

Inexorably, the patch of clear water advanced towards shore, slowly annihilating the unidentifiable muck. Not pushed forward, but extended. As the sluggish lake met the bubbling barrier all contaminants disappeared, and only impossibly pure water remained. The likes of which Humanity had not seen since dinosaurs trampled on Vikings taking a pee in a stream.

Gradually coming into visibility, the bottom was an irregular expanse of rocks, plus the occasional steam locomotive. Obviously its iron body was immune to the ravaging effects of the clean-up. Now in full operation, completely unleashed, and hungry as hell, the mutated microbes of Y.U.M. 123 tied tiny napkins about their throats and really went to lunch. Rapidly, the zone of clean water began spreading in every direction. Relentlessly it went into a true primordial feeding frenzy, the Y.U.M. eating everything not physiologically alive, thermally warm, or chemically dead in the abandoned lake.

Just then a gasping fish dove out of the mire and splashed happily into the cool blue. Amused, the observers smiled at each other. Life was indomitable, even on Titan.

Filling half the sky, the ringed majesty of Saturn reflected like fresh diamonds off the sparkling lake within a lake. Unstoppable, the patch of shiny blue, heralded by its bubbling green cuff, raced off in every direction. In only minutes, the entire surface turned a beautiful deep azure blue. And the zone of visibility descended deeper and deeper into the murky lake with every passing second. More fish were exposed, along with a turtle and a very surprised-looking octopus, who promptly swam away.

However, the surface color change did not stop as it reached the river feeding into the lake, and the grayish water of the contaminated tributary underwent the same incredible transformation as the microbes raced upriver into a sewer pipe and out of the protective dome. The Y.U.M. had a lot to do in its remaining six hours, and every second of that was going to be spent feeding and breeding.

A soft wind blew over the sticky reporters, and it did not make them cringe. It smelled faintly of air conditioning. But fresh was the operative word. Clean and fresh.

"Holy Joseph, Mary, and Zeus, it worked," whispered Erik, the filthy microphone dangling limply in his hands.

Polishing his laser, Sergeant Zane suddenly stopped and snapped his fingers for attention. The anchor looked, gasped, smiled and then resumed his more formal stance of a news reporter. Ah, now they had some answers.

Although the water of the lake was perfectly clear, the center of Underdunk was too deep to see. But lining the shoals and along the shallow banks leading to the shore was a forest of underwater skeletons, their feet in tubs of concrete. Over in a sandbar was a collection of automobiles with more skeletons handcuffed to the steering wheels. There were stacks of letters, piles of knives, and a small mountain of pistols. Everything was in remarkably good condition.

"And now we know why the project had secret enemies," announced Dr. Bentley looking into the crystal clear expanse of the new water.

Near the bubbling locomotive on the bottom of the lake, resting on a bed of golden sand, were boxes and file cabinets. Old and rusty but many, most, appeared still intact.

"Evidence," guessed Kaye out loud for his unseen audience. "Most likely, organized crime has been using this place as a dumping site since time immemorial. Or at least since 2245 when the United Planets colonized Titan."

"And if this process works here, it'll work anywhere. Even on Earth!"

"Or Choron." A clean Choron! Both his brains boggled at the concept. What a wild notion. His children could actually go into either of the oceans and not explode. Wow.

"Honorary Dr. Bentley, old pal," smoothly began the alien, retracting his eye stalks. "May I humbly ask for the formula of these amazing microbes to clean my own homeworld of our pollution?"

"Yeah?" asked the woman suspiciously. "And how much will you sell it to them for?"

Words burned like fire in his mind, but summoning some secret hidden inner strength, he heroically said them anyway. "I . . . I shall not sell it."

"You? Do something for free? Ha!" snorted Zane.

The fresh lake air wafted over him and the alien happily filled his lung. Ah! "Doctor, there are some things even more important than . . ." Immediately, his throat constricted. No, he couldn't say it. What the hell, he'd give the Y.U.M. to his government as a charitable donation to lower his taxes. Ah, much better. To his race *free* was the only four-letter f-word not used in polite company.

"Well, you have been instrumental in helping us complete the project," murmured the scientist. "So, yes, agreed. But no blackmarket reselling."

"Never!" cried the alien in horror. His honor was on the line here. Besides, there were witnesses. And a verbal contract was always as good as the police force that backed it up.

Finished making a report to his superiors, Officer Zane released his collar button and smiled at the dirty group on the shore. "Tactical support groups from the local police, UP military, and InterPlanPol will be here in six minutes. Even the president of Mars and his dog are coming."

"This," he added unnecessarily, "is big!"

Bentley nodded. "Excellent. Thank you, officer."

"No problem, ma'am." Walking to the edge of the lake, Erik Kaye swabbed the toe of his boot in the water. Instantly the leather was washed clean and the polish removed. "And just consider what other criminal delights we will find at the bottom of the Hudson River in Newer York, the Thames River in England, the Rhine of Germany, or the Sea of Japan?" Running a hand through his matted hair, the big officer smiled. "How much critical evidence in capital cases are we going to reclaim? And how much of this will be linked to organized crime?"

"Yes, indeed," said Kaye swinging mike and HoverCam to face the police officer. "Exactly how many unsolved crimes are about to become solved? How many murder raps cleared, innocent prisoners set free, and drug-lord bosses sent to jail? What is your professional opinion, sergeant?"

The Titan officer grinned. "I think the warden at the United Planet's penitentiary better dust off the electric chair, because it's gonna get mighty busy real soon."

Finally understanding, Rocky pursed his forehead. Criminals had been disposing of evidence in the polluted water? Hmm, damn clever actually. "No wonder somebody tried so hard to stop us. Hell, every criminal organization probably wanted us dead."

Gleefully happy, Alice Bentley agreed. Although not designed for it, Y.U.M. was in the process of removing more than one type of human pollution.

"Ha ha, we win!" she laughed, arms akimbo.

The next day on Earth, a growing crowd of people waved and cheered on the Hudson River shoreline, while a bold few even dove into the fantastically pure expanse of water filling the mouth of the river. Where sparkling waves lapped at the banks, trash was no longer visible, graffiti gone from rocks, wood pilings and ancient concrete embankments appeared new and strong. Even the ever-present, pungent cheese smell was thinning from the air. More than a few onlookers started hacking and choking at the invasion of oxygen to their weathered lungs. Immediately, their neighbors began selling coughdrops.

Then arcing over the horizon came dozens of horribly beweaponed UP Leviathan hovertanks. Maneuvering over the clear water, side hatches slid open and out dove hundreds of soldiers in armored spacesuits, which functioned perfectly well as diving suits. And had much better TV reception. Each trooper was carrying a very large wicker basket. Empty, for the moment.

Meanwhile, in countless luxurious penthouses across Manhattan, groups of well-dressed gangsters started packing for Pluto—when suddenly, an armada of police Tarantula helicopters lifted into view outside the windows, and from the front door there came a very official knock-knock.

Trapped, the crime lords slumped in resignation, some of them openly weeping. Outside the penthouse window could be seen a foaming green band racing up the Hudson River, eventually heading for the poisonous Finger Lakes, the undrinkable Niagara Falls, the toxic Great Lakes, the putrid Ohio River, the deadly Mississippi. . . .

Across the world, the common folk cheered and danced, while numerous industrialists underwent desperate plastic surgery in their racing limos and more than one drug lord simply shot himself in the head to save police the time and trouble of a trial. Unstoppable and uncaring of these antics, the microbes continued eating themselves to a glorious death across the entire world.

The terraforming of Earth had begun.

# THE PRODUCT OF THE EXTREMES

▼

## B. W. CLOUGH

When Hector Trollin's inter-office buzzer rang he picked up the phone without putting down *Time* magazine. "We got a live one, sir," Miss Fox chirped. "This guy has a device to eliminate racism."

"Can't Mr. Herry take him? I did the last *two* perpetual motion machines."

"Sorry, sir. Mr. Herry's gone to the dentist."

"Oh, all right then." Wearily Mr. Trollin hung up. Eyes have their eyelashes, nightclubs have their bouncers, and editors, if they are lucky, have slush-pile readers. The U.S. Patent Office has what is unofficially called the Nut Division—those bureaucrats whose duty it is to discourage frivolous applications. They explain the laws of conservation of energy to inventors of perpetual motion devices. They inspect recipes for elixirs of eternal life. They listen to wordy scientific rationales

204 ▼ B. W. Clough

propounded by quacks wishing to patent copper bracelets that cure cancer. It is soul-shriveling work.

The man who strode into Mr. Trollin's office didn't look especially nutty. His glasses slid down his nose, his high pink forehead shaded into a receding hairline, and his three-piece gray suit did not fit well. Miss Fox followed to put the case file on Mr. Trollin's desk. She was tall and statuesque, her sleek ebony skin emphasized by a white linen dress.

"Aha," Mr. Trollin said, reading. "You are Doctor Roberto Wist. Suppose you explain your invention to me, doctor?" He leaned back in his swivel chair and made a steeple of his pale fingers, an attitude which Mr. Herry had assured him created a very intimidating atmosphere.

Dr. Wist pushed his glasses up. "Well, Mr. Trollin! May I ask you a personal question?"

"Surely." Mr. Trollin steeled himself. The jolly enthusiastic sales pitches were the worst. And Dr. Wist had a peculiarly annoying voice, braying and nasal, like a minor TV star shilling used cars.

"Have you ever considered having sex with your sister?"

Mr. Trollin blinked. "I must say I have not."

"Do you know *why* the concept is unthinkable to you?"

Mr. Trollin toyed with the idea of saying that he was an only child, but discarded it. "No."

"Because Nature encourages exogamy."

"Aha," Mr. Trollin repeated, confused.

"You understand that out-breeding, marrying outside the family, encourages genetic diversity and vigor. That is why the incest taboo is almost built into the human brain. That is why young lions leave their pride, while young lionesses stay on. That is why herd animals, horses and so on, oust young males when they become sexually mature."

"Perhaps we could move on to your invention," Mr. Trollin suggested, since Dr. Wist seemed to have an endless fund of examples.

"Well, Mr. Trollin! What about this racism problem? The situation in South Africa is a positive tinderbox. Even in this land of the free civil rights have not progressed as much as one might like. Busing of school children, quotas for firemen, racial lynchings outside of gas stations—"

"The invention," Mr. Trollin prompted.

"Well! My idea is to harness this drive for exogamy, in the cause of social justice. This is what I wish to patent." From his large shabby briefcase Dr. Wist whipped out an oversized mason jar. Inside a greenish-gray fluid slopped around.

"And this is—?"

"A concentrated culture of genetically engineered bacteria," Dr. Wist said, setting it tenderly on the desk. "Tough little things, aren't they? Have you heard the saying that the only vital sex organ is the brain? Well! These bacteria have been painstakingly designed to alter the receptivity response of the brain to certain factors—the incest taboo, to be precise. And in a very calculated direction! We are told that all men are brothers. Consider what would happen if you regarded all white fair-haired women, you yourself being white, as sisters. Is not a favorite racist comment, 'Would you want your sister to marry one?' Well, with the help of my little culture here, your sister will be much more likely to marry one! And you, her brother, will be in no position to cast nasturtiums, since your own matrimonial instincts will be inclined towards ladies of other races and nationalities. The product of the extremes, to paraphrase a mathematic aphorism, will be a happy mean!"

"I see," Mr. Trollin said, although he didn't. He leaned forward with a slightly wolfish smile. This was the fun part. "Tell me, Dr. Wist, are you a medical doctor? From what medical school did you obtain your degree? Are you licensed to do research in genetic engineering? Hmm?"

An hour later Dr. Wist trudged out of the Patent Office building to the nearby bus kiosk. Half a dozen commuters already waited there, and the bus was just coming round the corner. His personality did not readily become downcast, but Dr. Wist had to admit that the complete eradication of racism had been delayed. "For one day only!" he vowed, in a trumpeting nasal tone.

Right behind his legs a huge dog leaped out from where it had lain unnoticed under the kiosk bench. It bayed like the Hound of the Baskervilles.

"Aah!" Dr. Wist pirouetted clumsily. His glasses fell off and he caromed off two other commuters.

"Quiet, Billie!" the blind woman commanded, jerking the dog's seeing-eye harness.

The bus slowed with a loud hiss of air brakes. But it was too late. Dr. Wist slipped, and with a piercing yelp fell under the front wheels. The big briefcase tumbled into the gutter, where the tow truck backed over it as the police tried to free Dr. Wist's body. A greenish-gray fluid dripped slowly from the torn leather.

The first herald of humanity's new age came in the person of Hector Trollin himself, when he proposed to Miss Fox a month after Dr. Wist's accident. The Nut Division chipped in to buy the happy couple a pair of silver-plated salad tongs. No one in authority was alarmed or even interested, unless one counts Miss Fox's former boyfriend, an executive at the United Negro College Fund.

More public manifestations became plain only gradually. Interracial couples became more and more common in discos and bars in the D.C. area. Diplomats from impoverished Third World countries, who had always heretofore struggled with tiny entertainment budgets and the consequent social indifference, found themselves inundated with ritzy invitations. Blond senators fired their fair-haired secretaries, who were in turn rehired by Congressmen with dark hair.

In five years the demographers noted a startling increase in interracial births on the Eastern seaboard. By the turn of the century America could truly call herself a melting pot. Due to the Mendelian laws of inheritance there were still plenty of persons of marked coloring. But the tint of nearly half the population under the age of thirty could be described as coffee with cream.

Nor was Dr. Wist's legacy confined to his native shore. After a convulsive but mercifully brief societal upheaval South Africa became fully enfranchised, boasting that it made love and not war. In England William, the prince of Wales, announced his engagement to a lovely commoner named Emily Singh. King Charles and Mommy Di gave their full blessing. Overnight Miss Singh became the toast of the tabloids, and the sari was a red-hot trend in British fashion designer collections.

Less ethnically diverse nations tried to stave off the inevitable. Japan unveiled a new policy of stringent quarantine. No foreign foot would ever touch Japanese soil again. Export products were floated out to sea on barges, while the money to pay for them was transmitted electronically. The seclusion policy held for a decade, but in the end collapsed. To the increasing legions of medium-brown persons of marriageable age, the thought of Japanese spouses was intoxicating. In 2051 every marriage registered in Osaka was Japanese-Japanese. Not a single marriage was, in 2059.

By the year 2094 the World Government was in place. On the surface its task was an easy one. War had become extinct. The word *racism* could be found only in unabridged dictionaries, followed by the classification "obsolete." Travel was the basis of the world economy, since persons ready to settle down felt impelled to tour distant corners of the globe to find the right mate. After decades of struggle the world's doctors had tamed most of the diseases that had taken advantage of man's new mobility. One especially virulent flu strain had circled the globe four times, carried by romance-minded travelers.

And then . . .

World President Marilys Chaka was worried. She consulted her cabinet. "Birth rates are dropping," she observed.

"I'm not surprised," said Powys Bol. He grimaced around the table. "Look at us, to take a random sampling. We all might as well be cousins."

The members of cabinet eyed each other with their light brown or hazel eyes. Medium brown hair predominated, and skin of a dark biscuit color—perfectly pleasant, of course, but how dull! And the cabinet was representative in more than that. Only two of the nine members were married.

"Something must be done," President Chaka said. "Otherwise the human race will die out. I want to present two proposals, a very short-term attack, and a long-term solution." She pressed a button and said, "Anette, will you come in please? Anette Mohammed," she added for the benefit of her cabinet, "is one of the data management secretaries."

The door opened, and the cabinet gaped. Anette, a short stout woman, smiled seraphically. Her skin was of the all-too-common medium tan, and she wore conservative knee pants and open-toed clogs, as a professional woman should. But her hair! It glowed with a glorious orange hue, a copper color such as had not been seen even in Ireland for a decade. The four male cabinet members felt a distinct lightness somewhere around the chest region and a distinct heaviness elsewhere.

"Striking, isn't it?" President Chaka said. "It's dye, of course. We tried it out over lunch hour."

"Amazing!" Mr. Bol, a bachelor, swallowed hard.

"What reactions have you gotten, Ms. Mohammed?" one of the female ministers asked a little peevishly.

"Nearly caused an accident when I crossed the street after lunch," Ms. Mohammed said smugly. "So far this afternoon I've had fourteen propositions."

"And have you accepted any?" Mr. Bol asked.

"Only one—my fiancé's."

"Oh." Faces fell.

"Thank you, Anette," President Chaka said. "Well, what do you think?"

The cabinet almost burst into applause. "We can start manufacturing hair dye immediately," the commerce minister said, rapidly punching numbers into her hand-held computer.

"And I saw on an old microfiche something about contact lenses that change your eye color," Dr. Theophile said. "It never became more than a fad, that died out in the twentieth century."

"Look into it," President Chaka nodded. "As for the long-term . . ." She leaned back in her chair a little, and her gaze drifted to the window.

Under President Chaka's program, it took humanity twenty years to perfect a hyperspace drive. Another decade sufficed to build the first interstellar fleet. By 2125 the fleet reached the Centauri system, and discovered life on a planet orbiting Beta Centauri. Captain Dante Voss, leader of the expedition, was delighted to see the native population turned out in force to see his flagship's landing.

The hatch opened and Captain Voss climbed down the

ladder. He was immediately surrounded by the dominant life-form, willowy bipedal aliens who towered well over his head. Their skins were furred with a fine lime-green fuzz, and they chattered at him in a clicking, squirrellike tongue.

Captain Voss felt no fear at all, only excitement and interest. How attractive these aliens were! Their slim grace put him in mind of tall grass swaying in a March breeze. All his life everyone around Voss had, boringly, resembled himself. Earth was nothing but an enormous hall of mirrors these days, a hall with a plummeting birthrate. Only elaborate virtual reality sex games sustained the human race.

But this planet was the wrong one. These aliens were *too* alien, even to a casual inspection. A man could no more interbreed with them than he could with a sequoia tree. The ship, the entire fleet, ought to leave immediately and find another race, on some other planet. But Captain Voss felt his long-frustrated emotions leading him astray. He could see himself, directing the entire human race down a miserable and fruitless blind alley that ended, ultimately, in extinction. It was up to him to save humanity, and he could do it simply by turning and climbing back up that ladder, right now. . . .

But this was the last time he would ever objectively know that to be true. The dead hand of Roberto Wist was too strong. Captain Voss slid without noticing into self-delusion. After all, appearances were deceiving, everybody knew that. Perhaps, just perhaps it could be done. Didn't they say that true love conquers all? He wouldn't mind a little girl or boy with light green hair. . . . Automatically he thumbed his radio control. "I'm in love," he announced happily to the waiting ship. "Bring them all in, the entire fleet. The invasion starts today. The code word is, Make love, not war."

# My Soul to Keep

## Jerry Oltion

The patient in exam room three was a mess. They'd brought him in by helicopter from Yellowstone, which in itself gave a pretty good indication of how serious his condition was. West Park Hospital in Cody, Wyoming, was a small facility, the kind of place you flew critical patients *from*, not to, unless you were afraid they wouldn't survive the extra thirty minutes to DePaul in Billings.

This one had taken at least six inches of buffalo horn in his side, rupturing his spleen and stirring his intestines around like a fork full of spaghetti. He'd taken all the blood the mede-vac copter carried, and his pressure was down to forty over nothing by the time they wheeled him into the emergency room. Pamela Dempsey, the physician on duty, had poured seven more units through him while removing his spleen and gluing him back together, doing the surgery right there on the exam table rather than taking the time to prep him for the operating room, and even though she had stopped the bleeding she was still reluctant to let him out of her sight.

Except for the contagion problem. That had her wishing she could flee the entire hospital and never come back until every employee had been screened and found negative, but that wasn't part of the job description. She was the attending physician, and he was her patient; warts, diseases, and all.

He was a short, thin man in his late sixties or so, his muscles soft and what hair he had left forming a gray fringe around the sides of his head. Not a candidate for superhuman stamina. By all rights he should have been out cold, either from blood loss or from general anesthesia, but this one was a mumbler. He'd been conscious when they brought him in, and though he wasn't responsive he'd been awake enough to give away his condition. Wendell, the anesthesiologist, had given him sodium pentothal, but they didn't call the stuff "truth serum" for nothing. While it had put him under for surgery, it hadn't stilled his tongue; only the ventilating tube down his throat had managed that.

He'd been reciting the same prayer over and over again; Pamela could quote it now herself. It began, "Out of the depths have I cried unto Thee, O Lord: Lord hear my voice," and went on from there about his soul waiting for God to come for it. Pamela tried to put it out of her mind, concentrating on her work, speaking loudly to Marilyn, the nurse, when she needed clamps or a sponge or more cryoglue; but when she finished closing his wounds she backed away from the exam table and waved another team into the room to clean up.

"Come on," she said to Marilyn and Wendell. "Let's get out of here while we've got the chance." In passing, she said to the replacement team, "Watch out when you take him off the ventilator. If he starts talking, shut him up immediately. He's extremely contagious."

"With what?" Tony, one of the new nurses asked.

"Catholicism, it sounds like," Pamela answered. "He's got the worst case I've ever seen."

Tony's forehead and cheeks—all that showed above his surgical mask—paled, but he nodded and went on in. Pamela, Wendell, and Marilyn pushed past into the hallway and down to the dressing room where they peeled off their gloves and masks.

Pamela realized Marilyn was looking at her curiously, as if she'd missed a joke or something. "What?" she asked.

"Well of course he's the worst case you've ever seen," Marilyn said. "Don't you recognize him?"

Pamela pulled off her paper cap and shook free her shoulder-length red hair. "No, who is he?"

Marilyn laughed. "Nobody special. Just the pope, that's all."

His retinue—five men and a woman, all dressed in the same sort of flannel shirts, blue jeans, and pointy-toed boots that the patient had worn beneath the MAS trousers the medevac team had put on him—sat quietly in the waiting room's molded plastic chairs. A nervous-looking deputy sheriff stood at parade rest in front of the exit. When Pamela walked through the doorway from admissions, all but the deputy had their heads down and their eyes closed. The woman was holding a beaded necklace, and three of the men were fingering their knotted bolo ties while they prayed. Pamela recognized the symptoms from a film she'd seen in one of her diagnosis classes. They were saying the rosary. At least they were doing it silently.

They looked up when they heard her approach. "He's going to make it," she told them.

"Oh, thank God," the tallest of the men said. He let his tie fall back to his chest and pushed his gold wire-framed glasses higher up his nose.

Pamela ignored his comment. She said, "He lost a lot of blood, but we've got him stabilized now. He'll be as good as new in a few weeks. It's a good thing he isn't a Christian Scientist, though."

Nobody laughed. Six pairs of eyes watched her somberly. Pamela shrugged and said, "As soon as we get him set up in the Intensive Care Unit, we'll let you see him, but probably just for a few minutes. Tomorrow, when he's had a chance to rest, you can stay a little longer."

The man with the glasses nodded, but still no one spoke. Their aloofness made Pamela's neck hairs tingle. Had they all suddenly taken a vow of silence? She tried the direct approach. "So tell me, what was the pope doing getting gored by a buffalo in Yellowstone National Park?"

The bespectacled one looked to his companions, then back at Pamela. "Taking a picture," he said.

"Right." Pamela sat down across from him and waited.

After an uncomfortable few seconds, he added, "We were on vacation."

"Incognito." Pamela gestured at his clothing.

He blushed. "His Holiness wanted to meet some regular Americans, which your government would not allow."

"For good reason," Pamela said. "You do realize that the six of you are a walking epidemic?"

That finally provoked a response from another of the group: a younger, heavier man who snorted before saying, "We have heard this Satanic prattle before. Religion is not a disease."

Pamela nodded her head. "Well, actually, it is. We've mapped the affected cerebral sites pretty thoroughly. Belief in Satan and other demons, for instance, comes from neural remapping in a part of the brain's limbic system called the amygdala, just above the pituitary."

"And belief in God is a malfunction of the third ventricle connecting the thalamus and the hypothalamus. Yes, yes, we know your theories. They prove nothing."

"Not to you, maybe," Pamela said, keeping her voice as free of challenge as she could manage, "but the AMA is pretty well convinced."

Stony silence.

She leaned forward. "Which brings us to the next subject. As foreign citizens, whether or not you want us to cure your religion is entirely up to you, but if you chose to remain infected you'll all have to be quarantined for the duration of your stay here in the States. And in either case, we'll need you to fill out a list of your contacts since you came here so we can track down people who might have been infected."

"We will never betray our brethren!" the heavyset man said. "And I'd sooner have my heart ripped out of my body than have my faith ripped from my mind."

Pamela allowed herself a chuckle. "Lucky for you nobody experienced a sudden conversion while you were in the park, or somebody might have tried just that. The disability that causes psychotic violence is pretty closely linked to the one that causes religion, and we take willful dissemination of mental disease pretty seriously in these parts."

The taller man said tiredly, "Just do what you can for His Holiness's wounds, and we'll get out of your hair as quickly as possible. We've seen what we came here to see."

"Fair deal," Pamela said. She got up and took some blank contact forms from the admissions desk, leaving them and half a dozen pens on the coffee table in front of the Catholics just in case they decided to cooperate, then went upstairs to see about finding them a place to stay.

\* \* \*

Later, after the pope had been taken to Intensive Care and his companions had been locked into rooms on the third floor, Pamela, Marilyn, and Wendell met in the break room.

"What do you think?" Marilyn asked as she sloshed coffee into and over the side of a stoneware mug. "Are we in any danger?"

"I don't think so," Pamela said. "The exposure was short, and we had a lot of other things on our minds." She slumped down in one of the padded chairs and blew out a long breath.

"If sheer terror can keep you from catching it," Marilyn said, "then I'm certainly safe."

Pamela sighed. "Actually, fear only increases the likelihood."

Wendell frowned. "I don't know what all the fuss is about. I mean, believing in God isn't all that horrible, is it?"

Pamela sat straight up in her chair. Marilyn, who'd been just about to swallow, blew coffee halfway across the room.

"Gotcha!" Wendell shouted, slapping his thighs and bursting into laughter.

"You son of a bitch!" Marilyn yelled. She banged her coffee cup down on the counter and grabbed a napkin from the wall dispenser, wiped her chin with it, then wadded it up and threw it at him.

Pamela pursed her lips. "Hmm. Practical jokes are symptomatic of a malfunction in the ludicrium humorium. Maybe we'd better run a brainwave profile on you and see how extensive the damage is."

Wendell bent over and picked up the napkin. "Hah—there's no such thing as the ludicrium humorium."

"Well then, I guess that means you're just a pain in the ass." Pamela leaned back again and closed her eyes, glad she didn't have to live with a guy like Wendell, but she didn't have ten seconds of quiet before the break room door opened and the E.R. receptionist stuck her head around the jamb. "The word's out that we've got the pope here," she said. "Who wants to talk to the press?"

They hadn't made it past the waiting room. Pamela could hear them squabbling from clear down the hall by the lab, and when she turned the last corner she could see two ambulance drivers guarding the door against a couple of dozen reporters, half of whom wore forehead cameras and were apparently jockeying for the best angle to film the absolutely unchanged admissions desk, which was all they could see from the waiting room.

Pamela spread her arms wide and shooed them back toward the chairs. "Have a seat," she said, walking through them to the other side to draw them away from the door. She felt a twinge of instinctive fear at walking into a mob, but she quashed it immediately. Most of these people were local citizens; some of them were her own patients. They might look like a mob, but of course any tendency they might have had toward violence had been cured by neuro-enhancement reconditioning long ago.

But there was no stopping curiosity. The questions started immediately. Was it true that the pope was here? How long had he been in the country before he'd been caught? How far had the infection spread? Would the government declare martial law to control it?

"Whoa, whoa, now hold on just a minute there," she said, waving her hands to head them off. "First off, nobody's saying the pope is here. And even if he was—"

"We know he is, Pam," said Jeff Wilkes, the local stringer for the *Casper Star Tribune*. "There's no sense trying to hide him."

"I'm not trying to hide anybody," Pamela told him, "but there's such a thing as patient confidentiality. I can't tell you who's here unless they okay it."

Annie Goldstein, the new editor of the local paper, the *Enterprise,* said, "All right then, how 'bout we just say you have a Catholic patient here? That bein' the case, how long before we all start sayin' Hail Marys?"

Pamela laughed. "I don't think that's going to be a problem. The buffalo got him before he had a chance to do much. We don't have any evidence yet of anyone being infected, so—"

A babble of questions drowned her out. She waited until they'd shut up, then continued as if she'd never been interrupted. "As I was saying, we don't know if there's been any secondary infection at all, so it would be extremely irresponsible for any of you to suggest that there might be. Religion is spread by missionary contact *and idea repetition,* so the best thing to do is to forget this ever happened."

"We can't do that," cried Jeff. "It's our duty to report the news."

"Then report it responsibly," Pamela told him. "Stress the fact that casual contact with a religious person can't do any permanent harm. It's like advertising; it takes continual repetition of the core concepts to burn the brain pathways into the right configuration to accept the concepts as truth. So unless the po ... uh ... patient used the same kind of drugs and neural repatterning techniques we use to cure mental diseases, then he didn't have time to spread more than the idea that religion exists."

"That alone can be dangerous enough, can't it?" asked another reporter Pamela didn't know. The winking red activity light of her forehead camera momentarily made Pamela think of a devil's eye blinking at her.

She shook her head, trying to suppress a shudder. "*You* know it exists, don't you? That by itself isn't a problem. It's only when you start taking it seriously that it becomes dangerous."

"So you're saying there's no danger of an outbreak of Catholicism?" somebody else asked.

Pamela laughed. "That's really up to you people. If you say there isn't, then there won't be. But if you say there is, you're going to get people worried about it, and fear is one of the quickest routes to religion there is."

Annie, the *Enterprise* editor, snorted. "Damn it, Pam, you're dancing all over our freedom of speech here. Ever since the goddamned AMA decided violence in the media was causin' all the world's problems, we've just had one restriction after another put on us. Can't write more than three hundred words about murders anymore; got to run a goddamn Surgeon General's warning on any article that even mentions it, or war or racism either—it's ridiculous. My paper's starting to look like a goddamned scandal rag. And now you tell me I can't even say the pope's in town."

Pamela winced at all the "goddamns." A couple of other people had inched away during the tirade as well. "Uh, Annie," Pamela said, "I know it probably doesn't mean anything, but your vocabulary sounds kind of symptomatic. Have you had a checkup lately?"

"Of course I have!" Annie sputtered. "I couldn't run my goddamned paper without the stinkin' certificate of health. I tell you, this country's going to hell in a handbasket."

Annie's speech was cliché enough; Pamela figured she was probably just using the religious swear words out of old habit. And swearing was usually a fairly good indicator—though by no means a certain one—of a low level of religious indoctrination.

But if Annie was old enough to have picked up those swear words, then she was old enough to remember what the world had been like before they were recognized as disease vectors, too. "You'd rather have people killing each other, and stealing from each other?" Pamela asked. "You'd rather start locking your door at night again?"

"I'd rather not have somebody else telling me what I can and can't think," Annie said.

Pamela ran her fingers through her hair, then shook it out. "I imagine surgeons back in Lister's and Pasteur's day were kind of mad about having to wash their hands before operating on people, too, but that doesn't mean they had a right not to. Once we understood how bacterial infection was spread, we had a moral obligation to keep from spreading it, even if it meant changing our methods."

Jeff said, "What if censorship turns out to be a mental disease? Then what?"

Pamela laughed. "It is, actually. It's part of the whole complex of neuroses dealing with domination." She let herself slip into medicalese for effect: "But the realization that we can't spread pathogenic information survives even when the domination pathways are normalized. Which means it's just an intelligent choice in this case." She held up her hands before anyone else could speak. "Look, I've got to get back up there and see how my patient is doing. Write what you want, but let your conscience be your guide."

The reporters burst into mediababble again, but she waded back through them without responding. She felt a brief image of herself as the messiah, pushing through a crowd of worshippers, but she immediately suppressed it.

The sun was already down behind Rattlesnake Mountain, but soft evening light still filled the I.C.U. when Pamela pushed through the doors from the hallway. The pope was awake, sitting up and examining the vital signs transmitter strapped to his left forearm. He had gotten his color back, and looked ten years younger than when she'd seen him on the exam table.

"How are you feeling?" Pamela asked him.

"A bit sore," he said, lowering his arm and leaning back against his pillow. His voice was surprisingly strong and resonant for someone just out of surgery.

Pamela glanced at the telemetry screen on the crash cart, noting that his blood chemistry was balancing nicely, then sat down in the chair beside his bed. "You should be sore," she said. "We had to remove your spleen and a couple feet of small intestine."

He made a little fatalistic shrug. "The price of ignorance, I suppose." He looked directly at Pamela with his silvery blue eyes and added, "Thank you for not removing my religion as well."

Pamela felt herself shiver under his gaze. Looking away, she said, "It's not a life-threatening condition. Not on an individual scale, anyway."

"I'm sorry your country believes it to be so at all."

Pamela looked back at him. He seemed completely at ease, as if he were granting her an audience in his own home, rather than sitting in a hospital bed in a foreign land. "You should have lived here when we let it spread without check," she told him. "We were one of the most violent, aggressive societies on Earth."

The pope chuckled drily. "Religion isn't the only path to violence."

"Nope, and violence isn't the only way to kill people, either. Overpopulation alone is responsible for more deaths than all the wars combined, and you can't deny religion's influence on that."

Now the pope was smiling outright. "Ah, yes, birth is indeed the primary cause of death. However, I believe there are a few complicating factors along the way."

Pamela smiled too. "Probably. Whatever, we're doing a lot better now that we've begun treating religion and aggression and things like that as mental diseases. But this isn't really the time to—"

"Could you cure someone's love?" the pope asked her.

"What?"

"What about their sense of wonder? Could your medicine cure that?"

Pamela nodded slowly. "We can remove just about any recognizable compulsion, if that's what you mean."

"And who decides which ones are diseases, and which are beneficial?"

"Ah," Pamela said, nodding again. "I see where you're headed. The short answer is, our society decides. When the benefits outweigh the drawbacks, we keep our neuroses. It's actually a little more complicated than that, but this isn't the time to go into the epidemiology of mental disease. You need to rest and regain your strength."

The pope cocked an eyebrow. "I thought I was doing rather well."

He was. Pamela had never seen someone recover from surgery so quickly. "You're doing great," she told him. "Better than you have any right to be after what you've been through, which is why I don't want to risk wearing you out. Your body needs time to repair itself."

In an amused tone of voice, the pope said, "Don't discount the value of prayer."

Pamela sighed. "Go ahead if you have to, but please do it quietly. I don't want my nursing staff to come down with it."

The pope nodded. "I will be discreet." He looked over at

his bedside table, then back at Pamela. "Could I trouble you to get my rosary from wherever it's been taken?"

She wondered why the pope should need a reminder to keep his prayers straight, but she didn't suppose it was worth arguing with him. He was going to pray whether or not he had his rosary.

The clothing he'd been wearing when he arrived had been thrown away after they'd cut it off him, but there was a duffel bag in the closet with more clothes and his other personal belongings in it. Evidently it had come with him in the helicopter. Pamela took his bolo tie from the top of the bag and held it in her hand, feeling the smoothness of the cord and the different sized knots for the different prayers. It was well worn. The pope had been praying a lot since he came to America; probably from fear of being in such a godless land.

She shivered at the thought. Fear and repetition. The surest way to burn the pathways into the brain. She doubted if she could cure a case of indoctrination as deep as his, not without years of therapy.

"Be careful with this," she said as she handed the disguised rosary to the pope. "Every time you use it, you reinforce your condition."

He smiled beatifically. "That's the whole point."

Pamela's dreams that night were full of bloody crosses and burning bushes. She woke feeling more exhausted than when she'd gone to bed, but the headline on the day's *Enterprise* cheered her up immediately. It read: BUFFALO SAVES U.S. FROM RELIGIOUS INFECTION, in letters an inch high, and Annie had somehow gotten hold of a photo of the goring, which she'd doctored to show the pope wearing his scarlet robe and pointy hat. Pamela laughed when she saw it. Considering what Annie could have printed, this was perfect.

The hospital was pretty quiet when Pamela got there, considering the notoriety of her patient. The waiting room still held a few die-hard reporters, but nothing like the crowd from the previous night. In earlier days, having the pope in town would have triggered a deluge of politicians and religious leaders, but this time the only official to arrive was the agent from the Centers for Disease Control in Atlanta, who showed up late in the afternoon to investigate the possibility of an epidemic.

His name was Russell, and this was his first trip to Wyoming. After he had interviewed the pope and his retinue and confirmed Pamela's estimation of the problem, she took him out for an early dinner—late by his watch—to Cassie's, the most "western" of the supper clubs lining the road out of town toward Yellowstone.

"The place used to be a bordello," she told him as they crossed the empty dance floor toward the restaurant in the back. They took a table in one of the long, boxcar-style dining rooms and Pamela entertained him with tales of the restaurant's colorful past until the waiter brought their meals: two improbably thick filet mignons and enough side dishes to feed them for a week.

Just as she was about to take her first bite of steak, her pager went off.

"Never fails," she said. She popped the slice of meat in her mouth anyway, then pulled the pager from her purse and unfolded it into a phone while she chewed. "Dempsey here," she said around the mouthful of steak.

The ward clerk didn't waste any time. "Your patient is gone," she said.

Pamela swallowed. "Gone? How?"

"We don't know. His monitor stopped receiving just a few minutes ago, but that must have been when the remote went out of range, because when we went to check on him we found his bed empty and his duffel bag gone. It looks like he just got up and walked out."

"He couldn't have done that," Paula said, directing her words at the CDC man across the table from her as well as at the ward clerk. "He had major surgery just yesterday. He couldn't make it to the bathroom without help."

"Well then he had help," the ward clerk said, "because he's definitely gone."

"How about the other Catholics in quarantine?" Pamela asked. "Are they still there?"

"Locked down tight," came the response. "We haven't even told them yet that he's gone."

"Good. Keep it that way." Pamela looked around at the other diners. There were only four other occupied tables, but the people at all of them were listening to her half of the conversation. As calmly as she could, she said, "He's undoubtedly still in the hospital. Search the building, and call me back when you've found him. I'll be in to check on him as soon as I've finished dinner."

In a surprised voice, the ward clerk asked, "You're finishing your dinner first?"

"Remember the vector," Pamela told her quietly. "I'll be in as soon as I can." She folded the pager and slipped it back into her purse, then said to Russell, "Our patient has gone for a walk. We'll have to check him for internal injuries when we get back."

Russell made to get up, but Pamela stopped him with a hand on his wrist. "No, finish your dinner," she told him loudly. "He's not going anywhere." As he sat back down, she leaned forward and whispered, "We don't want to start a panic."

His confused expression gave way to realization, then a

conspiratorial grin spread across his face. "Ah, of course." He picked up his knife and fork and carved another slice of filet. Around them, conversations started again.

Even so, they ate quickly, hardly tasting the food, and skipped coffee and dessert. Pamela dropped a fifty on the table without waiting for the bill, and she and her companion walked back out through the dance floor—busier now that the evening bar patrons had begun to arrive—to her car.

There was some kind of commotion going on in the parking lot. Two jacked-up pickups were nosed together at an angle; evidently a couple of Saturday night cowboys had been playing chicken for the same parking spot and neither of them had given up until they'd wedged their fenders together. Now they were shouting at each other and waving their arms in wild gestures, and for a moment Pamela wondered if it would come to blows. She was just about to call for an ambulance when one of the cowboys dug into his pocket, produced a coin, and flipped it into the air. Both faces followed it up and back to the ground, then the cowboy who'd flipped it picked it up, shrugged, climbed back into his truck, and backed up to let the other one have the parking spot.

After they'd both stowed their rigs, the two cowboys shook hands and, laughing now, sauntered on into the bar.

"Looks like people live a little close to the edge around here," Russell said as Pamela drove them back to the hospital.

"Welcome to the Wild West," she said with a sigh. She watched the oncoming cars, most of them full of tourists from all over the country, the rest full of bored cattlemen and unemployed oil field workers, all of them searching for some kind of meaning to their lives. *Dear God,* she thought, *don't let the pope get loose in this town.*

\* \* \*

He wasn't in the hospital. They found his wrist remote in the grass outside the front doors; evidently he had worn it that far to cover his disappearance, then ditched it and fled.

The other Catholics were no help in finding him. The talkative one claimed that God had called him to heaven, but the others simply shrugged and professed ignorance of the whole situation. None admitted to having any connections in town.

With no idea of where he might have gone, Russell reluctantly alerted the sheriff's office, which promptly put up roadblocks and began the process of scaring the town into the very panic that Pamela had been trying to avoid. There was no holding back the press this time; within hours the airport was busier than La Guardia, all of the incoming planes full of national news anchors.

Pamela had no choice but to call a disaster alert, clearing out an entire wing for a psych ward and making sure the hospital's neural reconditioner was calibrated to flatline both panic and religion. She and Marilyn and Wendell—her surgery team—set themselves up for business in one of the three emergency rooms and prepared for the siege.

They didn't have long to wait; patients started arriving within minutes of the first CNN broadcast. Most of them were uninjured, arriving in the company of concerned friends or relatives, and most were hysterical cases who couldn't recite a single prayer, but a few of the older patients had suffered genuine relapses. One purple-haired, wrinkled woman in her eighties or so sang a surprisingly operatic version of "Onward Christian Soldiers" in the waiting room.

The reconditioner had trouble with those cases until Pamela realized she had to address their guilt complexes as well; after that the job became routine. They hadn't had time to rebuild their religious neural patterns to any extent, so a single session under the net was enough to erase their short-term urges. In some cases the guilt had been building for years, though; those patients would have to return every few days for weeks before they were completely cured.

Then the spontaneous conversions started showing up. Those were the ones Pamela had been dreading: humanity had lived with religion so long that the brain had actually begun evolving to accommodate it, and some people were extremely susceptible. Under the right circumstances, a mere suggestion could trigger an entire belief system. Those usually weren't as internally consistent as established religions, and they were easy to spot because the infected person usually considered themselves to be God or the new Messiah, but they were even more difficult to treat than ordinary indoctrination cases. One out of ten would never be the same again no matter how many times they tried repatterning.

Worse, their delusions gave them such intense personal magnetism that an entire cult could spring up around them in hours.

Some of their belief systems included violence, and Pamela began to see broken bones, even a few knife wounds. The impromptu psych ward began filling up, as did the emergency rooms and the waiting area. Pamela and the other doctors were running patients through the reconditioner like cattle, settling for partial reversals when the line began to stretch down the hallway from the ER. The air was filled with the soft susurration of dozens of people praying while they waited for their turn.

Then a commotion of banging and shouting erupted out in the direction of the admissions desk, and a collective gasp rippled through the crowd. "They found him!" someone shouted, just as someone else hollered, "Let go of me, god-damn it!"

That hadn't sounded like the pope, but Pamela went to the door to see what was going on and there indeed was the man, flanked by sheriff's deputies. Bright red blood stained his face and the front of his shirt. Four more deputies were marching two more captives along behind him, and as the crowd in the hallway parted to let them through, Pamela saw that they were the two Saturday night cowboys from the parking lot at Cassie's.

One of them wore the now-familiar expression of religious bliss, but the other was struggling furiously, tugging and swearing at his captors and shouting, "I'll kill the son of a bitch! Look what he did to Joe-Bob."

"Where do you want 'em?" one of the deputies holding the pope asked. Horrified at the thought of a surgery patient being manhandled like that, she chased everyone out of the closest exam room and had them lay the pope down on the table there. Marilyn and Wendell took the two cowboys, along with the four deputies holding them, into another exam room.

"Where does it hurt most?" Pamela asked the pope.

"By dose," he said, touching his still-bleeding nose.

"What? No, no, I'm talking about internal injuries." Pamela took a pair of scissors from the crash cart and began slicing off his clothing. "Good God, man, you can't count on surgical glue to hold you together while you're walking around. It's a wonder you haven't split open like a—"

"Lige a whad?"

Pamela was staring at his abdomen. Pink, healthy, with a fresh scar where the buffalo horn had entered. The incisions she'd made were just faint lines.

"This isn't the pope," she said to the deputies.

"What? Of course it is," one of them said. He pulled a crumpled picture from his shirt pocket and held it out to her.

The man in the picture sure looked like the one on her exam table, but . . . "Then the man we had in here yesterday was a ringer, because *this* guy didn't have surgery recently."

"Agshully, I did," the pope said. "I juzt healed myzelf."

"Sure," Pamela said sarcastically, but the scar on his belly drew her attention again. This guy *had* met up with a buffalo not long ago, and those incision lines followed the same angles as the ones she'd made.

Could it be? Unless the pope had an identical twin, then it almost had to be. Pamela had heard of faith healing before, but she'd always dismissed it as just another example of religious self-deception. The placebo effect. But if the pope could really heal a surgical incision in a day, then the implications were staggering.

Blood dripped from his bleeding nose, and he sniffed to keep more from following it. "Could I ged a Kleedegs?" he asked.

Pamela handed him a couple of gauze pads, but as she helped tend his wound she asked him, "Why don't you just heal your nosebleed, too?"

"Because I can't use the Lord's gift for trivial things," he answered, speaking clearly now that he had a nostril clear.

Any other excuse wouldn't have convinced her, but that one sounded true. Pamela felt herself tingling all over, as if she could actually feel her world view undergo a paradigm shift.

A loud thump from the next exam room brought her back to reality. The cowboy, most likely, objecting to sedation.

"What happened out there at Cassie's?" she asked.

The pope was busy with his nose again, so one of the deputies said, "Near as we can figure, he managed to convert Joe-Bob somehow, and when his buddy Dale found out about it he got mad enough to punch him out."

"Is that so?" Pamela asked.

The pope nodded.

"Well, now maybe you can see why we consider religion a disease. It almost always leads to violence."

"*Life* leads to violence," the pope replied.

"Not in the U.S. of A.," Pamela told him. She gave him some fresh gauze, and saw that his bleeding had nearly stopped. "Look, we're going to want to talk with you some more about this whole faith-healing business, but right now thanks to you I've got a hospital full of mental patients that need my help. So if you guys—" she nodded to the deputies "—could take him upstairs to the I.C.U. and make sure he stays there this time, I'll get back to work. With a little luck, maybe we can get this thing under control by midnight."

That hope died only a few minutes later, along with the overworked neural reconditioner. Pamela had just set it up to erase Dale the cowboy's violent tendencies—pointing out to him that he'd never have given in to his anger the way he had if he hadn't already been close to the line—and she was berating him for not coming in for regular checkups when a warning buzzer sounded on the machine and the master brainwave profile that had been dancing across the monitor went flat.

"Oh hell, what now?" she asked, wiggling the pattern selection knob. When that didn't produce results, she started working her way back through the settings, flipping switches and checking connections, but nothing she did brought it back on line.

"Damn it, you can't die now," she said, banging the side of the monitor with the flat of her hand.

Russell, the CDC man, had just entered the room, carrying a clipboard of patient contact forms. He frowned when he saw what Pamela was doing, and asked, "What's the matter?"

"The godforsaken thing died on me, that's what," she

snapped, banging it harder this time. Something rattled inside the plastic case, and the monitor died completely.

"Ha, tha's it, give 'er another whack," said the cowboy, who was drugged to within an inch of unconsciousness.

"Uh oh," said Pamela.

Russell asked, "Do you have another reconditioner?"

"No," she whispered. Her anger had vanished as quickly as it came.

"Where's the nearest replacement?"

"Powell," she said, and when he didn't respond she added, "That's about twenty miles east of here."

He relaxed a little. "Call them up and tell them we need to borrow it."

"Right." Pamela switched off the broken instrument and headed for the doctor's lounge where she could hear to use the phone.

Powell, it turned out, was having a miniature revival of its own, and the hospital administrator refused to part with their reconditioner. Likewise the hospitals at Greybull, Lovell, and Worland. Pamela finally managed to track down a free machine in Billings, but considering loading and unloading time as well as flight time, it would be nearly two hours before it would arrive. In the meantime, the only thing they could do for patients was sedate them.

And if the word got out that the hospital was powerless against the religious plague, the conversion rate would soar. When people lost faith in medicine, they would turn to spiritual leaders without a backward glance. Cults would thrive, violence would spread alongside them—Pamela could imagine normal civic rivalry between Cody and Powell erupting into a jihad by morning.

After she hung up the phone, she stared at the book-lined walls of the doctor's lounge, imagining how quickly they would burn when the mob reached the hospital. If only she hadn't lost her temper. *Damn* the pope for rattling her so; if he hadn't pulled that faith healing stunt she wouldn't have lost it.

She stood up suddenly. Holy Christ, the pope! He could heal people! She left the doctor's lounge at a run.

"No, I'm sorry," he said when she'd told him what she wanted. "Even if I wanted to, there's no way I could 'heal' anyone's religion. It's not something I can possibly think of as an illness." He smiled as he leaned back against his upraised bed, clearly amused at the very concept, and Pamela, who had swallowed a lot of pride in order to ask him for help, had to bite down on an angry outburst as well.

"Then teach *me* how to do it," she said. "*I* can certainly heal people."

"Not with your faith," the pope said sadly, "for you have none."

"I'm not so sure about that," Pamela said. "I've seen what you can do; I believe it's possible. What more do I need?"

The pope sighed. "You need to believe in the divine power of the Lord. It's *His* power I wield, not my own."

"Hmm." Pamela looked over to the two deputies standing in the doorway, then back at the pope. "Okay, tell you what. Suppose I let you convert me. Could I do faith healings then?"

One of the deputies whispered something to the other, but Pamela ignored them.

"What do you say?" she asked. "I'm making you a straight offer. I'll believe in your God if you'll teach me how to heal people your way."

The pope shook his head. "God doesn't bargain with us. You have to accept Him on His terms, not your own."

"You're saying I might not be able to do it even if I convert?"

"I'm saying you cannot make it a condition of your faith. You must acknowledge our Lord as your savior without reservation, and only then, if your faith is strong enough, will you be able to work miracles."

Pamela looked over at the deputies again, but only one of them stood in the doorway now. The other had probably gone to alert the administration that one of their doctors had wigged out. But damn it, she was onto something here, she knew she was.

She turned back to the pope. "Fair enough," she told him. "I'm willing to try it. What do I have to do?"

"More than you are capable of, I fear," the pope said.

"Don't underestimate the power of prayer," Pamela told him. "Come on, where do I start? Confession? Communion? A dozen Hail Marys?"

The pope laughed softly. "No, that all comes later." He gazed into Pamela's eyes for a moment, pinning her down like a deer in a car's headlights, then he blinked and released her from his spell. "Your reason for accepting the Lord isn't what I would hope for, but the Church doesn't turn away suppliants. In time you will come to understand the true value of faith." He reached out and took her hand. "Were you ever baptized?" he asked.

"I think so," she said. "When I was a baby. My parents were Baptists, anyway, and I was almost seven before the surgeon general declared religion a disease."

"Then you undoubtedly were. So, if you truly want to accept the Lord, I suppose we could start with the Apostles' Creed. Repeat after me, but only if you can do so honestly: I believe in God the Father Almighty, Creator of heaven and Earth, and in Jesus Christ his only son, Our Lord."

Pamela hesitated, aware that she was going against all her medical training, but equally aware that she had witnessed something miraculous. She *had* to learn how to do it, not just for herself but for the entire town. Hell, given the explosive potential of a religious outbreak, for the entire *country*. If it took believing in God, then that's what it took.

"I—" she said, but her voice cracked. She cleared her throat and tried again. "I believe in God the Father Almi—"

"No you don't!" Rough hands grabbed her and pulled her backwards. She spun around, and there stood Russell. "That's enough," he told her sternly.

"No it isn't," she said. "I have to say the whole thing. Then I'll be able to do miracles."

"You're not going to do anything but go to bed. You're already infected, can't you see?"

"Of course I'm infected!" Pamela wailed. "It's been getting worse ever since I took him to surgery. So what difference does it make now? As long as I'm already sick, let me at least learn how to use it to heal people."

The pope shrugged apologetically. "I tried to tell her it doesn't work that way."

"It doesn't work at all," Russell said. He pulled Pamela toward the door. "Come on, let's get you to bed."

"No!" She squirmed in his grip, trying to break free. "I broke the reconditioner. We *need* this. Besides, think of the possibilities for study! If we can learn to harness it, we can—"

"We can what? Even assuming it works, which I'm not, what could you do with faith healing that we can't already do with conventional methods?"

"You could heal your immortal soul," the pope offered.

"You stay out of this," Russell told him. "You've already caused enough trouble."

One of the deputies helped him pull Pamela from the pope's room, but she continued to struggle as she said, "We could heal people faster, with fewer complications. We could probably save people that we couldn't save otherwise. If we taught it like CPR, anyone at the scene of an accident could heal the wounded."

Russell and the deputy marched her down the hallway toward the psych ward. "Teach it like CPR, eh?" Russell said. "Wouldn't that be wonderful. Everyone in America believing in God again. And having half a dozen babies per family, and sending them off to war with the Arabs. Oh yes, it sounds absolutely divine."

"It doesn't have to be that way," Pamela protested. "We can learn to control it. We can use just the good aspects, and suppress the others. Listen to me! We can save the world!"

Nurses and doctors and even some of the ambulatory patients peered out of doorways at her as she passed, her toes dragging on the floor when she refused to walk any farther. She recognized Marilyn's face, her eyes and mouth as round as saucers, and Wendell, no mirth in his expression now. "Help me!" she called to them, and Wendell came forward, but when he got close he saw the subcutaneous injector in his hand and she screamed, "Get away!"

"Sorry, Pam." He pressed the injector to her shoulder and pulled the trigger, and Pamela felt a sting on her skin. Russell and the deputy pulled her into one of the rooms, where four beds were crammed into a space normally used for two, and laid her down on the only empty one left. Her vision began to swirl with tracers, and she realized she was about to lose consciousness. She couldn't let it happen; she needed to finish her conversion, and then she could fight the drugs in her system. In desperation she tried to remember the words the pope had just asked her to repeat, but the commotion had wiped them from her memory. Likewise the prayer that had echoed in her mind all through surgery yesterday. The only prayer she could remember was the one her parents had taught her, back in those primitive days before medicine had learned to diagnose and treat mental illness as easily as any other infection.

Not knowing what else to do, she closed her eyes and whispered, "Now I lay me down to sleep . . ."

# DEFENSE CONVERSION

▼

## DOUG BEASON

Losing voice contact with his assistant on his cellular phone between Denver and Vail was the best thing that could have happened to Fred Marshall. Fresh in from Washington, D.C., Marshall drove the hundred miles straight from the sprawling new Denver airport to the trendy ski resort in Vail. He did not drive fast. Purposely late for his meeting, he was content to be distracted by the purple mountains of Colorado's front range, their snow-peaked caps pushing against the blue sky; a mountain stream tumbled next to the highway on his left. It felt good to be back home.

As Marshall's car cruised down I-70 he knew he had beaten the rush-hour traffic spreading out from the high-tech city as the weekend approached. So with clear roads ahead of him, he concentrated on speaking on his cellular phone with his assistant waiting in Vail. He kept talking, knowing that finding a "null" in communications was a long shot, but he hoped his gamble would pay off.

The car dipped into a shallow depression and he lost contact. It was like someone had suddenly pulled the plug. And it made Marshall's day.

He jammed on the brakes. The white rental car fishtailed as it skidded to a stop, coming to rest by the road's shoulder. Marshall unstrapped his seat belt, clutched the cellular phone and stepped away from the traffic into the weeds crowding onto the road. Static came from the speaker. ". . . You're breaking up, Dr. Marshall. I didn't hear that last comment. Do you want me to switch to the satellite link?"

Marshall could barely control his elation. "No, not yet— wait until the second time I'm cut off before bringing me up over the satellite. Are the PhoneAir representatives there?"

The voice hesitated, then sounded puzzled. "Sure. They're waiting for you in the lobby. As for the satellites, they're overhead but I can't guarantee they'll still be in view when you get here for the demonstration. Everyone is here but you—"

"Get PhoneAir on the line, *now!*"

"Yes, sir."

"And keep talking. I want to pinpoint just where I lost communications. Just make sure you switch over to the satellite link the *second* time I lose contact with the PhoneAir people. Got it?"

"Right. Not the next time, but the second time."

Marshall stomped back toward Denver, keeping to the side of the road. Cars whooshed past him; a few honked, and Marshall fought the temptation to wave back at them in his excitement. He was uncomfortable in his dark suit, red tie, and long-sleeved white shirt, typical of the dress required deep in the bowels of the Pentagon, but totally out of place in the western mountains. He remembered thinking as a younger man, before moving away from Colorado, how he'd sworn he'd never wear anything more than a bolo tie. Times change.

"They're on the line, sir."

"Good. Hello, PhoneAir? I'm using one of your cellular phones right now, can you hear me?"

A new voice came over Marshall's speaker. "Of course. Jay Pennington, CEO of PhoneAir here. You're coming over clear as a bell, Dr. Marshall. As you should be—PhoneAir's coverage extends from the front range out to the western slope. Does this call have anything to do with the tech transfer conference you've called together in Vail?"

*This guy sounds like he just stepped out of a TV commercial,* thought Marshall. He was close to the radio-null and reception was a little shaky. Time to make his point.

"In a way. I've been tasked by the Pentagon to ensure that our military research and development is transferred to the civilian sector. The Department of Defense has some things that are guaranteed to blow your socks off—so to speak."

"I'm sure they have," came back Pennington's dry voice. He sounded unconvinced. "But I understand you won't be here in time to give the opening speech. I'm disappointed. From your invitation I was looking forward to hearing what you had to say. But I can't see our company using anything as militarily oriented as what the Pentagon has been developing."

Another car whooshed by, driving wind over Marshall. He turned away from the road and looked up at the steep granite rocks lining the narrow valley. "Maybe I can change your mind. I've got something you should be interested in."

"Oh?" Again, the slight skepticism.

"What would you say if I could guarantee expanding your cellular phone system to cover the entire US?"

"What? With satellites?"

"That's right."

"Impossible. The only system that can come close to doing what you're claiming was proven to be too expensive years ago. The satellites are too big, too unwieldy, and cost too much. The transmission coverage we have now is adequate to cover any situation."

"So tell me how you would cover this." Marshall stared around him. "I'm standing just outside Denver, only miles from your headquarters on Interstate 70—over which, by the way, you currently guarantee coverage. Now, suppose I'm injured. I need to call for help on my cellular phone." He paced quickly down the roadside. As he moved into the radio-null his speaker filled with static. He allowed the static to continue for a few seconds before moving back toward his car. The static cleared up. "You heard that? I can't let anyone know I'm hurt."

"That's not a fair example, Dr. Marshall, and you damn well know it. Every cellular phone system in the world has radio-nulls where the transmission momentarily lapses."

"How're injured people going to respond to the idea of 'fairness,' Mr. Pennington," said Marshall softly. "Especially if they're dying and can't move out of the radio-null? The point I'm trying to make is that there *is* a better way, something developed by the military that your company can use." He started walking back to the null area. "Our satellites aren't the ten-ton, five-hundred-million-dollar dinosaurs used by the telephone company; they're cheap, three-hundred-pound satellites—smallsats—launched in low-Earth orbit, with at least one satellite guaranteed to be overhead at all times. Since the smallsats are always overhead relaying signals, instead of attached to the ground like your antennas, there's never a null . . . like this."

Marshall stepped away into the null, and once again, radio static filled the speaker. But just as soon as the white noise began, it stopped and the transmission *really* sounded clear as a bell this time; it was so quiet over the connection that Marshall could hear the PhoneAir CEO's breathing.

Marshall spoke quickly. "My signal's being picked up by a smallsat, seven hundred and fifty miles above the Earth, and relayed down to an earth station. My signal will be handed off to the next smallsat crossing over my position, in approximately five minutes. We've launched an array of them, Mr. Pennington. They're in various orbits, all calculated to hand off communications from one satellite to another."

"And what did this cost?" Pennington sounded unconvinced. "Half the GNP just to pull off this little stunt?"

"Hardly. That's why we're using small satellites. We can launch up to twenty of them at once."

"I still can't believe that these smallsats of yours are powerful enough to cover a large enough area for our cellular phones to work."

Marshall started walking back to his car. He had to play this just right. Like anything and anybody associated with the Defense Department, he knew he was viewed as being "tainted"; people believed that he had an agenda mapped out, a scheme to militarize the country. It was a bias he had to fight constantly.

"To be quite honest, Mr. Pennington, we've taken advantage of electromagnetic focusing technology to boost the microwave signals from the satellites."

"You mean from the military's weapons work."

"Yes. But what you're seeing in this demonstration is *not* a weapons application. It's a civilian application of the high-power microwave technology the military developed to conduct electromagnetic warfare. The satellite's solar arrays are huge enough to draw as much power as an orbiting cellular system will need. The government is willing to sponsor a large-scale calibration test of this technology . . . if PhoneAir will make a commitment to use the satellites and pay royalties. It's nothing more than what you'd expect from working with any entrepreneur; it's just that the Pentagon is willing to give you this technology in return for a guaranteed cut of the profits."

Pennington didn't answer. As he approached his rental car, Marshall thought that he could hear arguing in the background over the phone.

"Well, Mr. Pennington. What do you say?"

"How soon can you get to Vail?"

"Within an hour."

Marshall could hear more arguing over the link. Finally, Pennington's voice came back. "We'll talk when you get here."

It had been years since Marshall had been to the mountain resort of Vail, but it had changed little. Small, Swiss-like buildings lined the road; people crowded the sidewalks; and the ever-present mountains, with brown ski-slope scars running down their sides, stood silent vigil over the area.

Marshall was steered to Jay Pennington by his assistant and got right to the point. "Have you thought it over? What do you say?"

"You've convinced me we should look into this technology. But not everyone at PhoneAir agrees—we've spent a lot of time and money developing our ground-based infrastructure, and it would be foolish to throw it all away on a halfbaked Pentagon scheme. Every ground-based transmission antenna we have has cost us on the order of half a million dollars."

"All I'm asking for is a chance to prove this technology. Put it to a test, just like you would any other improvement. Then make your decision."

"Fair enough. But I've got one last question for you."

"Go ahead."

"What's in this for you?"

"As I said, I'm in charge of tech transfer at the Pentagon—"

"No, Dr. Marshall," interrupted Pennington. "For you. What do *you* gain by doing this?"

Marshall felt shocked, but he knew it was related to a suspicion of his defense background. "These are hard times, Mr. Pennington—you know that. The military can't steer the commercial sector into using new technologies unless there's a clear profit to be made. We need the technological advances that companies like yours will make in this area. The days of defense-only uses are gone."

"I'm well aware of that, Dr. Marshall. I just want to know what I'm getting into."

Memories of a cold winter night in Colorado raced through Marshall's head. He felt as though he could hear the pitiful cry for help, the old home that didn't have any heat, and the long, oppressive cold . . . if only *she* had been able to call for help. . . .

Marshall shook free from the memory. "Satellite communications can help everyone—especially with these new focusing technologies."

"Well, we're willing to test that statement. Count us in."

"It's a deal." *But that's only the beginning.* Marshall was careful to smile as the two men shook hands.

\* \* \*

"Seems like one hell of a way to test a phone system. If I didn't know better, I'd have thought you were getting ready to hook this antenna farm up to the power grid."

Marshall ignored that comment from Jay Pennington as they left the PhoneAir chauffeured car. The two men walked into a field of small whiplike antennas that covered an area three hundred yards in diameter. Constructed of metal rods poking up three feet high from the ground, the telecommunication antennas made the patch in the northern Colorado town of Diamondrough look like a giant pin cushion.

Mountains completely surrounded the small community. The bowl of blue sky capping the snowy peaks made Marshall feel like he was at the bottom of a giant fishbowl; the mountainsides showed the yellow aspen leaves and dark orange of scrub brush turning with the coolness of fall. The telecommunication antennas shared the dirt field with sage brush and wild grass.

Marshall and Pennington reached the middle of the antenna farm. Marshall put his hands on his hips and surveyed the site. Thousands of tiny wires ran from the antennas to a central receiving point, a half mile from where they stood. The wires twisted into a thick, black strand that disappeared into a weather-beaten trailer, set off from the array of antennas.

Marshall felt a sudden chill from a gust of fall wind. The trip home to Diamondrough brought back the cold memory of finding his mother dead in her unheated house three years ago. He'd have to stop by that old house before driving back to Denver with Pennington. He pushed the thought from his mind. "If the Pentagon is going to back this project, we have to have detailed calibration data. The only way to achieve the sensitivity we need is to use the largest antenna array possible. This just isn't something we can kluge together."

Jay Pennington grunted and picked up a stalk of grass. He surveyed the site while chewing. "I understand—but it still seems that it would be a hell of a lot easier to forget the calibration tests and use our cellular phones." He shrugged. "I should have known that getting in bed with the government wouldn't be easy. My first clue was your orbiting microwave weapons; there's still a lot of people in PhoneAir upset that we're using them. We've even had to cancel our contracts to build more transmission antennas. My second clue was conducting the test in this out-of-the-way place."

Marshall took off his sunglasses and squinted at the lithe CEO. Pennington was dressed in dude ranch clothes, and his blue jeans looked as though they had been freshly starched. He seemed out of place in the wilderness area.

"There aren't many places like this for the test: isolated, with mountains around that stymie ordinary cellular phone systems. This keeps stray microwave emissions away. Another six months and we'll have all the questions answered. And by spring you'll have access to our satellites."

Pennington started back to his chauffeured car. Marshall followed, stepping over the wires that ran along the ground. "My staff tells me you grew up around here, Dr. Marshall. Is that why you chose Diamondrough for the test site?"

"My mother passed away a few years ago. She owned a house here that I still use over the holidays. But Diamondrough satisfied all the criteria we were looking for to hold the tests. It's not like this hasn't been done before. There are precedents—Los Alamos was selected by Oppenheimer for the atomic bomb project because of its remoteness, not because he spent his summers there. Besides, this is probably the best location for your technicians."

They reached the car and the driver opened the door for them. Pennington stamped his feet on the ground, shaking loose clods of dirt from his boots before climbing in. "How's that?"

"Your men know that out here Washington can't interfere with the tests. Left alone, they'll be able to complete their work without any bureaucrats breathing down their throats. That's the real reason you'll be up and running next spring."

"As long as I don't have to stay with them, it's fine with me. Are you coming back for the holidays?"

"Yes." Marshall fastened his seat belt. "I'll be here over Christmas. It's a chance to get away from D.C., and I can check up on the calibration tests. If we're lucky, the pass will get snowed in and we'll be left alone for a few days. That happens every so often. It's nice and quiet."

As they settled back into their seats, Pennington sighed. "Nice and quiet. But I can't help thinking about your Los Alamos story."

It was Marshall's turn to be surprised. "Oh?"

"Yeah. Remember what kind of genie we let out of *that* bottle."

Trainloads of coal surrounded the old power plant eighty-three miles south east of Diamondrough, making the old three story building look like it was nestled in the middle of the moon. Billows of steam tumbled up into the air from the conversion unit where the heated water met the cool mountain air.

The coal-fired plant provided power for communities for a hundred miles around—rural electricity was an expensive necessity. Inside the coal-fired stokers, three microchips controlled the heating rates to optimally purge the system of any pollution build-up. Each microchip conferred with the other, and if one had conflicting orders, a "veto" by the remaining two chips would correctly run the operation. The microchips functioned as programmed, unceasingly checking their internal "clock" once every thousandth of a second to ensure their timing was precise. If the timing was off, the scrubbers would automatically shut down to halt the operation of the power plant.

Programmed into every chip lurked a version of the Christmas Day virus, a simple program that once initiated would randomly redefine the timing interval of each internal clock. The virus watched from the bowels of each chip, counting and comparing, waiting to claw up through its levels of hidden code.

The drive from Denver to Diamondrough took six hours longer than Marshall anticipated. Snow dumped down in thick, wet flakes that cut visibility nearly to zero on the winding mountain road. He had lost the classical music channel on the radio hours ago, and now the only sounds that he could hear in the four-wheel drive rental car were the windshield wipers and the hot air blowing from the heater.

Marshall had left the ski traffic behind when he had pulled off to the side and put chains on his tires; he couldn't remember when he had seen another car, but that didn't bother him. He had driven these roads in worse weather, racing home to Diamondrough from the University of Colorado after the end of each semester. As long as he kept moving he knew that soon he would be home.

During the three years since his mother had died he had thought of her again and again, alone in the house without any heat. Phone service had been cut off. He could imagine her trying to call for help. She must have been confident that *someone* would eventually come; but no one did.

A week without any heat, and she had died . . . and now Marshall's yearly trek to the tiny mountain town only served as a macabre reminder of the harsh reality of living in an isolated area. At least he knew that the satellite-based phone system would prevent anyone from ever losing touch again.

The blizzard this Christmas Eve seemed especially bad. He pulled into Diamondrough late in the afternoon. The town was dark, but that wasn't unusual. He drove past the town center and realized that he hadn't even made an effort to acquaint himself with the new people who had taken over the town. Now with Christmas morning just hours away, he decided to wait a few days before checking in with the PhoneAir representative and his team.

The snow had drifted head-high into the driveway. Marshall left the rental car parked next to the snowbank by his mother's old house. It felt good to be back . . . cold, but good. He had a week with nothing to do but recharge.

At the powerplant eighty-three miles southeast of Diamondrough, precisely three-thousandths of a second past midnight, Christmas Day, the virus residing under five layers of subroutines compared the time-date group issued by a microchip's internal clock to a preset parameter. Two other identical microchips performed the same operation; one of the microchips, however, had been impacted the week before by a 17 TeV cosmic ray, masking out the effects of the implanted virus.

Fifty-six milliseconds past midnight, two of the microchips compared their new instructions and voted to override the third microchip. Within another clock cycle, all of three milliseconds, the timing sequences of the microchips controlling the main pollution scrubber units at the Colorado power plant diverged.

Unable to coordinate the heating rates of the coal emission, a half second later the scrubbers shut down. After the scrubbers stopped, the power plant ceased to function.

Lights blinked off all over town; music stopped playing at ShotGun Willie's Buffalo Grill, the only bar within thirty miles. The town was bathed in starlight casting a soft glow over the snow covered buildings. Every rural town within a hundred miles lost power.

Within minutes, the fans forcing heated air generated by natural gas whirled to a stop in every house throughout the tiny mountain town of Diamondrough. Isolated by impenetrable, drifting snow brought by a blizzard flowing over the continental divide, the seven hundred residents of Diamondrough were without power. . . .

Or heat.

Marshall woke to someone pounding on the door. It took a moment for him to realize what was going on. He remembered driving through a snowstorm, drifts piling higher and higher through the pass to Diamondrough. It was *still* cold inside the house.

"Marshall, open the door!" The voice seemed to come through layers of cotton. He groped for his watch. Midmorning. Christmas Day. He stumbled out of bed. Sunshine splashed on the wooden bedroom floor; he could see clear sky through the window. The snow had stopped and it was crystal clear outside. And it felt as cold as a metal fork left in the freezer.

Marshall fumbled with a thick robe, but the cold wouldn't go away; he'd have to check the heater. He opened the door and two men dressed in thick, fur-lined parkas entered, stomping their feet free of snow. The air in the room seemed to be sucked outside by the cold.

As the men threw back their hoods, Marshall recognized the PhoneAir representative and the mayor.

The PhoneAir rep started speaking right away. "I'm patching in a call through the satellite link. The phone lines are intermittent, so thank God satellite communications are still up and running—"

Marshall shook his head, trying to make sense of the conversation. "Slow down. What's the problem?"

The PhoneAir rep twisted his face in astonishment. "What's *not* the problem! Where have you been, Marshall? We've lost all power out here. We have enough juice in the batteries to keep the satellite link up for awhile, but unless we get some help out here fast, people are going to be in deep trouble. From what the power company says, it may take a *week* to bring the plant back up—they had to shut it down cold!"

Marshall was fully awake by now. A dark vision of an old woman sitting by herself in a cold room nearly overwhelmed him. He whispered, "Who else have you notified?"

"The mayor's keeping in contact with the governor, but the phone lines could go down at any time—the phone company's battery backup isn't nearly as sophisticated as ours. I've offered to let the mayor use the satellite link as long as our batteries hold out. But until the electricity comes back on, it will be touchy."

Marshall stiffened. "The pass?"

"Iced over," said the mayor. "You know how that gets. Even with an all-out effort, it might take days to punch through the drifts. I was telling the PhoneAir crew that they can't even fly a helicopter in here—the altitude's too high."

Marshall tried to sound calm. "The military can airdrop coal and oil to hold us over. The Colorado Air National Guard can help us—"

The mayor interrupted. "Without coal or oil furnaces, what good is that going to do us? Look. Enough houses have fireplaces and wood heaters to be able to keep people from freezing, even if it takes a week to get the power back up." The Mayor shook his head. "What I'm worried about are the sick people, the elderly. How is Doc Fitzgerald going to take care of those who need emergency attention?"

Marshall ran a hand through his thinning hair. The men stood in the center of his tiny living room. A rug thrown across the wooden floor made the room feel inviting, but no one sat on the furniture. Marshall wasn't even sure that his mother's frail old couch would hold the men's weight.

His mother . . . how long had she waited in this very room, without any heat, before she died? All she needed to do was to call for help. It was years ago, but the memory was still vivid.

"Why did you come here? Why me?"

The PhoneAir rep squinted at Marshall and looked almost indignant. "Who else? If there's anyone in Diamondrough who can figure out how to pull a rabbit out of a hat and get us out of this mess, it has to be you, Dr. Marshall."

Marshall shook his head, trying to shake loose the memory, skirting just in and out of his peripheral vision. "There are no rabbits—"

"I've got a team of technicians that can engineer just about anything. Come on, Dr. Marshall, you brought the satellite test here—what can my people do to help? Build a makeshift power plant? Rig up some car engines to run a generator?"

Marshall clenched his jaw, feeling a surge of frustration well up inside him. "The satellite calibration test is the only working system in Diamondrough—but it's not a power plant, and certainly not a damned rabbit. Face it, we're in for a tough week. If things work out, the weather may hold up and it won't get any worse. Some people may die, but what can we do? If you can use the satellites in lieu of the phone lines, then go for it, but I can't think of anything else."

The mayor shrugged. "It's kind of funny that some people didn't want your satellite center in here, Dr. Marshall. They thought that the microwaves would harm people; now it's the only way we can communicate with the outside world."

Marshall dismissed the observation. "There's more danger standing next to a microwave oven than there is because of the microwaves from our satellites." He felt surly—upset at the world for expecting too much from him, and angry because his satellite communication system couldn't help them. Worse, the memory of something sat just below his grasp, as if he saw something out of the corner of his eye, only to turn, and have nothing be there.

"Say—" the PhoneAir rep looked up. "The microwaves—the satellites have a focusing capability. Didn't you say they were developed for the military?"

"Yeah," said Marshall. "But how's that going to help us? They're *weapons,* remember? We don't have any electronic equipment to jam."

"Can't you tune the microwave frequency to the water absorption band? You know, like in a microwave oven? It doesn't take much to make water boil." He looked excitedly to the mayor, then back to Marshall. "Why can't you focus the microwaves and melt the ice and snow in the pass? We've got a satellite somewhere overhead all the time. It should help, shouldn't it?"

Marshall shook his head. "The problem with that is that the water in the atmosphere would absorb the microwaves, and the microwave energy would never reach the ground. Besides, it's too inefficient. The sun will melt the snow and ice quicker than we can."

The PhoneAir rep looked crestfallen. The Mayor shook his head. "Too bad—all those microwaves and no use for them. So much for dual-use technology."

Marshall's mind wandered, lighting upon what brought him here: his mother's death, the remote calibration site. *So much for dual-use technology.* His background in defense didn't make any difference; all the communications and weapons in the world couldn't help them. Microwaves everywhere, and no way to use them.

What was it that he was trying to remember?

Something that Jay Pennington had said surfaced in his mind: *I'd have thought you were getting ready to hook this antenna farm up to the power grid.*

"A power grid!"

The PhoneAir rep shook his head. "It won't be up for a week."

"No. I mean what the mayor said . . . and what you said. I've got an idea. The microwaves are all around, but only at very low intensity. We can focus them to a high energy density."

"But you said the atmosphere would absorb them," protested the PhoneAir rep. "I don't understand."

"We'll keep them at a frequency transparent to the atmosphere. The calibration antennas are designed to collect microwaves, and they're already set up to dump all the energy into our diagnostic trailer. Pennington said it reminded him of a power grid. So why not focus the microwaves onto the antenna farm and hook *that* up to the power grid?"

"Huh?"

"We're already transporting energy through the atmosphere, but at a low level. We know the system works. All we have to do is to use the satellite's focusing elements and focus a hell of a lot more energy onto the antennas. Hook it up to the power grid, and we'll be able to have power to run some of the critical devices in town—like what Doc Fitzgerald needs, for example."

"But that's using power-switching technology, which we don't have."

"We're talking a megawatt at the most. And if we don't do anything fancy, we can have continuous power. The satellites were designed to broadcast microwaves even at night by being at an oblique angle to the surface, and being high enough in orbit to get out of the Earth's shadow." Marshall turned to the mayor. "We're going to need your help."

The mayor shrugged. "Whatever. I don't know what the hell is going on anyway, so just tell me what to do."

"Get a team of people to sweep through the town and throw the circuit breakers on every house so we won't draw any unnecessary power once the grid is up. We've got to conserve electricity like crazy so that old Doc Fitzgerald gets first dibs on whatever power is available. The next thing is to gather the people to where the most efficient heating systems are located—we can supply the necessary juice to keep the heat going."

The PhoneAir rep was still looking dubious. "What about my technicians? This isn't going to be an easy job."

"Get them hopping then. They can take care of the details—like I said, we're already transporting power, we'll just increase the intensity. The hook-up to the power grid should be straightforward."

"If you say. But will it work?"

Marshall grinned, suddenly feeling useful—and free of the guilt that haunted him. "If it doesn't work, we'll just act like sheep and huddle the whole town together so no one freezes!"

Jay Pennington, chief executive officer of PhoneAir, sat in the overstuffed VIP chair in the old "Star Wars" conference room, directly across from Marshall's office. Pictures of satellites, exotic weapons, and a Delta Clipper, the first single-stage-to-orbit spaceship, covered the wood-paneled walls. They were alone in the blue-carpeted room.

Pennington rocked back and said, "After you showed us how easy it is to transmit energy through the atmosphere, PhoneAir has decided to diversify into the solar power business. Do you realize how much money there is to be made in the public utility field? Who'd have ever thought we could use low-flying satellites to transmit power? This will be a godsend for rural communities, especially in Third World countries."

Marshall nodded. "Sometimes we have to have our noses rubbed in it to discover the obvious."

Pennington snorted. "You know, sometimes I wonder if you had that application in mind all along. Were you just waiting for an emergency to come along where people were forced to rely on solar power transmitted from satellites?"

"How could I have known? It was *your* disgruntled employee who sabotaged the power plant. It was *your* investigation that showed he received kickbacks on transmission antennas purchased to support your cellular phone system. Our satellites would have made the transmission antennas obsolete, and he would have stopped collecting the kickbacks. But I knew nothing of any of that."

"I guess every technological advancement meets some sort of resistance," said Pennington.

Marshall opened his mouth to speak, and closed it again when Pennington went on. "Especially from folks who don't think they'll benefit from the change. But if we kept that attitude, we'd still be back with the dinosaurs. I never thought I'd be here negotiating for more defense technologies." He rocked forward and placed his elbows on the conference table. "And that's the real reason I'm here. What else have your wizards developed that might have some sort of dual-use in the civilian sector? We're open to trying just about anything."

Marshall thought for a moment. There were literally dozens of technologies he could throw out, but he didn't want to overwhelm Pennington. At least not now. "Well, there's something we've put in orbit to support the ballistic missile defense program that might be useful—Brilliant Eyes."

"What's that?"

"Thousands of optical sensors, able to detect everything from rocket launches to satellites."

"Got any uses in mind?"

Marshall leaned back. He thought about Pennington's comment about the dinosaurs: an asteroid had killed off those creatures, and there wasn't anything around to prevent another asteroid from striking the Earth again, any time. How much money would people be willing to spend on being able to detect a killer asteroid tumbling in to destroy civilization? He didn't know, but he imagined the price was one that many—especially the old and wealthy—would be willing to pay.

"Yeah." Marshall grinned. "I've got a terrific idea."

# THE GUATEMALA CURE

▼

## MARY A. TURZILLO

Althea sat propped in a green velour chair in her housemate's perfectly domestic bedroom. Her ribs didn't actually hurt anymore; with Sativatol they just felt stiff, tired. Her black eye and bruises were fading. She was almost well enough to go back to the lab.

The psychic wounds would take longer to heal.

"I'm not worried," she was saying. "I used that vending machine in the student center lavatory. It said negative. Anyway, I've got my period."

"Trust me, you are. I'm Irish. I'm psychic. With your training, how can you trust a machine that takes five suzies and a urine specimen?" Kelly folded another tissue, inserted it between her fourth and her smallest toe and reached for the nail enamel. "Your period? Spotting. Or bleeding from, you know, violence."

Althea felt a sick, hot shudder crawl across her skin. "It isn't that kind of bleeding."

"Have it your way, ladybug. But go to the clinic, won't you?"

Althea owned the small duplex, an investment from her modest inheritance, but Kelly had settled in as if the place had been in her family for generations. Between Althea's grad fellowship and Kelly's salary as an insurance ombudser, they had a cozy life. Cozy as life could be in a grimy world simmering in a carbon dioxide blanket, resentful and enraged with its human burden.

Althea's friendship with Kelly started when they were placed in the same foster home when both were twelve. Both felt uprooted, torn from normalcy and family. Althea always believed that one morning Daddy would drive up in the old gas-powered Buick, somehow reconstructed from the twisted wreck, and take her home to Mom. Kelly, in contrast, had never known her mother, whose Irish ancestry, Althea was pretty sure, was a fantasy. Her father had never actually sexually assaulted her, but inflicted blows and burns, then abandoned her.

Both yearned for a home. Althea made a home out of her career, while Kelly lavished her nesting impulses on the duplex, trying to create the home she had never had as a child.

Kelly's bedroom was a personality statement. The wallpaper was intertwined shamrocks, art deco. Ferns and African violets flourished by the window, despite smog that killed even mother-in-law-tongue for Althea. The bedspread was pale green candlewick, the carpet lichen green. Watercolors of Irish landscapes and a portrait of Maud Gonne decorated the walls. A cat-litter box was concealed by a moss-colored wicker screen. The greenery was supposed to suggest a garden. To Althea, tonight, it suggested a hospital room.

Kelly herself, pretty with pale freckled skin and sleek cap of black hair, sat spraddled on the bed, wearing a sexy slip, painting her toenails. Althea could never figure out why her friend wasted money on lingerie; about once a year Kelly would bring home some man, and he would spend the night. Then she would pick a quarrel with him, and go into an irrational, frightening rage. If this didn't deter him, Kelly would act so crazy that he would soon flee.

Intimacy problems, Althea supposed.

"Would you consider abortion, if you were?" Kelly asked.

"I don't know." Althea shifted to ease pressure on her ribs. "Carl had an implant, but it still might be his."

"Carl. Who skated off to Utah to bio-engineer new weapons."

"Maybe." Althea studied her own short nails, unenameled, and picked at a frayed cuticle. "I called last night again. Left a message. He may have already left for Utah."

"Mister Environment. Two-faced creep. Hope he enjoys his DoD dollars. Probably trade his skateboard in on a car that runs on gas."

Althea smiled. "They only make gas-cars in Korea."

"Well, then, he'll get an antique Corvette." She pressed her tongue to the corner of her mouth, applying rose polish to her little toe. Pleased at her handiwork, she screwed the top back on the bottle. "Ever think what a great world this would be without men?"

Althea felt slightly sick.

"I'm sorry," Kelly said. "You've had enough talk about men."

"Ordinarily," said Althea deliberately, "I would laugh and agree and not really mean it, because I like men, and I think you like men, but, yes, tonight it seems less than funny."

Kelly pulled one foot toward her face and blew on her toes. Althea thought the move would look innocently provocative to a man.

Kelly carefully stretched her feet out and continued, "I mean, let's not mention rape and abandonment. Let's just talk about the environment. Like, who invented the internal combustion engine?"

"Kelly, that's not—"

"But there might have been a better way, right? And who invented dynamite? And most of the other weapons in the world?"

"Men."

"And who conceived and constructed the first atom bomb?"

"Men, Kelly. I get your point."

"Who led the nation that killed twenty million men, women, and children, and caused World War II?"

"Hitler. A man."

"Which sex is more likely to kill somebody in a DUI accident?"

"Men, I suppose."

"Most of the world's problems. They make guns, they make fat, dirty vehicles, they take short-cuts that destroy the ozone layer or make greenhouse gasses and immortal plastic trash. Industry?"

"Mostly led by men."

"Always. Drug cartels?"

Althea sighed. "Male-dominated, I suppose."

"Which sex is more likely to commit violent crimes?"

"Well, men."

"Okay, and who invented the world's first computer program?"

"A man, I guess. But what's wrong with—"

"No, it wasn't. It was a woman. Lord Byron's daughter, who got little love from old George cause he was always off rattling sabres or writing poems in honor of Don Juan. Point is, computers can solve a lot of environmental problems. That's where women shine."

"Men create more environmental problems because they're at the top of the power hierarchy." Althea's ribs really ached, now. She hated it when Kelly started obsessing. "Women would start wars and dump toxic waste if they had the chance."

"You don't really believe that!"

"Despite—everything."

"Hmmph. What's the number one cause of environmental problems?"

"I don't know, Kelly! You're badgering me. War? The internal combustion engine? Ah—overpopulation! But you can't pin that on men alone."

"Can't I? Do women want to have twenty-three babies all in a row? Most women in the world have more babies than they want."

"Why is that just the fault of men?"

"I mean, a male power structure dictates that a Third World woman marries, often unwillingly, to survive. The husband porks her as often as he wants, without asking if she wants it. Some male priest-shaman-dictator says, hey, birth control is a sin. It happens even here." She paused, her energy darkening. "Would my poor mother would have wanted me, knowing what my father was?"

Althea raised her eyebrows. "You would rather never to have been born?"

"I dunno. Maybe. Anyway, let me go on. There are species, aren't there, which have just a few males and after they've mated, the females kill them off and business is back to normal?"

"Kelly, what about love? Would you want to live in a world without love?" She repressed thoughts of Carl.

Kelly pulled the tissues from her toes and threw them into the wastebasket. They would go to a recycling center. Kelly was not only neat, she was Part Of The Solution. "Romantic love is a neurosis."

Althea felt a spike of anger. "What does that say about me?"

"It says you're a victim."

Althea thought about getting up and stalking out, but the gesture would take too much energy. "Most men aren't bullies or tyrants. My father was a good man."

"Your father was driving too fast on a country road."

"Don't judge the world by your case! You really were a victim. Your vision is warped!" Althea was angry now. Just as well because otherwise she might cry.

Kelly slid off the bed and came over to pat Althea's shoulder. "I'm sorry. I didn't mean to get so personal."

Kelly's aged black cat, Witch, wandered in and rubbed against Althea's uninjured ankle. Kelly used to own three cats, but Bitch and Itch had died of vaccine-resistant leukemia. Althea's tom-cat, Letch, had run away. Althea picked up Witch and scratched her forehead. Witch closed her eyes in ecstacy.

Althea's anger drained away. "So you think the world would be better off without men?"

"Isn't that what I'm saying?"

"But why? What makes men any worse than women?"

"You're the scientist, you tell me. Something in their brains." She settled cross-legged on the carpet at Althea's feet, careful of her pedicure. "Which kind of chromosome do they have that we don't?"

"Y." Clearly, Kelly was half-remembering a lecture by one of the so-called experts flown in to address Feminists to Save Earth, a rad-fem group into which she had been trying to recruit Althea.

"And that hormone. Testosterone?"

"Women have that, too, just not as much. It's what makes women horny. And you it makes feisty."

"Yeah. Well, you think that's what's wrong? Or you think it's cultural? Maybe it's women's fault? We raise them like little tin gods, so then they grow up and kill each other to prove who's best."

Althea nudged Witch into her lap and enjoyed the old cat's purr. "Not entirely cultural. There is a brain difference."

"Can it be corrected?"

Althea laughed. "You mean with drugs?"

"Sure. Could we feed them all estrogen or something? Or maybe do some kind of prenatal surgery to correct their genes. Doesn't your boss do that kind of stuff?"

"On bacteria, Kelly! And insects, when we get brave. Gene splicing can't yet work on human genes to correct bad manners. Though in the seventies they did diagnose redundant Y chromosome syndrome."

Kelly leaned forward, eyes bright. "Yeah? Is that what makes these bastards so mean?"

"Kelly, that's a serious chromosome defect. Less than one percent of the population has it."

"Oh. Well, are you telling me men think just like women? I mean, did Carl think just the same as you did? Sometimes men seem a little slow to catch on to things, right?"

"Researchers believe the corpus callosum in the male brain is not as well developed as in the female brain."

"Corpus—?"

"A connector between brain hemispheres. Makes it easier for a female to jump from linear thinking to integrative or global thinking. All that means, if it means anything, is that a man will do something that seems logical without immediately understanding the overall impact of his action."

"Like work on the Manhattan Project without stopping to think they were going to kill a couple hundred thousand people?"

"That's not a good example, because I'm sure they damn well knew what they were doing. But, yes, something seems logical to a male, so he does it without looking at long-term consequences. That kind of 'logic' would be at odds with ecological thinking."

"Can that be corrected with drugs?"

"You'd have to convince them to take the drugs, wouldn't you?"

Kelly studied Althea's face, then reached out and stroked Witch. "So we have to exterminate the brutes."

"I guess. Start with those guys that threw me downstairs and—" but she couldn't bring herself to say *rape*. "If you can find them."

"Aren't there diseases that kill just one sex?"

Althea ignored the vague awareness that she was being baited. "Sure. Toxic shock syndrome and breast cancer."

"No, I mean just men."

"Prostate cancer. You mean infectious? Legionnaire's disease has a preference for men. And my boss showed me a paper about some disease that hit a village in Guatemala and killed just adult men. The author thought it was spread by guano. That what you mean?"

"Guano?"

"Bat crap, bird crap. That kind of thing."

"Did you ever write to the author of the paper?"

"I never got to finish it. It was in my briefcase the night I met my macho buddies on the stairs." Althea had asked Kelly to search the area for the briefcase.

"Maybe I should have looked in the shrubbery at the edge of the parking lot," said Kelly thoughtfully. "It would be just like a man to carry it out there and dump it."

Althea abruptly found this talk of Y chromosomes, testosterone, and guano depressing. Her ribs hurt, and she wanted to sleep.

Althea dragged herself to the lab at noon several days later.

Lithe, cheerful Dr. Mani Banerji bustled around and offered her herbal tea and a samosa from his lunch. "Sorry, Althea. Carl must make his own decisions, but I am indeed disappointed. I did not envision him as a cog in the war machine." He seemed glad to see her, relieved that she was recovering.

Mani and his wife convinced her to go to the spring ox roast at Argonne Country Club. Althea's depression lightened; in her secondhand red sarong, she felt better than she had for months.

Until she saw Carl.

A girl in a skateboard tee shirt had her feet in his lap, and they were sharing a tall drink in a plastic foam cup.

Althea froze, like a possum caught in the headlights of an oncoming car. Carl. Back in town and he'd never called her. Never explained. His eyes widened as he noticed her. He scrambled to his feet, overturning the drink on the girl.

*Leave me alone,* she thought, and fled. He caught up with her.

"I'm just back in town for the weekend," he said. "I know I have a lot of explaining to do."

She broke into a run, tripped, and bit back tears. Carl bent to help her up, and she tried to backhand him, pulled something in her rib cage. Cursing, she got to her feet and ran to the parking lot. The car was like an oven, but the solar battery started it at once.

At home, she pounded on Kelly's door. She needed more sympathy than she could get from Witch. Then she remembered.

Kelly's vacation had started yesterday. She was off on a tour with some of her weird friends.

By the time Kelly got back, it was apparent that she had been right. Althea was pregnant. The light period had been spotting; the coin machine in the women's lavatory was a piece of junk. The rape counsellor suggested abortion, and when Althea rejected that, DNA fingerprinting to determine paternity.

"Oh, I'm so *sorry*," Kelly said, dropping suitcases and parcels in the hallway near the women's bicycles. Witch was doing frantic purring-rubbing against Kelly's ankles. "I should have thought about you. It's hard to telephone when you have trouble with the language and—oh, I know, that's no excuse."

"It's all right. I wouldn't have told you over the phone anyway. Why spoil your vacation?" Althea thought, *I would have too told her over the phone. I'm just being nice.* She also wondered why Kelly hadn't bothered to send her a postcard.

"Listen, I have a surprise for you." Kelly picked up Witch and scratched under her collar. "I set it up before I left and I think we can pull it off Monday. Can you take off from work Monday?"

"Aren't you going to tell me about your trip?"

Kelly waved the question away. "Tomorrow. Let me drag

this stuff into my room, then we'll discuss this pregnancy thing."

Kelly pushed Witch off, shoved parcels into her room, and closed the door. "Let's sit in the living room. Surprises in my luggage."

"I'm not sure I can take any more surprises."

"Good surprises. Honest." Kelly led Althea into the living room and pushed her into a chair. From the refrigerator she brought two tall glasses of tamarind seltzer. The television, on the interactive channel, blared, "How do *you* vote, Kelly and Althea? Choice A: allow radioactive waste to continue in orbit indefinitely. Choice B—"

"Off!" said Kelly, and it blinked out. She gave one drink to Althea and flopped down on the sofa with the other. "First of all," she continued, "you'll never guess what I found the day before I left for Central America."

"My briefcase," said Althea dully. "Thanks." Kelly had left the briefcase, which had obviously been run over by at least one car, on Althea's bed. It still contained most of her papers, although the one on the Guatemala virus had apparently been blown away.

"You're welcome." Kelly crossed her legs. "Now. You're definitely eating for two, Carl is—"

"Oh, Kelly, I saw him at the ox roast. This bimbo fluff-chick was all over him. He tried to chase me down and get me to approve of his stupid, male-chauvinist—"

"Definite case of Y-chromosome poisoning, hm? Or is it degeneration of the, what did you call it? Corpus delicti?"

"Corpus callosum, you mean? Oh, don't make me think about it. I know it's silly, but the really awful part was, he had this plastic foam cup. I didn't know they still sold them. So trivial, but a perfect symbol of how he sold out. He's ruined my faith in mankind."

"*Man*-kind? Is the choice of words deliberate?"

"No, no. I don't agree that men are the problem. Dr. Banerji is such a good man, an ethical scientist."

"Okay, name three ethical responsible men." Kelly sipped her drink. "You can use your father for one, I won't argue. Although he must have been speeding. It was a gas-burning car, wasn't it?"

"That's all they had back then!"

Kelly yawned and leaned over to pet Witch. "Well, anyway, Carl's abandoned you and your environmental work, and now he's building better diseases at Utahgenics."

Althea had a sudden memory of another paper missing from her briefcase: a draft of a paper Carl had written on the military use of bats as a vector for disease.

"Why didn't I see through him?" Althea threw a sofa pillow and it bounced off Kelly's closed door.

Kelly cocked her head to one side. "Aren't you the one that thinks problems have solutions?"

"I do. But I'm tired of solving problems." She felt a wall between her and Kelly. Kelly had never had a serious relationship. She used men as entertainment, validation of her attractiveness, and occasional sexual release. But she had never given her trust and respect to a man. Never had her trust and respect betrayed. Carl had skated on his Planet Earth board into Althea's heart, and then skated out of her life to a biological warfare lab in Utah.

She had an mental image of Carl standing at the mouth of a cave in a Third World country, releasing bats infected with some virus intended to kill guerrillas—and innocent villagers—as their droppings got into water supplies or dried to airborne dust. Carl, with his quirky smile. Wave after wave of bats, waking at twilight, moribund and deadly.

She opened her eyes. "Listen, let's discuss this tomorrow. I want to hear about your trip."

The next few days, Kelly was mostly out of the house running errands. She kept her room locked. Sunday, she shooed Althea out of the kitchen. Surprise for the next day, she said. Althea wondered what kind of surprise required an entire day of cooking.

Monday, Kelly woke Althea before dawn. "No breakfast. I packed a picnic. It's no good when you're pregnant to eat when you first get up." She shoved two green carpet-bags in the car and insisted Althea take a sweater. She only smirked at Althea's questions.

Althea had a moment of deja vu as they wound out of the city on the route Althea's family used to take to go to the cabin in Michigan. The memories of that last trip, the one that had ended in a crash on a Michigan blue highway, were no longer painful, so she rolled down the window. She remembered the country smells: timothy, cut grass, sometimes manure, clover, rain. Now she could only smell baked earth and fumes. Trucks still burned noxious fossil fuel.

Kelly was crazy to recommend against breakfast during pregnancy. Althea was simultaneously nauseated and famished.

So she closed her eyes and dozed. She dreamt of Carl on his board, skating a high ramp, blowing kisses at her.

She awoke abruptly as Kelly pulled up to a field beyond which a ruddy dawn broke. *One good thing about pollution,* thought Althea. *It makes for colorful dawns and sunsets.*

Then she saw the hot-air balloon floating, billowing, its basket still on the ground. The balloon was green and blue, and painted on it were the continents and oceans of the earth.

Althea rubbed her eyes and grinned. "Kelly, what a nut you are! Are we going up in that?"

"Yes, isn't it neat? We'll have breakfast and watch the dawn. Do you like it? Do you really like it?"

"I love it!" A thought, *I wish Carl could see this,* stabbed her soul, but she firmly repressed it.

The owner, wiry Mr. Woodrow, seemed brimming over with glee at the effect his balloon had on Althea. "You told me she'd love it, right?" shouted Kelly gaily over the roar of the methane burner. From a red truck a few yards off, a chubby woman wearing an I SURVIVED THE 2010 DROUGHT tee shirt smiled and waved.

"Oh, and I'll be sure you get your money's worth," said Woodrow.

"The basket doesn't look very strong," said Althea stupidly.

"Designed to hold me and four others," said Woodrow, puffing his scrawny chest. "Your friend paid extra to get it for just two."

Althea thought, *What a fun thing to do with a date.* Then, remembering Utahgenics and the fluff-chick, *Not!*

The methane roared off and on, and the ground receded.

"Don't be afraid, we won't fall!" said Kelly.

"Look! There's our car. And Mrs. Woodrow in the truck." Althea felt foolish, excited, giddy, tired, hungry, and morning-sick. Most of all, she felt ten years old.

"Isn't this neat?"

"I can't feel anything, but we really seem to be zipping."

"The higher we go, the faster the wind takes us," said Woodrow.

Althea shivered. Kelly pulled two green sweaters out of one of her bags and they donned them.

Fields, green with circles of intensive irrigation to fight the most recent drought, glided below them. After a while, the novelty wore off and Althea's stomach decided it was more hungry than morning-sick. "Didn't you say something about breakfast?"

The sun was up now. "Sure." Kelly dug in her bag and produced two croissants and a jar of orange juice with straws.

"This is it?" Althea said, then realized she sounded ungrateful.

Kelly glanced at her, attention elsewhere. "You're a light eater."

Althea smiled. "Um, I guess. But the air gives a person an appetite." And this embryo, she thought. It crossed her mind that she should politely offer Woodrow a croissant, but that would mean giving up hers, since Kelly had already gobbled one. She nibbled, yearning for butter or jam. She glanced at the carpet bag, wondering what in the world could take so much space.

"Ah," said Kelly finally. "We're getting near an urban area. There's a reservoir."

Woodrow turned off the methane. "Yes, and we'll have to land soon. My wife has a thermos of coffee in the truck." *How nice*, thought Althea, *he didn't mind that we didn't bring him a roll.*

Kelly opened the carpet bag and pulled out a mesh bag of something dark and heavy. From this, she began scooping out pellets.

Only they weren't pellets. Some of them took flight, and some fell to the deck.

"What are you doing, miss?" asked Woodrow.

"Never mind. It's a joke. Just a practical joke."

Althea bent over and picked up one of the pellets.

It was a dead hummingbird.

"Miss, you should have told me about this before we left the ground. You could injure someone on the ground."

"I sincerely hope so," said Kelly brightly.

"What?"

"It's all right. Just go back to your methane thing."

"I can't let you do this. This is my balloon and I'm responsible." He tried to wrest the mesh bag from Kelly. She let go and pulled another bag of hummingbirds out of her carpetbag.

Althea watched in horror. "What are you doing, Kelly? Why are you releasing these birds? Where did you get them? It can't be legal for you to have all these wild birds!"

"It's okay," said Kelly, shaking the mesh bag out over the edge of the basket. "I'm doing this for you. I'll explain later."

Woodrow was getting red in the face. "You won't explain to me later, young lady. You'll stop instantly and hand over that bag. What kind of trick is this?"

Kelly was releasing a third bag of birds. Some of them flew away. Others simply fell, like viridescent turds. *They must be terrified,* thought Althea.

"Why are some of them dead?" Althea yelled. Woodrow had turned the methane back up.

"It's okay, Althea. Some of them just don't survive. That's the way it is with hummingbirds."

Althea turned to Woodrow, who was now chalky white. "I'm sorry, Mr. Woodrow, I don't know what she's doing."

Woodrow set his bony jaw. "I was hoping that if we went higher it would discourage her." In a lower voice he added, "We can't be wrestling her for those bags. The best would be to bring her down."

"Yes," said Althea, "yes."

The green carpetbag was empty. Kelly looked seraphic, happy beyond mortal happiness.

"Kelly, this is all wrong. Why did you release those birds?" *And what*, thought Althea, *did it have to do with your little vacation to, was it Guatemala?*

*And what else could you have found in my briefcase? Carl's paper? References?* Althea tried to remember.

As the ground loomed upward, and the red truck sped parallel to their path, Kelly finally spoke. "He told me they do the rides at dawn or dusk. I chose dawn."

"Why?" asked Althea.

"Because my associate couldn't get the bat guano to work."

"Bat guano? To do what?" But she knew.

"It worked pretty well in the water, but we wanted the crap to dry and spread it by dust too. So we used hummingbirds."

"Wanted to spread *what* by dust?"

Kelly smiled slyly. "Feminists to Save Earth found another microbiologist, this woman who got fired from U. of San Carlos, to show me how to infect the birds. I wanted to surprise you."

Althea shivered, despite the sweater.

Kelly patted her arm. "If it had been bats, I would have done it at dusk."

# HIGHER EDUCATION

▼

## JERRY POURNELLE
## & CHARLES SHEFFIELD

At sixteen, Rick Luban's life was about to end. He didn't know it yet. He thought he was all set for a good time.

The first period had gone no differently from usual. Mr. Hamel had been teaching high school for thirty years—forever, in Rick's eyes. He looked like an old turtle, and like a turtle he had developed his own survival techniques. Nothing got to him; not talking in class, or eating, or farting, or sleeping. Gross and direct rudeness or violence, too much even for him to ignore, he passed up the line at once to the principal's office.

Hamel's rule: No fuss, no muss. And if that meant no work and no learning, too, he would settle for it. He usually reached that understanding with a class before the end of its first week.

"Test today." Hamel took no notice of the half-hearted groans. Failing an act of God, biology tests in his class came every Tuesday and everyone knew it. "Read the questions, mark the answers. You have forty minutes."

More out of boredom than anything else, Rick put on the earphones attached to the desk and slipped the written sheet of questions into the reader.

"Question one," said the voice in his ear. "Five point credit. One of the animals on your screen belongs to a different class from the others. Indicate which one. For assistance on the biological definition of *class*, or for name identification of any of the animals shown, touch the empty box."

The TV screen in front of Rick was divided into six rectangles. The first was empty. The second through sixth showed an ant, a butterfly, a mosquito, a spider, and a caterpillar. They were all in color, and all moved in natural settings.

Rick saw Dim Willy Puntin, Puntin the Pumpkin, reaching out to poke the icon of the caterpillar. It certainly looked grossly different from the other four. Rick snorted to himself. That was just like Hamel, trying a trick question. Rick had hardly been listening to the lesson about larval insect forms, but even a five-year-old knew that caterpillars turned into butterflies; and insects all had six legs.

Rick reached forward to touch the icon of the spider, at the same moment as Juanita Cesaro, two seats in front of him, removed her headset. She raised her hand and then stood up.

Hamel left the raised podium and moved over to her at once. Rick eased the earphones away from his head. Juanita was dim, but she was hot stuff. Half the boys in her year—including Rick—had been through Juanita; but you'd never know it from seeing her in class. She always sat demure and quiet, doing so poorly in every subject that her teachers all had trouble passing her. She *never* caused trouble.

"These." Juanita waved her hand vaguely at the headset, television, and reader. "Not working."

Hamel came around the desk and leaned over to examine the television picture. He was very careful not to touch Juanita, and careful to stand so that this fact would be apparent on the classroom videocamera recording.

*Wily old turtle. No sexual harassment charges for you.* Rick could see the empty box and the five icons on Juanita's screen, just like on his own. Another clapped-out reader, it had to be. The readers were junk, breaking down all the time. Even when they worked they would only handle one size of page. School was too cheap to buy decent equipment. Not like the school the telephone company ran. That one had great equipment, but it was just for kids whose mothers worked there. His mother had got herself fired for drugs six weeks after she started with the phone company, so Rick had only been at the company school a little while. That was back in kindergarten, but he still remembered the school.

Hamel had apparently made up his mind about the reader. He was glancing thoughtfully around the class, finally gesturing to a girl at the back. "Belinda. For this period I want you to change seats with Juanita."

As expected. Belinda Jacob was one of three people in the class who could read well enough to handle the test from the printed sheet without using a reader at all. *So see what reading does for you,* Rick thought, as the two girls changed places. *Not a damn thing.* Belinda was Hamel's star student. She had probably been halfway through her own test before she had to move—and now she was forced to start over, while Juanita would get the benefit of her right answers.

Rick grinned to himself as he settled back to listen to the rest of the questions. Unless Hamel went to the trouble of noting the point where the two had changed over, which wasn't at all likely, Juanita for the first time in her life was going to score—on a *test.*

\* \* \*

The broken reader was all that the first period could offer to relieve the boredom. That was predictable with Mr. Hamel. Dullness was the rule. What Rick and his friends had been looking forward to for a week was second period. They were supposed to get a new civics teacher then, right out of training.

"Willis Preebane, his name is. An' if I can't have some fun with him, I'm losing my touch," Screw Savage said.

Any one of the three might have offered the same statement, but Screw had special credibility. He was a school legend. Two years before, by a mixture of near inaudible insult and off-videocamera dumb insolence, he had made a new teacher take a swing at him on her very first day. She had been fired on the spot. Screw was provided with a groveling apology from Principal Rigden. His parents had sued school and county anyway, and been paid a hefty out-of-court settlement. Now Screw tended to get high grades without ever doing homework or handing in tests.

"But we'd all like to have first go at him," Screw went on, "so we do it fair an' draw lots."

Rick and the other two were walking between classes, heading for Room 33 with Screw Savage leading the way. The corridors were their usual confusion with backed-up lines in front of the metal and plastique detectors. Hoss Carlin, walking next to Rick, took a step to his left and reached out to brush his fingers over the breasts of a girl walking the other way. She slapped his hand away, but she turned to give him a big smile and said, "See you tonight."

"Watch it, Hoss," Rick warned. "You're in deep shit if they have that on camera."

"Nah." Hoss jerked his head upward. "Checked already."

The ceiling videocamera for the corridor was ruined, lens broken and body a shattered hulk. It was like this all over the school. Every time a corridor camera was repaired, within a day or two it would be smashed.

"Anyway," Hoss went on, "Jackie'd be on my side if they did see me. She'd tell 'em I was swattin' a wasp off her tit or somethin.'"

The three youths were almost at Room 33. Most of the class were already there, standing waiting outside the locked door.

"Mebbe Preebane's not as dumb as you think, Screw," Hoss said. "He knows at least that much. Lockin' the door stops us givin' him a welcome."

"So one of us has to get real inventive once we're inside." Savage turned around, three toothpicks sticking up from between the knuckles of his closed right fist. "Short one has first go at Papa Willis. Who wants first pick?"

"Me," Hoss said, and grimaced with annoyance when the toothpick he pulled was full length. "Lucky with women, unlucky in the draw. Go on, Rick. You got one out of two chance now."

Rick plucked the toothpick from between Savage's first and second finger, and grinned when he saw it was a fragment only an inch and a half long.

"Lucky bastard." Screw opened his hand to reveal a third, full-length toothpick. "You get Preebane all to yourself."

"Aha!" The voice, thin and with a definite lisp, came from behind Rick. "And do I hear thomeone taking my name in vain?"

Rick turned and stared. The man waddling along the corridor was too good to be true. He was pale, short, and grossly overweight. He had watery blue eyes in a pudgy face, and he sported a flat, gingery-brown mustache that looked as though it had been poorly dyed and pasted above his full upper lip.

Preebane's very appearance was an opportunity to have

fun. If Rick didn't get in quickly, some other class joker certainly would.

In fact, it was already happening. Rick heard a whisper, deliberately loud, from among the group of waiting students: "Quiet now. Here comes our new P.E. teacher."

Preebane, heading for the classroom door, paused uncertainly. After a moment he decided to pretend he had not heard the comment. He unlocked the door and waved the students inside. Rick, contrary to his natural instincts and usual practice, went to sit in the middle of the first row. Preebane, belly wobbling, moved to stand beneath the videocamera right in front of Rick. He beamed directly at him.

Rick gazed back and waited for inspiration. He, who usually had a thousand ideas for baiting teachers, suddenly found his mind a blank. Willis Preebane looked like a man who, if goaded to physical violence, would drop dead from the exertion before he could land a blow.

And that voice. "Good morning. I am Mr. Preebane, and I want to welcome you to my class on introductory civics." Or rather, it was "Mr. Pweebane," and "my clath on intwoductory thivicth."

"I told Pwinthipal Wigden of my approach, and she agweed with it completely. Begin by forgetting evewything that you have ever been told about the Conthtituthion."

"Done," said a girl's voice from the back of the room, followed by a loud male whisper, "Hire the handicapped."

The others were starting without Rick. He could feel Screw and Hoss glaring accusingly at his back. And still his brain was empty. It was an enormous relief to hear the click of the P.A. system, right above his head, and a voice saying, "I am delighted to announce that we have been paid an unexpected visit by Congresswoman Pearl, who as I am sure you know serves on our Board of Education. All students and teachers will please assemble at once in the main hall."

Principal Rigden didn't sound delighted to Rick. She sounded ready to shit bricks. But the interruption would give him time to think. He stayed in his seat until everyone except Mr. Preebane had left the room, then he moved out and held the door for the teacher. Preebane nodded his thanks. Rick closed the door; was careful not to lock it; and hurried after the rest of the class ahead of Preebane. He caught up with them as they were filing into the hall.

"What about some action, dipshit?" Screw Savage didn't wait until they were seated. "If I'd known you was goin' to just sit there like a dried-out dog turd, I'd never have held any draw. You can't hang old Willis out to dry, what the hell can you handle?"

"His dick." Hoss stood on the other side of Screw. "He's done it too much and softened his brain."

"Don't you believe it. I know what I'm doing. And it's something special." Rick glared at both of them. "But I need a little bit of help from you. You have to go sit down near the front."

"And where will you be?" Screw sounded suspicious.

"Right at the back. Near the door. The classroom's not locked, Screw. I was last out, I made sure it was that way."

"Ah!" The other two understood at once.

"What do you want us to do?" Hoss asked.

"Wait 'til the principal is ready to introduce Congress-woman Whatsit. It should get real quiet. Then you drop something."

"What?"

"Hell, I dunno. Anything. Anything that makes a decent noise."

Hoss dived into his pocket and came up with a handful of change. "This? People will scrabble around after 'em, too."

"Perfect."

"But the old Rigger will have my ass in a sling for interrupting her."

"For dropping money by accident, and losing some? Don't think so. Anyway, if you're going to help, get going. I can't wait much longer. Have to find a seat near the side door."

Hoss and Screw nodded. Rick turned at once and started easing his way against the main flow of students. The seats at the back, usually filled first, were today half empty. Everybody wanted to see Principal Rigden wriggle and grovel, the way she always did with board of education visitors. Rick sat at the end of a row he had almost to himself, close enough to the open door for a quiet getaway.

He waited impatiently while the stage filled with the senior teachers. Willis Preebane was up there with them—that was surprising for a new and junior staff member. The honor didn't seem to make him comfortable; maybe because his ass would hardly squeeze in between the arms of his chair.

There was one student on the stage, too. Daniel Rackett. As valedictorian (vale-dickhead-torian, as Hoss usually put it) Danny would be called upon to say something to welcome their guest. He didn't look comfortable, either. He was peering at the headset that was supposed to read his speech into his ear. From the expression on his face it wasn't working right. Even from the back of the hall Rick could see his Adam's apple bobbing up and down.

Finally Principal Rigden appeared, smiling broadly and leading a large, red-haired woman in a green pantsuit. They moved to two empty chairs at the front of the stage, Congresswoman Pearl sat down, and the principal turned to face the students. "I would like—"

There was the clatter of two dozen small coins falling onto

the wooden floor. Some of them were still rolling when Rick quietly rose and slipped out of the side door.

The principal would speak, then Danny Rackett, then the visitor. Rick probably had at least half an hour. But that wasn't long for what he had in mind.

First he headed away from Room 33, keeping his eyes open for working videocameras. The contraceptive dispensers were down by the cafeteria entrance. They needed a student name and ID code before they would operate, but Rick was prepared for that. He entered "Daniel J. Rackett" and "XKY-586", waited as the valedictorian's ID was confirmed, and took the packet of three condoms. He did it twice more. Nine should be enough. If anyone checked today's records, Danny would get quite a reputation.

The corridors were deserted as he hurried back toward Room 33, opened the door, and slipped through. The tricky piece now was to disable the classroom videocamera without being seen by it. The cable ran along the ceiling, well out of reach. Rick scaled the open door and balanced precariously on top of it. He had no knife on him—anything that might form a weapon would never get past the school entrance—but his nail clippers were enough for this job. He crouched on top of the door, reached up, and delicately snipped the thin gray cable.

He lost his balance as he did so and had to jump, but he landed easily. And finally he could close the classroom door. There was no way of locking it from the inside, but he felt a lot safer once it was shut.

He blew up eight of the condoms and tied their ends. They formed great balloons, a couple of feet long and nine or ten inches wide. He taped them all around Preebane's desk, stepped back, and surveyed his work.

It was a start, but it was not enough. He could imagine

Screw Savage's sniff and critical comment: "Kindergarten stuff." He had to try for the rest.

Rick went to the door, opened it, and looked along the corridor. He had no idea how much time had passed, but everywhere was still silent and deserted. He left the door unlocked and hurried along to the washroom at the end of the corridor. He placed the end of the remaining condom over a faucet, held it in position, and turned on the water.

It took forever to fill. Rick put in as much water as he dared, until he was sure that the thin skin would burst under the weight. At last he tied off the end. The bloated condom had become amazingly heavy. He cradled it in his arms and headed back to the classroom.

The most difficult part still remained. Somehow he had to balance the monstrous condom right above the door, so that it would burst as the door swung open. And he had to get out, himself, after the trap was set.

It sounded impossible. Rick puzzled over it, increasingly sure that he was running out of time, until at last he realized that he was trying to solve the wrong problem. He didn't have to leave the room at all. There was going to be total confusion after the door was opened. He could hide behind the desks at the back of the room, and leave when the excitement was over.

He spent ten nervous minutes arranging a harness of tape around the condom, then placed thumb tacks through the ends of the tape. Finally he dragged a chair over to the door and lifted the condom into position. He pushed the pins into the wall and made delicate adjustments. When the door was opened, its rough top had to just scrape the bottom of the condom enough to break it. But the condom felt so distended and tight, he was almost afraid to move it now.

At last he realized that he was doing more harm than good. The changes he was making were loosening both the pins and the tape. He returned the chair to its original position and forced himself to retreat to the back of the room. He found a place which allowed him a narrow view of the door, with a very small chance of his being seen.

And then he waited. And waited.

What could be going on in the hall? There was no way to know how long Congresswoman Pearl would decide to speak. Certainly, Principal Rigden would not dare to interrupt a visitor who was a member of the Board of Education. Suppose that she went on right until lunch time, and the class did not return to this room?

Rick's legs were stiff and his knees sore from crouching on the hard floor when at last he heard the sound of footsteps clattering along the corridor. He tensed. He had not been able to lock the door, as he had originally intended. Maybe Preebane would notice that.

Apparently not. The metal handle on the inside was turning. The door opened its first inch and Rick heard Preebane's voice saying, "After you, Aunt Delia. I am weally glad that my clath will have you—"

The door swung open. Rick had one glimpse of Willis Preebane, ushering a large, green-clad figure ahead of him into the room. Then the giant condom, scraped by the top of the door, burst with a soft, subdued plop. Water deluged down.

Rick, peering through the narrow slit, had the sudden feeling that the flood had decapitated Congresswoman Pearl. He could see her red hair, sodden with water, lying on the floor.

Then he heard her scream. She clutched at her head. The hair beneath the wig was revealed as short-cropped and gray.

Behind the congresswoman and Preebane, crowding now into the doorway, came Rick's whole class. They were buzzing with excitement and delight. Delia Pearl's secret would be all over the school by lunch time. Rick saw Screw near the front, standing open-mouthed with astonished glee.

He felt a huge satisfaction. He had promised; and he had certainly delivered.

Rick also believed that he was safe from discovery. In the melee that followed, the classroom had been total confusion. No one noticed when he joined the rest—even Hoss and Screw didn't realize that he had been in the room, and they had no idea how he had managed the trick until he explained.

It was a total shock to Rick when he was called out of class right after lunch and taken to Principal Rigden's office.

The principal was there. So was Congresswoman Pearl, the three assistant principals, Willis Preebane, and two other people whom Rick did not recognize.

The congresswoman had managed to dry her wig, and she was wearing it. That was a mistake. After its soaking it looked like a strip of cheap coconut matting wedged down onto her head. Beneath it, her blue eyes glared at Rick with undisguised hatred.

"This is the one?"

"We believe so." Principal Rigden wasted no time on formalities. She turned to Rick. "Ricardo Luban, do you know of the outrage that was perpetrated on Congresswoman Pearl this morning?"

"Yes." Rick felt uneasy, but he could not see how anything could be pinned on him.

"Will you admit that you were responsible for it?"

"I didn't do it."

"Were you in Mr. Preebane's class before the assembly to greet the congresswoman?"

"Yes."

"And you were the last to leave that class?"

"Yes. I think so."

"Mr. Preebane?" The principal turned her head.

"He was the last. Definitely. He held the door for me."

"Did you?"

"I guess so."

"And you locked the door after you, as you were supposed to?"

"Sure."

Rick felt easier in his mind. They were going to try to
prove that he hadn't locked the door. He didn't think they
could. And even if they did, that was a long way from proving
that he had set the booby trap. But the principal didn't pursue
that line. She merely nodded, and asked, "Mr. Preebane tells
us that you then went on ahead of him, toward the hall. Is that
right?"

"Yes." Rick was uneasy again.

"And you attended the general assembly?"

"Yes."

"And remained there throughout?"

"Yes." If they were going to ask him what happened in the
hall, he was on solid ground. Hoss and Screw Savage had
briefed him pretty thoroughly over lunch. Danny Rackett's
headset hadn't worked right. He had tried to read his speech
of welcome from printed sheets, stumbled over every word
longer than one syllable, and made an ass of himself until Principal Rigden finally cut him off. She had then made a short
speech herself, explaining what a wonderful person the visit-
ing congresswoman was. And finally Congresswoman Pearl
had offered her own contribution, telling the audience how
pleased she was that her own nephew, Willis Preebane, had
decided to teach here, how talented he was, and how lucky the
school was to have him. She hoped he would be really happy
with his choice.

She had said it all twice, to make sure that the principal and the other teachers got the message, added that she was looking forward to seeing an actual class being taught, and at last sat down.

If Principal Rigden wanted anything more detailed than that, Rick would plead ignorance. He was sure that was all anyone else remembered. Most wouldn't know that much.

"So where did you sit during the assembly?"

The question was totally unexpected. It left Rick floundering.

"I dunno—"

"That's silly, of course you remember. Now, where?"

"I guess maybe I was near the back. Near the side door."

"Very good." The principal turned to the screen that covered one wall of her office. "Right here, in fact." She touched the wall. "This is you, is it not?"

The screen showed a videocamera still. The resolution was not good. Rick sitting way at the back of the hall was barely recognizable.

"Yeah, that's me."

*Mistake. Should have said maybe, not sure.* He thought of changing his story, but it was too late. The picture had flashed off, to be replaced by another, and Principal Rigden was saying, "The first image I showed was taken at the beginning of the assembly. This one was taken close to the end of it. The seat where you were sitting originally is now empty. Where are you sitting now, Ricardo Luban?"

"I moved." Rick spoke automatically, but he knew he was doomed. If they had been able to locate him on the video image . . .

"We are quite sure that you moved." The principal stepped away from the wall screen. "But where did you move to? During the lunch period we managed to identify every student in school today, in both the first and the second picture. I should say, every student except one. You are present in the first image, and absent in the second. Now would you like to confess?"

Rick shook his head. They had him on ice, but he wasn't going to admit it. He would plead innocent today, and tomorrow, and if necessary for the whole of the next two years, until the end of his time in school.

It was with disbelief that he heard Principal Rigden saying, "I quite agree with you, Congresswoman Pearl, and with the other board members. Guilt is established beyond reasonable doubt. Such people have absolutely no place in this school or in our school system. We will take action for expulsion as soon as the necessary signatures can be obtained and the paperwork completed."

"For the final, official decision." Delia Pearl stared stonily at Rick. "But unofficially, pending that decision, expulsion will happen today, and the Welfare Department will be notified today."

"Today?" Principal Rigden hesitated. "Very well. Of course." She turned to Rick. "You are expelled from this school, effective immediately. The final notification will follow in a day or two. Please collect your possessions and leave the premises as soon as possible."

"You can't do that!" Expulsion, for a simple practical joke that had really hurt no one? Rick knew a student who had broken his language teacher's arm, and another who had deliberately run over a science teacher in his car. Explosive booby traps for other teachers had been set, filled with shit or warm tar. But those people had received only trifling punishments.

"I think you must let us decide what we can and cannot do."

"I'll sue. I will."

For a second everyone stared at him. Then they all smiled.

"Sue a congresswoman?" The principal laughed aloud. "And what lawyer will take your case? Get out, Luban. Go."

Delia Pearl's mouth twisted with satisfaction, and she turned to Preebane. "Willis, I do not feel that we can trust this young man one little bit. Would you please accompany him when he collects his possessions, and then escort him off the premises."

"Of course." Preebane did not even look to the principal for confirmation.

Rick was led away. He was too dazed to resist. He hardly saw Hoss or Screw or the other members of his class as he picked up his school bag, and he did not say a word when he was escorted to the front door and his ID was canceled from the entry system. He walked out into the afternoon sunlight and stared around him as though he was on an alien planet.

He went to the side of the school, walked out beyond the sports field, and sat on the grass. He was still sitting there when school was released for the day. Occasional students passed by. No one spoke to him. He did not stir or speak to them. Only when a long afternoon shadow fell across him, and silently remained there, did he look up.

It was Mr. Hamel, more like a turtle than ever as he stood motionless with his head pushed slightly forward. He nodded at Rick.

"Caught at last, Luban. And not before time."

"You heard what happened?"

"The whole school heard. Would you like to talk to me about it?" And, when Rick shook his head, "Very well. That is your option." He began to walk away across the grass.

"Wait!" Rick struggled to his feet and hurried after him. "I don't want to talk, but I want to *ask.*"

"Better yet. We learn by asking, not by talking." Hamel

continued, slowly pacing out of the school grounds and into the street. "So ask."

"Why *me*? I mean, why did the motherfuckers dump on *me* like that? What I did wasn't any big deal compared to the other shit that goes down all the time in this school."

They had come to a bench. Hamel sat down on it and gestured to Rick to join him.

"Must you use that language?"

"What'll you do, expel me? You never heard people talk like that?"

"I hear people talk that way every day," Hamel sighed. "It's unpleasant. Do you want people to wish you were not around them? It's easy enough to do. Or do you want answers?"

"Answers. Why'd they dump on *me*?"

"Very well," Hamel said. "Luban, you are not stupid. But you are a fool. For one thing, you consort with people like Savage and Carlin who really are stupid. You are also ignorant, cynical, amoral, and unthinking. Wait a moment." He held up his hand. Rick was starting to stand up. "I am going to answer your question—or rather, I am going to let you answer it. You are—how old? Sixteen? So you have been in the education system for eleven years. And what have you learned?"

"My grades are all right."

"Certainly. Because nothing is required of you. It is easy to hit a target pasted to the end of the rifle. We are also required to help you feel good about yourself. The technical term is to raise your self-esteem. While you were in school I could not have spoken to you this way, because you had to be protected from the truth. Now I can. Despite all the work we have done to raise your self-esteem, surely you must know you've learned very little."

"I do all right," Rick protested again.

"You do all right. What does that mean? Let us examine what you know.

"You can read short, simple words, but only those you have seen before. You have a reasonable speaking vocabulary, but you cannot read more than half of the words you know. You have a rudimentary knowledge of simple science, and you can do simple arithmetic. I've hammered some biology into your skull, but you know little mathematics, and no economics, geography, history, arts, or languages. You can recite all manner of song and rap lyrics, but no poetry or literature. And you would be little better if you stayed here another two years and graduated."

"Reading from books is a waste of time," Rick said. "Like adding up numbers. I got a calculator that does that. Reading's ancient history. The readers do it for us fine."

"They do when they work, and when you have one available. But you miss a point. A person who cannot *read* also cannot *write*. Writing—and revision—is essential for completeness and clarity of expression. But I do not want to digress. You have been in the education system for eleven years. How much, in that time, have you learned about the system itself, and how it works?"

Rick considered the question. He had never had the slightest interest in the education system. Nor did anyone else in his right mind.

"Not much."

"But you have enough information to work things out for yourself. For instance, whom do I work for—to whom do I report?"

"Principal Rigden."

"And to whom does she report?"

"I dunno. I guess the Board of Education."

"Good enough. There are a couple more layers in there, but that will do. Now another question. How much of the county and state's total budget goes to education? I don't expect you to know the answer to that, so I will tell you. It is about four-tenths. That's an awful lot of money, a huge vested interest at work. Now, who decides what that amount will be and how it should be allocated?"

"Congress?"

"For all practical purposes. Very good. So let us climb the ladder of our status society. If you play one of your unfunny 'jokes' on a teacher, and are caught, you pay a price. But a teacher, most students are amazed to learn, is the lowest form of life in the school system. Do something to the principal, that's worse, and the punishment is more severe. To a board of education member, worse yet. And to a *congresswoman,* who is also a member of the board of education—"

"I didn't know I was doing nothing to a congresswoman."

"That is the plea of the foolish through all of history: *I didn't know what I was doing.* But, speaking as a teacher, I tell you that I have no sympathy for you. Is it better to insult and offend and diminish me or Willis Preebane, rather than Congresswoman Pearl, simply because the punishment is less? That is the logic of a coward."

"I ain't no coward!"

The sun was setting in their faces, and Hamel shielded his eyes with his hand. Rick could see the deep lines on his cheeks and around his mouth. Hamel seemed ancient, far older than when he was teaching his class, until suddenly he lowered his hand and turned to face Rick. His eyes were alert and astute, changing his whole face.

"You want some good news? Until today you had two more years of schooling here. Did you have any thought of continuing beyond that?"

Rick shook his head. For the past three years he had wanted to finish school and get out of it more than anything. "Mick makes me stay in school because Mom gets the education incentive bonus in the welfare. I'd be long gone if I could."

"So now what happens to you?"

"I don't know. Watch the virtual tube, I guess. Only Mick will kill me. Throw me out on the street anyway. The education incentive was nine-forty a month and we only get sixty-two hundred."

"A good part of the money. Of course you don't get the money."

"Naw, Mick takes it. He's gonna hate losin' that nine-forty. Fifteen percent—"

"It is that. You do percentages in your head?"

"Sure, that's easy."

"I see. So now you're out. Suppose you had stayed in. At eighteen, you would graduate. Even with your minimal skills and application, you would receive your diploma. Then you emerge and offer your talents to a waiting world. Did you have any plans as to what you would do?"

"Find a job, I guess. There's supposed to be plenty of jobs around."

"In laundries, or fast food places. Or running a scanner, there are usually jobs in data entry. There is also the Job Corps, makework jobs, cleaning litter from parks. Plenty of those. That sound good?"

"Naw, but there's other stuff."

"Not for you," Hamel said sadly. "The fact is that perhaps two dozen of your classmates will have any skills anyone wishes to pay for. Of course nearly everyone has the grades to go on to junior college."

Rick shuddered.

"You wouldn't learn anything there, of course," Hamel continued. "But it would keep you off the streets, and separate you from the genuinely stupid. Better than nothing, but still pretty much a dead end."

"Education incentive, too. Goes up to a grand a month."

"A thousand a month to stay in junior college for two years. Do you think you would learn anything you could sell?"

"I don't know," Rick protested. He shook his head. "The way you talk, I guess not. So who gets the real jobs?"

"Who do you think? Those who have salable skills. A few of your classmates, perhaps, but mostly students from Company schools." Hamel shook his head sadly. "I have lived to see the transformation of the United States from a republic to a feudal aristocracy. Not pretty."

"I don't know what you're talking about."

"No, I don't suppose you do. You ask who gets the real jobs. Simple: people with real knowledge and drive. There are jobs for them. Not for an arrogant, semi-literate, unfocused, troublemaking know-nothing. Not for amoral, idle, cynical wasters, which is what you'd be if you stayed here. I told you I had good news, but you may find it hard to see it that way. Here it is: you are fortunate to be expelled from this school. Had you remained you would have wasted another two years, and at the end of it you'd have no more knowledge or capability than you have today."

Rick stood up. "I don't need to take this crap from anybody. I'm going."

"Very well. Going where?"

Rick shook his head. "I dunno, Mick's going to kill me." He knew how it would happen. When they found out that the education incentive would stop, his mother would scream and Mick—Rick's "stepfather," though he certainly wasn't—

would tell her to shut her yap. Then they would start in on each other. Finally when the fight between them cooled off they would gang up and turn it all on him.

"Going home, I guess. I got a truce with the gangs but I can't be out after dark unless I pay, and I don't have any money."

"And tomorrow morning, when you get up and school is closed to you?"

"I don't know. Look for a job."

"Selling dope?"

"I don't know, what else is there?"

"Theft. Shoplifting. Working for a pimp. Admittedly those don't pay as well as being a pusher, but they stay out of jail somewhat longer. Live longer too."

Rick knew what that meant. Most rackets were controlled by gangs, or even by adult mobsters. Mick, his current stepfather, claimed to have mob connections, but nobody believed him. Especially not Rick, because Rick had asked about getting set up in a good racket, and Mick kept stalling him off. Rick was sure that Mick didn't know jack shit about real rackets. And if you didn't have connections, you wouldn't last long, either get busted or shot, or maybe both. "All right, I don't know," Rick said.

"I assumed as much. However, I have a suggestion." Mr. Hamel handed Rick a small yellow card. "Can you read what is written there?"

Rick stared at the card in the fading light. "Eight-one-five-two." He paused. The numbers were easy but the words were long and unfamiliar. At last he shook his head. "Not without a reader."

"Then I will tell you. It says, eighty-one fifty-two Chatterjee Boulevard, suite five hundred. Can you remember that, and find the place?"

"Sure." Rick stared at the card. "Say it again."

"Yes, eighty-one fifty-two Chatterjee Boulevard, suite five hundred."

"Got it." Now that he'd heard the words he could sort of read the card, at least enough to remind him.

"If you go there tomorrow there is a possibility of useful employment."

"A job?"

"Exactly. Not an easy job, but a worthwhile one. You may keep the card."

Rick studied the words, silently mouthing them to himself. "I know how to get to Chatterjee Boulevard. If I went there tonight, would someone be in suite five hundred?"

"I cannot say, but it is not impossible." Hamel stood up. "I must go now. But you have the right idea. Action is usually preferable to inaction."

Rick stood up too. He wanted somehow to thank Mr. Hamel, but he did not know how. "Why are you doing this for me?"

Hamel paused. "Certainly it is not because I like you, Luban. I do not. As I said, you are a fool. And you are—"

"Ignorant, cynical, amoral, and unthinking. I heard you."

"Correct. Did I omit lazy? But you are not stupid. You are, I think, basically very intelligent. However, all forms of intelligence and aptitude tests that might suggest one student is more able or talented than another were long since judged discriminatory, and banished from our school system. Therefore, I have no objective basis for my conjecture. But I do hate waste. You and your friends have been wasting your lives."

Hamel nodded and started to walk away, a small, stooped figure in the twilight. "Do you think I'll get a job?" Rick called after him.

"I cannot say." Hamel did not pause or turn around. "But if you do, wait a while before you thank me for it."

Mr. Hamel had sensed the truth: Rick could not face going home. The school might not have called his mother, but somebody would have called, and they'd make sure she knew there wouldn't be any more education incentive money. Nine hundred and forty bucks a month. Fifteen percent. He never got any of that money, but it would be his fault they weren't getting it, and they'd make him pay. Mick would wait up for him, drunk or drugged but anyway in a foul temper. If only, when Rick finally had to go to the apartment, he could tell them that he already had some sort of job, some way to bring home some money . . .

It seemed like the thinnest of straws to grasp at as he descended from the overhead Public Vehicle at the corner of Chatterjee Boulevard and began to walk along toward number 8152. He had to push his way through crowds of young men and women, standing or wandering aimlessly along the littered street. They were part of the Pool. Not more than one in ten of the Pool would have a job of any kind—ever. Yet most of them had graduated high school and junior college, and some of them a real college. Rick had already known most of the things that Mr. Hamel had told him. He had just never thought about them.

*They didn't want us to think about them.* Rick remembered what Mr. Hamel had said about self-esteem. He'd heard some of that before, too, but hadn't understood. *They want us to feel good and not think about the future. It works, too, why should we?*

Number 8152 was a ten-story windowless building, its featureless walls made of gray lightweight carbon composite.

Rick waited stoically as his ID was verified by the automatic guard and the card given to him by Mr. Hamel was read. It was close to eight o'clock at night. On the way here he had convinced himself that suite 500 would be empty.

That conviction grew when he at last stood outside the entrance of the suite. He could see through the shatterproof glass door that it was just one room. It had plenty of computers and displays inside, but no people.

He touched the attention panel anyway, and was astonished when after about ten seconds a woman's voice responded, "You are at an office of Vanguard Mining and Refining. Please identify yourself."

Rick went through the ID process all over again. He showed the little card and stumbled through the explanation that it had been given to him by Mr. Hamel, and why. The woman did not say another word, but at last the door swung open. Rick went in. The door closed behind him and one of the television monitors came alive.

"Sit down right here."

Rick took the only seat near the monitor. Now he could see the woman on the screen. She was small, thin, and sharp-featured, and somehow reminded him of an animal. A rat? No. Not quite.

She was examining something in front of her, not visible to Rick. "You are sixteen years old. You have been expelled from school. And it is eight o'clock your time. Right?"

Each of the statements was true enough, but taken together they made little sense.

"That's right."

"I want you to tell me exactly why you were expelled from school. Take your time and give as much detail as you can. I'll try not to interrupt. If I do there will be a delay of about five seconds between what you say, and my comment or question. So you may have to back up occasionally and say things over. Go ahead."

There was a temptation to lie, or put things in a way more favorable to Rick. Some instinct warned him that would be a mistake. He recounted the whole episode, from the arrival of Willis Preebane to Rick's interrogation and expulsion by Principal Rigden. It was difficult to talk about the condoms and the booby trap. After the fact it sounded so stupid and pointless and unfunny. Rick was sure that any hope of employment with Vanguard Mining was evaporating with every word he said. He plowed on, ending with his decision to come to this office tonight even though it was so late.

"Not late where I am," the woman replied. "I got up just two hours ago. But are you tired?"

Just got up. She had to be somewhere on the other side of the Earth! The speech delay must be caused by the satellite link. "I'm not tired."

"Good. Can you read?"

"A little bit." But five seconds was far too long for a satellite link delay. Rick struggled to remember things that had never before been of the slightest interest to him. Radio signals traveled at the speed of light. But how fast did light travel?

"Can you write?"

"Just a few things."

"Hell." The woman's opinion of his reply showed more in her tone of voice than in her comment. "Well, no matter. Anyone can learn to read and write. We'll manage. I want to give you a whole set of things called aptitude tests. First, though, we have to deal with a few formalities. You never had tests like this in school, because they're forbidden in public programs. We're a private company but still the tests can't be given to you without suitable consent. In the case of someone like you, less than eighteen years old, that consent has to come from a parent or guardian."

Rick felt an awful sinking feeling. He was going to be sent home after all with nothing to tell except his expulsion from school.

"Problem with that?" The woman must have been studying his face. "Tell you what. Suppose that we give you the tests anyway, see how you do. If the results are good you can get consent later and we'll postdate the tests. If they're not good, we purge the test results from our files and you're no worse off."

What she was suggesting sounded illegal—but if that didn't worry Vanguard Mining, it sure didn't worry Rick. He took a deep breath.

"I'm ready."

"Any last question before we begin?" Rick shook his head, then changed his mind. "You said you just got up. Is it morning where you are?"

"Morning, afternoon, evening, anything you choose to call it." The woman smiled, to show small, sharp teeth. Rick suddenly caught the right animal resemblance. Not a rat, but a weasel—though he had never actually seen a live weasel. Mr. Hamel had somehow taught Rick more biology than either of them realized.

"I'm on CM-2, one of Vanguard Mining's translunar training stations," the woman went on, "about seven hundred thousand kilometers away from Earth. But the tests will be delivered where you are by a local program. I'll still be here if you get stuck. Don't call me unless you absolutely have to, though—the tests are timed. Ready to go?"

Rick nodded. His heart was racing and his mouth felt too dry to speak. The woman's picture vanished from the screen and was replaced by a sequence of numbers.

"Good luck," said her disembodied voice. "Do well on your tests—and one day maybe you'll come out here and see this place for yourself."

Seven weeks of mind-numbing briefings, endless questions, and bruising physical tests and conditioning; they were all converging, collapsing now to a single, final minute.

Rick had been strapped into his seat for more than an hour. Next to him sat Deedee Mao, another of Vanguard Mining's recent recruits. Like him she had been expelled from her school at sixteen years old, but beyond that they had little in common. She was from the East Coast, three thousand miles away from Rick. She was big, loud, and self-confident, just the sort of aggressive female that he hated. They had taken all their courses together, and she and Rick had argued furiously and continuously during the final three weeks; but since boarding the LEO transfer vehicle neither of them had said a word.

That silence suited Rick. He didn't want to talk to anybody. He could not take his eyes from the changing digits of the display.

Sixty-two—sixty-one. A siren began to wail inside the ship. Only one more minute to liftoff.

He knew, intellectually, that riding the single-stage-to-orbit ship was not much more dangerous than taking a PV across the city. So why was he gripping the arms of his seat so hard? He tried to move his mind to other things. All he could think of was the bitter memory of his last hours at home.

His stepfather didn't try to hide his relief at getting rid of Rick, the "troublemaker" too bad even for the school system, the extra mouth not even good for the educational incentive. On the first night, when Rick came home and told them that he had done well on the Vanguard Mining tests and needed parental consent to accept a job with them in the Belt, Mick had asked, "When do you go, and how much do they pay to get you?"

No congratulations; no discussion of the job itself, no worry about possible hazards of an off-Earth assignment. No query as to how long it would be before Rick returned. Just, "When do you go?"

His mother had moaned and wept, but she could not keep her eyes away from the credit slip provided by Vanguard Mining—the "sweetener" that expressed the company's financial appreciation of her willingness to sign over to them the parental control of her child.

There was an odd whirring sound and a vibration of the metal surface beneath Rick's feet. The hatch was moving to its final sealed setting. That meant that the lasers were powered up, waiting for their first discharge. The cover beneath the SSTO would have opened, to reveal the ablative layers.

Forty, thirty-nine, thirty-eight . . .

Rick tried to concentrate on factual matters. The first minute would be the most uncomfortable. That's when he and Deedee and fourteen others would feel the highest acceleration. After that the ground lasers would be switched off and the onboard nuclear rocket would cut in. The acceleration force on them would drop to two gees.

Thirty-two, thirty-one, thirty . . .

There were voices in the background. The ground crew for the ship, only five people. Their duties had been explained as part of the "informed consent" briefing.

The moving display in front of him seemed to have slowed, minutes passing between each second. Before he started training, Rick had imagined that travel to and in space would be conducted wearing spacesuits. The briefings had taught him that was an idiotic idea, as out-of-date as the notion that aircraft passengers all wore parachutes. Rick was dressed in the same informal uniform of blue shirt and slacks that had become familiar to him since the day he signed up with Vanguard Mining.

Twenty, nineteen, eighteen . . .

Almost as safe as a trip on the PV, the briefings said. But every day the media carried news of PV accidents. The vehicle he was sitting in felt far more vulnerable. Laser power could fail; the nuclear rocket could refuse to cut in; or it could refuse to turn off at the right time and hurtle the passengers away to nowhere. You could sometimes walk away from a PV accident. Had anyone ever walked away from a transfer vehicle failure?

Rick tried to steel himself for anything. He failed. It was with total astonishment that he suddenly felt a hand on his thigh.

You were supposed to keep your arms and hands flat on the padded seat support during launch. Rick turned. Deedee Mao was staring straight ahead of her. Her yellow face was oddly pale and rigid, but her fingers were squeezing and rubbing his leg.

"Wanna get it on when we're on the training station?" She could only be speaking to him, but he could hardly hear her or see her lips moving. "Y'know, in free fall. I hear it's somethin' special."

It was the worst possible time for a sexual proposition. Even if he had liked Deedee, Rick was far too nervous to feel horny.

But he wasn't going to admit to her or anyone else just how he did feel.

"Sure." His voice sounded like an old man's. He cleared his throat. "Sure." Then he couldn't say any more.

Twelve, eleven, ten . . . "I'll be in c-cabin t-t—." Deedee's fingers on his thigh were trembling. "Cabin t-t-twenty-eight."

Five, four, three—

"Oh, sweet Lord—"

Her hand was trembling worse. With fear, not passion. Rick felt a strange sympathy. Deedee was looking for distraction, anything to help her through the first seconds of launch.

"She's tracking," a crewman's voice said.

"Mirror's free."

Two, one . . .

Anything. And he needed distraction as much as she did.

Zero. "Up ship." As the final digit flickered into sight, Rick broke the rules, too. He lifted his arm from the padded support, and placed his hand on top of Deedee's.

Within half a second he knew that he had made the mistake of the century. Lift had begun. Deedee's hand and his own were suddenly welded together, pressed down by more than five gees of acceleration. His leg was tilted slightly upward and their joined hands inched up his thigh toward his groin.

Rick gasped with pain. If that monster weight kept moving up his body, it would turn him into a eunuch. He tried to lift his hand and arm and found them sheathed in lead. He could not raise his hand, let alone Deedee's. All he could do, with one desperate jerk, was push their hands a couple of inches away along his leg and hold them there.

The pain and pressure was excruciating. Deedee's whole forearm lay across his thigh. He could feel bruises forming there in real-time. He sat silent and sweating, pushing and pushing forever, until without warning all weight vanished completely. His stomach at once came free of its moorings and started to float up into his throat, but before he had time to gag he was again pressed back into his seat.

"Power's on."

This time the force was endurable. It had to be the two gees of the nuclear drive, though compared with the laser-boosted liftoff it felt like nothing.

Rick lifted his hand away from Deedee's, closed his eyes, and relaxed. After a few moments he felt her hand leave his thigh.

"Luban."

"Yeah?" He opened his eyes and glanced across at her. Deedee Mao's smooth yellow face was still pale but now it bore its usual belligerent expression.

"Don't get no funny ideas, Luban."

"Like what?"

"I mean, about what I said back there at liftoff."

"I won't."

"I mean, I was just making conversation."

"Like hell. You were scared white. You should change your name from Deedee to pee-pee. You were ready to pee in your pants."

"Making love to you appeals less than screwing a swamp toad."

"I guess you've tried that. Tough on the toad."

She reached over and grabbed his arm. "Listen, if you want to have this out when we get to the station that's fine by me. I've eaten smart-ass jerks like you—"

She paused. The steady roar beneath them had ended. Suddenly they were in free fall, gliding upward in dead silence. Rick once more felt his stomach start to move up his throat.

"—eaten them for breakf—" Deedee couldn't complete the word. Her brown eyes bulged and her mouth clamped shut. She turned away from Rick, reaching forward and trying to hold off long enough to get her suction mask into position.

Rick clenched his own teeth and closed his eyes again. He wished he could close his ears, too. Any smart-ass jerks that Deedee had eaten for breakfast were coming up again, along with everything else; and from the sound of it Deedee was just getting into her stride. Rick didn't want to watch.

Sex in free fall—or, fighting, or anything else with the possible exception of dying—didn't seem to be in Rick and Deedee's immediate future.

Rick had been told many things about Vanguard Mining's operations, but he lacked the glue to put the pieces together. For instance, he knew from his briefings that franchises for commercial mining of the Belt had bogged down in endless debate within the Council of Nations. That deadlock had continued until the Council's own international (and multilingual) mining effort had ended in disaster, with the loss of all equipment and personnel.

At that point, business interests were suddenly permitted to mine the Belt—and welcome to it. The Council had decided that there was no profit to be made there, although they were more than ready to accept franchise fees. They were astonished when Vanguard Mining's prototype mine and refinery, in 2028, turned out to be profitable. In the sixteen years since then the company had established commercial mining and refining operations on thirty-eight different planetoids out in the Belt.

Rick knew all that. He had also been told, at the time of his first tests by Vanguard, that the woman speaking to him was located on a place called CM-2, in translunar orbit. It never occurred to him to connect those facts until the translunar vehicle carrying the trainees was close enough for Rick to actually see CM-2.

He had been expecting some sleek, clean-lined structure. Instead he found their vehicle was closing on a vast irregular lump of dark rock.

"That thing?" Rick spoke to Deedee, who was standing between him and Jigger Tait, a Vanguard miner who was hitching a ride back from Earth with the trainees. "That can't be the training center."

In the two days since first liftoff, Rick and Deedee had been observing a sort of armed truce. Neither one was sure enough of stomach stability to risk an assertion of superiority. So it was Jigger, big-boned, iron-stomached, unaffected by freefall, and apparently totally self-confident in every way, who raised his pale eyebrows, sniffed disdainfully, and said, "Don't you guys know *anything*? That's CM-2 out there—commercial mine number two."

"But I thought the mines were all in the Belt."

"They are. But this one has been worked out commercially. When the nickel and iron and platinum and iridium were all gone they attached low-thrust engines and moved it to translunar, so now it's the headquarters for the training school."

"I don't remember that from the briefings." Rick looked questioningly at Deedee, who shook her head.

"Me neither."

"Then you didn't use the browse feature on your reader."

"We weren't told we had to."

Jigger sniffed again. "I'm sure you weren't. But I'll give you some free advice that I had to learn the hard way when I was a trainee: If you only do what you're told to do, you'll soon be in trouble at Vanguard Mining." Jigger lifted from his seat, moving effortlessly in the zero-gee environment. "Okay kids. Better get your act together and strap in. We'll be docking in a couple more minutes."

He floated away toward the rear of the ship. Rick and Deedee lingered at the screen for a few seconds longer, peering at the object ahead of the transfer vehicle. Now that they were closer they could see how big it was. Each of the wartlike bubbles that covered the surface of the planetoid was actually the exit point for a three-meter mine shaft. The whole object must be riddled with tunnels. CM-2 was more like a whole world than a training station.

The now-familiar warning siren began to wail. Thrust was coming in sixty seconds. Rick led the way back to their seats, striving to mimic the easy free-space motion of Jigger Tait. He couldn't do it. After a few seconds of aimless drifting he was forced to pull himself along using seat backs as handholds. Convinced that Deedee was watching him and laughing, he turned his head. She had just bounced off a wall and was turning end-over-end with a bewildered expression on her face.

One thing about free fall, Rick thought as they reached CM-2 and went through docking, pressurization, and disembarkation: it made you a lot less likely to laugh at somebody else—because you never knew how soon your turn would come to look like an idiot.

As he left the pressurized dock he turned and caught a glimpse of Earth through the transparent overhead dome. It hung above him, about twice as big as a full Moon.

He halted and stared up at it for a long time. Somewhere on that globe was his school, with Screw and Hoss and Juanita and Jackie, with Mr. Hamel and Mr. Preebane and Principal Rigden. They were seven hundred thousand kilometers away.

They felt more like seven hundred million.


"Let me introduce myself." The man was plump and balding, with fleshy cheeks and drooping jowls. "I'm Turkey Gossage, chief of the training program on CM-2. You can think of me as the principal here—the head teacher. You don't know it yet, but I'm the best thing that ever happened to you."

Rick had taken a position near the back. He craned for a better look. The man in front of the group was dressed in a black tank top and jeans rather than the standard blue jacket and slacks. He scowled aggressively as he stared at them, but his blue eyes were sparkling. There had been a low general mutter from the group, and he was reacting to it.

"You heard me, sweethearts? The best thing. So if you got something to say, get it off your chests now."

No one spoke.

"You, sweetheart." Gossage pointed a finger at a woman in the front row. "I see your mouth moving, but I don't hear you. Don't whisper. Tell all of us."

"Don't you call me sweetheart!" It was Deedee, not much to Rick's surprise. "You can't do that."

"I can't, eh?" Gossage was grinning, but his neck and jowls turned red as turkey wattles. It was suddenly obvious how he got his nickname. "Why not?"

"Because it's degrading, and it's insulting. It's also sexually discriminatory. Do it one more time, and I'll take you to court." Deedee paused.

"You mean you'll sue me?" Gossage grinned again, but now it was unexpectedly friendly. "Sweetheart, that word is music to my ears. It proves we've got innocent new blood out here on CM-2, and it leads me straight in to what I have to say to all of you. Let's get a few things out of the way right now. First, forget the sexual discrimination talk. I call everyone sweetheart. You, and bluebeard standing next to you, and the one at the back with the shitface grin on his chops." Gossage was looking right at Rick. Rick stopped smiling.

"Far as I'm concerned," Gossage went on, "you're all sweethearts 'til you prove otherwise. As for suing me, the best of British luck to you. You're not on sue-'em-all Earth now. We got exactly two lawyers out beyond the Moon, and they're up to their asses in mineral depletion allowances and tax codes. If you can afford their time, you don't belong here. And if you did manage to sue, you'd lose for reasons that I'll go into in a minute. So tell me what else is on your mind. You were angry before I ever called you sweetheart."

Deedee shook her head. It was another youth in the second row who spoke up. "What's this teacher bullshit? I done with school three months ago. Nuthin' 'bout school in anythin' anybody said to me."

"I see. What's your name?"

"Cokie Mulligan."

"All right, Cokie Mulligan. Nothing about school in anything anybody said to you. Right. You read your contract, did you? The one that you and your parents or guardians signed."

"Sure I did."

"The whole thing? Including the fine print?"

Mulligan hesitated. "Yes."

"Then you noticed the place where it says that Vanguard Mining, and in particular its authorized instructors—people like me—are *in loco parentis* to you for the duration of your contract."

"Whaz zat mean?"

"*In loco parentis* means in place of your parents." Turkey Gossage smiled horribly at Mulligan. "So now I'm like your daddy and your mommy, all rolled up into one. And I'm going to take better care of you than they ever did."

Mulligan shook his head. "Maybe. But I don't want no teacher, an' I'm not goin' to no dumb school. I hate school and I'm done with school. I never signed up for that."

There was a general mutter of agreement from everyone in the group.

"I see." Turkey Gossage turned, floated across to a chair facing the front of the room, and straddled it with his forearms folded along the back. "What we have here, I suspect, is a simple failure to communicate. It's that hated word, *school,* isn't it? It suggests the wrong thing to all of you, and I shouldn't have used it.

"All right. Let's agree that this isn't a school. Let's say it's a survival course for off-Earth mining operations. The Belt is a dangerous place. You can fuck up bigtime out there, eat vacuum, OD on radiation, blow yourself up, get flattened by an ore crusher, get stranded and starve to death. No legal liability for Vanguard Mining—read your contract. But Vanguard doesn't want you dead, because it cost us money to get you here, and it'll cost more to send you out to the Belt. We have an investment in you. So it's my job to make sure that by the time you leave here you know how to avoid killing yourself. That means learning a few new rules. Anybody object to the idea of surviving?" Rick shook his head and glanced around at the others. Everyone was doing the same.

"Good." The smile had never left Turkey Gossage's face. "Now we get down to details. I'm going to give you assignments that have to be completed before bedtime. But before we talk about them I want to talk about you. I'm sure you all think you're hotshot and special and smarter than most people. And you actually are—otherwise you wouldn't be here at all. But smart or not, at the moment you're still zeroes. No skills means no value.

"Before we're through here, that will change. You'll have skills. You'll have value. Out here you'll earn that self-esteem they shovel at downers. If you live long enough you'll have a reason to think you're hot-shot and special. And it all starts with the assignments. Today it will be reading. All right?"

Nods all round.

"Just one thing." Turkey Gossage was deliberately casual. "I said reading, and I meant reading. By you. Not with a reading machine. There will be times out in the Belt where a knowledge of complex instructions is vital and no electronic readers are available. So you have to be able to read. I'll let you into a big secret, something you'd never be told in an Earth school: reading is easy. Practically everyone can learn to read with a bit of effort. All of you can, or you wouldn't be here. And we won't go too fast at first. Short words, easy sentences." There was a stir at the back of the class. A short-haired and overweight blond girl was moving toward the door.

"Now where are you going?" Gossage did not raise his voice. "Leaving us already?"

She turned angrily at the doorway. "Yes, I am."

"What's your name?"

"I'm Gladys de Witt. I didn't read none when I was in school, and I'm damned if I'm going to start now I'm out of it. Go fuck yourself, Gossage. You think you're the boss, but you're not. You can't stop me leaving. I seen the contract. I don't have to stay. It says you can't use violence on me, neither."

"That's quite true. I can't prevent anyone of you from leaving. I can't be violent with you. And I can't make you complete your assignments." Gossage nodded slowly. "Very true. All I can do, Gladys de Witt, is explain these to you." He held up a handful of small pink cards. "They are meal vouchers. You need one to obtain food from the cafeteria service system. When you complete your assignment satisfactorily— by this evening, or tomorrow morning, or tomorrow midday, or whenever—you will receive one voucher. But if you fail to complete your assignment to my satisfaction, you will not."

"You can't do that to me!"

"I'm afraid I can. Read your contract. Vanguard Mining, *in loco parentis,* decides the manner and extent of trainee nutrition. Now, Gladys. Are you going to leave? Cookie has some oatmeal and vitamin pills, you get all that you want. Or would you like to stay here with the rest of the trainees while I explain today's assignment? Dinner is lasagna with mushrooms, peppers, and garlic bread. The choice is yours."

Turkey Gossage could smile and coax with the best of them, but he was one tough son-of-a-bitch. He hadn't been kidding about the food voucher policy. After a couple of missed meals, even the toughest and most ornery—and hungriest—trainee came into angry line.

Rick observed closely, then put Turkey Gossage into his "handle with care" category. What he couldn't understand, though, was how Gossage had found himself such a pleasant, easy-going—and droolingly sexy—assistant.

Gina Styan was a graduate trainee from three years back, returned for two months to work with Gossage on CM-2 before she went to her post on the newest of the thirty-eight Belt mines. She had a figure that made Juanita Cesaro look like a boy, clear dark skin, and cropped black hair that emphasized delicate bone structure and high cheekbones. Those, plus what Rick read as an unmistakable interest in her brown eyes whenever she looked at him, bristled the hair on the back of his neck. The sight of her made him catch his breath.

She had the hots for him, too. He was sure of it. All it would take was a quiet place and an opportunity.

Which seemed to be exactly what CM-2 was designed not to provide. It was just as well that Deedee Mao's liftoff invitation to cabin twenty-eight had been bogus, because it now proved to be impossible. She shared cabin twenty-eight with three other trainess. Rick was no better off. His cabin had five recruits in it, including Cokie Mulligan who snored like a saw in free fall, though he swore he hadn't when he was back on Earth.

It was no better during work periods. The recruits were never out of each other's sight, except when they were busy on their assignments. Then they were permitted the privacy of a single small cubicle. After the first week Rick suspected Turkey Gossage of doing that on purpose. When the only way to be alone was to sit in a little room by yourself and pretend to study, you found yourself actually studying much of the time out of sheer boredom.

Almost against his will, Rick found himself reading. He still wasn't good, and he resented every word, but within a couple of weeks he'd have beaten everybody in his old class and most of his fellow trainees. He was in no hurry to rush on ahead of them. After reading, Turkey Gossage threatened pure and applied mathematics—"the high spot of all your training," as he put it, without convincing anyone.

But all this left Rick's problem with Gina Styan unsolved. How was he ever going to make out with her if they were never alone?

A possible answer came in the third week, when the pure theory of space operations gave way to practical experience. All the trainees had become accustomed to free fall, so nausea was a thing of the past. But manual work in space was another matter. That took lots of practice.

And practice they were going to get, in assignments that Turkey Gossage described as "manual coordination and control in a weightless environment." A euphemism, as Rick soon discovered, for unpaid hard labor. *Weightless environment.* Moving things around in space, where an object didn't weigh anything, sounded easy as breathing. Nothing to it. Jigger Tait, staying awhile on CM-2 with Turkey Gossage before shipping to the Belt again, assured Rick as much. Then he and Rick went together to the deep interior of CM-2 to clear one of the chambers. They moved massive pilings and metal I-beams and irregular chunks of rock.

After four hours of that Rick ached in every bone. His burdens might have no weight, but they still possessed inertia. And inertia was *worse* than weight. Back on Earth, once you had lifted something you could just let it drop and gravity would do the rest. Here you had to start a rock moving, then put in just as much work to stop it.

But Jigger had not been lying. He did the work effortlessly. It was easy as breathing—for him.

Rick wondered how many other half-truths and hidden catches were tucked away in the Vanguard Mining training program. Turkey Gossage was sticking to his policy on the meal vouchers. Rick had handed in his last assignment late, and been handed a meal ticket just before he had to leave with Jigger. It sat burning a hole in his pocket while his stomach growled in protest. He could hardly wait for the word to quit.

But when Jigger Tait told him they were done for the day, Rick still had enough energy and curiosity to notice something when they emerged through the airlock from the planetoid's stony interior. It was a different lock from their entry point and next to it sat another small chamber. It was like no other structure that Rick had seen. There were flat, solid, windowless walls and a massive close-fitting door.

Rick's question produced no more than a shrug and a dismissive "Historical interest only." Jigger Tait would have continued back around the planetoid toward the training facility quarters, but Rick stopped in front of him and swung open the heavy door.

"Hey! Padded floor and walls. What's the deal?"

"Bolt-hole." Jigger followed him inside. The interior

lights had come on automatically. "Before the mining produced deep interior tunnels, the miners always faced a radiation danger. Our suits aren't enough to protect us."

"Solar flares?"

"Yeah." Jigger stared at Rick. "I thought you couldn't read."

"Movies. Show it as standard hazard for space travel."

"Well, for once they got it right. If you're out on the surface of an asteroid and a big flare hits, you have three choices: you can move to the interior tunnels, if there are any, or you can head for a special shielded chamber like this one. Me, I'll take this any day. Your own air, see, the interior fills by itself when the door is locked. And there's plenty of reserves of food and drink. Stay here for a week if you had to."

"But there's no airlock."

"There is on the inside. That was put in later. When they built this they figured anyone coming in from space might be in one hell of a hurry."

"You said there are three choices?"

"Sure." Jigger was already moving back through the thick door. "You can stay outside and fry if you want to. Freedom of choice. Isn't that what people back on Earth are all so proud of?"

"Freedom to die?"

"Sure. Most basic right of all." Jigger started around the planetoid, swinging easily along on the fixed network of cables. "Hell, you should be free to die when you want, where you want, how you want. If you're not, your body and your life don't belong to you at all. They belong to your keepers."

"You can die any way you want to?"

"Sure. Anyone works for Vanguard Mining has that right. But dying is a right, not an obligation. So watch your step, Rick. Space is more dangerous than you think."

✻  ✻  ✻

Rick remembered those words, more or less. But what he thought about a lot more in the next few days was that shielded chamber. Radiation-proof—and soundproof. He visited it a couple more times when he had no other duties. Thick walls, padded floor, and tight-fitting door. Total privacy. Just what he needed.

It took four days before he could trade with Gladys de Witt for her next one-on-one training session with Gina Styan in the interior of CM-2. Fortunately Gladys had her own hot ideas about Jigger Tait. She didn't tell Rick what this particular training was for, and Rick didn't ask. He'd move a lot of rocks for a chance at Gina.

This time his job turned out to be both easier and harder than manual labor. Rick had to learn to operate remote-controlled cutting equipment, and Gina proved to be a hell of a tough teacher. She ran him through scores of operating steps again and again, watching him with that slightly mocking, sexy, and intimate look on her face whenever he messed up a sequence.

"There's a hell of a lot to this." Rick felt obliged to defend himself when the session ended with the cutter under his control waltzing wildly sideways to gouge a hole in the tunnel side wall. "How long did it take you to remember all the variations?"

"I'm not sure I ever did."

"You have a pictorial prompt in your suit helmet? Then why in hell didn't you give me one?"

"No prompt." Gina waved a small red book at Rick. "The control steps are in here, along with a lot of other stuff. But it's all in words and formulas. Once you can read—"

"This is really dumb. A few simple pictures, that's all it would take."

"You think so? Listen to this, then you tell me how you would put it into pictures. 'Pressure equalization between old and new drilling is best achieved by releasing stored air into the evacuated chamber. The cutting equipment normally produces a straight cylindrical cavity three meters in diameter, so the volume to be filled is simply 2.25 *pi* L cubic meters, where L is the length of the new drilled tunnel in meters.' You know what *pi* is?"

"I think so. I'm not sure." Rick was actually quite sure. Sure he didn't.

"It's a mathematical constant. Draw me a picture of that if you can. Do you know its value?"

Rick shook his head. This wasn't going the way he had imagined it, but he'd bide his time. Let Gina feel superior for the moment. She would find out soon enough who was the real boss.

"Why should I bother to know any of that math stuff? If I ever need it I'll pull it up on a calculator."

"*Pi* is equal to 3.14159." She didn't seem to have heard him. "That's to six significant figures. It's as accurate as you'll probably ever need unless you get into orbit work. You'll have the value of *pi* engraved on your brain stem and your butt before you leave CM-2, along with a lot of other numbers you've never heard of yet. And while we're at it, let me tell you what happens to a calculator or an electronic prompter during a blowout or a big radiation storm: they die, or they become totally unreliable. But this"—Gina held up the red book—"can stand more than radiation, heat, and cold than you can. By the time a book like this became unusable, you and I would be long dead." She tucked the book into a pocket on her suit. "You'll learn. Let's go."

Rick had learned, at least some things. He had spent many hours studying and committing to memory the network of passages and chambers that criss-crossed the interior of CM-2. Without saying anything to Gina he headed for the surface along a particular set of passages. He emerged, just as planned, right beside the shielded chamber. The door was as he had left it, slightly ajar.

He stopped when he came to it.

"You ever been in one of these before?"

"Ages ago. This, or one just like it." Gina was glancing around her with no particular interest. "I don't know why they keep this place in working order. It has no uses since the interior was excavated."

"It does." Rick swung the heavy door into position and pressed the sealing button. Interior lights came on at once and there was a hiss of released air. He went across and checked that the inner door was also sealed.

"Not needed for radiation protection," he went on, "but it has other uses." He took off his suit helmet and gestured to Gina to do the same.

"You're wasting air." But Gina did not sound much concerned by that, and she followed Rick's lead and removed her own helmet. "Other uses? Like what?"

"Like this." Rick had been sizing up their positions and rehearsing his own next action. He knew the moves and he was pretty experienced, but that had been back on Earth. He had to do things differently in free-fall.

The smart thing was to make the first step one that he knew very well. He was close to the chamber wall. He kicked off from it, drove hard across the room, and pinned Gina against the opposite wall. He had to use both arms and legs to hold her there, but they had finished face to face.

"Gina." He spoke in a whisper, though he could have screamed and no one else would have heard a thing. "Gina, you're really something special. Let's get out of these dumb suits and have some fun." He tried to kiss her, but she turned her head away.

"Dammit, Rick, that's enough fooling. And it's not funny. Let me go."

He almost did. Then he remembered Screw Savage's advice to him and Hoss. *"No* never means no with a woman. They say it because they like to play hard to get, but they really want it bad as you do. You gotta ignore what they *say* and keep chargin'. Go for the gold!"

Rick moved his left arm quickly to turn Gina's head back toward him, pressed his mouth to hers, and started to give her a French kiss. His right hand felt at the same time for her breast.

It was as though he had pressed a starter button. As his fingers met her left nipple through the resilient material of the suit, her right knee pistoned up between his legs. It hit him squarely in the crotch like a bony hammer.

Rick gasped and curled up into a ball, hanging in midair. He was sure that the blow had burst his testicles, or driven them right back inside his body. He vaguely heard Gina speak through his fog of pain.

"You little shit! *Nobody* does that to me, ever. Apologize." She had him by the ear, pulling it off his head. "Apologize, right now, or I'll really hurt you."

Rick was curled up, forehead close to his knees. He could hardly breathe, and he certainly couldn't apologize. But if he didn't, she might do the same thing to him again.

"Sorry!" It was more a gasp than a word. "Sorry."

"I don't know what made you think I'd be interested in a semi-literate oaf like you, but here's news: I'm not."

She let go of his ear, then clapped his helmet onto his head hard enough to make his ears ring. While he hung dizzy and helpless, she flipped his suit seals into position. "You can find your own way back, dummy, or die trying. I don't much care which."

Rick heard the inner door slam shut and the airlock cycling. He tried to lift his head to see if Gina had gone, until a worse worry took over. Nausea swept over him. He felt ready to vomit—inside his suit.

He swallowed hard, closed his eyes, and fought the urge. The spasm slowly faded. By the time it was over his forehead was beaded with cold sweat and the sickness had been replaced by an agonizing throbbing in his belly and groin.

Fifteen minutes passed before he felt well enough to leave the chamber. Then it was a miserable splay-legged crawl back to the training facilities. He paused before entering.

What had Gina told Turkey Gossage? Surely, the whole horrible episode. Rick was done for. He was going to be kicked out of this place, just as he had been kicked out of school. And where could he go now? Back to join the Pool on Earth?

He couldn't hang around outside forever, and there was no real point in trying to avoid Gossage. Better to get it over with.

Rick eased his way out of his suit and limped to Turkey's office. He didn't see anyone else on the way, and he almost changed his mind when he was right at the entrance. But Gossage had already seen him on the threshold and waved him in.

"You took your time." Gossage nodded to Rick and at once returned his attention to the screen in front of him. "I didn't think you'd make it before I closed for the day. Help yourself to your meal voucher."

Rick, tensed and ready for a storm of anger, stared at Gossage open-mouthed. "What did Gina say?"

Turkey really looked at Rick for the first time. "Say? Why, what do you think she said? You did well. I know you rammed the wall with the cutter at the end, but Gina said that the test she gave you was harder than anything in the standard course. So you passed. Now, go and eat. You must be starving."

Rick grabbed the voucher and left before Gossage could ask him anything. But he didn't feel in the least like eating, and still less like going into the cafeteria where he might have to face Gina. He was sore, exhausted, and bewildered. He started for his cabin, knowing that he needed rest. Then he visualized Cokie Mulligan and the other trainees, watching him stagger in and starting the questions.

He couldn't stand that, either. Where could he go?

The only place he could think of was the gym. It should be deserted. There was light centrifugal gravity, and showers. He could examine and bathe his bruised and tender parts, stretch out on a couch, and not move until it was time to wake up and use his meal voucher for breakfast.

He dragged his way toward the outer circle of the training area where the gym was located, thankful that it was a time when few people were about. Safe inside the bathhouse, he removed all his clothes and took a warm bath. He examined himself closely. So far as he could tell everything down there was perfectly normal. He didn't even seem to be swollen, though it felt that way from the inside. Finally he went into the shower, set the water temperature as hot as he could stand, and simply let the stream run over his head and back for a long time.

By the time he dried himself and put on a change of clothing he was feeling human again. He emerged from the shower area and stopped. The gym was no longer deserted. Jigger Tait was running laps, round and round the inside of the big hi-gee wheel. He must have been there for a while, because his blue tee-shirt was stained with sweat.

He nodded down at Rick when he caught sight of him and ran around the hoop of the track toward him. "Want to join me?"

Rick shook his head and started toward the exit. But he couldn't help moving in an awkward bow-legged fashion.

"You all right?" Jigger stepped closer.

"Yeah. I'm all right."

"You sure don't look it. You walk like you got a case of hemorrhoids or you just took a dump in your pants. What happened?"

"I just—" Rick paused. He didn't have a lie in his head. Anyway, Jigger would find out soon enough, along with everybody else. He sighed. "I just did something really dumb."

And suddenly it all came spilling out, even worse in retelling than in reality. Jigger stood and listened without saying a word, the sweat cooling on his moon face and steam rising from his damp tee-shirt. It was only after Rick told how he had made his move on Gina, and she had kneed him in the testicles, that Jigger shook his head and said, "Wish I'd been there."

"You'd have stopped her?"

"No. I'd have broken you in two." Jigger grabbed Rick by the arm and led him to a pair of rowing machines, the only place where the two of them could sit down facing each other. "How old are you, kid?"

"Sixteen."

"Thought so. Know how old Gina is?"

"Nineteen?"

"She's twenty-two. You're like a baby to her. Hell, you *are* a baby. Back in school you probably felt like a real big shot—I know I did. I'd had girls, busted teachers, the whole bit. But to Gina a kid from Earth is still in diapers. I'd say each year in space, 'specially in the Belt, is like three on Earth. You were a little kid making a pass at a grown-up."

"But she didn't report it to Gossage. And she passed me on the test I took."

"So it didn't really upset her. How'd you feel if a ten-year-old came on strong to you? You'd think it was ludicrous. And you were being tested for proficiency, not maturity. Anyway, believe it or not, Gina likes you. If she didn't she'd have ripped your balls off and stuffed them down your throat. Got away with it, too. What ever made you think for one second that she might be interested in you?"

"She looked at me like she was really fond of me."

"Yeah. Know why? Because you remind her of her kid brother. He's back on Earth and going nowhere, just the way she was before she was sent out here. Gina admits it, she used to be a real tearaway. Her parents couldn't do a damn thing with her. But her brother's less of a rebel, and she's afraid he'll just stick in school to the end and finish up in the Pool."

"You don't think she'll tell anyone about what I did?"

"Don't see why she should. But I'll talk to her and make sure."

"Will she listen to you?"

"I think so." Jigger stared at Rick for a second, his head to one side. "You're not too observant, are you? I mean, you've never noticed that Gina and I are an item, have been for a year and a half. That's why I came to CM-2 instead of heading right out for the Belt. That's why I know about her, and what a hellcat she used to be, and all about her kid brother."

Rick gazed at Jigger in horror. He had just remembered what Jigger said about breaking him in two. "I didn't know— I didn't notice. I'm sorry. I mean, if I'd had any idea that you two—"

"You know now. Nothing wrong with feeling horny, either—it means you're physically adjusting to space. But stick to trainees. And don't forget one other thing. California where you came from has the strongest laws in the known universe against sexual harassment and rape, but they still don't work worth a damn. Out here we do things differently. A woman is taught a few tricks so she can look after herself. Deedee and the rest of the women have had special training. Remember that if you want to keep your balls." Jigger stood up from the rowing machine, came across, and patted Rick on the shoulder. "And while your jewels are still sore, use what happened with Gina to remind you of one other thing: If you want to survive in space, it's not enough to be able to read and write and calculate. You have to learn to *notice* things—the sort of stuff you won't find in any book."

Rick skulked for a week. He hid away in the privacy of the study cubicles, until finally and inevitably he had the dreaded face-to-face meeting with Gina. She came into the cafeteria with a group of trainees while he was taking a hurried meal.

Rick froze. But her casual greeting suggested that nothing unusual had ever happened between them. Rick breathed a prayer of thanks and decided that he could return to a normal life.

He was wrong. That same afternoon he was summoned to Turkey Gossage's office. Worried again, he was in no hurry to get there and only a little relieved to find Deedee Mao arriving at the same time.

Gossage nodded them to seats on the other side of the circular table that he used as a desk. He went on studying a monitor, invisible to Rick and Deedee. He was muttering to himself, until at last he looked up.

"I guess you two think you're real hotshots. Or don't you know?" Rick glanced at Deedee. She seemed just as puzzled as he was.

"I guess not." Gossage was studying their faces. "So I'll tell you. The pair of you are sitting at the top of the trainee heap. You've done well. You'll have to screw up big time to avoid graduating."

Rick's pleasure at that news lasted for only a second, because Turkey was continuing. "Naturally, since you're such hotshots we want you to have a specially good chance to make a mess of things. For the pair of you the training course just moved beyond theory and supervised instruction. Tomorrow morning you'll be partners on a practical exercise in space ore mining. And I promise you, it won't be easy. I suggest you spend the rest of today studying the problem. You have until the close of the work day tomorrow to complete the assignment."

Rick and Deedee exchanged grimaces. They had pretty much avoided each other since their first liftoff into orbit. Now they were supposed to cooperate—even *depend* on each other.

"Studying *together*." Gossage had read their faces. "The more you know about each other's strengths and weaknesses, the better. And remember something else: in the real world you don't always get assigned to projects with your best buddies. Go get to work. The universe doesn't care how much people like each other."

The "practical exercise" that Gossage and his staff had prepared did not sound too hard. Rick and Deedee would load a five-hundred-ton ore carrier with low-grade tailings, controlling a semi-smart mining robot to do all the heavy work. They would fly the carrier to CM-2's refinery, drop off the ore, and return to the mine area on the empty carrier. Their own safe return through CM-2's interior would mark the end of the exercise.

But as Deedee remarked, the devil was in the details. Smartness in a mining robot was a mixed blessing, and the instructions given to it must limit its initiative. That meant learning the interaction manual and understanding the robot's powers and limitations. The ore carrier was no better. Examining its flight path and fuel needs, Rick and Deedee learned that the fuel supply provided for the round trip was barely enough. One mistake, even a small one, would leave them drifting helplessly away from CM-2 and calling for help from an empty carrier. Turkey Gossage, obviously by intention, had provided no precomputed flight trajectory.

Finally there was a hidden variable mentioned nowhere in the project description: according to training course rumor and legend, Gossage always threw in some extra problem on a practical test, a zinger that could not be predicted ahead of time. You found out about it when it hit you in the face.

Working with Deedee, Rick grudgingly had to admit that she was *smart*. She seemed less cocky and belligerent than he remembered her, and she caught on to new ideas at least as fast as he did. He suspected that in a pinch she could read and remember better. And she never seemed to get tired.

Rick tried to match her. He drove himself harder than ever before, until late at night they found themselves sitting side by side and staring helplessly at a set of schematics. The lines on the screen seemed to blur and curve as Rick watched. The circuit had to be completed correctly before the display would advance but nothing seemed to work.

"It *can't* be that hard," Rick muttered at last.

"It isn't." Deedee sighed and reached forward to turn off the display. "It's us. We've saturated. At least, I have. How about you?"

"An hour ago. I just didn't want to admit it." Rick stood and reached up to rub at his stiffened neck muscles. "Better get some sleep. We've got a big day ahead."

"Yeah." Deedee stretched. "I'm in cabin twenty-eight. Wanna get it on? Y'know, in free fall. I hear it's somethin' special."

Her tone of voice was casual and she wasn't looking at Rick. But she was smiling.

He shook his head. "Better with a swamp toad. God. That was us. Only a couple of months and it seems like ten years ago."

"It *was* ten years. Ten real years." Deedee headed for the exit. "Who said that time proceeds at a uniform rate? Whoever it was, he was crazy."

"Or she was."

"Fair enough. Good night, Rick."

"Night, Deedee. Sleep well."

Maybe she did. Rick certainly didn't. He woke long before he needed to, the details of the project swarming through his mind. After half an hour of tossing and turning he rose, dressed, and headed for the cafeteria. He was still ordering a meal when Deedee wandered in. Her face was calm but a little pale.

She came straight up to him. "Anything in the rules that says we can't start early?"

"Nothing I know of."

"Right. Let's get going."

"No." Rick gestured to the place opposite him. "First you eat."

"Hunger sharpens the brain."

"And low blood sugar turns it off." Rick keyed in a huge meal for her, then felt obliged to increase his own order. "We eat. Then we go."

They chewed doggedly, without enjoyment, watching

each other's plate until both were empty. By the time they had finished it was close to official breakfast time. Unwilling to talk to other trainees they hurried out and headed for the lock that led to the interior of CM-2.

The hardest thing of all was to avoid rushing. They put their suits on carefully and checked each other's seals. No little surprises there from Turkey Gossage. But as Deedee pointed out, he was not likely to do anything so obvious.

"Which means if he *did* do something obvious," Rick pointed out, "it *would* surprise us. No assumptions."

"Agreed. No assumptions."

They drifted together through the deep interior of CM-2, heading for the side of the planetoid opposite to the main training facilities. The corridor by now seemed as familiar as home. They did not need to consult maps or tracers. The ore carrier and the mining robot, as promised, were waiting in the main loading chamber. The tailings had already been sintered to form oddly shaped but identical solid blocks, each weighing half a ton. At a pinch, Rick and Deedee could load each one themselves; but that was a sure way to flunk the exercise.

They put the mining robot through its paces on a dummy run, checking that each movement corresponded exactly to that pictured. Finally, and gingerly, Deedee directed the machine to begin loading. She watched the pick-up stage, while Rick counted blocks and monitored their stowing aboard the ore carrier. There were still a hundred more to go when he came out and told Deedee to stop.

"Why? The robot's doing fine."

"Maybe. But we have a problem. The carrier is nearly full. It won't take more than another couple of dozen and we've only loaded nine hundred."

"That can't be right. The carrier is rated for at least five hundred tons cargo mass. Maybe the blocks are heavier than they're supposed to be? Or maybe they're less dense and bigger."

They checked the mass of a sintered block. It was half a ton exactly. Its density was as it should be. Then they crouched in the loading chamber, helmet to helmet, and pored over the electronic and printed manuals. At last Rick sighed. "I get it. I'm a dummy. I should have realized it as soon as the loading started."

Deedee was still staring at the electronic layout diagram of the carrier. "Well, I don't. Everything looks just fine."

"The carrier's fine. The ore blocks are fine, too."

"So what's the problem?"

"It's the *shape* of the blocks. I noticed they looked odd when we first came in. They have the right mass and density but they don't pack tight. There's too much space left between them."

"So what do we do?"

"We look for a better packing arrangement, one that fits the blocks together more tightly."

Ten minutes of useless brainstorming was enough to prove that they would never find the answer by abstract thought. Under Deedee's direction the mining robot began to fit blocks one on another, turning them every way to seek the best fit of the irregular faces. The right answer, when they finally reached it, seemed absolutely obvious. With one particular arrangement the sintered blocks keyed in together tightly and seamlessly.

Then the carrier had to be unloaded, and the whole operation begun over. This time the five hundred tons fitted with room to spare. Deedee came over to watch the last block go in. She ordered the mining robot in on top of it before she closed the hatch.

"Think that was the Gossage surprise?" she said as she followed Rick into the ore carrier's control room.

"The first one, maybe. Nobody said he keeps it to one. There could be another right here."

They examined the carrier's status indicators one by one with enormous care, until at last Deedee shrugged. "We can't stay here forever just looking. Do it, Rick."

Under Rick's nervous control the carrier crept forward out of the loading chamber and into open space. By all Belt standards the journey was a trivial one: a couple of hundred kilometers through unobstructed vacuum, to rendezvous with another body having negligible velocity relative to CM-2. The training facility's refinery was in an essentially identical orbit around the Earth-Moon system.

That fact did not offer Rick any sense of security. He was keyed tighter than he had ever been until at last the carrier was snugly into the refinery's dock. Then it was Deedee's turn. She unloaded the robot and it carried the sintered ore blocks one by one to the refinery's gigantic hopper. They stared at each other as the final block went in.

"Smooth," Deedee said at last.

"Too smooth?"

"There's no such thing."

"You know what I mean." Rick stared at the distant bulk of CM-2, its outside lights clearly visible from the refinery. "Let's get back. If there are surprises here I don't want to hang around and wait for them to find us."

He checked the fuel as he switched on the drive. More than enough. He could cut off power after a couple of minutes, coast all the rest of the way to CM-2, and finish with a little fuel to spare. And even with the delay in loading they had plenty of time to complete the assignment before the end of the work period. Maybe the only Gossage surprise was the sintered block shape.

That comforting thought was still in his head when he realized that the star field outside was slowly rotating. Instead of heading straight for CM-2 the ore carrier was yawing, turning its blunt prow farther and farther away from the planned heading.

Rick slapped at the controls and turned all thrust power off.

"What's wrong?" Although Rick had not said a word, Deedee caught the urgency of his movement.

"Drive. We're crabbing." Rick was already calling up onto the control display the rear perspective layout of the carrier, to show the six independent but balanced units that provided the ship's drive. "Something's wrong with one of the modules. We're getting no thrust from it."

Deedee was watching the changing starscape in the front port, noting the exact direction of rotation of the ship. "We're tilting to the right and down." She touched her gloved hand to the display, one finger on the stylized image of a module. "If it's a problem with just one thrustor, it has to be this one. Any of the others would turn us in a different direction."

"Agreed."

"So turn off the opposite one of the six, directly across from the bad one. Do it, Rick! That will balance us again."

"I can't." Rick gestured at the control panel. "The thrust modules aren't separately controllable. It's all or nothing."

"So what do we do?"

Rick did not answer. He had called up a section of the ship's manual onto the display. More than anything he had ever wanted in his life, he wanted to read that manual. And he couldn't. The words were too long and unfamiliar, the sentences seemed too complex. He strained to understand, willing the words to make sense. And still he couldn't read them. The ship was drifting along, but CM-2 was not directly ahead.

Their present course would miss the planetoid.

"Help me, Deedee." Rick was sweating inside his suit. "Help me to figure this out. The manual will tell us what to do. It has to. Help me to read. You read better than me."

"I don't. You know I don't." But Deedee was following Rick's lead, reading each word on the screen aloud, stumbling over the hard ones.

They struggled on, reading in unison, cursing unknown words, correcting each other. Until finally Deedee cried out and pointed at the display, "Att-it-ude. That's what that word is. Attitude control. This is the part we want. Come on, Rick. Read it!"

Rick was certainly trying; but he had already discovered that simple need and urgency didn't let you read any faster. They ground on together, word by word, through the next three paragraphs. And, at a certain point, groaned in unison.

"It's obvious!" Rick slapped his knee with his gloved hand.

"And we're idiots." Deedee repeated the important sentences, gabbling them on the second time through. "In the event of thrust module imbalance, the carrier must be returned to the main maintenance facility.'—Yeah. Thanks a lot.— 'However, should a thrust module fail and a temporary course adjustment be necessary in space, this can easily be performed by the use of minor lateral control jets. These can be used to spin the ship about its long-it-ud-in-al'—hell of a word— 'axis, so that the mean thrust is maintained in the desired direction. The same elementary technique can be used to make general direction adjustments, by halting longitudinal rotation after any suitable angle.' Do it, Rick!"

"I am doing it." Rick was already using the lateral thrustors, turning the ship about its main axis to bring the failed thrustor module onto the opposite side. "I'm going to have to juggle this. If I thrust too long in the other direction we'll swing too far and miss the base on the other side."

"Do it in—little bits." The main thrustors fired, this time in a pattern as jerky as Deedee's speech. "We still have plenty of time. Go easy. You can afford to go easy."

"I will go easy. Trust me."

Rick was eyeing CM-2 as it swung back into view in the forward port. Under his control the drive was stuttering uneasily on and off while the ship rotated unevenly about its main axis. He knew exactly where he wanted to go—into the hard-edged aperture that sat like a bullet hole in the planetoid's rugged side. But getting there, exactly there, was another matter. It was another half hour before Rick could turn off all power, shiver in released tension, lift his hands from the controls, and wait for the magnetic arrest system to guide the carrier to a berth within CM-2.

Before the grapple was complete Deedee was out of her seat and heading for the lock. "Come on. We have to go."

"What's the hurry?" Rick was moving more slowly, stretching cramped hands as he eased himself from the pilot's chair. "You said we had plenty of time."

"I lied." Deedee was already in the lock, waiting impatiently. "I didn't want you worrying about time when you were flying the carrier. But it's going to be touch and go."

Rick took a glance at his helmet chronometer and leaped for the lock. "We only have twenty-three minutes left!"

"I know." The lock was cycling. "We can do it, though— so long as we don't meet any more snags."

They flew side-by-side from the docking berth to the mine entry point to CM-2. "Say, two minutes each end." Rick hit the entry combination. "Twelve minutes to get through the tunnels—that's about as fast as we can go. But we still have a seven minute cushion." He keyed in the entry combination again. "What's wrong with this thing? It shouldn't take this long."

"The power has been turned off." Deedee pointed to the telltale set in the great door. "And it's too heavy for manual operation."

"Turkey. The bastard. He's screwed us. We can't get in."

"Then we'll have to go around. Or use one of the side tunnels?"

"No good. They all lead outside, not to the training facility."

"That's our answer." Deedee had turned. "We can go right around the outside. Don't waste time with that door, Rick. Come on! We're down to twenty-one minutes."

She led the way, zooming at maximum suit speed for the open entrance of the mine loading chamber. Rick, close behind, did the calculation. They had to make their way right around CM-2 to almost the opposite side of the planetoid. Say, three kilometers. If they could average ten per hour, they would do it. If not . . .

All Rick could think of was that early this morning he had made Deedee sit down and eat breakfast when she was hyped up and raring to go. If they were too late now, it was his fault.

They came to the edge of the loading chamber and burst out from the darkness. As Deedee, still ahead of Rick, emerged into full sunlight she reversed suit jets and came to an abrupt dead halt.

"Keep going, Dee. I'm right behind you."

But she was not moving. "Listen to your dosimeter, Rick."

He became aware of a tinny rattle in the background. It was his suit's radiation monitor, operating well above the danger level.

"Back inside." And when he hesitated, "We have to, Rick.

Right now." She had him by the arm of his suit, towing him. "It must be a solar burst, a sudden one and a big one. We're safe enough as soon as we get some rock shielding around us."

They were already out of sight of the Sun. Safe enough. And failed. Rick glanced at his chronometer. Eighteen and a half minutes.

"Deedee, we wouldn't be outside for very long. I'll bet the integrated dose would be small enough, it wouldn't harm us."

"Maybe. But are you sure?"

He wasn't. Worse than that, he didn't know how to make sure. The calculation couldn't be very difficult, no more than a formula and a few simple summations. Jigger would probably have done it in his head. But Rick didn't know how to do it at all. He groaned.

"We're safe enough here." Deedee had misunderstood the reason for his misery. "Rock is a perfect shield."

"I know. I don't want a shield. I want to beat the deadline."

"We can't possibly. A solar storm could last for days, and we have only seventeen minutes left."

*Rock is a perfect shield.* "Dee, we still have a chance. The sun is shining almost directly into the loading chamber. The training facility is on the opposite side. We can go through a side tunnel to a point where we're out of direct sunlight, then jet the rest of the way outside shielded by CM-2 itself."

"Sixteen minutes. We'll never do it in time." But she was following Rick as he plunged back into the dark interior. He picked one side tunnel and went into it without hesitating. Fortunately Deedee didn't ask why Rick knew so well the network of passages and chambers that criss-crossed the interior of CM-2. He certainly wasn't going to mention it or the disastrous episode it had led to with Gina.

The passageways had been designed for mining rather than

rapid travel through them. The trip through the interior seemed to take forever. At last Rick and Deedee were at the surface again, about a quarter of the way around the planetoid, but they were running out of time. Five minutes left. A kilometer and a half to go on the outside, hugging close to CM-2 to avoid the solar flare. It didn't sound far. But it meant averaging eighteen kilometers an hour. You couldn't do that. Not in a suit, zooming around the irregular exterior of a planetoid.

Rick knew it. Deedee probably knew it, too. Neither said a word as the final minute flashed past and the deadline expired. They kept going, bitterly, all the way to the lock that would lead them into the training facility.

As the lock opened, Rick halted. "No good. Six minutes late. Sorry."

"I know." Deedee came to his side, put an arm around him, and hugged him. She leaned her helmet against his as they moved into the lock together. "We gave it our best shot. Nobody can take that away from us."

The lock pressure equalized. They reached up to remove their helmets as the inner door opened—and found themselves staring at the anxious face of Turkey Gossage. Turkey glanced at once at his watch.

"Don't say it." Rick moved out of the lock. "Six minutes late."

"I wasn't going to. Did you come around the outside?"

"Part of the way." Deedee came to stand at Rick's side.

"Let me see your dosimeters so—"

"No problem. We did the first part in the interior, and we only came outside when CM-2 was shielding us from the Sun."

"Smart move." Gossage relaxed visibly. "Of course, even in the Sun the dose you'd have received in the short time you were there would have been tolerable."

"We weren't sure." Rick was suddenly more tired than he had ever been. "We didn't know how to calculate it."

"I can show you that in five minutes."

"Not today, sir." Rick slumped against the chamber wall and allowed his arms and legs to go limp. "We did our best, we really did."

"And we came so close." Deedee flopped down by Rick's side. "If there had been one less problem to solve—just one."

"I see. Would you agree with that, Luban?" Turkey seemed more amused than sympathetic.

"Yes. But I don't see why it matters."

"It matters very much. To me, at least." Gossage squatted down so that he was facing the two of them. "You see, it's not every day that people mistake me for a deity." And, when Rick and Deedee stared at him with dull and exhausted eyes, "I gave you a test that I thought would stretch you right to your limits. If you did everything right, and fast, and clean, you could make it back before the deadline—just. I rigged the shape of the sintered blocks. I fixed the drive so it would go wonky on the return trip. I turned off the power on the main entry door so you couldn't get back inside and would have to come around the outside. But if there's one thing that even Turkey Gossage can't do, it's to arrange a solar flare for his special convenience. I'd have to be God Almighty to do that. The flare wasn't in my plans, any more than it was in yours."

He reached out, taking Deedee and Rick's right hands in his. "If it hadn't been for the flare you'd have beaten your deadline with time to spare. That's good enough for me. You did well, better than I expected. You've passed. Now, don't go to sleep on me!"

Rick and Deedee had simultaneously closed their eyes. They showed no sign of opening them again.

"All right." Gossage stood up. He was still holding their

hands and his movement lifted them to their feet. "You've passed, the pair of you, but you don't seem to care. Eat and rest, rest and eat. Then things will seem different. We'll talk later about what you'll do when the training course is over." He released them, turned, and headed for the tunnel. As he reached it he added, without turning his head, "Just don't think life is going to be this nice and easy all the time."

The trainees had been bubbling over with excitement for three days. They could hardly wait for graduation. But the ceremony, when it finally came, was another mystery. It represented the culmination of four brutal months of tests, briefings, hectic study, and final practical examination. They had expected—and Rick at least had dreaded—all the pomp and circumstance of a high school graduation ceremony, with robes and pictures and diplomas and celebrities and boring speeches *ad nauseam.*

What Rick got, along with every other graduate of the training program, was one quick handshake from Turkey Gossage.

"What would you do with a certificate if you had one?" Turkey was beaming. "You can't hang it on the wall where you're going—none of you will have a wall."

"Treasure your signature, sir." Gladys de Witt had been forced to perform a southpaw handshake with Turkey. A loose cable had broken her right arm on the final stage of her practical test; but she had finished, flying the ship home to base one-handed. Now she waved her white cast in the air. "Sign this for me instead."

Turkey did so, to enormous applause. As he finished he caught Rick's eye and walked across to him. "No big rush." He spoke softly. "But when you get a free minute you have a visitor. Back in my office."

A visitor? Rick was more than surprised. He was baffled. Everyone he knew on CM-2, including Jigger and Gina, was right there at the graduation ceremony and all set to party.

As soon as he could do it without anyone noticing he slipped away. He headed for Turkey's office. When he got there he realized that he had been wrong. He did know one other person on CM-2. What he had not known—still did not know—was her name.

The woman nodded to him. In person, the sharp features were much more attractive. Or maybe his standards had changed. Anyway, she no longer made him think of a weasel.

"Congratulations, Rick. You've come a long way from Chatterjee Boulevard. This time I ought to introduce myself. My name is Coral Wogan." She held out her hand. Rick, still baffled, shook it. "At the moment the training course feels like an end to you," she went on. "As it surely should. But it is really a beginning."

"I know that. I have tons to learn. I feel I've just started."

"Which is wonderful, and appropriate." She paused, and Rick realized that Turkey Gossage had come in quietly behind him. "The big question is, what are you going to learn? What should you learn, for a satisfying life? And that leads to the next question: What brings real satisfaction? I would say, the toughest job is also the best job."

Turkey had moved forward and could see Rick's face. "Coral, I know you think you're making sense. But actually you're being as clear as mud. Let me try for a moment."

He turned to Rick. "I've been pumping you up during the training course, telling you that the most challenging job in the solar system is out in the Belt, mining and refining and carrying finished products back to the Earth-Moon system. And that is one hell of a job, no denying it. But it's not the real leading edge. Know what is?"

"Yes, sir. The Jovian system mining expedition. The mission to explore and map the moons of Jupiter."

"Turkey!" Coral Wogan spoke accusingly.

"I didn't, Coral. I swear I didn't say a word." Gossage turned to Rick. "Where did you hear about that?"

"From Jigger and Gina. They've applied. They hope to go as a team." Rick was suddenly filled with enormous excitement. Coral Wogan and Turkey Gossage must be having this conversation with him for a reason. "Sir, can I apply to go?"

"See, Coral? I told you." It was Gossage's turn to sound accusing. He shook his head at Rick. "You could apply, but you'd have no chance. Anyone selected must have at least three years of real Belt experience. If you stay the course you could apply for the second expedition in five years time. Ms. Wogan hopes you won't do that, because in five years you could be ready for a different job. Over to you, Coral. This one is your area, not mine."

She nodded. "You see, Rick Luban, the Jovian project may be the most exciting job in the system but it's not the toughest one. The toughest one is to fight a monster that's effectively immortal, a monster with a billion arms and a million times more power than Vanguard Mining. A monster that's not in space, but back on Earth."

"No fancy speeches, Coral." Turkey had read Rick's puzzled look. "Get to the point."

"Right. Do you remember what it was like for you in school before you came to space?"

"Very well."

"Do you think you're smarter now than you were then?"

Rick had to consider that. He wasn't sure just what she was asking. "Smarter, no. My brain's the same. But I know a lot more, and I understand more of what I know."

"Very true. And do you know why that's true? I'll tell

you. Back on Earth you were being strangled by the biggest, most inefficient, best entrenched bureaucratic system in the history of the world. You were in public school, adrift within an education system that has itself lost any interest in the value of knowledge, or truth, or discipline, or self-evaluation. Like all big monopolies, it is more interested in perpetuating and protecting its own territory than in anything else. The men and women who emerge from the school system know less and less—and then wonder why they find themselves unemployable."

"Do you understand all that?" Turkey Gossage showed more interest in Rick's facial expression than in Coral Wogan's flow of words.

"I understand what Ms. Wogan is saying. But I don't know why she's saying it. I mean, you both work for Vanguard Mining. And you train your own people the way you want to."

"We do—by starting over from scratch with good raw material. We can live with that, but it's not the right way. For every bright bored kid like you, Rick, kicked out of the system, another thousand stay inside it and are stifled for life."

"We'd like to change that." Coral Wogan was smiling at Rick in a way that he did not like at all. "We know it's going to take generations, but we want to make a start. And it has to be done from within. The toughest, most challenging job in the solar system isn't in the moons of Jupiter. It's to go back down to Earth, infiltrate the public school system, and find the children who belong out here. And, eventually, we have to transform and either improve or destroy the whole mess."

"No!" Rick saw in his mind the patient turtle, bowed down by thirty years of frustration and indignity. "If you think I could ever go back to Earth and be like Mr. Hamel, to put up with all the bullshit—"

"I don't. Mr. Hamel is someone sympathetic to us, but he is not an activist. We are looking for someone who—"

"No. I'm not interested."

"Told you, Coral. But I promised you a shot." Turkey Gossage came to stand right in front of Rick, shielding him from Coral Wogan. "All right, Rick. The party is starting and you've earned the right to be there. Any statement or question for me or Ms. Wogan before you go?"

"I'd like to find out all I can about the Jovian mining expedition."

"We'll get that for you. I promise. Anything else?"

"No." Rick started for the door, then hesitated. "I'm sorry, Ms. Wogan. I really appreciate being considered. But that sort of thing's not for me."

"I understand. One thing I didn't get to mention is that even if you were interested, we wouldn't think of beginning for another five or six years. You had some of the qualities we need before you left Earth—you knew what it was like to be amoral, cynical, and violent—but anyone who takes this job also needs to be devious and subtle and *very* knowledgeable. That takes time. Is it all right if I ask you again in another five years?"

"Sure. But my answer will be the same." Rick started out of the door, but again he hesitated. "Can I ask one more question?"

"Of course."

"Did you ask anyone else in the training course?"

"One other person. Deedee Mao."

"I see. Can you tell me what she said?"

"Yes. First she said no, no way. No fucking way, to be precise. Then she asked if we had talked to Rick Luban about it. I told her we had not, but we were going to."

"I see. Thank you."

"Thank you, for listening. Now go party." Turkey Gossage waited until Rick was out of sight and out of earshot. "That's it, Coral. Twenty *noes* in a row, and no sign of a *yes.*"

"Think I don't realize that?"

"You know why?"

"Because they're young. Because Rick and the rest of them all had terrible experiences in the Earth education system. Because the Belt and Jovian exploration feel far more exciting."

"All those. And one other thing." Gossage came forward to sit at the big round table opposite Coral Wogan. "The trainees haven't watched the Earth system fail, year after year after year. They haven't had the frustration of unlearning lessons in new recruits, before real teaching can begin. The only people who should go down and take on the Earth bureaucracy are ones who have seethed over it and hated it for a long time."

"People like?"

"People like you."

"And you."

"Right. We are the ones who know the job needs doing. You and I, and a few others. And we keep trying to talk other people into doing it for us, when we should be starting it ourselves. The trainees don't say it, but underneath they must be thinking, if the job's so all-fired important why aren't *they* down there in the trenches, instead of asking us? Well, Coral?"

"No. It's not for me."

"Right. Me neither. But think of the effect on Deedee, and Rick, and all the others, if they found that you and I were down there ahead of them, starting the job. What do you say?"

"I say, no way. No fucking way, to quote Deedee Mao. I have a million things to do here."

"Right. Me too. So let's go join the graduation party." Turkey led the way to the door.

As they left the room Coral Wogan said thoughtfully, "I can't go now. I really can't. But in five years' time, or maybe even in one year's time . . ."

Turkey laughed; and then they were gone. The room that formed the nerve center of the training program became silent and empty.

Far away along the corridor the party was at last getting into its stride. From the training room the sound was just a confused hubbub, like the first distant swell of a revolution.

# ABOUT THE AUTHORS

**James P. Hogan** began to write in the mid-1970s and is one of today's outstanding writers of hard science fiction. His fifteen novels, together with his articles and short stories, contain some of the field's most provocative ideas and interesting scientific speculations. He is a full-time writer who currently divides his time between Ireland and Florida.

**Lawrence Watt-Evans** is the author of over two dozen novels, more than four score short stories, and large numbers of articles, poems, and comic book scripts. He is equally at home in the fields of science fiction, fantasy, and horror, and is the current president of the Horror Writers of America.

**Dr. Geoffrey A. Landis** is a practicing scientist working in support of the nation's space program. Equally at home writing science fact or science fiction, he has produced short stories that have won both the Hugo and Nebula Awards.

**James Kirkwood** is the president of an aerospace research corporation in the nation's capital. His more reasonable speculative exercises are published as science fiction. His more outlandish ones are submitted as research proposals to the United States Government.

**Larry Niven** is one of the best and best-known living writers of hard science fiction and fantasy. He has published at every length, and is a multiple Hugo and Nebula Award winner. He is fond of writing both solo and in collaboration, and notes that he has "collaborated with every kind of writer except ignorant and stupid."

**Kathe Koja** is the author of *Skin, Bad Brains, The Cipher,* and *Strange Angels.* Her short fiction has appeared in a variety of magazines and anthologies, both solo and in collaboration with Barry Malzberg.

**Barry N. Malzberg** has been a leading figure in science fiction as novelist, short story writer, essayist and critic for more than a quarter of a century. His novel *Beyond Apollo* (1972) was the first winner of the John W. Campbell Memorial Award, and his nonfiction book, *The Engines of the Night* (1982), provides one of the field's most profound commentaries.

**Dr. Arlan Andrews, Sr.,** is Manager of Advanced Manufacturing at the Sandia National Laboratory, and served as a Presidential science advisor in both the Bush and Clinton administrations. He is the author of more than a hundred speculative articles and science fiction stories over the past twenty-five years.

**Nick Pollotta** is a former stand-up comic from Manhattan whose science fiction novels contain some of the field's rare real humor. He has published a dozen science fiction novels, and his short stories have appeared in horror, mystery, and science fiction magazines and anthologies.

**B. W. Clough** saw most of the world in her much-traveled childhood, and her writing reflects her global experience. Her first novel appeared in 1984, and since then she has published three more books. Her first published short story was selected for a best-of-the-year science fiction collection.

**Jerry Oltion** has published three novels and more than fifty short stories in the science fiction field's leading magazines.

He has been a Nebula finalist, and is also a winner of the *Analog* Readers' Poll.

**Dr. Doug Beason** is Director of Research for the Air Force Academy, and served as a Presidential science advisor in both the Bush and Clinton administrations. He has authored or co-authored eight science fiction novels, including the Nebula Finalist *Assemblers of Infinity.* His short fiction has appeared in *Analog, Amazing Stories, Full Spectrum, New Destinies,* and other anthologies.

**Mary A. Turzillo** is a relatively new writer in the science fiction field. Her works have appeared in *Asimov's* magazine, *SF Age, Tomorrow Fantasy and Science Fiction, Xanadu,* and *The Ultimate Witch.*

**Dr. Jerry Pournelle** is one of science fiction and science fact's best-known and best-selling writers, both alone and in collaboration with Larry Niven. He is a past president of the Science Fiction Writers of America, winner of the John W. Campbell Award, and a regular columnist in the leading computer magazines.

**Dr. Charles Sheffield** is a past president of the American Astronautical Society and also past president of the Science Fiction Writers of America. He is a best-selling writer of both fact and fiction, and a winner of the John W. Campbell Memorial Award, the Hugo Award, the Nebula Award, and the Japanese Sei-un Award.